BALTHASAR'S ODYSSEY

Amin Maalouf

BALTHASAR'S ODYSSEY

Translated from the French by
Barbara Bray

THE HARVILL PRESS
LONDON

08807877

First published as *Le Périple de Baldassare* by Editions Grasset & Fasquelle, 2000

2 4 6 8 10 9 7 5 3 1

Copyright © Amin Maalouf, 2000 and © Editions Grasset & Fasquelle, 2000
English translation copyright © Barbara Bray, 2002

First published in Great Britain in 2002 by
The Harvill Press
Random House, 20 Vauxhall Bridge Road,
London SW1V 2SA

Random House Australia (Pty) Limited
20 Alfred Street, Milsons Point, Sydney,
New South Wales 2061, Australia

Random House New Zealand Limited
18 Poland Road, Glenfield,
Auckland 10, New Zealand

Random House South Africa (Pty) Limited
Endulini, 5A Jubilee Road, Parktown 2193, South Africa

The Random House Group Limited Reg. No. 954009
www.randomhouse.co.uk

A CIP catalogue record for this book
is available from the British Library

This edition has been published with the financial assistance of the French Ministry of Culture

ISBN 1 86046 992 2

Map drawn by Emily Hare

Papers used by Random House are natural,
recyclable products made from wood grown in sustainable forests;
the manufacturing processes conform to the environmental
regulations of the country of origin

Typeset in New Baskerville by Palimpsest Book Production Limited,
Polmont, Stirlingshire

Printed and bound in Great Britain by
Biddles Ltd, Guildford & Kings Lynn

To Andrée

N

Atlantic Ocean

WEST

London

Amsterdam

Cologne

Calais

Paris

E U R O P E

Venic

Agde

Nice

Genoa

Lisbon

Barcelona

Marseilles

Anconа

Valencia

Mahon

Gibraltar

Tangiers

Algiers

M e d

1666

The scale of miles

100 200 300 400 500

S

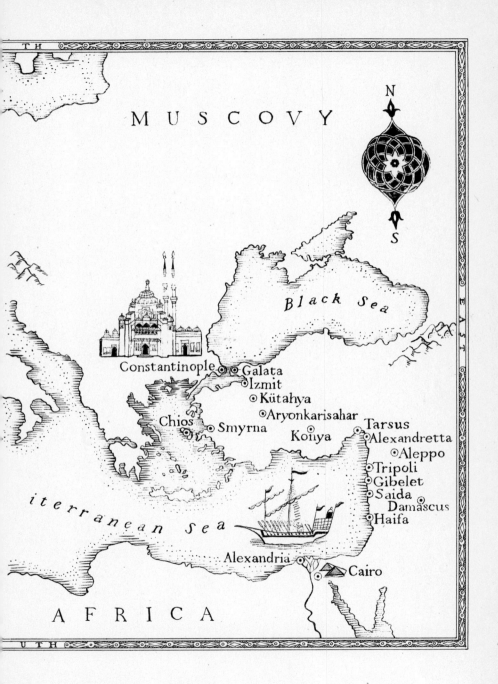

NOTEBOOK I

The Hundredth Name

Still four long months until the Year of the Beast, and it's already here. Its shadow dims our hearts and the windows of our houses.

The people round me can talk of nothing else. The coming year, the signs, the portents . . . Sometimes I say to myself, Let it come! Let it finally empty out its pouch of prodigies and disasters! Then I change my mind and think of all the decent ordinary years when each day was spent just looking forward to the evening's pleasures. And I roundly curse the doom-worshippers.

How did this foolishness start? In whose brain can it have sprouted? Under what skies? I couldn't say for certain, and yet in a way I know. From where I am I've seen the fear, the monstrous fear born, grow and spread. I've seen it creep into people's minds, into those of my nearest and dearest, into my own. I've seen it overthrow reason, trample it underfoot, humiliate it, and then devour it.

I've watched the good days vanish.

Up till now I have lived in peace. I prospered in figure and fortune, every season a little more. I wanted nothing I couldn't get. My neighbours admired rather than envied me.

Then suddenly everything started to happen.

That strange book, appearing and then disappearing, and all my fault . . .

Old Idriss's death. True, no one blames me for it . . . Except myself.

And the journey I'm to set out on next Monday, despite my qualms. A journey from which I have a feeling I shan't return.

3

So it's with some apprehension I write the first lines in this new notebook. I don't know yet how I'll record the things that have happened, or those that already loom ahead. Just a simple account of the facts? A journal? A log? A will?

Perhaps I should say a word to begin with about the person who first made me anxious about the Year of the Beast. His name was Evdokim. A pilgrim from Moscow who came knocking on my door about seventeen years ago. Why "about"? I've got the exact date down in my ledger. The twentieth day of December 1648.

I've always written everything down, especially details, the sort of things I'd have forgotten otherwise.

Before he came in he made the sign of the cross with two outstretched fingers, and stooped so that his head would clear the stone lintel. He had a thick black cloak, woodcutter's hands with thick fingers, and a thick fair beard, but tiny little eyes and a narrow forehead.

He was on his way to the Holy Land, but he hadn't stopped at my house by chance. He'd been given the address in Constantinople, and told it was here and only here that he had a chance of finding what he was looking for.

"I'd like to speak to Signor Tommaso," he said.

"He was my father," I replied. "But he died in July."

"God rest his soul!"

"And those of your kin likewise!"

This exchange had taken place in Greek, the only language we had in common, though it was clear neither of us used it much. The conversation was rather tentative, anyhow: my father's death, still a painful subject for me, was also a shock to my visitor. Moreover, since he was speaking to a "Papist apostate" and I to a "misguided schismatic", we were anxious not to offend one another's susceptibilities.

After we had both been silent a moment, he went on:

"I am very sorry your father is no longer with us."

As he spoke he looked round the shop, trying to make out the jumble of books, antique statuettes, glassware, painted vases, stuffed falcons; and wondering – to himself, but he might just as well have said it aloud – if, since my father was no longer there, I might not be in need of help. I was already twenty-three years old, but my face was plump and clean-shaven and must still have looked rather boyish.

I drew myself up and thrust out my chin.

"My name is Balthasar, and I have taken over my father's business."

My visitor showed no sign of having heard. He went on gazing at the thousand marvels around him with a mixture of wonder and apprehension. Our curio shop had been the best stocked and most celebrated in the East for a hundred years. People came from everywhere to see us – Marseilles and London, Cologne and Ancona, as well as Smyrna, Cairo and Isfahan.

After looking me up and down one last time, my Russian seemed to have made up his mind.

"I am Evdokim Nikolaevitch, from Voronezh. I have heard great things of your business."

I assumed an easy manner – my way, then, of making myself agreeable.

"We've been in the trade for four generations. My family comes from Genoa, but we settled in the Levant a long time ago."

He nodded once or twice to show he knew all that. In fact, if he'd heard about us in Constantinople this was probably the first thing he'd been told. "The last Genoese to come to this part of the world" – with some remark or gesture suggesting madness or eccentricity handed down from father to son. I smiled and said nothing. He turned to the door, bawling out a name and an order, and a servant hurried in, a small stout fellow in baggy black clothes, with a flat cap and down-turned eyes. He took a book out of a box he was carrying and handed it to his master.

I assumed he wanted to sell it to me, and was immediately on my guard. In my trade you soon learn to beware of people who start by putting on airs about their fancy origins and acquaintances, give orders right, left and centre, and in the end just try to palm off some old piece of bric-à-brac on you. Unique in their own eyes, and so naturally unique for everybody. If you offer them a price that's less than they had in mind, they take offence and claim you're not only cheating them but insulting them too. And go off breathing fire and slaughter.

But this visitor soon reassured me: he wasn't here to sell or haggle.

"This book was printed in Moscow a few months ago. And everyone who can read has read it already."

He pointed to the title, which was in Cyrillic characters, and began reciting earnestly, "*Kniga o vere*", before realising he needed to translate for my benefit: "The Book of the Faith, unique, genuine and orthodox." He glanced at me out of the corner of his eye to see if the words had made my Papist blood run cold. I remained impassive, inside and out. Outside, the polite smile of the merchant. Inside, the wry smile of the sceptic.

"This book tells us the apocalypse is at hand!"

He showed me a page near the end.

"It is written here that the Antichrist will appear, in accordance with the Scriptures, in the year of the Pope, one thousand six hundred and sixty-six."

He kept repeating the figure, slurring over the words "one thousand" a bit more every time. Then he looked at me to see my reactions.

I had read the Apocalypse of St John the Divine the same as everyone else, and had paused over the mysterious passage in Chapter 13: "Let him that hath understanding count the number of the beast: for it is the number of a man; and his number is Six hundred threescore and six."

"It says 666, not 1666," I ventured.

"You'd have to be blind not to see such an obvious sign!"

"Sign!" How often had I heard that word, not to mention "portent"! Everything is a sign or a portent to someone always on the look-out for them, ready to marvel at and interpret anything and imagine parallels and coincidences everywhere. The world is full of such tireless seekers of omens – I'd had them in the shop, some of them quite delightful, some really appalling!

Evdokim seemed vexed at my lack of enthusiasm, which he saw as reflecting ignorance and impiety. Not wishing to offend him, I made an effort and said:

"It is certainly all very strange and disturbing . . ."

Or something of the kind.

"It is because of this book that I am here," he answered, evidently reassured. "I am looking for other texts that may help me to understand it."

Now I understood. I'd be able to help him.

I should explain that the success of our business in recent decades was largely due to the craze throughout Christendom for old Oriental books – especially those in Greek, Coptic, Hebrew and Syriac – which seemed to contain the most ancient truths of the Faith, and which the royal courts, particularly those of France and England, tried to acquire in order to back up their point of view in the quarrels between the Catholics and the supporters of the Reformation. For nearly a century my family scoured the monasteries in the East in search of such manuscripts, hundreds of which are now to be found in the Royal Library in Paris or the Bodleian in Oxford, to mention only the most important repositories.

"I haven't many books dealing specifically with the Apocalypse," I said, "and especially not with the passage about the number of the Beast. But you might care to look at . . ."

And I listed ten or twelve titles in various languages, indicating their contents and sometimes the chapter headings. I like this aspect of my profession, and think I have a gift for it. But my visitor didn't seem as interested as I'd expected. Every time I mentioned a book he would show his disappointment and impatience by fidgeting with his fingers or gazing around.

Finally I understood.

"Oh, you were told of a particular volume – is that it?"

He mispronounced some Arabic name, but I had no trouble making it out. Abu-Maher al-Mazandarani. To tell the truth, I'd been expecting to hear it for some while now.

Anyone with a passion for books knows Mazandarani's. By reputation, that is, for very few people have actually held it in their hands. I'm still not sure, as a matter of fact, if it really exists, or ever has done so.

Let me explain, for it will soon look as if I'm talking in contradictions. When you study the works of certain famous and recognised authors, you will often find them mentioning the book in question, saying that one of their friends or teachers had it in his library once. But I have never come across a reputable writer who clearly confirms he's seen it. No one who says, "I own it", "I've looked through it", or "I've read it". No one who actually quotes from it. So the really serious merchants, and most scholars, believe the book has never existed, and that the few copies which show up from time to time are the work of forgers and hoaxers.

The title of this legendary volume is *The Unveiling of the Hidden Name*, but it is usually known as *The Hundredth Name*. When I've explained what name that is, you will see why it has always been so much sought after.

As everyone knows, the Koran mentions ninety-nine names of God, though some prefer to call them "epithets". The Merciful, the Avenger, the Subtle, the Apparent, the Omniscient, the Arbiter, the Heir, and so on. And that figure, confirmed by Tradition, has always provoked the obvious question in curious minds: Must there not be a hidden, hundredth name to round off the number? Quotations from the Prophet, which some doctors of the law contest though others recognise them as genuine, say there is indeed a supreme name that someone has only to utter to avert any kind of danger or obtain any favour from Heaven. It is said that Noah knew it, and so was able to save himself and his family at the time of the Flood.

It is easy to see the attraction of a book that claims to reveal such a secret nowadays, when men live in fear of another Deluge. I've had all sorts of people through my shop – a barefoot friar, an alchemist from Tabriz, a Turkish general, a cabalist from Tiberias – every one of them looking for that book. I've always thought it my duty to tell them why I thought it was only a mirage.

Usually my visitors resign themselves once they have heard my explanation. Some are disappointed, but others are relieved: if they can't have the book, they prefer that nobody can.

The Muscovite reacted neither one way nor the other. At first he looked amused, as if to convey that he didn't believe a word of my patter. When I got annoyed at this and stopped short, he suddenly grew serious and begged in a low voice:

"Sell it to me and I'll give you all the gold I possess without a murmur!"

"My poor fellow," I felt like saying, "think yourself lucky you've come across an honest merchant! There are plenty who'd relieve you of your money in no time!"

I patiently started explaining again why, to the best of my knowledge, the book didn't exist, and how the only people who claimed otherwise were either naive and gullible authors or swindlers.

As I spoke, his face grew flushed; like that of a doomed man whose doctor is airily explaining that the medicine the patient hoped would cure him has never been invented. I could see in his eyes not disappointment or resignation, not even incredulity any more, but hatred, the daughter of fear. I cut short my explanations with the cautious conclusion:

"What the truth of the matter is, God only knows!"

But he had stopped listening. He stepped forward, grabbed at my clothes with his mighty hands and crushed my chin against his giant chest. I thought he was going to strangle me, or smash my skull against the wall. Luckily his servant hurried over, touched him on the arm and whispered something in his ear. Soothing words, I suppose, for his master let go of me at once and thrust me disdainfully away. Then he left the shop, muttering imprecations in his own language.

I never saw him again. And I'd probably have forgotten all about him, even his name, if his visit hadn't marked the beginning of a strange procession of callers. It took me some time to realise it, but I'm certain now: after Evdokim, the people who came to the shop were different from before, and behaved in quite another way. Hadn't the pilgrim from Moscow had a look of terror in his eye, a look of the sort of terror some might describe as "holy"? I could see it now in everyone. And with it the same attitude of urgency and impatience, the same mixture of persistence and apprehension.

These are not mere impressions. It's the merchant speaking now, with his hand on his ledger. After the Russian's visit, not a day went by without someone coming and talking to me about the Apocalypse, the Antichrist, the Beast and the number of the Beast.

Why not admit it outright? It's the Apocalypse that has brought in most of what I've earned in the last few years. Yes, it's the Beast that clothes me and the Beast that feeds me. As soon as its mere shadow crops up in a book, buyers come running from all over the place, purses at the ready. It all sells for a fortune, learned treatises and far-fetched squibs alike. At one time I even had on my shelves a tome called *An accurate description of the Beast and many other monsters of the Apocalypse* – in Latin, with forty drawings into the bargain.

But while this morbid enthusiasm makes me well off, it also makes me uneasy. I'm not the kind of man to go along with the follies of the moment. I keep my head when others are losing theirs. On the other hand, I'm not one of those arrogant fools who form their opinions as oysters form their pearls, and then shut them away where nothing can touch them. I have my own ideas and beliefs, but I can hear the rest of the world breathing. I can't ignore the fear that's spreading everywhere. Even if I thought the world was going mad, I couldn't ignore its folly. I may smile and shrug my shoulders and execrate foolishness and frivolity, but I can't help being disturbed.

In the struggle that goes on inside me between reason and unreason, the latter has won some points. Reason protests, mocks, insists, resists, and I'm still clear-sighted enough to observe the confrontation more or less impartially. But it's precisely this vestige of lucidity that forces me to admit that unreason is gaining ground in me. One day, if things go on like this, I'll no longer be able to write as I'm writing now. I might even turn back through these pages and erase what I've just set down. What I call unreason now will have become what I believe in then. If that Balthasar should ever come into being, which God forbid!, I hereby hate and despise him, and muster all the intelligence and honour I have left to curse him.

I know this all sounds rather wild. That's because the rumours that are dinning around the world have seeped into here. The sort of thing Evdokim said then I hear in my own house now.

It's my own fault.

Eighteen months ago, as business was still flourishing, I decided to ask my sister Pleasance's two sons to come and give me a hand. My idea was that they should get to know the antiquities trade so that eventually they could take over from me. I had high hopes of Jaber, especially. He was the elder of the two. A diligent, meticulous, studious youth, already almost a scholar before he was a man. The opposite of his younger brother Habib, who neglected his books to roam around the back-streets. I didn't expect much of him. But at least I hoped he might settle down a bit if I gave him some unaccustomed responsibilities.

A waste of time. As he has grown up, Habib has become an incorrigible womaniser. He does nothing but sit at the window of the shop, ogling, smiling and paying compliments, and disappearing at all hours for mysterious appointments the object of which I can easily guess. How many young women who live nearby find, when they go to fetch water, that the quickest way to the fountain passes by our window! Habib means "beloved" – names are rarely neutral.

Jaber stays well inside the shop. His skin grows paler all the time, so rarely does it see the sun. He reads, copies, makes notes, arranges, consults, compares. If his face ever lights up, it's not because the shoemaker's daughter has just come round the corner and is sauntering this way. It's because young Jaber has just read something on page 237 of the *Commentary of Commentaries* that confirms what he thought was meant by a passage he found yesterday evening in *The Final Exegesis*. I'm quite satisfied to skim through the most difficult and abstruse volumes out of duty, and even then I often stop for a yawn. Not he. He seems to revel in them, as if in the most delicious sweetmeats.

So much the better, I thought at first. I wasn't sorry to see him so industrious. I quoted him to his brother as an example, and even started entrusting some of my own tasks to him. I didn't hesitate to let him deal with the most pernickety customers. He'd spend hours chatting to them, and though he wasn't primarily interested in business he usually ended up selling them masses of books.

I'd have been perfectly satisfied with him if he too hadn't begun – and with all the ardour of youth – to irritate me with talk of the imminent end of the world and of the omens heralding its coming. Was it the influence of the books he read? Or of some of my customers? At first I thought I could settle the matter by clapping him on the shoulder and telling him to pay no attention to such nonsense. He seemed a very biddable lad, and I believed he'd obey me in that as in other things. Little did I know him, and little did I know the age we live in, and its passions and obsessions.

According to my nephew, we have an appointment with the end of the world that dates from its beginning. Those alive today will have the dubious privilege of witnessing that macabre culmination of History. As far as I can see, this doesn't make him feel sad or depressed. On the contrary, I think I detect a sort of pride – tinged with fear, no doubt, but also with a certain amount of exultation. Every day he finds some new confirmation of his predictions in Latin, Greek or Arabic sources. Everything is converging, he says, towards a certain date. The date cited in the Russian book of the Faith – if only I hadn't told him about it! – 1666. Next year. "The Year of the Beast", as he likes to call it. He backs up his belief with a whole array of arguments, quotations, computations, learned calculations, and an endless litany of "signs".

I always think that if you look for signs you find them, and I write this down once again lest, in the maelstrom of madness that is seizing the world, I should one day forget it. Manifest signs, speaking signs, troubling signs – people always manage to "prove" what they want to believe; they'd be just as well off if they tried to prove the opposite.

That's what I think. But I'm rattled just the same by the approach of the famous "year".

I still remember a scene that took place two or three months ago. My nephews and I had had to work late to finish the inventory before the summer, and we were all exhausted. I'd collapsed on to a chair, with my arms circling my open ledger and a nearby oil-lamp beginning to dim. Then suddenly Jaber came and leaned over the other side of the table, so that his head touched mine and his hands pressed down painfully on my elbows. His whole face glowed red, he threw a huge shadow on the walls and furniture, and he whispered in a lugubrious voice:

"The world is like this lamp. It has burned its ration of oil. Only a drop is left. See how the flame flickers! The world will soon go out."

What with being so tired, and with all that gossip about the coming Apocalypse, I suddenly felt quite crushed by these ominous words. As if I hadn't even the strength to sit up straight. As if I must just sprawl there and wait for the flame to die away before my eyes and the darkness to swallow me up.

Then the voice of Habib rose up behind me, laughing, cheeky, sunny, salutary.

"When are you going to stop tormenting poor Uncle – eh, Boumeh?"

"Boumeh", meaning owl or bird of ill-omen – that's what the younger brother has called the elder since they were children. And as I stood up that evening, suddenly crippled with aches and pains, I swore I'd call him that too from then on.

But though I do so, and curse and swear, and mutter to myself, I can't help listening to what Boumeh says, and his words nest in my mind. So that I too start to see signs where before I saw only coincidences. Tragic or instructive or amusing coincidences – but where once I'd have just exclaimed in surprise, now I start, I'm worried, I tremble. And I even think about changing the peaceful course of my existence.

Admittedly, recent events were bound to unsettle me.

Just take the business of old Idriss!

Just to shrug my shoulders as if that didn't concern me would not merely have been unwise. It would have been reckless and blind.

Idriss came and sought refuge in our little town of Gibelet, sometimes known as Byblos, seven or eight years ago. In rags, and with practically no belongings, he seemed as poor as he was old. No one ever really found out who he was, where he came from, or what he had fled. Persecution? Debt? A family vendetta? As far as I know he never told anyone his secret. He lived alone in a hovel he was able to rent cheaply.

The old man, whom I rarely came across and with whom I never exchanged more than a couple of words, came to the shop last month clutching to his chest a large book that he awkwardly suggested I should buy. I leafed through it. An undistinguished anthology of the work of little-known poetasters, copied out in shaky and irregular calligraphy, badly bound and badly preserved.

"A unique treasure," said the old man. "It's all I have left from my grandfather. I'd never have parted with it if I wasn't in such dire . . ."

Unique? There must have been something similar in half the houses in the country. It would remain on my hands till the day I died! I thought. But how could I show the poor wretch the door when he'd swallowed his pride and his shame in the hope of getting some money to buy food?

"Leave it with me, hajj Idriss," I said. "I'll show it to some of my customers who might be interested."

I knew already how I'd proceed. Just as my father would have done, God rest his soul, if he'd still been in my place. For conscience's sake I made myself read a few of the poems. As I'd seen at first glance, they were mostly minor works, with a few well-turned lines here and there; but on the whole the book was completely trite and unsaleable. At best I might get six maidins for it – more probably three or four – from a customer really keen on Arabic poetry. But in fact I found a better use for it. A few days after Idriss's visit, an Ottoman dignitary who was passing through came to buy a few things from me. And as he insisted on having a discount, I got myself a satisfied client by giving him the book free as well.

I waited for just under a week, then went to see the old man. God, how dark his house was! And God, how empty and poor! After I'd pushed open the rickety wooden door I found myself in a room with a bare floor and bare walls. Idriss was sitting on a mud-coloured straw mat. I sat down cross-legged beside him.

"An important personage came to my shop," I told him, "and he was pleased when I offered your book to him. I've brought you the money that's due to you."

Please note that I told him the exact truth! I can't bear to lie, though I may occasionally cheat a little by leaving something out. But I was only trying to save the poor man's dignity by treating him as a merchant rather than a beggar! So I took three one-maidin coins out of my purse, then three five-maidin pieces, pretending to calculate the total carefully.

He stared at me wide-eyed.

"I didn't expect all that, my son. Not even half as much . . ."

I shook my finger at him.

"Never say that to a shopkeeper, hajj Idriss. He might be tempted to diddle you."

"No danger of that with you, Balthasar effendi! You are my bene-factor."

I started to get up, but he stopped me.

"I've got something else for you," he said.

He disappeared behind a curtain for a few moments, then came back carrying another book.

What, more? I thought to myself. Perhaps he's got a whole library in the other room. What the devil have I got myself into?

As if he'd read my thoughts, he hastened to reassure me.

"It's the last book I've got left," he said, "and I want you to have it! You and nobody else!"

He placed it on my hands, open at the first page, as if on a lectern.

Good heavens!

The Hundredth Name!

Mazandarani's book!

I'd never have dreamed of finding it in such a hole!

"But hajj Idriss, this is a very rare book! You ought not to part with it like that!"

"It's no longer mine – it's yours now. Keep it! Read it! I never could."

I turned the pages eagerly, but the room was too dark for me to make out more than the title.

The Hundredth Name!

God in Heaven!

As I came out of the shack with the precious tome under my arm, I felt quite drunk. Was it really possible that this book, sought after by the whole world, was in my possession? How many men had come from the ends of the earth in search of it, and I'd told them it didn't exist when all the time it was in that dilapidated hut a stone's throw away! And a man I scarcely knew was making me a present of it! It was so disturbing, so unimaginable! I found myself laughing aloud in the street, like an idiot.

I was still like that, tipsy but incredulous, when a passer-by hailed me.

"Balthasar effendi!"

I recognised the voice straight away: Sheikh Abdel-Bassit, imam of Gibelet's mosque. But how he could have known who I was, when he's been blind from birth and I hadn't said a word?

I went over to him, and we exchanged the usual greetings.

"Where do you come from, dancing along like that?"

"I've been to see Idriss."

"Did he sell you a book?"

"How did you know?"

"Why else would you have gone to see the poor fellow?" he laughed.

"True," I said, laughing too.

"An irreligious book?"

"Why should it have been?"

"If it wasn't, he'd have offered it to me!"

"To tell the truth, I don't know much yet about what's in it. It was too dark to see in Idriss's place. I'm waiting to get home to be able to read it."

The sheikh held out his hand.

"Show me!"

His lips are always half open as if he's about to smile. I never know when he really is smiling. Anyhow, he took the book, leafed through it for a few seconds as he held it in front of his closed eyes, then handed it back.

"It's too dark here too," he said. "I can't see anything!"

This time he laughed aloud, looking up at the sky. I didn't know if politeness required me to join in. That being so, I just gave a little cough, halfway between a stifled laugh and a clearing of the throat.

"So what sort of book is it?" he asked.

You can hide the truth from a man who can see; lying is sometimes a necessary skill. But to lie to someone blind is base and unworthy. A certain sense of honour, and perhaps some superstition, obliged me to speak the truth. Though I did wrap it up in some careful conditionals.

"It may be the book that's attributed to Abu Maher al-Mazandarani. *The Hundredth Name.* But I'm waiting until I get home to check that it's genuine."

He tapped the ground three or four times with his stick, breathing heavily.

"Why does anyone need a hundredth name? I was taught all the names *I* needed to pray with when I was a child. What would I want a hundredth one for? Tell me, you who've read so many books in every language!"

He took a string of prayer beads out of his pocket, and started telling them rapidly as he awaited my answer. What could I say? I had no more

17

reason than he to champion the hidden name. But I felt obliged to explain:

"As you know, some people claim the supreme name allows you to perform miracles . . ."

"Miracles? Idriss has had that book for years, and what miracle has he performed for himself? Has it made him less poor? Less decrepit? What misfortune has it saved him from?"

He didn't wait for my reply to that, but went off lashing at the air and the dust with his angry stick.

My first concern on reaching home was to hide the book from my nephews. Especially from Boumeh: I was sure if he actually saw and touched it he'd go out of his mind. So I slipped it under my shirt, and when I got indoors I hid it safely under an old and very fragile statuette that no one was allowed even to dust, let alone move.

That was last Saturday, 15 August. I promised myself I'd spend Sunday examining Mazandarani's book closely.

As usual I rose rather late on Sunday – an infidel hour, some would call it. But as soon as I was up I went along the little corridor that leads from my bedroom to the shop, got the book out and sat down at my desk as nervous as a child. I'd bolted the door on the inside so that my nephews shouldn't take me by surprise, and drawn the curtains to discourage visitors. So I had quiet and cool, but when I opened the book I realised there wasn't enough light. So I decided to move my chair nearer the window.

While I was doing so, someone knocked at the door. I let out an oath and listened, hoping whoever it was would tire of waiting and go away. Unfortunately he knocked again. Not just a timid tap – an imperious thump, and then a volley of them.

"Coming!" I shouted. I quickly put the book back in its hiding-place, then went and opened the door.

My caller's insistence had made me think it must be someone important, and so it was: Chevalier Hugues de Marmontel, emissary

18

of the court of France. A most cultivated person, a connoisseur of Oriental literature and objets d'art, who had often come to my place in the course of recent years and made substantial purchases.

He was on the way from Saida to Tripoli, he told me, whence he would take ship for Constantinople. And he could not possibly pass through Gibelet without knocking at the door of the Embriaci's noble dwelling. I thanked him for his compliments and his concern, and naturally asked him in. After drawing back the curtains, I let him browse about at leisure among the curios as was his habit, following him at a distance so as to be able to answer any questions, but not bothering him with any unsolicited comments.

He began by glancing through a copy of Samuel Bochart's *Geographia sacra*.

"I bought it as soon as it was published," he said, "and I keep referring to it. At last a book that deals with the Phoenicians, your ancestors – that is to say, of the people of this country."

He moved forward a pace or two, then halted.

"These statuettes are Phoenician, aren't they?" he asked. "Where are they from?"

I was proud to say that I myself had found and excavated them, in a field close to the beach.

"I'm very fond of this one," I admitted.

The Chevalier merely said, "Oh", surprised that a merchant should speak so of something offered for sale. I was slightly offended at this, and said no more, merely waiting for him to turn and ask me to explain my attachment. When he did so, I told him that the two statuettes had once been buried side by side, but with time the metal they were made of rusted in such a way that a hand of each had become welded to a hand of the other. I like to think of them as two lovers separated by death, but reunited for ever by time, rust and the earth. Everyone else who sees them speaks of two statuettes, but I prefer to speak of them as one: the statuette of the lovers.

The Chevalier put out his hand to take hold of it. I begged him to be careful, as the least shock might break them apart. No doubt thinking I had been rather abrupt with him, he signed to me to handle my statuette myself. So with the greatest possible care I started to carry it nearer to the window. I expected him to follow, but when I turned round he was still standing in the same place. In his hands he was holding *The Hundredth Name.*

He was as white as a sheet. I too turned pale.

"How long have you had it?" he asked.

"Since yesterday."

"Didn't you once tell me you didn't think it existed?"

"That's what I've always thought. But I must have told you forgeries appeared from time to time."

"Is this one of them?"

"Probably. But I haven't had time yet to make sure."

"How much do you want for it?"

I almost said "It's not for sale!" but I changed my mind. One should never say that to an important personage. He'll only say, "In that case, I'll borrow it." And then, for fear of giving offence, you have to lend it to him, and of course it's highly likely you'll never see your book again, nor your customer either. I've learned that to my cost.

"As a matter of fact," I stammered, "it belongs to a crazy old fellow who lives in the most broken-down hovel in Gibelet. He's convinced it's worth a fortune."

"How much?"

"A fortune, as I said. He's insane!"

At this point I noticed that my nephew Boumeh had come up behind us and was observing the scene in stunned surprise. I hadn't heard him enter. I asked him to come over and be introduced to our eminent visitor. I hoped this would allow me to change the subject and escape from the trap closing in on me. But the Chevalier just nodded briefly and repeated:

"How much is the book, Signor Balthasar? I'm waiting."

How much should I say? The most I ever charged for the rarest volumes was 600 maidins. Sometimes, very exceptionally, the price went up to 1,000, which in sols tournois came to . . .

"He's asking 1,500! But I can't let you pay all that for a forgery!"

Without a word my visitor opened his purse and counted out the sum in sound French currency. Then he handed the book to one of his servants, who went and stowed it away in the midst of his baggage.

"I'd have liked to take the statuettes, too. But I suppose I haven't enough money left for that!"

"Take the two lovers as well, then. They're not for sale, but please have them as a gift. Take good care of them!"

I then invited him to stay to lunch, but he briefly declined. One of his escort told me he had to get on with his journey as soon as possible if he wanted to reach Tripoli by nightfall. His ship sailed next day for Constantinople.

I accompanied the party to Gibelet harbour, but without getting another word out of the emissary, nor so much as a farewell glance.

I reached home to find Boumeh weeping and wringing his hands with rage.

"Why did you give him that book? I don't understand it!"

I didn't understand it either. In a moment of weakness I'd lost *The Hundredth Name*, the statuette I was so fond of, and the respect of the emissary. I had even more reason to lament than my nephew. But I had to defend myself somehow.

"What can I say? It just happened! I had no choice! He *is* the envoy of the King of France, after all!"

My poor nephew was sobbing like a child. I took him by the shoulders.

"Cheer up! It was a forgery, as you and I both know."

He pulled himself free.

"If it was a forgery, we committed a fraud by selling it to him at that price. And if by some miracle it wasn't a forgery, we shouldn't have parted with it for all the gold on earth! Who sold it to *you*?"

"Old Idriss."

"Idriss? How much for?"

"He gave it to me."

"In that case, he certainly didn't mean you to sell it."

"Not even for 1,500 maidins? With that he could buy a house, new clothes; hire a maid; perhaps even get married."

Boumeh didn't feel like laughing. He seldom does.

"If I understand you correctly, you intend to give all this money to Idriss."

"Yes – without even putting it in our till!"

I stood up, put the coins in a leather purse, and left the house.

How would the old fellow react?

Would he reproach me for selling what was meant as a present?

Or would he see the incredible amount of money I was bringing him as a gift from Heaven?

As I pushed open the door of his hut I found a neighbour sitting on the threshold with her face buried in her hands. Before going in, I asked her if hajj Idriss was at home. She looked up and spoke one word.

"Twaffa."

He is dead!

I'm sure his heart stopped beating at the very moment when I gave his book to the Chevalier de Marmontel. I can't get the idea out of my head.

Hadn't I asked myself how the old man would react to what I'd done? Now I knew!

Is my bad conscience preventing me from thinking straight? Alas, facts are facts – the coincidence is too striking. I have acted very, very wrongly, and I must make amends!

It didn't occur to me at once that I ought to follow the book to Constantinople. As a matter of fact, I'm still not sure there is any point in it. But I have allowed myself to be persuaded it's the best thing to do.

To begin with, there were Boumeh's moans and groans. But I expected and was annoyed by them in advance, so they didn't really affect my decision. Especially as the foolish fellow wanted to set out straight away! To hear him, you'd think all that had just happened was made up of signs from Heaven especially directed at me. And despairing of seeing me interpret them correctly, Providence was supposed to have sacrificed the life of poor Idriss with the sole object of opening my eyes.

"Opening my eyes to what? What am I supposed to understand?"

"That time is short! That the accursed year is at hand! That death is lurking around us! You've held your own salvation and ours in your hands, you've had *The Hundredth Name* in your possession, and you couldn't hold on to it!"

"Well, I can't do anything now. The Chevalier's miles away. That's the work of Providence too."

"We must catch him up! We must set out right away!"

I shrugged. I didn't even intend to reply. There was no question of my going along with such childish behaviour. Set out at once? Ride all night? And get our throats cut by brigands?

"As for dying, I prefer to die next year with the rest of my fellow-men rather than anticipate the end of the world!"

But the boy wouldn't budge.

"If it's too late to catch him in Tripoli we can still meet him in Constantinople!"

Suddenly a lively voice from behind us:

"Constantinople! The best idea Boumeh ever had!"

Habib! Now *he* was putting his oar in.

"So *you've* deigned to honour us with your presence! I always knew it would be my unlucky day when you and your brother agreed about something for once!"

"I care nothing for your tales of the end of the world, and I'm not in the least interested in that confounded book. But I've been wanting to go to the Big City for a long while. Didn't you say that when you were my age your father, our grandfather Tommaso, wanted you to see Constantinople?"

This had nothing to do with the case, but it touched me on my weakest spot – the reverence I'd felt for my father since he died, and for all he'd ever said or done. As I listened to Habib, a lump came into my throat, my eyes glazed over, and I heard myself murmur:

"True, true. Perhaps we should go to Constantinople."

Next day Idriss was buried in the Muslim cemetery. There weren't many mourners there – my nephews and me, three or four neighbours, and Sheikh Abdel-Bassit, who conducted the service. When it was over he took me by the arm and asked me to go home with him.

"I'm glad you came," he said as I helped him over the little wall round the cemetery. "This morning I wondered if I'd have to bury him on my own. He had no one, poor man. Neither son nor daughter, nephew nor niece. No heir at all – though it's true that if he'd had one he'd have had nothing to leave him. His only bequest was to you. That wretched book."

This left me deep in thought. I'd seen the book as a token of thanks, not as a bequest. But, in a way, that was what it was – or had become. And I'd gone and sold it! Would old Idriss, in his new abode, forgive me?

We walked in silence for a while, up a steep and stony road without any shade. Abdel-Bassit was plunged in his thoughts and I in mine – or rather in my remorse. Then he said, straightening his turban:

"I hear you're leaving us soon. Where are you going?"

"To Constantinople, God willing."

He stopped and put his head on one side, as if to catch the din of the distant city.

"Istanbul! Istanbul! To those who have eyes it's hard to say the world has nothing to show. Yet it's the truth, believe me. If you want to know the world, all you need do is listen. What people see when they travel is never more than an illusion. Shadows chasing other shadows. The roads and the countries teach us nothing we don't know already, nothing we can't hear within ourselves in the peace of the night."

The man of religion may be right, but my mind is made up – I'm leaving! Against my better judgment, and to some extent unwillingly – but I'm leaving! I can't bear the thought of spending the next four months, then the twelve months of the fateful year itself, sitting in my shop listening to predictions, setting down signs, listening to reproaches and endlessly mulling over my fears and regrets!

My beliefs haven't changed. I still execrate stupidity and superstition. I'm still sure the lamp of the world isn't about to go out . . .

But that said, how can I, who doubt everything, not doubt my own doubts?

Today is Sunday. Idriss was buried last Monday. And we're to set off tomorrow at dawn.

There'll be four of us – me, my nephews, and Hatem my clerk, who'll see to the animals and the provisions. We're taking ten mules, no less. Four for riding, the others to carry the baggage. That way, none of the beasts will be overloaded, and we should, God willing, be able to keep up a good pace.

Khalil, my other clerk, who is honest but not very resourceful, will stay behind to help Pleasance look after the shop – my excellent sister Pleasance, who takes a poor view of this impromptu journey. It makes her sad and anxious to be parted like this from her two sons and her brother, but she knows it would be no use trying to oppose it. Nonetheless, this morning, when we were all caught up in the bustle of last-minute preparations, she came and asked me if it wouldn't be better to put off our departure for a few weeks. I reminded her that we must cross Anatolia before the winter. She didn't insist – just muttered a prayer, and began to weep silently. Habib did his best to tease her out of it, while her other son, more horrified than sympathetic, told her to hurry up and go and bathe her eyes with rose-water, because tears shed on the eve of a journey are an evil omen.

When I'd first told Pleasance I planned to take her children with me, she hadn't objected. But it was only natural for her maternal instincts to break out in the end. Trust Boumeh to imagine a mother's tears could bring bad luck.

Pages written in my house at
Gibelet on the eve of my departure.

I'd gathered together my notebook, ink, reeds and blotting powder ready for the journey, but this same Sunday evening I've had to set them out on my desk again for use. A stupid incident occurred at the end of the afternoon which nearly prevented us from leaving. Something I find not only highly exasperating, but humiliating as well. I'd have preferred not to mention it, but I promised myself I'd record everything in my journal and I mean to keep to my resolve.

The cause of all this bother is a woman called Marta, known around here, with a tinge of sarcasm, as "the widow". A few years ago she married a fellow everyone knew to be a lout. He was from a family of louts, all of them crooks, pilferers, scoundrels, footpads, wreckers – every single one of them, old and young alike, as far back as anyone can remember! And pretty Marta, then a pert young thing, impish, wilful, mischievous but not a bad girl, fell in love with one of them. His name was Sayyaf.

She could have had any eligible young man in the village – I'd have been more than willing myself, I don't deny it! Her father happened to be my barber, and a friend of mine. When I went to his place in the morning for a shave and caught a glimpse of her, I'd come away humming a tune. There was something in her voice, her walk, the way she fluttered her eye-lashes – something no man with blood in his veins could resist. Her father had noticed how attracted I was, and had given me to understand that he'd be delighted, even flattered, at such a connection. But the lass had fallen for the other fellow, and one morning we heard she'd let him carry her off and a renegade priest had married them. The barber died of grief a few months later, leaving his only daughter a house, an orchard, and more than 200 gold sultanins.

Marta's husband, who'd never worked in his life, then decided to go into trade in a big way and charter a boat. He persuaded his wife to let him have all her father's savings, down to the last penny, and off he went to Tripoli. He has never been seen again since.

At first the story went that he'd made a fortune with a cargo of spices, and built a whole fleet of ships for himself, and planned to come and show off sailing past Gibelet. People said Marta spent all her days by the sea with the girls she knew, proudly waiting for him. But in vain – no ships, no fortune and no husband ever turned up. After a while, other less splendid rumours began to circulate. He'd been drowned in a shipwreck. He'd turned pirate, been captured by the Turks and hanged. But some said he'd got a hideout on the coast near Smyrna, and by now had a wife and children. This mortified his wife, who'd never got pregnant during their brief life together and was reputed to be barren.

For the unfortunate Marta – alone for six years already, neither married nor free, without resources, without brothers or sisters, without children, spied on by all her louts of in-laws lest she think of sullying the honour of her vagabond of a husband – every day was agony. So she started to maintain, with a persistence bordering on madness, that she'd heard from a reliable source that Sayyaf was dead, so she really was a widow. But when she dressed in black, the family of the alleged departed attacked her mercilessly, accusing her of bringing the absent Sayyaf bad luck. After being the victim of several blows, the marks of which anyone could see on her face and hands, "the widow" resigned herself to wearing colours again.

But she did not admit defeat. In recent weeks, it was said, she'd told some of her girlfriends that she planned to go to Constantinople to check with the authorities whether her husband was really dead, and that she wouldn't come back without a firman from the Sultan proving that she was a widow and free to begin a new life.

And it seems she carried out her threat. This Sunday morning she didn't attend mass. It was said she'd left Gibelet during the night, taking her clothes and jewels with her. Rumours at once arose, implicating me. This is annoying and insulting, and above all – do I have to swear it on the Gospel? – it is simply untrue, absolutely and entirely untrue. I haven't exchanged a single word with Marta for years – since her father's funeral, I think. At the most I've greeted her in the street from time to time, furtively raising my hand to my hat. That's all. For me, on the day I heard she'd married that rascal, it was all over.

But hearsay now has it that I've made a secret arrangement to take her with me to Constantinople. And as I couldn't do so openly before the whole village, I'm supposed to have told her to go ahead in advance and wait for me to pick her up at an appointed place. It's even said that it's because of her that I've never re-married, which has nothing to do with the truth, as I may one day have the opportunity to explain.

Untrue though it is, this story looks quite plausible, and it seems to me most people believe it. Beginning with Marta's brothers-in-law, who claim to be sure of my guilt, insulted by my alleged tricks, and determined to avenge their honour. This afternoon Rasmi, the most excitable of them, burst into my house brandishing a gun and swearing he was going to do me in. It took all my self-possession, and that of Hatem my clerk, to calm him down. He insisted I delay my departure to demonstrate my good faith. It's true that would have done away with all the rumours and suspicions. But why should I guarantee my honesty to a gang of louts? And for how long would I have to postpone my journey? Until Marta showed up again? And what if she'd gone away for good?

Habib and Jaber were against any delay, and I think I'd have gone down in their esteem if I'd weakened. Besides, I didn't for a moment feel inclined to give in. I simply weighed the pros and cons, as a sensible man should, before giving a firm refusal. Then the fellow said he was going to come with us in the morning: he wanted to make sure the runaway wasn't waiting for us in some nearby hamlet along the way. My nephews and my clerk were all outraged at this, and my sister even more so, but I made them see reason.

"The road belongs to everyone! If he wants to travel in the same direction as us, we can't stop him," I said loudly and clearly, so that the fellow should understand that he might follow the same route as us, but he wouldn't be travelling *with* us.

I'm probably overestimating his sensibility, and we certainly can't count on his manners. But there are four of us and he's on his own. His tagging along annoys me rather than worries me. Heaven grant we don't have to deal with any more formidable threats on our journey than this bewhiskered braggart!

The village of Anfé, 24 August 1665

The country round Gibelet is not very safe in the half-light, so we waited till daybreak to pass through the gate of the town. Rasmi was there waiting for us, tugging at the bridle of his mule to make it stay quiet. He seems to have picked a very skittish mount for the journey; I hope it will soon make him tired of trying to keep up with us.

As soon as we reached the coast road, he turned off and rode to the top of a headland, whence he gazed around the landscape, smoothing his moustache.

Watching him out of the corner of my eye, I wondered for the first time what could have become of the unfortunate Marta. And I was suddenly ashamed of myself for, up till now, thinking only of the trouble her disappearance had caused me. It was her fate I ought to have been worrying about. Might she have done something desperate? Perhaps her body would one day be washed up on the beach. The whispering would stop *then*. A few tears would be shed. Then oblivion.

And I – would I mourn the woman who almost became mine? I found her attractive, I wanted her, I used to watch out for her smiles, the way her hips moved when she walked, the way she tossed her hair, the tinkling of her bracelets – I might have loved her dearly, clasped her to me every night. I might have grown fond of her, her voice, her step, her hands. She might have been with me this morning when I left. She, too, might have wept, like my sister Pleasance, and tried to make me give up the journey.

My mind, distracted by the jolting of my mount, wandered further and further afield. I could now see the the woman I hadn't really looked at for years. Once again she flashed me the playful glances that were hers in the blessed days when she was still only the barber's daughter. I upbraided myself for not having desired her enough to love her. For having let her marry her misfortune.

Her valiant brother-in-law had ridden up several more of the hills that border the road. He gazed in all directions, and once he even called out: "Marta! Come out! I saw you!" But there was nothing there. His moustache is bigger than his brain!

The four of us rode forward at the same pace, pretending not to notice his gallops, his stopping and starting, or the clapping of his legs against the flanks of his mule. But at noon, when Hatem prepared some food – only local flat bread stuffed with local cheese, seasoned with oil and oregano – I invited the intruder to share our meal. Neither my nephews nor my clerk approved of my generosity and, given the ill-mannered oaf's behaviour, I must say they were right. For he grabbed what we offered him, took it to the other side of the road, and devoured it all alone like a brute beast, with his back to us. Too uncouth to eat with us, but not proud enough to go hungry. What a pathetic wretch!

We are going to spend this first night at Anfé, a village on the coast. A fisherman has offered us food and shelter. When I went to open my purse to give him a token of thanks, he declined, then took me aside and asked me instead to tell him what I knew about the rumours concerning next year. I spoke in as learned a manner as I could to reassure him. They are only empty rumours, I told him – the kind that always circulate when men lose courage. Don't be taken in by them! Does it not say in the Scriptures, "Ye know neither the day nor the hour"?

My host was so comforted by these words that, not content with having offered us hospitality, he took my hand and kissed it. I blushed with shame. If the good fellow only knew the absurd reason for my journey! And there I was pretending to dispense wisdom!

Before going to bed I made myself write these few paragraphs, by the light of a rank-smelling candle. I'm not sure I've selected what's important. It's not going to be easy to distinguish the essential from the trivial every day, the significant from the incidental, the true paths from the blind alleys. But I mean to go forward with my eyes open.

Tripoli, 25 August

We seem to have shaken off our unwelcome fellow-traveller. Only to meet with other troubles.

This morning Rasmi was waiting for us outside the house where we'd spent the night, moustache bristling, ready to go. He must have slept in another house in the village, I suppose – some brigand of his acquaintance. When we set out he followed us for a few minutes, then rode to the top of a headland, as he had done yesterday, to scan the landscape. Then he turned back and went off in the direction of Gibelet. My companions are still wondering if it wasn't a ruse, and if he won't try to surprise us further on. But I don't think so. I don't think we shall see him again.

We reached Tripoli at noon. This must be the twentieth time I've been there, but I never pass through the city gates without emotion. It is here that my ancestors first set foot in the Levant, more than 500 years ago. In those days the Crusaders were besieging the town, unsuccessfully.

Ansaldo Embriaco, one of my ancestors, helped them build a citadel designed to overcome the resistance of the beleaguered defenders, and offered the aid of his ships to blockade the harbour. In return he was given the seigniory of Gibelet.

The domain remained in my family for a good 200 years. And even when the last Frankish state in the Levant was destroyed, the Embriaci managed to persuade the victorious Mamelukes to let them hold on to their fief for a few more years. We had been among the first Crusaders to arrive, and we were the last to leave. We didn't quite go even then. Am I not the living proof of that?

When the reprieve was over and we had to abandon our domain of Gibelet to the Muslims, what remained of the family decided to return to Genoa. "Return" is not the right word: they had all been born in the Levant, and most of them had never set foot in the city their forefathers came from. However, once back in Genoa, Bartolomeo, my ancestor at the time, soon fell into a state of depression. For a while, at the time of the first Crusades, the Embriaci had been one of the city's most prominent families, with their own private mansion in their own quarter of the town, their own followers and supporters, a tower named after them, and the biggest fortune in all Genoa; they had now been supplanted by other families: the Dorias, the Spinolas, the Grimaldis and the Fieschis had all become more eminent than they. My ancestor felt degraded, exiled even. He might be a Genoese – he *was* one, in his speech, his dress, his way of life – but he was only a Genoese from the East!

So my people went to sea again, and weighed anchor in various ports – Haifa, Alexandria, Chios – until Ugo, my great-grandfather, had the idea of going back to Gibelet, where in return for services rendered the authorities gave him back a plot of land in what had once been his family fief. We had to abandon our seignorial pretensions and go back to commerce, our original occupation; but the memory of our days of glory survived. According to documents still in my possession, I am the eighteenth descendant in the direct male line of the man who conquered Tripoli.

So when I go to the booksellers' district, how can I fail to feast my eyes on the Citadel, where once fluttered the banner of the Embriaci? When they see me coming, the merchants make fun of me and start to call to one another, "Watch out, the Genoese is here to take the Citadel again – don't let him by!" They come out of their booths and really do stop me, but only to embrace me rowdily and offer me coffee and cordials at every step. They are naturally a hospitable people, but I must say I'm a sympathetic colleague too, and an extremely good customer. If I don't come to them, they send me any items they think might interest me but which are not in their line – that is to say, mostly relics, icons and old books relating to Christianity. They themselves are for the most part Muslims or Jews, and their customers are chiefly their co-religionists, mainly concerned with their own faith.

Today, arriving in the city at noon, I went at once to see Abdessamad, a Muslim friend of mine. He was sitting at the door of his shop, surrounded by his brothers and a few other booksellers from the same street. But when, following the usual elaborate exchange of courtesies, and after I'd introduced my nephews to those who didn't already know them, I was asked what brought me here, I was tongue-tied. Something told me it would be best not to say: it was the voice of reason speaking, and I should have listened to it. Surrounded by these respectable characters, who all had a high opinion of me and regarded me rather as the most senior member of our group, if not because of my age and erudition then at least because of my fame and fortune, I realised it would be unwise to reveal the real reason for my visit. Though at the same time another, less prudent voice was urging me to take a different course. After all, if old Idriss in his hovel had had a copy of this coveted work, why shouldn't the booksellers in Tripoli have one too? Theirs might be no less of a forgery than his, but it could save me having to go all the way to Constantinople!

After some seconds of reflection, during which all eyes rested weightily on mine, I finally said:

"I suppose one of you wouldn't happen to have a copy of that treatise by Mazandarani that people are talking about these days – *The Hundredth Name*?"

I'd spoken in as light, detached and ironic a tone as I could manage. But an immediate silence fell on the small company – and, it seemed to me, on the whole city. All eyes now turned on my friend Abdessamad. He was no longer looking at me, either.

He cleared his throat as if about to speak, but instead he let out a forced, staccato laugh, which he suddenly cut short, to take a sip of water. Then he said to me:

"We're always glad to see you!"

This meant that my present visit was over. I stood up sheepishly and said a word of farewell to those closest to me; the rest had already scattered.

Stunned, I began to walk back to the hostelry where we were to spend the night. Hatem came and told me he was going to buy some provisions. Habib whispered that he was off for a stroll by the harbour. I let them both go without comment. Only Jaber stayed with me, but I didn't speak to him either. What could I have said? "A plague on you, Boumeh – it's your fault I've been humiliated!" His fault, and Evdokim's, and Idriss's, and Marmontel's, and the fault of many others, but most of all it's mine. And it's first and foremost up to me to preserve my reason, my reputation and my dignity.

I wonder, though, why those booksellers reacted as they did. Their attitude was very cold and curt toward someone who's always found them friendly and prudent. I expected amused smiles at most. Not such hostility. And I framed my question so carefully! I don't understand. I simply don't understand.

Writing these lines has calmed me down. But that incident put me in a bad humour for the rest of the day. I went for Hatem because he didn't buy what I meant him to buy. Then I scolded Habib for not coming back from his excursion till after dark.

To Boumeh, the main cause of my discomfiture, I couldn't think what to say.

On the road, 26 August

How could I have been so naive?

It was staring me in the face and I didn't see it!

When I woke up this morning, Habib wasn't there. He'd risen early and whispered to Hatem that he had to go and buy something in the Citadel market and would meet us afterwards near the Bassatine gate to the north-east of the city.

"I just hope he gets there before we do," I exclaimed, "because I shan't wait for him! Not a single minute!" And I gave the order for us to leave at once.

The gate isn't far from the hostelry so we were soon there. I looked around. No Habib in sight.

"Give him time," pleaded my clerk, who has always had a soft spot for the boy.

"I shan't wait long!" I replied, tapping my foot impatiently. But I had to wait for him. What else could I do? We were setting out on a long journey – I couldn't very well abandon my nephew on the way!

After an hour, by which time the sun was high in the sky, Hatem, pretending to be all excited, called out to me: "Here comes Habib, running and waving his arms! He's a good lad really, God save him! Always smiling and affectionate. The main thing, master, is that he hasn't come to any harm."

All this, obviously, to try to spare him a trouncing! But I wouldn't be mollified. An hour we'd been waiting! There was no question of my greeting him or smiling at him; I wouldn't even look in the direction he was coming from. I just waited another minute, long enough for him to come up with us, and then I stalked off towards the city gate.

Habib was now behind me: I could feel his presence and hear his breathing. But I kept my back turned on him. I'll start talking to him again, I thought, when he's kissed my hand respectfully and promised not to stay away again without my permission! If we're to continue this journey together I need to know all the time where my nephews are!

When we reached the officer keeping the gate, I greeted him formally, told him who I was, and slipped him a suitable coin.

"And is this your son?" he asked, nodding towards the person behind me.

"No, I'm his nephew."

"And this woman?"

"That's his wife," said Habib.

"Right! You may proceed."

My wife?

I decided to get through the gate and away from the customs post and the soldiers, still looking straight in front of me. Then I turned round.

It was Marta.

"The widow."

Dressed in black, and smiling all over her face.

No, I admit I didn't understand anything till now, didn't even suspect. And Habib handled it well, I agree. He's usually up to all sorts of tricks in order to charm both men and women, but in the last few days he didn't indulge in one knowing smile or a single teasing allusion. He pretended to be as shocked as I was by Rasmi's accusations. Which turned out in the end to be less flimsy than I thought.

I suppose in due course my nephew will tell me how it was all arranged. But what's the point? I can guess most of it. I can guess why he so surprisingly sided with his brother to urge me to make this journey to Constantinople. I imagine he then hurried off to tell "the widow", and she must have thought that was a good moment to run away. So she left

Gibelet, and must have spent one night in Tripoli staying with a cousin or in a convent. That's all so plain I don't need any confessions. But until the whole thing was put right under my nose, I didn't have an inkling.

So what should I do now? For the rest of the day I just walked straight ahead, without expression, without saying a word. Sulking solves nothing, I know. But unless I want to lose all dignity and all authority over my family, I can't act as if I hadn't been led up the garden path.

The trouble is, I'm forgetful by nature, easy-going, and always inclined to forgive. All day I've had to make an effort to keep up my attitude of injured innocence. And I'll have to keep it up for another day or two, even if it hurts me more than the people I'm trying to punish.

The four of them trail along behind me, not daring to speak to one another above a whisper. Good.

The village of the tailor, 27 August

Today we've acquired another unexpected companion. But a respectable one this time.

We had a terrible night. I knew this inn we stopped at, but I hadn't been there for a long while. Perhaps I'd stayed there at a more auspicious time: I didn't remember those swarms of mosquitoes, those cracked and mouldering walls, that stench of stagnant water. I spent the whole night tossing and turning, clapping my hands together every time I heard that menacing drone approaching.

In the morning, when it was time to set out again, I'd hardly closed my eyes. Later on during the day, I fell asleep in the saddle several times, and nearly fell off my mule. Fortunately Hatem came and rode close beside me, to prop me up from time to time. He's a good fellow – I'm not really cross with *him*.

Towards noon, after we'd been travelling for a good five hours and I was looking for a shady spot to have our midday meal in, we found our way suddenly barred by a big leafy branch from a tree. It would have been quite easy to move it out of the way, or just to go round it, but I halted, puzzled. There was something strange about the way it had been put there, right in the middle of the road.

I was looking around to find some explanation when Boumeh came up and suggested in a whisper that it would be best to turn off on to a path on the right that rejoined the main road a bit further on.

"If that branch was blown off its tree," he said, "and the wind dropped it there just like that, it must be a warning from Heaven, and we'd be mad to disregard it."

I derided his superstition but followed his advice. True, as he was speaking to me I'd noticed, some way along the path he wanted me to take, an inviting-looking copse. Just looking at the greenery from a distance, I seemed to hear the cool plash of running water. And I was hungry.

As we started along the path we saw some people riding away in front of us – three or four of them, I thought. They'd probably had the same idea as us – to leave the road and have their meal in the shade. But they were moving fast, and flogging their beasts as if in a hurry to get away from us. When we reached the copse they'd already disappeared over the horizon.

Hatem was the first to yell:

"Brigands! Highwaymen!"

A man was lying in the shade of a walnut tree. Naked, and showing no sign of life. We called out to him as soon as we saw him, but he didn't stir. We could already see that his brow and beard were streaked with blood. But when Marta cried, "My God, he's dead!" and let out a sob, he sat up, apparently reassured by hearing a woman's voice, and hastily covered his nakedness with his hands. Until then, he told us, he'd been afraid his attackers had come back to finish him off.

"They'd laid a branch across the road, and I thought that might signal some danger further on, so I turned off along this path. But it was here that they were lying in wait. I was on my way back from Tripoli, where I'd been to buy cloth. I'm a tailor by trade. My name's Abbas. They took all I had: two asses and their load, my money, my shoes, and my clothes! God curse them! May everything they stole from me stick in their throats like a fishbone!"

I turned to Boumeh.

"So you thought that branch was a warning from Heaven, did you? Well, it was only a highwayman's trick!"

But he wouldn't change his mind.

"If we hadn't taken this path, God knows what would have become of this poor man! It was because they saw us coming that the robbers made off!"

Hatem had just offered the victim one of my shirts, and he said as he put it on:

"Only Heaven could have sent you here to save me! You are decent people – I can tell by your faces. And only honest folk travel with women and children. Are these two fine young men your sons? May God watch over them!"

He was talking to Marta, who was wiping his face with a moistened handkerchief.

"His nephews," she answered after a slight hesitation and a quick apologetic glance in my direction.

"God bless you," the man repeated. "God bless you all. I shan't let you go on without offering each of you a suit of clothes. Don't say no – it's the least I can do. You saved my life! And you shall spend tonight at my house, and nowhere else!"

We couldn't refuse, especially as it was nightfall by the time we reached his village. We'd made a detour to take him home; after all he'd been through, we couldn't let him travel on alone.

He was very grateful, and despite the late hour insisted on giving a veritable feast in our honour. From every house in the village, people brought us the most delicious food, some with meat and some without. The tailor is loved and respected by everyone, and he described us –

my nephews, my clerk, my "wife" and me – as his saviours, the noble instruments of Providence to whom he'd be beholden for the rest of his life.

We could not have imagined a more congenial place to stay: it has made us forget the annoyances that beset the beginning of our journey, and smoothed away the tensions between me and my companions.

When it was time to retire, our host swore an oath that my "wife" and I must sleep in his room, while he and his wife would spend the night in the main room with their son, my nephews, my clerk, and their elderly maidservant. It was too late, of course, for me to reveal that the person travelling with me was not my wife: I would have gone down in the estimation of all these folk who had just been singing my praises. No, I couldn't do that. It was better to go on pretending until the morning.

So the "widow" and I found ourselves together in the one room, with only a curtain separating us from the others, but very much alone, and for the whole night. By the light of the candle our host had left us, I could see the laughter in Marta's eyes. There wasn't any laughter in mine. I'd have expected her to be even more embarrassed than I was. Not at all! It wouldn't have taken much to make her split her sides. It was downright indecent. I was feeling embarrassed enough for two.

After a few false starts, we ended up stretching out on the same couch under the same blanket, but fully clothed and a long way apart.

Then came some long minutes of silent darkness and unsynchronised breathing. Then Marta moved her head close to mine.

"You mustn't be angry with Habib. It's my fault if he hid the truth from you. I made him swear not to say anything – I was afraid that if my plans for running away got out, my brother-in-law would have cut my throat."

"What's done is done."

I'd spoken coldly. I had no desire to start a conversation. But after we'd both been silent for a while, she went on:

"Of course, it was wrong of Habib to tell the officer I was your wife. But he was taken unawares, poor lad. But you're very well respected, and all this is embarrassing for you, isn't it? I your wife! God forbid!"

"What's said is said!"

I hadn't thought before I spoke. It was only afterwards, when Marta's words and my own had echoed together in my head, that I realised the meaning that could be attributed to my reply. In the comical position we'd been put in, every word was as slippery as an eel.

"I your wife?"

"What's said is said!"

I almost started to correct and explain myself. But what was the good? I'd only have sunk deeper in the mire. So I looked in my neighbour's direction to try to make out if she'd understood. It seemed to me she wore the mischievous expression of her youth. I smiled too. And, in the dark, waved a hand in resignation.

Perhaps we needed that exchange to be able to sleep peacefully side by side, not too near and not too far from one another.

28 August

I was in a very good humour when I woke up, and so was my "wife". My nephews kept staring at us all day, intrigued and suspicious. But my clerk seemed amused.

We'd planned to set out again at dawn, but we had to give up that idea. It had started to rain in the night, and in the morning it was still pouring down. The day before had been pleasantly cloudy for anyone travelling, but we knew the clouds wouldn't be content with bringing us only shade. So we had no choice but to stay another night or two with our hosts. God bless them, they made us feel welcome every moment we were there, and as if our presence gave them no trouble at all.

When bedtime came around, the good tailor swore again that as long as we were under his roof, my "precious wife" and I would sleep nowhere else but in his room. For the second time I offered no objection. Too meekly, perhaps . . . We lay down side by side again, Marta and I, without any fuss. Still fully dressed, still some distance apart. Just neighbours, as we were yesterday. The difference being that now we chatted away without stopping – about this and that, about how welcome our hosts were making us, about what the weather would be like next day. The "widow" was wearing a perfume that I hadn't noticed the night before.

I'd just begun telling her some of the reasons why I'd decided to go on this journey when Habib came into the room. He approached soundlessly, barefooted, as if he'd hoped we wouldn't notice him.

"I've come to sleep in here because of the mosquitoes," he said when he realised I knew he was there. "I was getting eaten alive in the other room."

I sighed.

"You were right to come. The door here's too small for the mosquitoes to get in."

Had I let my annoyance show in my voice? My neighbour moved her head closer to mine and said in a whisper as quiet as she could make it:

"He's still only a child!"

Again she was trying to make excuses for him. Perhaps, too, she wanted to show me that Habib's jealousy was unfounded. For I might think that if he'd plotted with her to help her escape from her in-laws and join up with us, it was not only out of a spirit of chivalry but also because he felt something for her, and that she hadn't discouraged him even though she was seven or eight years his senior.

I think he *is* jealous. First of all he lay down close to the wall, wrapped up in his blanket. Even though he didn't say anything, I could hear his irregular breathing – he wasn't asleep. His presence annoyed me. On the one hand I said to myself that in the morning I must explain to him clearly that my two nights' proximity to the "widow" was merely the result of circumstances that he knew all about, and no one should make anything of it. On the other hand, I didn't see, and still don't, why I should have to justify myself to this urchin. I didn't put *myself* in this embarrassing situation! I may be easy-going, but I mustn't be pushed too far! If ever I did feel like wooing Marta, I wouldn't ask permission from my nephews, or from anyone else!

I turned to her firmly and whispered, not too softly:

"If he really is still a child, I'll punish him like one!"

As I moved near her I could smell her perfume more strongly, and I felt like moving nearer still. But Habib, if he hadn't been able to make out my words, at least had heard me whisper. And, still wrapped up in his blanket, he wriggled over and lay down at our feet. Yes, he stretched himself right up against our feet so that we couldn't move an inch.

I was tempted to give him good thump, "accidentally on purpose", while I was supposed to be asleep. But I preferred to take my revenge differently: I took Marta's hand in mine and held it there, under the blanket, till morning.

Near the Orontes, 29 August

By this morning it had stopped raining and we were able to resume our journey. I'd been so annoyed by my nephew's unseemly behaviour that I'd had very little sleep.

But perhaps it was best that the night should end as it did. Yes, on second thoughts it's better to wake up amid the pangs of desire than amid those of remorse.

We took leave of our hosts, who put us even more in their debt by loading down our mules with provisions – enough for several days' journey. May Heaven give us the chance to return their hospitality!

The going is more pleasant after the rain – no sun, or excessive heat, or clouds of dust. Some mud, of course, but that affects only the hooves of our mules. We kept going until it started to get dark.

We skirted the town of Homs and halted for the night at a monastery on the banks of the Orontes. I'd stayed there twice before, on a trip to Aleppo and back with my father; but no one here could remember that.

In the evening, as I was strolling beside the river, in the monastery gardens, a young monk with bulging eyes came up and questioned me excitedly on the rumours circulating about next year. Vehemently though he condemned "false reports" and "superstition", he seemed distraught. He spoke of disturbing signs recounted by local peasants – a calf born with two heads, the sudden drying up of an ancient spring. He also mentioned the hitherto unheard-of behaviour of certain women, but he did so in such a roundabout style that I couldn't understand what he was driving at.

I did my best to reassure him, quoting the Scriptures once more and reminding him of man's inability to foretell the future. I don't know if my arguments helped him. No doubt he went away from our encounter having imbibed something of my apparent calm; but *I* brought away from it a tremor of *his* fear.

On the road, 30 August

I've just read what I've written in the last few days, and I'm appalled.

I undertook this journey for the noblest of reasons, concerned about the survival of the universe and the reactions of my fellow-mortals to the dramatic events now being foretold. And because of that woman I find myself embroiled in the filthy byways beloved of the vilest of men. Jealousies, intrigues, petty tricks – when the whole world might be annihilated tomorrow!

Sheikh Abdel-Bassit was right. What is the good of travelling all over the world just to see what is inside me already?

I must pull myself together! I must get my original inspiration back, and dip my pen only in the most venerable ink, even if it is also the bitterest.

We often speak of sea-sickness, but rarely of riding-sickness, as if it was less degrading to suffer on the deck of a ship than on the back of a mule, a camel or a nag.

But riding-sickness is what I've been suffering from for the last three days, though I haven't got to the point of deciding to interrupt the journey. However, I haven't written much.

Yesterday evening we reached the little town of Maarra, and it was only in the shelter of its half-ruined walls that I felt myself come alive again and got my appetite back.

This morning, as I was sauntering through the shopping streets, something very strange happened. The local booksellers had never seen me before, so I could question them freely about *The Hundredth Name*. All I met with were expressions of ignorance – whether genuine or feigned, I couldn't say. But by the last booth, next to the main mosque, just as I was about to turn back, a very old seller of secondhand books, whom I hadn't yet spoken to, came up to me, bare-headed, and handed me a book. I opened it at random and, following an impulse I still can't explain, began to read aloud the lines my eyes first fell upon:

> *They say Time is soon to die*
> *That the days are short of breath*
> *They lie.*

The author of the book is Abu-l-Ala, the blind poet of Maarra. Why did the old man put it into my hands? Why did it open just at that page? And what made me read aloud from it like that, right out in the street?

Is it a sign? But what sort of a sign is it that refutes all other signs?

I bought the old man's book. No doubt it will be the least unreasonable of my travelling companions.

Aleppo, 6 September

We got here yesterday evening, and had to spend all today haggling with a sly and greedy caravaneer. He claimed, among countless other tricks, that the presence in the party of a wealthy Genoese merchant and his wife meant he had to take on three more men to strengthen the escort. I said we were four men to one woman, and could defend ourselves against bandits if necessary. He looked us over meaningly, raising an eyebrow at the puny shanks of my nephews, the mild demeanour of my clerk, and especially my own prosperous paunch. Then he gave a disagreeable laugh. I felt like turning on my heel and applying to someone else, but I restrained myself. I hadn't much choice. I'd have had to wait a week or two and risk running into the first winter cold of Anatolia, and even then I might not find a more amiable guide. So I swallowed my pride and pretended to share the joke, tapping my belly and holding out the thirty-two piastres he was asking for – the equivalent of 2,500 maidins, no less!

Weighing the coins in his hand, he tried to make me promise that if we all arrived at our destination safe and sound, together with our merchandise, I'd pay him something extra. I reminded him that we had no merchandise, only our personal effects and our provisions. But I still had to undertake to show my gratitude if the whole journey passed off without incident.

We leave at dawn the day after tomorrow, Tuesday. If God wills, we should reach Constantinople in about forty days.

After the tribulations of the journey so far, and before those yet to come, I'd been hoping for a quiet day, an oasis of calm, rest and cool, enlivened by a gentle stroll or two. But today hasn't been in the least like that: fatigue, one scare after another, and an as yet unexplained mystery is all this Monday has produced.

Having woken up early, I left the inn and went to the old tannery district to look for an Armenian wine-merchant whose address I still had. I found him quite easily and bought a couple of pitchers of malmsey from him for the journey. As I left his shop I suddenly had a strange feeling. On the steps leading up to the door of a nearby house there was a group of men, talking and glancing furtively in my direction. Something glinted like a blade in the eyes of one of them.

As I walked on through the narrow streets I felt more and more as if I was being followed, spied on, encircled. Was I just imagining it? I was sorry now that I'd ventured here alone, without my clerk or my nephews. I was sorry I hadn't gone back to the Armenian's shop as soon as I scented danger. But it was too late. Two of the men were now walking in front of me, and when I turned round I saw two more of them cutting off my retreat. The street I was in had emptied as if by magic. A few moments before it had seemed quite busy – not crowded, but not empty either. Now there was no one. A desert. I could already see myself being stabbed and then robbed of all I had. This is where my journey ends, I thought with a shudder. I'd have shouted for help, but I couldn't utter a sound.

Looking round desperately for some way of escape, I noticed, on my right, the doorway of a house. With a last effort I clutched at the door-knob, and it opened. Inside, all that was to be seen was a dark corridor. To hide there would be no better than choosing the place to have my throat cut. So as my pursuers followed me into the passage at one end, I hastened along it towards the other. There I came upon a second door, slightly ajar. I didn't have time to knock. I just shouldered it open and burst in.

I can hardly find words to describe the scene that then unfolded. I can smile at it now, but at the time it made me tremble almost as much as the blades of the rascals behind me.

There lay prostrate before me a dozen men, barefoot and deep in prayer. And I, not content with interrupting their ceremony and trampling on their prayer mat, tripped over someone's leg, let out a fruity Genoese oath, and measured my length on the ground. My two pitchers of wine crashed together as I fell. One of them broke, and its unholy contents splashed with a loud gurgle over the rugs on the floor of the little mosque.

God in Heaven! Before I had time to be afraid I was ashamed. How could I, in such a few seconds, have been guilty of so much profanation, boorishness and blasphemy? What could I say? How could I explain? What words could express my regret and remorse? I hadn't even the strength to get to my feet. Then the eldest of those present – he was in front of the rest and leading the prayer – came over, took me by the arm, and helped me up, disconcerting me further by saying:

"Forgive us, Master, if we finish praying before attending to you. Be kind enough to wait for us behind the curtain."

Was I dreaming? Had I misunderstood? This affable tone might have reassured me if I hadn't known how the sins I'd just committed were usually punished. But what could I do? It was impossible for me to go out into the street again, and I didn't want to make matters worse by perturbing their orisons further with apologies and repinings. All I could do was withdraw obediently behind the curtain. There I found a bare room lit by a small window looking on to a garden. I leaned against the wall and folded my arms.

I didn't have long to wait. When they'd finished praying they all came into my cell and gathered around me in a half-circle. They gazed at me silently for a moment, exchanging glances with one another. Then the oldest among them spoke to me again, as amiably as before:

49

"If the Master introduced himself in that manner in order to test us, he knows we are ready to welcome him. And if you are a mere passer-by, may God judge you according to your intentions."

Not knowing what to say, I took refuge in silence. In any case, he hadn't asked me a question, even though his eyes, like those of his companions, were gulfs of expectation. I assumed an enigmatic expression and walked towards the door. They stood aside and let me pass. When I got out into the street I found my pursuers had taken themselves off, and I could go back to the hostelry without further hindrance.

I do wish someone would explain to me what just happened. But I've thought it best to say nothing to my companions about my misadventure. If my nephews found out how rashly I'd acted, my authority over them would probably suffer. And then they'd think they could commit whatever folly they liked without my daring to criticise.

I'll tell them about it later on. Meanwhile, I'm content to confide my secret to these pages. Isn't that what this journal is for?

But sometimes I ask myself: why keep a diary, and in this ambiguous language, when I know no one will ever read it? When in fact I don't even *want* anyone to read it? I do it precisely because it helps me to clarify my thoughts and memories without having to tell my travelling companions about them.

Other people write as they speak. I write as I stay silent.

On the road, 8 September

Hatem woke me too early, and I still feel I didn't finish my dream. But although I hadn't had enough sleep, I had to hurry to join the caravan by the Antioch gate.

In my dream I was being followed by some men, and every time I thought I'd shaken them off I saw them in front of me again, barring my path and baring their teeth at me like wild animals.

It's hardly surprising I had such a dream after my experience of yesterday. What does surprise me, and disturb me somewhat, is that I still feel I'm being spied on even now I'm awake. But by whom? By the brigands who wanted to rob me? Or by that strange congregation whose prayers I interrupted? I don't suppose I'm really being pursued by either group, but I can't help turning round all the time.

I only hope this aftermath of last night will fade as I get farther away from Aleppo!

9 September

This morning, after we'd camped out all night in a field strewn with ancient ruins – broken columns buried under sand and grass – the caravaneer came and asked me point-blank whether the woman with me was really my wife. Trying to look offended, I said she was. He apologised, assuring me he hadn't meant any harm but had forgotten whether I'd told him or not.

This has put me in a bad mood for the rest of the day. I keep turning it over in my mind. Does he suspect something? There are about a hundred travellers in the caravan; might one of them have recognised the "widow"? It's not impossible.

But it's also possible that the caravaneer overheard a snatch of conversation or caught a meaning look between Marta and Habib, and that his question was intended to warn me.

As I write these lines my doubts increase, as if my pen, scratching at the paper, was also scratching at the wounds to my self-esteem . . .

I shan't write another word today.

11 September

Today there was one of those demeaning incidents I promised myself I wouldn't mention. But because it bothers me, and I can't confide in anyone, I might as well write it down.

The caravan had halted for the travellers to have a meal and a short rest before starting out again when it was cooler. We'd spread out at random, a few people lying or sitting under each tree, when Habib leaned over and whispered something in Marta's ear that made her laugh aloud. Everybody nearby heard, and turned to look, first at her and then, with pitying expressions, at me. Some exchanged remarks under their breath with their neighbours: I couldn't hear what was said, but their smiles and titters were not lost on me.

I need not say how hurt and humiliated and embarrassed I felt. I decided I would have it out with my nephew and make him understand he must behave better in future. But what could I say? What had he done wrong? Wasn't it I who was behaving as though the lie linking Marta and me together gave me special privileges?

And so it does, in a way. Since the people in the caravan think she's my wife, my honour will be tarnished if I let her behave irresponsibly.

I'm glad I confided in my journal. Now I know that the feelings upsetting me are not unjustified. They've got nothing to do with jealousy; it's honour and respectability that are at stake. I can't just let my nephew whisper in public to the woman everyone thinks is my wife, and make her roar with laughter!

I'm not sure whether putting all this into words makes me angrier or calms me down. Perhaps writing only arouses the passions in order to allay them, as beaters flush out the game in order to expose it to the hunters' arrows.

12 September

I'm glad I didn't give in to the desire to tell Habib or Marta off. Anything I might have said would only have sounded like jealousy. Though as God is my witness it isn't that! Anyhow, I'd only have made myself ridiculous, and made them whisper and laugh together at my expense. Trying to defend my respectability, I'd just have damaged it.

I preferred to deal with the matter quite differently. This afternoon I invited Marta to ride beside me, and as we went along I explained why I'd undertaken this journey. Habib may already have told her something about it, but if so she gave no sign, listening attentively to my explanations, though she didn't seem very worried about next year.

I wanted our conversation to be rather formal and serious. So far, I'd thought of Marta's presence in our party as an unavoidable accident, sometimes annoying or embarrassing, at other times comical, amusing and almost reassuring. By taking her into my confidence as I did today, I've in a way made her one of us.

I'm not sure if I did right, but at any rate I felt relieved and much more comfortable after our conversation. After all, I'd been the only one that suffered because of the tensions that had sprung up in our little group since we broke our journey in Tripoli. I'm not the sort of person who thrives on adversity. I want to travel in the company of affectionate nephews and a devoted clerk . . . As for Marta, I don't yet know what I really want. A kind of considerate neighbour? Something more? I can't just listen to my own longings as a lonely man, though every day I spend on the road will make me feel them more. I know I ought to do my best not to pester her with my attentions, though I'm well aware too that they spring from my soul as well as my body.

I haven't spent a night alone with her since we left the tailor's house. Sometimes we've slept under canvas, sometimes at an inn, but always all five of us together, or even with other travellers as well. Though I haven't done anything to change things, I have sometimes wished circumstances would arrange for Marta and me to be alone with one another again.

To tell the truth, I wish it all the time.

13 September

Tomorrow is Holy Cross Day, and this evening I had a serious argument on the subject with the caravaneer.

We'd stopped for the night at a khan on the outskirts of Alexandretta, and I was strolling round the courtyard to stretch my legs when I overheard a conversation. One of the travellers, a very old man, from Aleppo judging by his accent, and very poor judging by his patched clothes, was asking the caravaneer what time we were to set off tomorrow. He said he'd like to be able to go, even if only for a moment, to the Church of the Cross, which according to him contains a piece of the True Cross. He spoke timidly, with a slight stammer, and this seemed to bring out the arrogance of our caravaneer, who replied in a scornful manner that we were going to start at the crack of dawn and had no time to waste in churches. If the old man wanted to see a bit of wood, he need only pick up that one – and the caravaneer pointed to a rotten old bit of tree stump lying on the ground.

Then I went over and said firmly that I wished us to stay on in Alexandretta a few hours longer so that I could attend mass on the feast of the Holy Cross.

The caravaneer, who'd thought he was alone with the old man, started when he heard me. He would probably have avoided talking like that in the presence of witnesses. But after a slight hesitation he recovered and answered – more politely, however, than to the other poor fellow – that the time of departure could not be put off: the other travellers would object. He even said it would harm the whole caravan, hinting that I'd have to pay compensation if I wanted a postponement. Then I raised my voice further and insisted that the caravan should wait for me until mass was over, otherwise I'd complain to the Genoese Resident in Constantinople, and even to the Sublime Porte.

I was taking a risk when I said that. I am in no position to approach the Ottoman Court, and even the Genoese Resident hasn't much influence these days: he himself was subjected to harassment last year, and would be quite incapable of protecting or obtaining redress for me. But, thank God, the caravaneer didn't know that. He didn't dare take my threats lightly, and I could see he was wavering. If we'd been alone, I'm sure he'd have tried to smooth things over, but the sound of our voices had attracted a circle of travellers, and he couldn't climb down in front of them without losing face.

All of a sudden one of the travellers went up to him. He had a green scarf wound round his head, as if we were in the middle of a sand-storm. He put his hand on the caravaneer's shoulder, and stood there looking at him for a few moments without a word – or if there was one, it was uttered in such a low voice I didn't hear it. Then he walked slowly away.

Then my adversary, his face screwed up as if in pain, spat on the ground and said:

"We shan't be leaving tomorrow, because of him!"

"Him" was me. By pointing me out, the caravaneer meant to identify the guilty party, but everyone present realised he was designating the victor.

Am I pleased with my victory? Yes, I'm not only pleased – I'm delighted, happy and proud. The old Christian from Aleppo came and thanked me, praising me for my piety.

I didn't want to disabuse him, but piety has nothing to do with it. I was acting out of profane prudence. In the ordinary way I seldom go to mass, I don't celebrate Holy Cross Day, and in my view relics are worth no more than their equivalent in piastres. But people would have stopped respecting me if I'd stood by and let the symbols of my religion and my country be insulted.

It's the same with Marta. Whether she's my wife in fact or only in appearance, my honour is involved with her, and I owe it to myself to protect it.

14 September, Holy Cross Day

I keep thinking about that incident yesterday. It's rare for me to act so violently, and it gives me a pang to remember it, but I don't regret my boldness.

Reading over the account I wrote yesterday evening, it seems to me I didn't say enough about how fast my heart was beating at some points. There were some long moments of silent struggle when the caravaneer was wondering if I really had as much protection as I claimed, and *I* was asking myself how I could get out of this confrontation without losing face. Of course I had to look him in the eye, to disguise my weakness and make him think I was sure of myself.

That said, there was also a moment when I was no longer afraid. When I stopped being a merchant and took on the spirit of a conqueror. Brief as that moment was, I'm proud of it.

Was it my will-power that brought about the decision? Or was it the intervention of the Arab in the head-dress? Perhaps I ought to thank him . . . Yesterday I didn't want to approach him, in case people thought I'd been at a loss and he'd saved the situation for me. But today I did look for him, and I couldn't find him.

I keep thinking about him, and because I'm not engaged in any contest now, and this notebook isn't an arena and I'm not surrounded by spectators, I can say here that I was immensely relieved when he took a hand: my victory is partly his, and I am somewhat in his debt.

What could he have said to our caravaneer to make him give in?

I almost forgot to say that I, together with my nephews, my clerk, the "widow", and about a dozen other travellers, duly went to the Church of the Cross. For the first time, Marta was wearing a coloured dress – a blue one with the neck edged in red. I'd seen her in it as a girl, when she went to church in Gibelet on feast days with her father the barber. Up till then, ever since she joined us on our journey, she'd always worn black – out of bravado, because her in-laws objected to it. She must have decided the gesture was no longer necessary.

All through the celebration of the mass, the men kept looking at her – some furtively, others openly. But as God is my witness, it didn't bother me, and I didn't feel the slightest twinge of jealousy.

16 September

A Jewish jeweller from Aleppo, Maïmoun Toleitli by name, came to see me this morning. He'd heard how learned I was, he said, and was eager to meet me. Why hadn't he approached me before? I asked. There was an embarrassed silence. I realised at once that he'd preferred to wait until after Holy Cross Day. So far, admittedly, when some of my co-religionists meet a Jew, they feel obliged to act in a very hostile manner towards him, as if such behaviour constituted a just revenge and an act of great piety.

I explained tactfully that I wasn't like that, and that if I'd insisted on staying on for a day in Alexandretta it was not to demonstrate that my religion was more important than other people's, but simply to insist on being shown some respect.

"Quite right," he said. "With the world the way it is . . ."

"Yes," I agreed. "If it had been different, I'd have demonstrated my doubts rather than my beliefs."

He smiled, then lowered his voice to say:

"When faith preaches hate, blessed are the doubters!"

I smiled back, and lowered my voice to say:

"We are all lost sheep."

We spoke for only about five minutes, but it was enough to make us brothers. Our whispered exchanges generated the spiritual kinship no religion can create, and no religion can destroy.

17 September

Today our caravaneer decided to make us depart from the usual itinerary and go round by the bay of Alexandretta. He claims a fortune-teller told him he'd have his throat cut if he went through a certain place on a Thursday, so the delay I'd insisted on forced him to change our route. The other travellers didn't protest. What could they have said? You can argue about a difference of opinion. You can't argue about superstition.

I said nothing, for fear of causing another incident. But I suspect the rogue of re-routing the caravan for some nefarious purpose. Especially as the inhabitants of the village he took us to have a dreadful reputation. As wreckers and smugglers! Hatem and my nephews bring me all sorts of rumours. I tell them to be careful.

My clerk has put up the tent, but I'm in no hurry to go to bed. Marta will stretch out on her own along one side of the tent, and we four men will lie cramped together at right angles to her, with our heads nearest and our feet pointing away from her. I'll smell her perfume and hear her breathing all night long, without being able to see her. Sometimes the presence of a woman can be torture!

To pass the time till I felt drowsy, I went and sat on a stone to write a few lines by the light from one of our camp fires. Then I caught sight of Maïmoun. He wasn't yet ready to retire, either, so we went for a stroll along the beach. The lapping of the waves encourages confidences, and I told him all about my strange adventure in Aleppo. He lived there, so

I expected him to offer some explanation. And he did provide one that satisfied me for the time being.

"Those men were more frightened of you than you were of them," he began. "They practise their religion secretly and are persecuted by the authorities. They're suspected of rebellion and sedition.

"But everyone in Aleppo knows about them. Their enemies nicknamed them 'The Impatient Ones', to make fun of them, but they liked it and now they use it themselves. They believe that the Hidden Imam, God's ultimate representative on earth, is already among us, ready to reveal himself when the time is ripe, and to put an end to the sufferings of the faithful. Other groups say the Imam will come, sooner or later, some time in the future, but the Impatient Ones believe his advent is imminent, and that the saviour is here already, in Aleppo or Constantinople or elsewhere, going about the world, watching, and getting ready to tear aside the veil of secrecy.

"People wonder how they would recognise him if they met him. I've been told the Impatient Ones are always discussing this among themselves. Because the Imam is hidden and must not be found by his enemies, we must be ready to recognise him in the most unexpected disguises. He who will one day inherit all the world's riches might come in rags. He who is the wisest of the wise might appear in the form of a madman. He who is all piety and devotion might commit the worst sins. For this reason these men make it their duty to revere beggars, fools and profligates. Thus, when you intruded on their worship, and swore, and spilled wine on their prayer mat, they thought you were trying to test them. They weren't sure, of course, but they didn't want to make you unwelcome in case you were the Expected One.

"Their faith requires them to be friendly to everyone, even to Jews and Christians, because the Imam might assume a different religion as camouflage. They must even treat their persecutors well . . ."

But if they are so pleasant to everyone, why are they persecuted?

"Because they are waiting for the one who will topple all thrones and do away with all laws."

59

I had never heard of these strange sectarians, but Maïmoun told me they'd existed for a long while.

"But it's true they're becoming more numerous and more fervent now. More careless too. Because of all the rumours going round about the end of the world, which the weak-minded are taken in by."

These last words have troubled me. Have I myself become one of the "weak-minded" people my new friend condemns? Sometimes I check myself and anathematise credulity and suspicion, smiling with scorn or pity . . . when I myself am hunting for *The Hundredth Name*!

But how can I remain entirely rational when I'm always coming upon signs and portents? Isn't my recent adventure at Aleppo very disturbing? Doesn't it look as if Heaven, or some other invisible force, is trying to increase my bewilderment?

18 September

Today Maïmoun told me he contemplated going to live in Amsterdam, in the United Provinces.

I thought at first he was speaking as a jeweller, and that he hoped to find more beautiful gems to carve there, and wealthier customers. But he was speaking as a sage, a free man, and also as one who had been hurt.

"I'm told it's the only city in the world where a man can say 'I'm a Jew' as others, in their countries, say 'I'm a Christian' or 'I'm a Muslim' – without fearing for his life, his property or his dignity."

I'd have liked to question him further, but he seemed so moved by what he'd said already that he had a lump in his throat and his eyes filled with tears. So I said no more, and we walked on side by side in silence.

Further on, when I could see he was calmer, I put my hand on his arm and said:

"One day, God willing, the whole world will be an Amsterdam."

He smiled bitterly.

"That's your pure heart speaking. The world mutters something different. Quite different."

Tarsus, dawn, Monday 21 September

I talk away to Maïmoun for hours every day. I tell him about my fortune and my family. But there are two subjects I still shrink from broaching.

The first concerns my real reasons for coming on this journey. All I've said is that I needed to buy some books in Constantinople; and he's been considerate enough not to ask me which ones. As soon as we met it was our doubts that drew us together, as well as a certain love for wisdom and reason. If I now went and confessed that I'd given credence to vulgar delusions and common fears, I'd forfeit all his esteem. So shall I keep it all to myself for the whole of the journey? Perhaps not. Perhaps a time will come when I can tell him everything without harming our friendship.

The other subject is Marta. Something has kept me from telling my friend the truth about her.

As is my habit, I haven't said anything that's untrue. Not once have I uttered the expression "my wife". Either I avoid referring to her, or if I must do so I use vague terms like "my people" or "my nearest and dearest", as the men in this country often do, out of an extreme sense of modesty in this connection.

But yesterday it seems to me I crossed the invisible line that separates *allowing* someone to think something and *causing* them to do so. And I feel rather guilty about it.

As we were approaching Tarsus, St Paul's home town, Maïmoun came and told me he had a cousin there of whom he was very fond, and in whose house he proposed to sleep, rather than in the caravanserai with the rest of the travellers. And he would be honoured if "my wife" and I, together with my nephews and my clerk, would join him.

I ought to have declined Maïmoun's invitation, or at least let him insist. But before I realised what I was doing I'd blurted out that nothing would give me more pleasure. If Maïmoun was surprised by my haste, he did not show it: he just said he was delighted by this token of friendship.

So this evening, as soon as the caravan arrived, we went to the cousin's house. His name is Eleazar, and he's past his first youth and very well-to-do. His prosperity is reflected in his dwelling – two storeys standing in a garden planted with olive and mulberry trees. I gather he deals in oil and soap, but we didn't talk of our business, only of our homesickness. He kept reciting poems praising Mossoul, the town where he was born. With tears in his eyes he recalled its narrow streets, its fountains, its colourful characters, and the tricks he got up to there as a boy. He's obviously never got over having to leave Mossoul to settle here in Tarsus, where he had to take over a flourishing business founded by his wife's grandfather.

While a meal was being prepared, he summoned his daughter and asked her to show Marta and me to our room. There followed a somewhat trivial scene, but one that I feel I ought to describe.

I'd noticed that my nephews – especially Habib – had been on the alert since I'd told them of Maïmoun's invitation. And even more since we'd entered Eleazar's house. For it was obvious at a glance that this wasn't a place where five or six people were going to be crammed together to sleep in one room. When Eleazar asked his daughter to show "our guest and his wife" to their room, Habib started to fidget, and I had the impression he was getting ready to say something unpleasant. Would he really have done so? I don't know. But at the moment it seemed to me that he might, and to avoid a scene I took a hand and asked our host if I could have a word with him in private. Habib smiled – no doubt thinking that his Uncle Balthasar, at last come to himself again, was going to find some excuse to avoid spending another "embarrassing" night. But, God forgive me, this was not at all what I had in mind.

Once out in the garden with my host, I said:

"Maïmoun has become like a brother to me, so as you are a beloved cousin of his I consider you a friend of mine already. But I feel awkward arriving here like this, with four other people."

"I am truly delighted to have you as my guest," he replied, "and the best way for you to show you're my friend is to make yourself as much at ease under my roof as if you were in your own house."

As he spoke he gave me a searching look. No doubt he was somewhat intrigued by my asking him to get up and go outside to talk to him in private merely to say something so trite, so much a part of ordinary politeness. Perhaps he thought I had some other, unavowable reason – connected no doubt with his religion – for not wanting to sleep in his house, and was expecting me to insist on leaving. But I quickly gave in and simply thanked him for his hospitality. And we went back into the house arm in arm, both wearing a solemn smile.

Meanwhile our host's daughter had gone back to the kitchen, and one of the servants had come in with cool drinks and dried fruit. Eleazar asked him to leave all that and show my nephews to their room upstairs. A few minutes later, the daughter of the house returned, and Eleazar asked her again to show "my wife" and me to *our* room.

So that was how it went. Then we had dinner, after which everyone retired to bed. I said I needed to go outside for a short stroll before I could go to sleep, and Maïmoun and his cousin came with me. I didn't want my nephews to see Marta and me go up to the same room.

But I was anxious to be with her, and a few minutes later I joined her.

"When you went outside with our host," she said, "I thought you were going to tell him everything – about you and me."

As she spoke I looked at her, trying to make out whether she wanted to reproach me or express relief.

"I think we'd have hurt his feelings if we'd turned down his invitation," I said. "I hope you don't mind too much."

"I'm beginning to get used to it," she replied.

And nothing in her voice or her expression betrayed the slightest annoyance. Or embarrassment.

"Let's go to sleep then!" said I.

And as I spoke I put my arm round her shoulders as if we were about to go for a walk.

And my nights with her are something like that – like a walk under the trees with a girl, when you both tremble whenever your hands touch. Lying there side by side makes us shy, considerate, restrained. Isn't it a more dubious matter to steal a kiss when you're in that situation?

Mine's a very strange wooing! I didn't hold her hand until our second meeting, and even then I blushed for it in the dark. At this, our third encounter, I put my arm round her shoulder. And again I blushed for it.

She raised her head, undid her hair, and spread the black tresses over my bare arm. Then she went to sleep without saying a word.

I want to keep on savouring this first taste of pleasure. Not that I mean to let it remain as chaste as that for ever. But I'm not in a hurry to end this ambiguous closeness, this growing complicity, this pleasurably painful desire, in a word this path we're going along together, secretly pleased but pretending every time it's Providence that's bringing us together. It's a delightful game, and I'm not sure I want to move on.

But it's also a dangerous game, I know. We could be consumed by fire at any moment. But how far away the end of the world was last night!

22 September

What did I do that was so reprehensible? What more happened last night in Tarsus than happened during the two nights we spent in the village of the tailor? Yet my people are treating me as if I'd just done something completely beyond the pale! None of them will meet my eye. My two nephews whisper to one another in my presence as if I didn't exist. And although even Hatem, admittedly, still fusses around me as attentively as any clerk fusses around his master, there is something affected and over-obsequious in his manner and expression that I read as a silent reproach. Marta, too, seems to avoid my company, as if she were afraid of appearing to be in collusion with me.

About what, for Heaven's sake? What else have I done but play my part in this farce written by my accusers themselves? What *should* I have done? Reveal to all our travelling companions, and first of all to the caravaneer, that this woman is not my wife – and have her insulted and driven away? Or ought I to have told Abbas the tailor, then Maïmoun and his cousin, that Marta really is my wife but that I don't want to sleep with her – and have all of them ask themselves unseemly questions? I did what a man of honour ought to do – protected the "widow" and didn't take advantage of her. Is it a crime if I get some satisfaction, some subtle pleasure, out of this comic situation? That's what I could say if I wanted to justify myself. But I shan't say anything. The blood of the Embriaci flows in my veins and tells me to be silent. For me it's enough to know I'm innocent, and that my loving hand remains pure.

Perhaps innocent isn't the word. I don't mean to say there's anything in what the scamps who condemn me suggest, but I must admit, in the secrecy of these pages, that I did rather ask for the trouble I'm in. I took advantage of appearances, and now appearances are taking advantage of me. That's the truth of the matter. Instead of setting my nephews a good example, I let myself be drawn into a kind of game, influenced by desire, boredom, the discomforts of the journey, vanity

– who knows? Influenced too, it seems to me, by the spirit of the age, the spirit of the Year of the Beast. When people think the world is about to founder, something goes wrong, and men lapse into either extreme devotion or extreme debauchery. I myself haven't got that far yet, thank God, but it seems to me I'm gradually losing my sense of propriety and respectability. Doesn't my behaviour to Marta reflect a touch of unreason that gets progressively worse, making me think it's quite an ordinary matter to sleep in the same bed as a person I pretend is my wife; making me take advantage of the generosity of both my host and his cousin; and all this under the same roof as four other people who know I'm lying? How long can I continue on this road to perdition? And, when it all comes out, how can I go back to my old life in Gibelet?

You see what I'm like! I've only been writing for a quarter of an hour, and already I'm on the point of seeing my critics' point of view. But these are only marks on paper, and no one will ever read them.

I'm writing by the light of a large candle. I like the smell of wax – I think it encourages thought, and confidences. I'm sitting on the floor, leaning against the wall, with my notebook on my knees. Through the window behind me, with its curtain billowing in the wind, comes the whinnying of the horses in the courtyard, and sometimes the guffawing of drunken soldiers. We're in the first khan in the foothills of the Taurus mountains, on the way to Konya. We'll be there in a week if all goes well. My people are sleeping, or trying to sleep, all round me, strewn in all directions. Looking at them like this, I can't still be angry with them – either with my sister's sons, who are like my own, or with my clerk, who serves me devotedly even if he disapproves of me in his own way, or with this little-known woman who is less and less a stranger.

This morning – a Monday – I was in a completely different mood. Cursing my nephews, neglecting the "widow", loading Hatem down with endless unnecessary errands, I steered clear of them all and rode peacefully along beside Maïmoun. As for him, he looked at me exactly as he had yesterday. Or so it seemed to me as the caravan moved off.

*　　*　　*

As we were leaving Tarsus a traveller walking in front of us pointed to a ruined hovel, near an old well, saying St Paul was born there. Maïmoun moved close to me and whispered that he doubted this very much, as the apostle of Jesus came from a wealthy family, belonging to the tribe of Benjamin and makers and merchants of goat's-hair tents.

"His family must have been as extensive as that of my cousin Eleazar."

When I expressed my surprise at his knowledge of a religion not his own, his answer was modest.

"I've just read a few books, to limit my ignorance."

Because of my profession and a natural curiosity, I too had read a few books on various contemporary religions, as well as on the ancient beliefs of the Greeks and Romans. So we began to compare the respective merits of all these faiths, though of course neither of us criticised the other one's religion.

But when in the course of our exchanges I said that in my opinion one of the most beautiful precepts of Christianity was "Love thy neighbour as thyself", I noticed Maïmoun hesitate. I urged him, in the name of our friendship and of our shared doubts, to tell me what he was thinking.

"At first sight," he said, "that exhortation seems irreproachable. And anyway, before it was taken over by Jesus, it was also to be found, expressed in similar terms, in Leviticus, chapter 19, verse 18. Even so, I have some reservations about it."

"What are they?"

"Seeing what most people make of their lives, and of their intelligence, I wouldn't want them to love me as they love themselves."

I was about to answer, but he raised his hand.

"Wait. There's something else, something more worrying, in my view. Some people are always sure to interpret this precept with more arrogance than magnanimity. They'll read it as saying: What's good for you is good for everyone else. If you know the truth, you ought to use every possible means to rescue lost sheep and set them on the right path again. Hence the forced baptisms imposed on my ancestors in Toledo in the past. And I myself have heard the injunction quoted more often by wolves than by lambs. So I'm sorry – I have doubts about it."

"You surprise me. And I don't know yet whether I agree with you or not. I'll have to think. I've always considered that the most beautiful saying . . ."

"If you're looking for the most beautiful saying to be found in any religion, the most beautiful that ever issued from the lips of man, that's not it. The one I mean was spoken by Jesus, too. He didn't take it from Scripture, though. He just listened to his own heart."

What could it be? I waited. Maïmoun stopped his mount for a moment to underline the solemnity of his quotation.

"Let him that is without sin among you cast the first stone."

23 September

Was there an allusion to Marta in the phrase Maïmoun quoted yesterday? I wondered about it all night. There was nothing reproachful in his look; but perhaps there was a subtle invitation to speak. And why should I still be silent, since in my friend's eyes Christ's saying absolved me of what little wrong I may have committed, as well as of my deceitful omissions?

So I made up my mind to tell him everything this very morning: who Marta is, how she came to be in our party, what kind of relations have taken place between her and me, and what kind of relations have not. After the somewhat grotesque episode at Eliazar's house, it became urgently necessary for me to stop dissimulating, otherwise the friendship between Maïmoun and myself might be damaged. What's more, the situation gets more and more complicated every time we halt for the night, and I was going to need the advice of a wise and sympathetic friend.

Well, I didn't get much advice from Maïmoun today, though I did press him. He only told me to keep saying and doing what I've been saying and doing since our journey began. But he did promise to think the matter over some more, and to tell me if anything occurred to him that might make things go more smoothly.

I'm very glad, though, that he didn't hold my deceit and half-truths against me. If anything, he seemed amused by it all. And it seems to me that he now greets Marta with even more deference than before, and with a sort of secret admiration.

It's true her behaviour shows courage. *I* am always thinking of myself, my own embarrassment and my own self-esteem, when all I really risk is the odd bit of mischievous or envious gossip. Whereas she stands to lose everything in this petty game, even her life. I don't doubt for a moment that if her brother-in-law had found her, at the beginning of this journey, he'd have had no scruples about cutting her throat and then going back to his people and boasting about it. And if Marta ever returns to Gibelet, even armed with the document she seeks, she'll still face the same dangers as before.

If that day comes, shall I have the courage to defend her?

25 September

This morning, seeing Marta riding apart from our group, solitary, pensive, melancholy, I decided to go back and ride beside her, as I had done a few days ago. But this time I wanted not so much to tell her of my own hopes and fears as to question her and hear what she had to say. To begin with she eluded my questions, but I pressed her to describe what her life had been like in recent years, and what had made her, too, come on this journey.

While I expected to hear a string of complaints, I didn't at all foresee that my taking an interest in her misfortunes would break down a dam and unleash so much rage. A rage I'd never suspected behind her pleasant smiles.

"People never stop talking to me about the end of the world," she said. "They think they're frightening me. But for me the world ended when the man I loved betrayed me. After first making me betray my own father. Ever since then the sun no longer shines for me, and it wouldn't matter to me if it went out. And the Flood they predict doesn't scare me either – it would just make all men and all women equals in misfortune. Let it come as soon as it likes, whether it's a Deluge of water or of fire! Then I shan't have to tramp the roads begging for a paper that will allow me to live, a wretched document from the powers-that-be certifying that I may love and be married again! Then I shan't have to go from pillar to post any more – or else *everybody* will have to run in all directions! Yes, everybody! The judges, the janissaries, the bishops, and even the sultan! All of them will be running about like cats trapped in a field that's caught fire! Oh, if only Heaven would let me see that!

"People are afraid of seeing the Beast appear. I'm not afraid. The Beast? It's always been there, lurking near me. Every day I've met its scornful look – at home, in the street, even in church. Every day I've felt its bite! It's never stopped devouring my life."

Marta went on in this vein for some time. I've reported her words from memory – not word for word, I expect, but near enough. And I thought: "My God, woman – how you must have suffered since that time, not so long ago, when you were still my barber's carefree, mischievous daughter!"

At one point I rode near her and put my hand affectionately on hers. At that she fell silent, gave me a swift glance of gratitude, then veiled her face and wept.

For the rest of the day I could do nothing but think about what she'd said and follow her with my eyes. Now, more than ever before, I feel an immense fatherly affection for her. I long to know she's happy, but I wouldn't dare promise to make her happy myself. The most I could do would be to swear I'd never make her suffer.

But it remains to be seen whether, to make such a promise come true, I'd need to get closer to her or further away.

26 September

Today I finally told Maïmoun what made me undertake this journey, and asked him to tell me, with all the frankness due from a friend, what he felt about it. I didn't omit anything, either the pilgrim from Moscow, the book by Mazandarani, the number of the Beast, Boumeh's bad behaviour, or old Idriss's death. I needed help from Maïmoun's jeweller's eye, used to telling the difference between true and false brilliance. But he only answered my questions with others, and added his anxieties, or at least those of his family, to my own.

At first he listened to me in silence. While nothing I said seemed to surprise him, he became increasingly thoughtful, even downcast, with every sentence. When I'd finished he took both my hands in his.

"You have spoken to me like a brother," he said. "Now it's my turn to open my heart to you. My reasons for embarking on this journey are not all that different from yours. I, too, came because of these wretched rumours. I came reluctantly, exclaiming against credulity, superstition and all the computations and so-called 'signs' – but I came all the same. I had no choice. If I hadn't come my father would have died. You and I are both victims of the madness of our nearest and dearest."

Maïmoun's father, an assiduous reader of sacred texts, has long believed the end of the world to be at hand. According to him it is clearly written in the Zohar, the book of the cabalists, that in the year 5408 those who are resting in the dust will rise up. In the Jewish calendar, that year corresponds to our 1648.

"But that was seventeen years ago, and the Resurrection didn't take place. Despite all the prayer and fasting, despite all the privations my father imposed on my mother, my sisters and me – which we accepted with enthusiasm at the time – nothing happened. Since then I've lost all my illusions. I go to the synagogue when I must, so as to feel close to my family and friends. I laugh with them and cry with them on the appropriate occasions, so as not to seem unsympathetic to their joys and sorrows. But I don't expect anything or anyone any more. Unlike my father, who is none the wiser. He wouldn't dream of admitting that the year foretold by the Zohar was just an ordinary year. He's sure something happened then that we didn't hear of, but that will one day be revealed to us and to the world as a whole."

Ever since, Maïmoun's father does nothing but search for signs, especially those concerning 1648, the year of disappointed hopes. As a matter of fact, some important things did happen then – but has there ever been any year in which no important things happened?

"'In the old days,' my father says, 'there was always a period of respite between one calamity and the next, but since that accursed year disasters have followed one another in an uninterrupted stream. We have never experienced such a succession of woes. Isn't that a sign in itself?'

"One day I lost patience and said to him, 'Father, I always thought that was supposed to be the year of the Resurrection. That it would put an end to our sufferings, and that we had to look forward to it with joy and hope!' He answered: 'These pains are just birth-pangs; this blood is the blood that goes with deliverance!'

"So for seventeen years my father has been on the look-out for signs. But not always with the same degree of enthusiasm. Sometimes he'd let months go by without mentioning them once, then something would happen – some trouble in the family, or plague, famine or a visit from an important person – and it would all start up again. These last few years, although he's had serious health problems, he's only referred to the Resurrection as a distant hope. But a few months ago he started to get agitated again. The rumours circulating among the Christians about the imminent end of the world have completely upset him. Our community never stops discussing what is going and what is not going to happen, what we should be dreading and what we should be hoping for. Every time a rabbi from Damascus, Jerusalem or Tiberias, Egypt, Gaza or Smyrna passes through Aleppo, everyone crowds round him in a frenzy to find out what he knows or predicts.

"And so, a few weeks back, tired of hearing so many contradictory opinions, my father got it into his head to go to Constantinople to seek the opinion of an ancient hakim originating, like us, from Toledo. He is the only person who knows the truth, according to my father. 'If he tells me the hour is come, I'll leave everything and spend all my time in prayer and meditation; if he tells me the hour is not come, I'll go back to my ordinary life.'

"There could be no question of letting him travel the roads – he's more than seventy years old and can scarcely stand upright – so I decided I'd go and see the rabbi in Constantinople, to put to him all the questions my father would like to ask and come back with the answers.

"So that's how I come to be in this caravan – like you, because of these crazy rumours. Though neither of us can help laughing, deep down inside, at people's gullibility."

It's very kind of Maïmoun to compare my attitude with his. They're only superficially alike. He took to the road out of filial piety, without changing his own convictions; whereas I let myself be influenced by the folly around me. But I didn't say so: why belittle myself in the eyes of someone I respect? And why should I stress the differences between us when he is always pointing out the similarities?

27 September

Today's stage of the journey will have been less arduous than the preceding ones. After four days on the steep paths of the Taurus mountains, with stretches that are often narrow and dangerous, we reached the Anatolian plain. And after ill-kept khans, infested with

73

rough janissaries – who were theoretically supposed to protect us from highwaymen, but whose looks were in fact so far from reassuring that we shut ourselves up in our quarters – we had the good fortune to come upon a respectable inn, patronised by travelling merchants.

The innkeeper soon took the shine off our satisfaction, however, when he told us of rumours reaching here from Konya, according to which the town has been struck by the plague, and its gates closed to all travellers.

Disturbing as these tidings were, they had the advantage of bringing me close to the rest of my party, who gathered round waiting for me to decide what to do. Some other travellers had already chosen to turn back at dawn without more ado. Admittedly they had joined us only at Tarsus, or Alexandretta at most. We, who come from Gibelet and are already more than halfway, can't just give in at the first alarm.

The caravaneer suggests going on a bit further and changing our route later on if circumstances require it. I still find him as unattractive as I did when I first set eyes on him, but that seems to me a sensible idea. So on we go, and the grace of God be with us!

28 September

Today I said some things to Maïmoun that he thought significant, so perhaps I should write them down.

He had just observed that people nowadays can be divided up into those who believe that the end of the world is at hand, and those who are sceptical – he and I being among the latter. I answered that in my opinion people can also be divided up into those who fear the end of the world and those who wish for it – the former thinking of flood and disaster, the latter of resurrection and deliverance.

I was thinking not only of my friend's father and the Impatient Ones in Aleppo, but also of Marta.

Then Maïmoun wondered whether people in Noah's day were just as divided between those who applauded the Flood and those who were against it.

At that we started to laugh, and laughed so heartily that our mules took fright.

29 September

From time to time I cull a few verses at random from the book by Abu-l-Ala that an old bookseller in Maarra put in my hands three or four weeks ago. Today I came upon these lines:

> *The people want an imam to arise*
> *And speak to a silent crowd*
> *An illusion; there is no imam but reason*
> *It alone guides us day and night.*

I made haste to read this passage to Maïmoun, and we exchanged silent and meaning smiles.

A Christian and a Jew led along the path of doubt by a blind Muslim? But there is more light in his dimmed eyes than in all the sky over Anatolia.

Near Konya, 30 September

The rumours about the plague have not, alas, been denied. Our caravan has had to skirt round the town and set up its tents to the west, in the gardens of Merâm. The camp is crowded, because a lot of families from Konya have fled here from the epidemic, to be in the healthy air amid the streams and fountains.

We arrived towards noon, and despite the circumstances there's an air – I was going to say a sort of holiday air about the place, but it's more like that of an improvised picnic. Everywhere vendors of apricot juice and cordials clink their glasses invitingly, washing them later on at the fountains. On all sides there are booths whose appetising fumes draw young and old alike. But I can't help gazing at the town nearby: I can see its walls, with their towers, and guess at its domes and minarets. There different fumes rise up, hiding and darkening everything. That smell doesn't reach us, thank God; we sense it, and it makes our blood run cold. The plague; the fumes of death. I put down my pen and cross myself. And then go on with my story.

Maïmoun, who joined our party for the midday meal, spoke at some length to my nephews, and for a little while to Marta. The atmosphere was such that we couldn't avoid talking about the end of the world, and I noticed that Boumeh knew all about the predictions in the Zohar concerning the Jewish year 5408, our 1648.

"'In the year 408 of the sixth millennium'," he said, quoting from memory, "'they who rest in the dust shall rise up. They are called the sons of Heth.'"

"Who are they?" asked Habib, who always likes to oppose his brother's erudition with his own ignorance.

"It's the usual name for the Hittites, in the Bible. But what matters here is not the actual meaning of the word Heth so much as its numerical value in Hebrew – which is 408."

Numerical value! I get angry whenever I hear the notion mentioned! Instead of trying to understand the significance of words, my contemporaries prefer to calculate the value of the letters that make them up. And these they manipulate to suit their own ends – adding, subtracting, dividing and multiplying, and always ending up with a figure that will astonish, reassure or terrify them. And so human thought is diluted, and human reason weakened and dissolved in superstition!

I don't think Maïmoun believes in such nonsense, but most of his co-religionists do, and so do most of mine, and most of the Muslims I've had occasion to talk to. Even wise, educated and apparently reasonable people boast of their acquaintance with this science for simpletons.

I express myself all the more vehemently here because during today's discussion I didn't say anything. I just looked incredulous whenever anyone mentioned "numerical value". But I took care not to interrupt the debate. That's how I am. That's how I've always been, ever since I was a child. When a discussion is taking place around me, I'm curious to see where it will end, who will admit he's wrong, how all the people involved answer or avoid answering the others' arguments. I observe and enjoy what I learn, and I register everyone else's reactions without feeling impelled to express my own opinion.

During the talk at noon today, while I was provoked into silent protests by some remarks, other things that were said interested or surprised me. As when Boumeh pointed out that it was precisely in 1648 that *The Book of the One True Orthodox Faith* was published in Moscow, referring without any ambiguity to the Year of the Beast. Was it not because of that book that Evdokim the pilgrim took to the road and passed through Gibelet?; and his visit was followed by a whole procession of scared customers through my shop. So it might be said that it was in that year that the Beast entered my life. Maïmoun's father used to tell him that something significant had happened in 1648 but no one had recognised its importance. Yes, I don't mind admitting that something may have started in that year. For the Jews and for the Muscovites. And also for me and mine.

"But why was an event announced in 1648 that's supposed to take place in 1666? That's a mystery I can't understand!" I said.

"Nor can I," agreed Maïmoun.

"I don't see any mystery," said Boumeh, with irritating calm.

Everyone waited with bated breath for him to go on. He took his time, then went on loftily:

"There are eighteen years between 1648 and 1666."

He stopped.

"So?" asked Habib, through a mouthful of crystallised apricots.

"Don't you see? Eighteen – six plus six plus six. The last three steps to the Apocalypse."

There followed a most ominous silence. I suddenly felt that the pestilential vapour was approaching and closing in on us. Maïmoun was the most pensive of those present: it was as if Boumeh had just solved an old enigma for him. Hatem bustled round us, wondering what was the matter: he'd caught only scraps of our conversation.

It was I who broke the silence.

"Wait a moment, Boumeh!" I said. "That's nonsense. I don't have to tell you that in the days of Christ and the Evangelists people didn't write six six six as you would today in Arabic: they wrote it in Roman figures. And your three sixes don't make sense."

"So can you tell me how they wrote 666 in the days of the Romans?"

"You know very well. Like this."

I picked up a stick and wrote "DCLXVI" on the ground.

Maïmoun and Habib bent over and looked at what I'd written. Boumeh just stood where he was, not even glancing our way. He just asked me if I'd never noticed anything particular about the number I'd traced. No, I hadn't.

"Haven't you noticed that all the Roman figures are there, in descending order of magnitude, and each occurs only once?"

"Not all of them," I said quickly. "One's missing . . ."

"Go on, go on – you're getting there. There's one missing at the beginning. The M – write it! Then we'll have 'MDCLXVI'. One thousand six hundred and sixty-six. Now the numbers are complete. And the years are complete. Nothing more will be added."

Then he reached out and erased the figure completely, muttering some magic formula he'd learned.

A curse on numbers and on those who make use of them!

3 October

Since we left the outskirts of Konya behind, the travellers have been talking not of plague but of a curious fable, spread by the caravaneer himself, which so far I have not thought worth reporting. If I do so at present it's because it has just had an exemplary ending.

According to our man, a caravan got lost a few years ago on the way to Constantinople, and ever since then it has been wandering miserably around Anatolia, the victim of a curse. From time to time it passes another caravan, and its disoriented travellers ask to be told the way, or else put other, very strange questions. Anyone who answers by so much as a single word calls down the same curse on himself, and must wander with the others for ever.

Why was the caravan the object of a curse? It's said the travellers of which it was composed had told their families they were going on a pilgrimage to Mecca, whereas in fact they planned to go to Constantinople. So Heaven is supposed to have condemned them to wander endlessly without ever reaching their destination.

Our man declared he had met the phantom caravan twice, but had not let it take him in. No matter how much the lost travellers crowded round him, smiling, plucking at his sleeve and trying to cajole him, he pretended not to see them. And so he managed to elude the spell and continue his journey.

How can the ghost caravan be recognised? asked some of our more nervous companions. It can't be recognised, said our caravaneer: it's just like an ordinary caravan, its travellers are just like any other travellers, and that's precisely why so many people are misled and get bewitched.

Some of our people shrugged when they heard this story, while others seemed scared and kept scanning the horizon to check that no suspect caravan was in the offing.

I, of course, was one of those who lent no credence to these tales. Witness the fact that although they have been spreading back and forth the whole length of the caravan for three days, I didn't think it worthwhile to mention such a vulgar fiction in these pages.

But today at noon we did pass another caravan.

We had just stopped by a stream for the midday meal. Servants and other attendants were busy gathering twigs and lighting fires when a caravan appeared over a nearby hill. In a few minutes it was almost upon us, and a whisper ran through our ranks: "It's them – it's the phantom caravan." We were all transfixed. A strange shadow seemed to darken our faces, and we spoke very softly, staring at the new arrivals.

They seemed to draw near unnaturally fast, in a cloud of dust and haze.

When they were close by, they all dismounted and hurried towards us, apparently delighted at finding some fellow human beings and a cool spot. They advanced bowing and smiling broadly, and uttering greetings in Arabic, Turkish, Persian and Armenian. Our people were ill at ease, but no one moved or stood up or answered. "Why don't you speak?" the others finally demanded. "Have we offended you somehow?" Still none of us made a move.

The others were already turning away, vexed, when suddenly our caravaneer let out a shout of laughter, which was immediately topped by an even louder guffaw from the other caravaneer.

"Curse you!" said the latter, coming forward with open arms. "You've been telling your tale about the ghost caravan again! And they swallowed it!"

Then everyone got up and started to embrace the others and invite them to share their meal, by way of excuse for the misunderstanding.

That incident is the only topic of conversation this evening. All of our travellers pretend they never believed the story. But the fact is, when the other travellers approached us, everyone went pale and no one dared speak to them.

4 October

Today I was treated to another fable, but this one doesn't make me smile.

At breakfast time a man came to see me, shouting and waving his arms. He claimed my nephew had been making up to his daughter, and he threatened to settle the matter in blood. Hatem and Maïmoun tried to calm him down, and the caravaneer added his efforts to theirs, though he must really have been delighted to see me embarrassed in this way.

I looked round for Habib, but he'd disappeared. I saw this as an admission of guilt, and cursed him for having put me in such a situation.

Meanwhile the man kept shouting louder and louder, saying he'd cut the culprit's throat and sprinkle his blood on the ground in front of the whole caravan to show everyone how tarnished honour is made clean.

A growing crowd gathered around us. This was different from the quarrel the other day with the caravaneer. Now I could not hold my head high, nor did I wish to emerge victorious. All I wanted was to nip the scandal in the bud, so as to be able to complete the journey without endangering the life of any of my party.

So I lowered myself so far as to go over to the fellow, tap him on the arm, smile, and promise him he'd be given satisfaction, and his honour would emerge from this business as unsullied as a gold sultanin. I should say in passing that a sultanin is not a paragon of purity: the emptier the Ottoman treasury becomes, the more the coin is debased. Even so, I made the comparison deliberately. I wanted the fellow to hear the word "gold" and realise I was ready to pay the price for his honour. He went on bellowing for a little longer, though not so loudly, as if emitting only the echoes of his last rantings.

Then I took his arm and drew him aside from the rest. Once we were out of earshot, I proffered more apologies and and told him in so many words that I was prepared to pay compensation.

While I was entering into this sordid bargaining, Hatem came and tugged at my sleeve, begging me not to let myself be duped. Seeing this, the other fellow resumed his lamentations, and I had to tell my clerk to let me settle the business in my own way.

So I paid up. One sultanin, together with a solemn promise to chastise my nephew severely and prevent him from ever hanging around the young woman again.

It wasn't until the evening that Habib presented himself, accompanied by Hatem and another traveller I'd seen them about with before. All three assured me I'd been swindled. According to them, the man to whom I'd given the gold piece was not a grieving father, and the girl that was with him was not his daughter at all, but a trollop well-known as such to the whole caravan.

Habib claimed he'd never visited her, but that's a lie – I even wonder if Hatem didn't go with him. But I think they were telling the truth about the rest. I gave each of them a good box on the ears, just the same.

So there's a travelling brothel in this caravan, frequented by my own nephew – and I didn't even notice!

I've been in business all these years, and I still can't tell a pimp from an outraged father!

What is the use of my scrutinising the universe if I'm incapable of seeing what's under my very nose?

What a misfortune, to be made of such fragile clay!

5 October

I'm more shaken than I'd have imagined by what happened yesterday.

I feel weak and tired and dizzy; my eyes are permanently misty and I hurt all over. Perhaps I'm suffering from travel sickness again. Every step is painful, and the whole journey is getting me down. I'm sorry I ever embarked on it.

All my people try to comfort and reason with me, but whatever they say or do is lost in a deepening fog. These lines, too, blur as I write, and my fingers grow slack.

Oh God!

Scutari, Friday 30 October 1665

I haven't written a line for twenty-four days. True, I've been at death's door. Now I take up my pen again at an inn in Scutari, the day before we cross the Bosphorus and reach Constantinople at last.

It was shortly after we left Konya that I noticed the first symptoms. At first I put my dizziness down to the fatigues of the journey, and then I blamed the upset over my nephew's misbehaviour and my own credulity. But my discomfort was not unbearable, and I didn't mention it to my companions or even in these pages. And then one day I suddenly couldn't hold a pen, and had to go apart from the rest twice in order to vomit.

My own people and a few of the other travellers had gathered round, proffering various bits of good advice, when the caravaneer and three of his henchmen came up. The fellow declared I'd caught the plague, no less. He said I must have been infected somewhere in or near Konya, and ordered me to isolate myself from the rest of the caravan without delay. From then on I must tag along behind, more than 600 paces from my nearest fellow-traveller. If I recovered he would take me back again; if I had to halt he wouldn't wait for me, but consign me to God and go on without me.

Martha protested, as did my nephews, my clerk, Maïmoun, and a few of the other travellers. But there was nothing to be done. The argument went on for a good half-hour, but I didn't say a word. I felt that if I opened my mouth I'd be ill again. So I assumed an air of wounded dignity, though all the time I was silently rehearsing all the Genoese oaths I could think of and wishing the caravaneer a painful death!

I remained in quarantine for four whole days, until we reached Afyonkarahisar, the Opium Citadel, a small town with a sinister name, overlooked by the sombre shape of an ancient fort. As soon as we were installed in the local khan, the caravaneer came to see me. To say he'd been wrong, I obviously hadn't got the plague, he'd noticed I was better and I could rejoin the caravan next morning. My nephews started to quarrel with him, but I made them stop. I don't like to see someone checked when he's trying to improve. Any reproaches he deserved should have been delivered before. So I answered politely and accepted his invitation to come back and travel with the others again.

What I didn't say, either to him or to my people, was that in spite of appearances I was by no means cured. Deep down inside I could feel a sort of generalised fever burning like a brazier. I was amazed that no one seemed to notice how flushed my face was.

The following night was dreadful. I kept shivering and tossing and panting for breath, and the sheets I lay in and the clothes I wore were drenched with sweat. Amid the confusion of voices and echoes that rang through my deranged head I could hear the "widow" whispering at my bedside:

"He must not set out again tomorrow. If he takes to the road again in the state he's in now he'll die before he gets to Listana."

Listana was one of the many names which the people of Gibelet used to refer to Istambul, or Byzantium, the Porte, Costantiniyé and so on.

And indeed, next morning I made no attempt to get up. I'd probably exhausted my strength in the course of the last few days, and my body needed time to mend.

But I was still far from convalescent. I have only the most shadowy remembrance of the three days that followed. It seems to me I must have been very close to death: some of my joints are still as stiff as those of

Lazarus must have been after he was brought back to life. In my struggle with illness I lost a few pounds of flesh to it, the way one throws a joint of meat at a wild beast to assuage its hunger. I can hardly find words to speak of it: my soul must still be rather stiff too.

But what remains in my memory about the enforced halt at Afyonkarahisar is not suffering or distress. I may have been abandoned by the rest of the caravan, and death may have cast covetous eyes on me, but whenever I opened my eyes I saw Marta sitting at my side with her feet drawn up under her, gazing at me with a smile of relief. And when I closed my eyes again, my left hand still lay grasped in both of hers – the lower one with its palm against mine, the other from time to time stroking my fingers in a gesture of comfort and infinite patience.

Marta didn't send for a healer or an apothecary – they would have finished me off more surely than the fever. She took care of me just by being there, just with a few sips of cold water and with her two hands, preventing me from going on with my journey. So I stayed, and for three days, as I've said, death lurked around me and I seemed its destined prey. Then on the fourth day it left, as if tired of waiting, or perhaps overcome with pity.

I don't want to give the impression that my nephews and my clerk neglected me. Hatem was never far away, and between strolls around the town the two young men would come and ask how I was, looking worried and apologetic: you couldn't expect much more from them at their age. God save them, I don't blame them for anything, except having dragged me into this expedition. But it's Marta I'm really grateful to, though grateful isn't the right word, and for me to think it adequate would be the height of ingratitude. Something that cost tears can't be repaid with mere salt water.

I'm still not sure how much those few days shook me up. For any man the end of the world is first and foremost his own end, and mine had suddenly seemed imminent. Without waiting for the fateful year itself, I was in the process of slipping out of the world when two hands held me back. Two hands, a face and a heart – a heart I knew to be capable of impulsive love and obstinate rebellion, but perhaps not of so powerful and perfect a tenderness. From the time when through a misunderstanding we found ourselves in the same bed, seemingly man and wife, I'd thought that one night, through the inescapable logic of the senses, I'd manage to disguise desire as passion and take matters to their natural conclusion, even though I might regret it next morning. But now I believe that Marta is much more my wife in reality than in appearance, and that, when the day comes that I'm united with her, it won't be for fun or because I'm drunk or my senses have got the better of me – it will be the most heartfelt and proper of acts. And this whether or not, when the day comes, she's free from the oath that once linked her to her blackguard of a husband.

But that day is not yet come. I'm sure she hopes for it as much as I do, but the occasion hasn't yet presented itself. If we were still on the way to Tarsus, and about to spend the next night in Maïmoun's cousin's house, we'd emerge as united in our bodies as we already are in our souls. But what's the good of looking back? I'm here, almost at the gates of Constantinople, alive in spite of all, and Marta is not far off. Love feeds on patience as well as on desire. Isn't that the lesson I learned from her at Afyonkarahisar?

A week had passed by the time we set out again, joining a caravan from Damascus in which by a strange chance there were a couple of people I knew – a perfumer and a priest. We halted one day at Kutahya, and another at Izmit, and reached Scutari today in the early afternoon. Some of our fellow-travellers decided to press on and take ship straight away, but I preferred to be careful and give myself time for a healing siesta, so as to be readier to confront the last stage of the journey tomorrow, Saturday. We'll have been on our way for fifty-four days since leaving Aleppo – instead of the forty expected : sixty-nine days since we first set out from Gibelet. I only hope Marmontel hasn't already gone back to France, taking *The Hundredth Name* with him!

Constantinople, 31 October 1665

Today Marta has stopped being "my wife". From now on, appearances are in accordance with reality, until the time comes when reality is in accordance with appearances.

This is not because I decided, after bitter reflection, to put an end to a confusion that had lasted two months and become a little more familiar to me at every halt. But today things worked out in such a way that to keep up the fiction I'd have had to deceive everyone in the most brazen fashion.

After we'd crossed the strait, in such a crush of people and beasts that I really thought the boat would sink, I started looking for an inn kept by a Genoese by the name of Barinelli, where my father and I stayed when we came to Constantinople twenty-four years ago. The man is dead now, and the house is no longer an inn, but it still belongs to the family, and a grandson of the former innkeeper lives there with one maid whom I've glimpsed briefly from a distance.

When I presented myself to the young Barinelli and told him my name, he made a moving speech about my glorious Embriaci ancestors and insisted that we stay with him. Then he asked me who my noble companions were, and I answered without too much hesitation that I was travelling with my two nephews; my clerk, who was outside looking after our mules; and a respectable lady from Gibelet, a widow who had come to Constantinople to attend to certain administrative formalities and had made the journey under our protection.

I don't deny this cost me a pang, but I couldn't have said anything else. Travel sometimes gives rise to fables, as sleep gives rise to dreams. So long as you see straight when you get back to normal . . .

For me the awakening has come in Constantinople. Tomorrow, Sunday, I shall put on ceremonial dress and present myself at the embassy of the King of France, or rather at the embassy church, in the hope of finding the Chevalier de Marmontel. I hope he wasn't too angry with me for charging him so much for the Mazandarani book. If need be I'll allow him a substantial reduction in exchange for permission to make a copy of it, though no doubt, to persuade him, I'll have to use all my wiles as a Genoese, a trader in curios and a Levantine.

I shall go to see him on my own – I can't really be sure of my nephews. A hasty word, or one that's too ingratiating, or a sign of impatience, and Marmontel, that haughty character, would be put off once and for all.

1 November

Lord, how am I to begin my account of what happened today?

Should I start at the beginning? I awoke with a start, and went to attend mass at the embassy, in the Pera district.

Or at the end? We have made this journey, all the way from Gibelet to Constantinople, for nothing.

The church was crowded. A sombre gathering. Ladies in black; mournful whispers. In vain I looked around for the Chevalier de Marmontel or some other face I knew. I'd hurried in just as the office was about to begin, and only had time to uncover my head, cross myself, and station myself at the back, at the end of a row of worshippers.

Registering how very forlorn the atmosphere was, I cast a few inquiring glances at my nearest neighbour, but he studiously and piously ignored my presence. It wasn't merely that it was All Saints' Day – there must also have been a recent bereavement, the death of some important person. I was reduced to conjecture. I knew that the former ambassador, Monsieur de la Haye, had been on the point of death for years. After spending five months imprisoned in the Castle of Seven Towers on the orders of the Sultan, he had emerged suffering from the stone, and so enfeebled that rumours of his death had circulated several times. That must be it, I thought. And as the new ambassador was none other that the former envoy's son, there was nothing surprising about the consternation I could see around me.

The officiating priest, a Capuchin, began his funeral oration by speaking of a person of noble lineage, a devoted servant of the great king entrusted with the most delicate missions, and when he then went on to make veiled allusions to the dangers incurred by those who performed their distinguished duties in countries not of the faith, I was no longer in any doubt. Relations between France and the Sublime Porte have never been so acrimonious as they are now – so much so that the new ambassador, though appointed four years ago, has still not dared to take up his duties for fear of being subjected to the same vexations as his father.

Every word of the sermon strengthened me in my supposition, until at the end of a lengthy period the name of the deceased was actually mentioned.

I then started so violently that all faces turned towards me, a whisper ran through the congregation, and the preacher himself paused for a second or two, cleared his throat, and craned his neck to see if the person so afflicted wasn't a near relation of the late Chevalier.

For it was Marmontel who was the subject of the oration.

To think I had come here to speak to him after mass, only to learn that he was dead!

I'd spent two long months on the road, crossing Syria, Cilicia, the Taurus mountains and the Anatolian plain, just in the hope of finding him and borrowing *The Hundredth Name* for a few days. And now I was told that the man and the book alike were no more – both had been lost at sea!

As soon as the service was over I went to see the priest. He told me he was known as Thomas of Paris. With him was a well-respected French merchant called Master Roboly. I explained why I was so upset, describing how the Chevalier had come to my humble shop several times to make purchases on His Majesty's behalf. This seemed to impress them, and they inquired with some anxiety about the Chevalier's visit to Gibelet in August, and about what he'd said on the subject of his last voyage and any premonitions he might have had concerning it.

Father Thomas was very circumspect, unlike Master Roboly, who soon told me that in his opinion the Chevalier's death was due not to bad weather, as the authorities claimed, but to an attack by pirates, the sea off Smyrna having been quite calm at the time of the incident. He had even started telling me he didn't believe the pirates were acting on their own initiative, when the priest frowned and said, "We know nothing about it! May God's will be done, and may Heaven deal with each of us as he deserves!"

It's true there was no point now in speculating about the true causes of the tragedy, let alone the machinations of the Ottoman authorities. For me, in any case, it was all of no importance whatsoever. Both the man I'd come to see and the book I'd hoped to buy back or borrow from him now reposed in the realm of Neptune, in the bowels of the Aegean Sea or perhaps in those of its fishes.

I must admit that after feeling sorry for myself and lamenting the fact that I'd gone to so much trouble for nothing, I started to ponder on what it all meant and what I ought to learn from it. After the death of old Idriss, and now the disappearance of both Marmontel and *The Hundredth Name*, shouldn't I give up on the book and go quietly back to Gibelet?

But that's not what our expert on omens thinks. According to my nephew Boumeh, Heaven certainly wanted to teach us a lesson. (Some logic! – to drown the envoy of the King of France in order to drop a hint to a Genoese merchant. But let that pass.) Heaven wanted to punish us, especially me, for letting the book go when I'd actually had it in my possession. But the object wasn't to make me give up. On the contrary. We ought to redouble our efforts and expose ourselves to yet more sufferings and disappointments in order to deserve the supreme reward – the book, with the salvation it contained.

So what does Boumeh think we ought to do? Go on searching. Doesn't

Constantinople contain the greatest and most venerable booksellers in the whole world? We must question them one by one, search their shelves and ransack their store-rooms, and in the end we'll find what we're looking for.

On this point – but on this point only! – I don't disagree with him. If there's one place where you ought to be able to find a copy, genuine or forged, of *The Hundredth Name*, then that place is Constantinople.

But this consideration has had little influence on my decision not to return straight away to Gibelet. Once I'd got over the first shock of the unexpected news, I decided it would be pointless to get depressed, and even more so to expose myself again – in the cold season and when I've still not quite recovered from my illness – to the rigours of travel. Let's wait for a while, I thought, and scour the bookstalls and curio shops; and also give Marta time to complete her business. Then we'll see.

Perhaps by prolonging the journey by a few weeks I'll make it mean something again. That's what I tell myself before I turn this page. I know very well it's only a device to distract me from my anxiety and confusion.

3 November

I keep thinking about the unfortunate Marmontel, and last night, for the second time running, I saw him in my dreams! I do wish we'd parted on better terms on his last visit. He must have cursed my Genoese greed when I charged him 1,500 maidins for the Mazandarani book. How was he to know I did so only because I had qualms about parting at all with something a poor man had given me as a present? My intentions were of the best, but he couldn't have guessed that. And now I shall never be able to win back his good opinion.

I only hope time will take the edge off my remorse.

*   *   *

This afternoon my pleasant landlord, Master Barinelli, came to see me in my room. He checked beforehand, by carefully opening the door a little way, that I'd finished my afternoon siesta, and when I beckoned him in he entered shyly, explaining that having heard what had happened he'd come to see how I was. Then he sat down formally, eyes downcast, as if offering his condolences. His maid followed him in, and remained standing until I pressed her to take a seat. While he offered wholesome words of consolation in the Genoese fashion, she remained silent, understanding nothing but concentrating on the sound of his voice as if it were the sweetest music. I listened as if grateful for his observations on the decrees of Providence, but in fact my chief solace came from watching the two of them.

I found them very touching. I haven't mentioned them before in these pages, having too much to say about Marmontel, but since we've been here I've often spoken of them under my breath to my companions, especially Marta, and we've joked amiably about them.

Their story is a strange one. I'll try to tell it as I heard it myself: perhaps it will distract me for a while from my worries.

Last spring, Barinelli, on his way to the gold- and silversmiths' quarter on business, was passing by the slave market, known here as the Esir-pazari, when he was approached by a dealer holding a young woman by the hand and lauding her virtues. The Genoese told the fellow he had no intention of buying a slave, but the other insisted, saying:

"Don't buy her if you don't want to, but at least look at her!"

To end the matter as swiftly as possible, Barinelli glanced at the girl, meaning to walk on without more ado. But when their eyes met he had the feeling, he said, that he'd "found a long-lost sister who'd been taken captive". He tried to ask her where she was from, but she could understand neither his Turkish nor his Italian. The dealer explained that she spoke a language no one here could understand, adding that she had another small defect – a slight limp caused by a wound in her thigh. He lifted up her dress to show the scar, but Barinelli firmly drew it down again, saying he would take her as she was – he did not need to see more.

So he returned home with the slave, who could only tell him her name was Liva. Strangely enough, Barinelli's given name is Livio.

Ever since then theirs has been the most moving love story. They hold hands all the time, and never take their eyes off one another. Livio looks at her as if she were not his slave but his princess and beloved wife. I've often seen him raise her hand to his lips, place a chair for her, or stroke her hair or brow, oblivious of our presence. Any married couple and any pair of sweethearts in the world would be jealous of these two.

Liva has slanting eyes and prominent cheekbones, but fair, almost blonde hair. She might well come from a tribe that lives on the steppes. I think she must be descended from the Mongols, but from one of them who carried off a woman from Moscow. She has never been able to explain where she's from or how she became a captive. Her swain tells me she understands every word he says now, but that's not surprising, given the way he speaks to her. She'll end up learning Italian, unless Barinelli learns the language of the steppes.

Have I mentioned that she's pregnant? So her Livio won't let her go up- or downstairs unless he's there to take her arm.

Reading through what I've written, I see I've called Liva his "maid". I vowed never to cross anything out, but I must correct this point. I didn't want to refer to her as a "slave", and hesitated to call her his concubine or mistress. But after all I've just said, it seems obvious that she should simply be called his wife. Barinelli regards her as that, he treats her much better than wives are usually treated, and she'll soon be the mother of his children.

4 November

This morning my people are scattered around the city, each in pursuit of his or her preoccupation.

Boumeh has gone rummaging among the bookstalls, having heard some rumour about a great collector supposed to own a copy of *The Hundredth Name*. He hasn't been able to find out anything more precise.

Habib and his brother both crossed the Golden Horn on the same boat, but they came back separately, and I doubt if they stayed together long.

Marta went to the Sultan's palace to try to find out if a man with the same name as her husband wasn't hanged as a pirate two years ago. Hatem went with her, as he speaks Turkish fluently and is better than any of us at coping with official ins and outs. They haven't discovered anything specific so far, but they did learn something of how to set about it, and they'll return to the charge tomorrow.

As for me, I went to see Father Thomas again in his church at Pera. When we met for the first time, on Sunday, I had neither the opportunity nor, I may say, the wish to tell him plainly why I was so affected by Marmontel's death. I made some vague mention of valuable articles that the Chevalier had bought from me and that we were supposed to have talked about again in Constantinople. Now I explained, as to a confessor, the real reasons for my discomfiture. He interrupted me by seizing my wrist and pausing for a while as he pondered or prayed. Then he said:

"The only way for a Christian to address God is through prayer. He must be humble and obedient and tell Him of his own grievances and hopes, concluding by saying Amen and trusting that His will may be done. Proud men, on the other hand, look in the books of magicians for forms of words that they think can alter or divert God's will. They imagine Providence as a ship, whose tiller they, poor mortals though they are, may manipulate to suit their own purposes. But God is not a ship – he is the Master of all ships, and of the seas, and of quiet skies and tempests alike. He cannot be ruled by forms of words invented by magicians, nor constrained by phrases or figures. He is incomprehensible and unpredictable, and woe to him who thinks he can tame Him!

"You say the book you sold to Marmontel has extraordinary powers . . ."

"No, Father," I corrected him. "I merely told you the foolish things that are said about it. If I myself believed it possessed unusual powers, I wouldn't have parted with it."

"You did well to part with it, my son, for you travelled under the protection of Providence and here you are in Constantinople, while the Chevalier, who set sail with the allegedly sacred book in his baggage, never arrived! God have mercy upon him!"

I asked Father Thomas for details about the disaster, but he told me nothing new. He did offer me much consolation, though, and I left the church with a lighter step than I had entered it, and with my recent melancholy cured.

Above all – why should I deny it? – his last comment was a comfort to me. So when Boumeh returned in the evening and started speculating about our chances of finding another copy of *The Hundredth Name*, I said with a sigh, shamelessly pretending I'd arrived at this sage attitude on my own:

"I don't know if we shall return from here with it, but it's fortunate that we didn't come here with it."

"Why do you say that?"

"Because the Chevalier, who did travel with it . . ."

Marta smiled, Hatem's eyes sparkled, and Habib actually laughed and clapped his brother on the shoulder. Boumeh shrugged his hand off disdainfully and snapped back at me, avoiding my eye:

"Uncle thinks *The Hundredth Name* is some holy relic supposed to perform miracles. I've never been able to make him understand that it's not the book itself that can save its owner, but the word hidden within it. The book Idriss owned was just a copy of a copy. And what had we

95

come here for? To borrow the book from the Chevalier, if he'd let us, and make yet another copy! But it's not the book we're looking for – it's the word concealed inside it."

"What word is that?" asked Marta innocently.

"The name of God."

"Allah?"

Boumeh answered in his most pedantic manner.

"'Allah' is just a contraction of 'al-ilah', which simply means 'the god'. It's not a name; it's just a designation. As if you were to say 'the sultan'. But the sultan has a name too – he's called Muhammad, or Mourad, or Ibrahim, or Osman. Like the Pope, who is called the Holy Father but has a name of his own as well."

"That's because popes and sultans die," said I, "and are replaced. If they didn't die they'd always be the same, and we'd no longer need to give them a name and a figure. Just 'the Pope' or 'the Sultan' would be enough."

"Just so. And because God doesn't die and is never replaced by another, we don't need to address Him in any other way. That doesn't mean he hasn't got another, secret name. He doesn't tell ordinary mortals what it is – only those who deserve to know. They are the real Elect, and they need only speak the divine name to escape all dangers and fend off all calamities. You will object that if God reveals His name to those He has chosen, there is no need to own Mazandarani's book in order to have that privilege. No doubt. The wretched Idriss had the book in his possession all his life, and may have learned nothing from it. In order to deserve to know the supreme name a person must demonstrate exceptional piety, or unparalleled knowledge, or some other unique merit. But it can also happen that God feels well disposed towards someone apparently quite undistinguished. He sends signs to him, entrusts him with missions, tells him secrets, and transforms his dull life into a memorable epic. We must not ask why one person is chosen rather than another. Our ephemeral considerations are irrelevant to Him who sees past and future all in one glance."

Does my nephew really believe he himself has been designated by Heaven? That's the impression I got as I listened to him. In that still childish face, beneath the fair down on his cheeks, there's a kind of quivering tension that bothers me. Shall I be able to take him home to his mother when the time comes, or will *he* keep trailing *me* along on the road as he has kept all of us so far?

No, that's not true – not all of us! Marta came on this journey for her own reasons. Habib came out of chivalry or for romance. And all Hatem did was follow his master to Constantinople, just as he would have followed me anywhere. I am the only one who gave in to Boumeh's promptings, and it's up to me to restrain him now. But I don't do it. I listen to him patiently, even though I know his reason is unreason and his faith impiety.

Perhaps I ought to act differently towards him. Contradict him, interrupt, make fun of him – in short, treat him as an uncle usually treats a young nephew, instead of showing so much consideration for him and his learning. The truth is that I'm rather scared of him, terrified even. I ought to get the better of this apprehension.

Anyhow, be he an envoy from Heaven or a messenger from Hell, he's still my nephew, and I mean to make him behave as such!

5 November

At her request I went with Marta as far as the Sultan's palace. But I soon left again at the request of my clerk, who thought my presence made his task more difficult. I'd put on my best clothes in order to make a good impression, but I'd only aroused greed and envy.

We had entered the palace through the outer courtyard, together with hundreds of other plaintiffs, all as quiet as if in a house of prayer. But this was because of their terror at being close to one who had the power of life and death over each one of them. I'd never been in such a place before, and was anxious to get away from that crowd of whispering intriguers, creeping diffidently across the sand and reeking of misery and fear.

Hatem wanted to meet a clerk in the Armoury who'd promised him information in exchange for a small amount of money. When we reached the door of the building, which was once the church of St Irene, he asked me to wait outside for fear the man would put up his price if he saw me. But it was too late. As ill luck would have it, the official was just emerging on some business or other, and took the opportunity to examine me from head to toe. When he returned a few minutes later, his demands had risen to fifteen times what they were before. You don't ask a wealthy Genoese for the same amount you'd gouge from a Syrian villager escorting a poor widow. Ten aspres had become 150, and on top of that the information wasn't complete – instead of telling all he knew, the fellow held back most of it in the hope of getting more money. He told us that according to the ledger he'd consulted, the name of Sayyaf, Marta's husband, didn't appear among those condemned to death, but there was another ledger he hadn't yet been able to look at. We must pay up and be grateful, and still be left in uncertainty.

Hatem wanted to go on and see someone else "under the cupola", through the gate of Salvation. But he begged me not to accompany them any further, and, more amused than annoyed, I went and waited for them outside in a coffee shop we'd noticed when we arrived. All this tangling with officialdom gets on my nerves; I'd never have gone if Marta hadn't insisted. From now on I'll save myself the bother. I hope they'll get on faster and more cheaply without me.

They rejoined me an hour later. The man Hatem wanted to see had asked him to go back again next Thursday. He is a clerk too, but in the Tower of the Law, where he receives innumerable petitions and passes them on to higher authorities. He charged a silver coin for making the appointment. If I'd been there he'd have demanded gold.

Friday, 6 November

Today what was bound to happen did happen. Not at night, not in the form of a surreptitious embrace in a bed of confusion, but right in the middle of the morning when the narrow streets outside were swarming with people. We were there in Master Barinelli's house, she and I, looking through the blinds at the comings and goings of the people of Galata, like a couple of idle women. Friday is a day of prayer here, observed by some as a holiday, an occasion for taking a stroll or resting. Our travelling companions were all abroad on their various errands; our host had gone out too. We'd heard the door bang to behind him, and watched him and his pregnant lady-love walking carefully along the alley beneath the window, avoiding the heaps of rubble. She moved with some difficulty and clung to his arm, almost tripping over at one point because she was gazing fondly at him instead of looking where she was going. He just caught her in time and scolded her gently, putting his hand protectively on her brow and drawing an imaginary line with his finger from her eyes to her feet. She nodded to show she understood, and they went on more slowly.

As we watched them coping with their difficulties, Marta and I broke into laughter tinged with envy. Our hands touched, then joined like those of the couple in the street. Our eyes met, and as if in some game in which neither must be the first to look away, we remained like that for some time, each gazing at the other as into a mirror. It might have become ridiculous or childish if, after a moment, a tear hadn't started to trickle down Marta's cheek – a tear all the more surprising because she was still smiling. I stood up, went round the low table where the steam was still rising from our two coffee cups, and stood behind her, clasping her tenderly in my arms.

She tilted her head back, parting her lips and closing her eyes. At the same time she breathed a little sigh of surrender. I kissed her forehead, then her eyelids, then either side of her lips, shyly approaching her mouth. At first I just brushed it with my own trembling lips, murmuring her name and all the Italian and Arabic words for "my dear", "my love", "my own", and then for "I want you".

And then we found ourselves entwined together. The house was still silent, the outside world farther and farther away.

We'd slept side by side three times, but I hadn't encountered her body nor she mine. In Abbas the tailor's village I'd held her hand all night out of bravado, and in Tarsus she'd spread her black tresses over my arm. Two long months of timid attempts and gestures, with both of us looking forward to this moment with a mixture of hope and fear. Did I say earlier on how beautiful the barber's daughter was? She's still just as lovely as ever and has increased in affection without losing any of her freshness. It must be said that she has increased in passion too. But every act of love is different. Before, her love-making must have been greedy and fleeting, bold and reckless. I didn't experience it, but you can tell how a woman makes love by looking at her and her arms. Now she's both tender and passionate. Her arms enfold you like those of someone swimming for dear life; she breathes as if her head had been under water till now; but any recklessness is just a pretence.

"What are you thinking about?" I asked her when we'd got our breath back and were calmer again.

"Our host and his maid. They ought to have nothing in common, yet it seems to me they're the happiest people in the world."

"We could be that too."

"Perhaps!" she said, looking away.

"Why only 'perhaps'?"

She bent over me as if to look more closely into my eyes and my thoughts. Then she smiled, and dropped a kiss between my eyebrows.

"Don't say any more. Come here!"

She lay on her back again and pulled me to her. I'm the size of a buffalo, but she made me feel as light as a newborn infant on her breast.

"Closer!"

Her body seemed as familiar to me as a man's native country, with its hills and gorges and pastures and shady lanes – a land that's vast and generous and yet suddenly very tiny. I held her tight, she held me tight, her nails digging into my back and leaving sizeable marks.

"I want you!" I panted again in my own language. "My love!" she answered in hers, almost weeping as she breathed the word "love". And then I called her my wife.

But she's still the wife of another, damn him!

8 November

I'd sworn not to go back to the palace, and to leave Hatem to work out his schemes in his own way. But today I decided to go with him and Marta as far as the High Gate and wait for them all morning at the same coffee shop as before. My presence may not have any effect on the proceedings, but it does have a new meaning now. Getting hold of the document that will make Marta a free woman is no longer a minor consideration for me amid all the other concerns arising out of the journey – in particular, the search for Marmontel and *The Hundredth Name*. The Chevalier is dead, and I now see Mazandarani's book as a mirage that I should never have pursued. But Marta is really here, no longer an outsider but the closest and dearest to me of all my companions – how could I just leave her to manage as best she can amid all these Ottoman complexities? I wouldn't dream of going home without her. And, for her part, she could never return to Gibelet and face her family without a document from the Sultan establishing her as a free woman again. She'd have her throat cut the very next day. No, her fate is bound up with mine now. And since I'm a man of honour, my fate is just as much bound up with hers.

There I go, talking about it as if it were an obligation. It isn't that, but it does involve a kind of obligation which it would be misleading to deny. Marta and I didn't come together by accident or sudden impulse.

I nurtured my desire for a long while, letting the wisdom that comes with time work upon it; and then one day, that blessed Friday, I stood up, took her in my arms and told her I wanted her with all my being. And she gave herself to me. What sort of person would I be if I abandoned her after that? What would be the good of bearing a venerable name like mine if I let Barinelli, the son of an innkeeper, behave more nobly than I?

But if I'm so sure of what I should do, why am I arguing about it, why am I reasoning with myself as if I needed to be persuaded? It's because the choice I'm in the process of making is of much greater consequence than I thought. If Marta doesn't get what she wants, if they won't give her a certificate saying her husband is dead, she can never go back home again, and if so, I can't either. What would I do then? Would I be prepared, in order not to forsake her, to abandon everything I possess, everything my ancestors worked to build up, and wander around the world?

The thought of it makes my head spin. It would probably be wiser to wait and take each day as it comes.

Hatem and Marta emerged from the palace at lunch time, exhausted and desperate. They'd been obliged to pay out every aspre they had, and to promise more, and still they'd got nothing to show for it.

The clerk in the Armoury told them at once he'd been able to consult the second ledger containing the names of people who'd been hanged, but he demanded more money before he would tell what he'd found in it. Once he'd pocketed the cash, he informed them that Sayyaf's name wasn't there. But he added in a whisper that he'd learned there was a third list covering the most serious crimes, though two very highly placed officials would have to be bribed in order to gain access to it. He demanded a deposit of 150 aspres for this purpose, but magnanimously agreed to take 148, which was all his visitors had left on them. He threatened he wouldn't go on seeing them if ever they were so improvident again.

What happened today makes me want to leave this city as soon as possible, and Marta herself begs me to do so. But where could we go? Without that accursed firman she can't go back to Gibelet, and it's only here in Constantinople that she can hope to get it.

We went back to the Sultan's palace, as we did yesterday, to try to advance Marta's case, and again I stationed myself in the coffee shop while my clerk and "the widow", swathed in black, disappeared amid a crowd of other petitioners into the outer courtyard, known as the Courtyard of the Janissaries. I was resigned to the prospect of waiting for three or four hours, as I had done yesterday, but the shopkeeper makes me so welcome now that I didn't mind. He's a Greek from Candia, and keeps telling me how glad he is to be able to talk to someone from Genoa about how much we both dislike the Venetians. They've never done me any harm, but my father always said people ought to despise them, so I owe it to his memory to do so. The owner of the coffee shop has more serious reasons to hate them. He hasn't said it in so many words, but from various allusions I gather one of them seduced and then abandoned his mother, and he was brought up to hate his own blood. He speaks Greek interspersed with snatches of Italian and Turkish, and we manage to have long conversations, punctuated by orders from his customers. These are often young janissaries who drink their coffee in the saddle and then throw the empty cups at the shopkeeper for him to try to catch them. He pretends to join in their laughter, but as soon as they have ridden away he crosses his fingers and curses them in Greek.

I didn't have much time to talk to him today. After half an hour Hatem and Marta returned, pale and trembling. I had to make them sit down and drink several glasses of water before they were able to tell me of their misadventures.

They went through the first courtyard and were making their way to the second and their interlocutor "under the cupola", when they noticed a crowd had gathered around the gate of Salvation separating the two courtyards. A severed head was lying there on a stone. Marta averted her eyes, but Hatem went up close.

"Look," he said to her. "Do you recognise him?"

She forced herself to look. It was the clerk from the Tower of the Law, the one they'd been to see last Thursday "under the cupola", and who'd made an appointment to meet them again next Thursday! They'd have liked to find out why he'd been punished in this way, but they didn't dare ask. Instead they helped one another to totter away, hiding their faces lest their expressions of horror be taken as a sign of complicity with the victim!

"I'll never set foot in the palace again," Marta told me on the boat taking us back to Galata.

I didn't say anything, so as not to upset her further. But she'll have to get that cursed paper somehow!

10 November

I took Marta for a trip across the city to drive the images of the severed head out of her mind's eye. When he left Afyonkarahisar with the caravan, Maïmoun left me the address of a cousin of his with whom he intended to stay, and I thought this might be a good time to go and inquire after him. I had some trouble finding the house, though it is in Galata, only a few streets away from where we are staying. I was kept waiting for a moment after I knocked at the door; then a man came and asked us a number of questions before inviting us in. By the time he finally stood aside, with a few cold words of formal welcome, I'd made up my mind not to set foot in his house. He pressed us a little, but for me the matter was settled. All I learned from him was that Maïmoun had stayed only a few days in Constantinople, and left again without saying where he was going – unless his cousin considered me unworthy of knowing his destination. I left my, or rather Barinelli's, address, in case Maïmoun should come back before we left, and so that I shouldn't have to come and ask for news again from this unfriendly fellow.

Then we crossed the Golden Horn and returned to the city, where Marta, urged on by me, bought two beautiful lengths of cloth, one black with silver threads in it, the other of raw silk with a pattern of sky-blue stars. "You have given me night and dawn," she said, and if we hadn't been surrounded by other people I'd have taken her in my arms.

In the new spice market I met a Genoese man who set himself up there a few months ago and already has one of the finest perfumeries in Constantinople. I may never have set foot in the city of my ancestors, but I can't help feeling proud when I meet a fellow-countryman who is respected, bold and prosperous. I asked him to make up a perfume for Marta – the subtlest scent a lady ever wore. I let it be understood she was my wife or fiancée, without actually saying so. The man closeted himself in the depths of his shop and came back with a splendid dark green bottle as round as a pasha after lunch. It smelled of aloes, violets, opium and both kinds of amber.

When I asked him how much I owed him he pretended not to want any money, but this was just a merchant's empty ploy. He soon murmured a price I'd have considered exorbitant if I hadn't seen the wonder in Marta's eyes when she sampled her latest present.

Is it vain of me to play the generous fiancé, spending money in a lordly fashion and ordering things without even asking the price? But what does it matter? I'm happy, she's happy. If I'm vain, I'm not ashamed of it!

On our way home we stopped at a seamstress's in Galata for her to take Marta's measurements. And again at a cobbler's shop with a display of elegant ladies' shoes. Marta protested every time, and then gave way, knowing I was determined. I may not be her lawful husband, but already

I'm more her husband than the other one was, and I regard the duties of my situation as privileges. It is up to a man to dress the woman he undresses and to perfume the woman he embraces. Just as it is up to him to defend with his life the fragile step that shadows his own.

I'm starting to sound like an amorous pageboy. Time to lay down my pen for this evening, and blow the skittish, sparkling ink dry.

14 November

For four days I've been pressing Marta to set aside her fears and go to the palace again. Only today did she finally agree. So, taking Hatem with us, we set out to cross the water, using an umbrella to keep off occasional showers of rain. To distract Marta I chatted gaily to her about this and that, pointing out especially fine houses and the strange attire of some of the passers-by. We exchanged glances to hold back our laughter. Until we got to the palace. Then her face clouded over and I could no longer make her smile.

I stopped off, as usual, at my friend from Candia's coffee shop, while "the widow" set out for the High Gate, casting farewell looks back at me at almost every step, as if we were never going to see one another again. Heartbreaking as this was, she had to get the wretched firman if we were to be free and able to love one another! So I pretended to be firmer than I felt, and signed to her to go on and pass through the gate. But she couldn't. She trembled and slowed down more at every step. Hatem, stout fellow, supported her and whispered encouragement, but her legs simply wouldn't carry her. He had to give up and practically drag her back to me, weeping, grief-stricken, apologising between her sobs for having been so weak.

"As soon as I get near the gate I seem to see the severed head. And then I can't breathe or swallow."

I comforted her as best I could. Hatem asked if he should go on anyway. On reflection I told him just to see the clerk in the Armoury and ask him what he'd found in the third ledger, then come back at once. He did so, and the answer from the official was as I'd feared: "There's nothing in the third ledger. But I found out there's a fourth one." He asked for another four piastres for his trouble. Our misfortune is providing this wretch with a regular income.

We set out for home so depressed and downcast that we didn't exchange three words the whole way.

So now what are we to do? I'd better let night soothe my worries. If I can manage to get to sleep.

15 November

Night having failed to come up with any solution to my problem, I tried to calm my anxieties with religion. But I already rather regret it. You can no more suddenly turn yourself into a believer than into an infidel. Even the Almighty must be tired of my mood swings.

I went to church in Pera this Sunday morning, and after mass asked Father Thomas if he would hear my confession. Assuming the matter must be urgent, he apologised to the members of the congregation gathered round him and led the way to the confessional, where I told him, very awkwardly, about Marta and myself. Before giving me absolution he made me promise not to approach "the person in question" until she was my wife, though he included among his admonitions some words of comfort. I shall remember these, but I'm not sure I shall keep my promise.

Before the service began I had no intention of going to confession. I was kneeling in the shadow, mulling over my troubles amid a cloud of incense and beneath the majestic vaulting, when the urge seized me. I think I was motivated more by a fit of anxiety than by an access of piety.

My nephews, my clerk and Marta had all come to church with me, and they had to wait some time. If I'd stopped to think I'd have put off my confession till later, when I was on my own. I don't go to confession often, as everyone in Gibelet knows. To keep the priest happy I occasionally give him some old prayer book, and he pretends to think I don't sin very much. So what I did today is almost tantamount to a public confession, as I could tell from the attitude of my companions afterwards. Hatem was laughing, and his eyes twinkled. My nephews alternately glared at me and refused to meet my glance. Above all, Marta's eyes accused me of treachery. As far as I know, she hasn't confessed.

When we got home I decided it was necessary for me to gather them all around me and solemnly announce that I intended to marry Marta as soon as she was quit of her first alliance, and that I had just spoken to the priest to that effect. I added, without much conviction, that if by chance she was declared a widow in the next few days, we'd get married here in Constantinople.

"I feel for you as if you were my children," I said, "and I want you to love Marta and respect her as if she were your own mother."

Hatem bent over first my hand and then that of my future wife. Habib embraced us both with a warmth that was balm to my heart. Marta clasped him to her, and this time, I swear, I didn't feel a single twinge of jealousy. I'm sure they never held one another so close before. As for Boumeh, he too came over and embraced us in his own more furtive and enigmatic way, apparently deep in reflections we'll never know anything about. Perhaps he was thinking that this unexpected turn of events was yet another sign, one of the countless spiritual upheavals that precede the end of the world.

This evening, as I write these lines alone in my room, I feel a pang of remorse. If I could have today over again I'd act differently. There'd be neither confession nor solemn announcement. But never mind. What's done is done. One can never be impartial about oneself!

16 November

I still felt the same regrets when I woke up this morning. To lessen them I told myself my confession had relieved me of a burden. But that's not really true. I wasn't troubled by the act of the flesh until I knelt down in church. Before, I didn't think of what happened on Friday as a sin. And I'm angry with myself now for speaking of it as such. I may have thought I was casting off a weight in the confessional, but in fact I was making it heavier.

What's more, the same questions still assail me. Where am I to go? Where should I take the people for whom I'm responsible? What should I advise Marta to do? Yes, what on earth is to be done?

Hatem came and told me that in his view the solution with the fewest drawbacks would be to pay some official handsomely to issue a false certificate stating that Marta's husband really was executed. I didn't turn the idea down as indignantly as an honest man should have done. I've acquired too many grey hairs in this world to go on believing in purity, justice and innocence. To tell the truth, I'm inclined to have more respect for a false certificate that sets someone free than for a genuine one, that imprisons somebody. But on reflection I said no: Hatem's solution didn't really strike me as feasible. How could I go back to Gibelet and get married in church on the strength of a document I knew to be a forgery? How could I spend the rest of my life waiting for my door to be flung open by the man I'd prematurely buried so as to live with his wife? I simply couldn't resign myelf to that!

Today, Tuesday, to take my mind off my worries, I indulged in one of my favourite pleasures: I strolled around the streets of the city on my own, browsing all day long among the bookstalls. But when, near the Solimaniah mosque, a trader asked me what I was looking for, and I openly mentioned Mazandarani's book, the man frowned and signed to me to lower my voice. Then, after making sure no one else had heard me, he asked me into his shop and sent his son away so that we could speak in private.

Even when we were alone he still spoke in a whisper, so that I had to strain my ears to hear what he said. According to him, the highest authorities had got wind of certain predictions concerning the Day of Judgement, allegedly at hand. An astrologer was supposed to have told the Grand Vizier that all tables would soon be overturned, all food removed from them, and the grandest turbans would roll on the ground, together with the heads that wore them, while all the palaces collapsed upon their inhabitants. For fear that such rumours would give rise to panic and subversion, orders had been issued that any book forecasting the end of the world should be destroyed. Anyone copying, selling, promoting or commenting on such works was liable to the severest punishment. All this was being done in deadly secrecy, the worthy fellow told me, pointing out the stall of a neighbour and colleague closed down because its owner was said to have been arrested and tortured, while his own brothers dared not inquire about his fate.

I am infinitely grateful to this colleague for taking the trouble to warn me of the danger, and for trusting me in spite of my origins. But perhaps it was because of them that he trusted me. If the authorities wanted to test or spy on him, they wouldn't have sent a Genoese to sound him out, would they?

What I've learned today sheds new light on what happened to me in

Aleppo, and makes me understand more clearly the strange reaction I met with from the booksellers in Tripoli when I mentioned *The Hundredth Name* to them.

I must be more careful in future, and above all not keep going and prating to booksellers about Mazandarani's work. That's what I tell myself now, but I'm not sure I'll be able to stick to such prudence. For while my excellent colleague's words encourage caution, they also make me more curious than ever about the accursed tome.

18 November

I visited the bookshops again today, and stayed till nightfall, looking around, watching and searching in corners, but not actually inquiring after *The Hundredth Name*.

I made a few purchases, including a rare book that I'd been trying to find for a long time – *Introduction to Occult Alphabets*, attributed to Ibn-Wahchiya. It contains dozens of different scripts that cannot be deciphered except by experts: if I'd been able to get hold of it sooner I might have used it to write this journal. But the time is gone by – I've got used to my own way of doing things and found my own method of concealment. I shan't change now.

Written on Friday, 27 November 1665

Through no fault of my own I've just been through a long nightmare of a week, and fear is still lingering in my bones. But I refuse to go. I refuse to leave after having been duped and humiliated.

I shan't stay on in Constantinople any longer than necessary, but nor shall I leave until I've obtained redress.

My ordeal began on Thursday the 19th, when Boumeh, exultant, came and told me he'd at last discovered the name of the collector who owns a copy of *The Hundredth Name*. I'd told him to stop looking for the book, but perhaps I hadn't done so firmly enough. And though I now rebuked him still, I couldn't help asking him what he'd found out.

The collector in question was not unknown to me. He was a noble fellow from Walachia, a vaivode named Mircea who had gathered together in his palace one of the finest libraries in the Empire, and who had even, a very long time ago, sent an emissary to my father to buy a book of psalms written on parchment, marvellously illuminated and illustrated with icons. It seemed to me that if went to see him he'd remember this purchase, and perhaps tell me if he owned a copy of Mazandarani's book.

We visited the vaivode late one afternoon, at the time when people are getting up after their siesta. Boumeh and I went on our own, dressed in Genoese style. I'd made my nephew promise to let me conduct the conversation. I didn't want to scare our host by questioning him straight away about a book of doubtful authenticity and with equally dubious contents. A roundabout approach was indicated.

Though sumptuous enough in comparison with the Turkish houses around it, the vaivode of Walachia's palace doesn't quite live up to that designation, which it probably owes to the rank of its owner rather than to its architecture. It looked like a shoemaker's house multiplied by twelve, or twelve shoemakers' houses someone had bought and joined together, its ground floor almost devoid of windows, while those of the second storey rested on wooden corbels and had brown slatted blinds. But everyone calls it a palace, and the name includes the network of alleys surrounding it. I mentioned shoemakers because the district is inhabited by cobblers and leather workers – also by well-known bookbinders, of whom our collector must be, I suppose, a regular client.

We were met at the door by a Walachian partisan wearing a long green silk jacket that failed to conceal a sabre and a pistol. As soon as we'd given our names and occupations – we weren't asked about the object of our visit – we were led into a small study. All the walls – even the space above the single door – were lined with books. I'd introduced myself as "Baldassare Embriaco, dealer in curios and old books, and my nephew Jaber." I imagined my profession would act as an open sesame here.

The vaivode soon joined us, together with another partisan dressed in the same way as the first, his hand resting on the hilt of his sword. Seeing the sort of people we were, his master told him he could withdraw, and sat down facing us on a divan. A maid then came in with coffee and cordials, set them down on a low table, and left, closing the door behind her.

Our host asked politely after the fatigues of our journey and said how honoured he was by our visit, though he didn't ask us the reasons for it. He's an elderly man, probably getting on for seventy; slender, with a gaunt face and a grey beard. He was dressed less richly than his men, in a long white embroidered shirt hanging loosely over trousers of the same material. He spoke Italian, explaining that in his many years of exile he'd spent some time in Florence, at the court of the Grand Duke Ferdinand. He'd left to avoid being forced to convert to Catholicism. He praised the intelligence and generosity of the Medicis at some length, but deplored their current weakness. It was while living among them that he'd learned to love beautiful things, and decided to devote his fortune to collecting old books rather than to princely intrigues.

"But many people, in Walachia and Vienna alike, believe I'm still involved in plots, and think my books are only a diversion. Whereas in fact these creatures of leather occupy my mind completely, day and night. Learning that a book exists, tracking it down from country to country, homing in on it at last, buying it, owning it, shutting myself away with it and making it yield up its secrets, then finding a place worthy of it in my house – those are my only battles, my only conquests, and nothing gives me more satisfaction than to chat with other connoisseurs here in my study."

After this encouraging preamble I felt I could tell him, in suitably chosen words, what brought me there.

"I share the same passion as your Lordship, but in me it is less praiseworthy, for I do for reasons of business what you do for love. When I look for a book it is usually to fulfil an order and sell it to a client. Only this journey to Constantinople was undertaken for a different purpose. An unusual one for me, and I hesitate to tell people what it is. But with you, who have given me a welcome worthy of your rank rather than my own, and are a genuine collector and savant – with you I shall speak plainly."

And I began, contrary to my own expectations, to tell him directly and without any guile about the prophecies concerning the imminent coming of the Beast in the year 1666, before Mazandarani's book, the circumstances in which old Idriss had given it to me, how I'd sold it to Marmontel, and how the Chevalier had been lost at sea.

At this the vaivode nodded to show he knew about it. He didn't react to the rest of what I'd said, but when I paused he said he'd heard the various predictions about the coming year, and he referred to the Russian book of the Faith, which to save time I had not mentioned.

"I have a copy of it," he said. "It was sent to me by the patriarch Nikon himself – I met him when I was young, in Nijni-Novgorod. It's a disturbing piece of work, I confess. As for *The Hundredth Name*, it's true I was sold a copy seven or eight years ago, but I didn't attach much importance to it. The seller himself admitted it was probably a forgery. I bought it just out of curiosity – it's one of those books collectors like to talk about when they meet. Like the fabulous beasts hunters describe in their cups. I kept it just out of vanity, I admit, and I never actually tried to read it. I don't know much Arabic, and I couldn't have made much of it without a crib."

"So did you get rid of it?" I asked, trying to quell the pangs that were making my voice tremble.

"No," he said. "'I never sell or give away a book. It's a long time since I actually set eyes on the one we're talking about, but it must be here somewhere – perhaps upstairs among the other books in Arabic."

I had an idea. I was revolving in my mind how to express it acceptably when my nephew, ignoring my instructions, broke in.

"If you like," said he to our host, "I could translate it into Italian or Greek for you."

I glared at him. There was nothing out of the way about his suggestion – I was about to propose something similar myself – but the abrupt manner in which he'd made it contrasted with the urbanity of the previous conversation. I was afraid our host might be put off: I could see he was hesitating about what answer to make. I myself would have introduced the subject more carefully.

The vaivode gave Boumeh a condescending smile.

"I thank you for your suggestion," he said, "but a Greek monk I know can read Arabic very well and has both the perseverance and the skill in penmanship to make a suitable version for me. He's a man of my own age – young people find that kind of work too tedious. But if you two gentlemen would like to look through *The Hundredth Name* yourselves and copy out some lines from it, I'll fetch it for you. On condition that it doesn't leave this room."

"We'd be most grateful."

He rose and went out, closing the door after him.

"You'd have done better to keep your promise and say nothing," I told my nephew. "As soon as you opened your mouth he cut the conversation short. And now he feels he can impose 'conditions'."

"But he's bringing us the book – that's all that matters. That's what we came all this way for."

"How much shall we have time to read?"

"At least we'll be able to check if it's like the copy we had. And I know very well what *I* shall look for first."

We were still arguing when we heard cries and the sound of running footsteps outside. Boumeh got up to go and see what was happening, but I stopped him.

"Stay where you are! And remember you're in the house of a prince!"

The cries faded in the distance, then after a while approached the study again, accompanied by the sound of violent thumps that made the walls shake. And by a disturbing smell. At this I opened the door a little way and added my voice to the shouting. The walls and carpets were on fire and the house was full of dense smoke. Men and women were rushing about in all directions with buckets of water, yelling to one another as they did so. As I was about to hurry out of the room, I turned and saw Boumeh still sitting there.

"We must stay where we are," he said sarcastically. "We're in the house of a prince."

The impudence! I boxed his ears for it, and for a lot of other things I'd been saving up inside me. But the room was filling with smoke and making us cough. We ran for the front door, crossing through three barriers of flame.

And when we found ourselves out in the street again, safe and sound except for minor burns on our faces and hands, we had time to draw breath we were confronted by another much more serious danger. It arose out of a misunderstanding that almost cost us our lives.

Hundreds of local people had already gathered round to watch the fire when the guard who'd opened the door to us pointed in our direction. He meant to convey to his master or another guard that we'd managed to escape and were no longer inside the house. But the bystanders interpreted his gesture quite differently: they thought he meant we were responsible for the conflagration, and began to hurl stones at us. We had no alternative but to run away, which of course seemed to confirm the crowd's suspicions. They chased after us, armed with sticks and knives and cobbler's scissors; there was clearly no point in stopping and trying to reason with them. The more we fled and the more terrified we seemed, the angrier and more numerous the crowd grew. In the end the whole neighbourhood was pursuing us. But we wouldn't get far before they were bound to catch up with us. I seemed to feel them breathing down my neck already.

Then suddenly two janissaries appeared in front of us. Normally the mere sight of their plumed caps would have made me dive down the nearest alley to avoid them. But now they were a godsend. They'd been standing in front of a shoemaker's stall and had turned round, their hands already on the hilts of their sabres, to see what the noise was all about. I shouted "Amân! Amân!" a plea for life to be spared, and threw myself into the arms of one of them like a child running to its mother. Out of the corner of my eye I could see my nephew doing likewise. The soldiers exchanged glances, then shoved us behind them, taking up the cry, "Amân! Amân!"

Our pursuers stopped short, as if they'd come up against an invisible wall. Except for one youth, who went on frantically shouting and bawling – on reflection I realised he must be a madman. Instead of halting, like the others, he rushed on, reaching out as if to grab Boumeh's shirt. A hissing sound, and before I had time to see my janissary draw his sword and strike out with it, there he was wiping the blade on the back of the poor crazy wretch now lying at his feet. The blow had been delivered with such force it had slashed the victim's shoulder from his body like a branch pruned from a tree. No dying gasp – just a dull thud as the corpse hit the ground. I stared at the dark blood gushing from the wound; it took some time to slacken. When at last I could tear my eyes away, the crowd had vanished. Only three men remained, trembling, in the middle of the street. The janissaries had ordered them to stay behind after the rest had fled, to explain what had happened. They pointed back to the fire, which was still burning, and then to my nephew and me. I said at once that we had nothing to do with the conflagration – we were respectable booksellers visiting the vaivode of Walachia on business, and could prove it.

"Are you sure these two are the criminals?" the elder of the two janissaries asked the locals.

They were afraid to say anything for fear of implicating themselves, but finally one of them spoke for all.

"Everyone says these foreigners set fire to the palace. When we tried to question them they ran away as if they were guilty."

I'd have liked to answer this, but the janissaries signed to me to say nothing, and ordered Boumeh and me to walk in front of them to an as yet unspecified destination.

I glanced back over my shoulder from time to time, and saw that the crowd had gathered again and was following, but at a respectful distance. From further back still came the glow of the flames and the noise of the fire-fighters. My nephew just strode ahead without the least glance at me to show solidarity or share my anxiety. No doubt his great mind was preoccupied with far more important matters than the vulgar fears that beset his unfortunate uncle, unjustly suspected of a crime and being led by two janissaries through the back streets of Constantinople towards an unknown fate.

Our escort led us to the residence of one Morched Agha, apparently a person of some importance. I'd never heard of him, but he led me to understand he was once a commandant in the janissaries, and as a result now occupied a senior position in Damascus. He addressed us in Arabic, but in an Arabic he'd obviously picked up late in life and spoke with a strong Turkish accent.

The first thing I noticed about him was his teeth. They were worn so thin they looked like a row of black needles. I found them repulsive, but they didn't seem to cause him any shame or embarrassment. He displayed them generously every time he smiled, and he was always smiling. Apart from that, I must admit he looked respectable enough: a bit portly, like me, with grey hair under an immaculate white cap trimmed with silver, a well-tended beard, and friendly manners.

As soon as we'd been shown in he welcomed us and said we were lucky the janissaries had brought us to him rather than to a judge or to the prisoners' tower.

"These young men are like children to me. They trust me. They know I'm a man of justice and compassion. I have friends in high places, very high places, if you see what I mean, but I've never used my influence to get an innocent person convicted. Sometimes, though, I have had a guilty person reprieved, if he's made me feel sorry for him."

"I can swear to you that we're innocent," I cried. "It was all a mistake. Let me explain."

He listened to me carefully, nodding several times as if in sympathy.

"You seem a respectable man," he said then. "Let me assure you I'll be your friend and protector."

We were in a huge room furnished just with rugs, curtains and cushions. It contained, apart from Morched Agha himself and our two janissaries, half a dozen armed men who looked to me like renegade soldiers. When a din arose outside, a guard left the room, then returned and whispered something to our host that appeared to worry him.

"The fire is spreading," he said. "They've lost count of the number of victims."

He turned to one of the janissaries.

"Did the local people see you bring our friends here?"

"Yes, a few of them followed us at a distance."

Morched Agha looked more troubled still.

"We must be on the alert all night. You must all stay awake. And if anyone asks you where our friends are, tell them we've put them in prison to await trial."

He gave us a meaning wink, revealing his black spikes, and said reassuringly: "Don't worry. Those ragamuffins won't lay a finger on you – take my word for it."

Then he signed to one of his men to bring some pistachio nuts. The two janissaries chose this moment to withdraw.

*　　*　　*

But I must interrupt my account for tonight. It's been a tiring day, and my pen's starting to feel heavy. I'll take it up again at daybreak.

Written on Saturday the 28th

Later on they gave us dinner, then showed us a room in the house where my nephew and I could sleep on our own. I didn't sleep a wink all night, and was still awake at dawn when Morched Agha came and shook me by the shoulder.

"You must get up straight away," he said.

I sat up.

"What's the matter?"

"The crowd has gathered outside. It seems half the neighbourhood has burned down, and hundreds of people have been killed. I swore to them on my father's grave that you weren't here. But if they go on asking I'll have to let some of them in to see for themselves. So you must hide. Come with me!"

He led us along a corridor and unlocked what looked like a cupboard door.

"You have to go down a few steps," he told us. "Be careful, there isn't any light. Go down slowly and hold on to the wall. There's a small room at the bottom. I'll join you there as soon as I can."

We heard him close the door and turn the key twice in the lock.

Having negotiated the stairs, we groped around for somewhere to sit, but the floor was muddy and there wasn't a chair or a stool. I was obliged to lean against the wall, praying that our host wouldn't leave us down in this hole for long.

"If he hadn't taken us under his wing we'd be in a dungeon by now," said Boumeh suddenly. He hadn't opened his mouth for hours.

In the dark I couldn't see if he was smiling.

"A fine time to make jokes!" I said. "I suppose you'd rather he threw us to the mob? Or handed us over to a judge who would have us strung up to satisfy public opinion? Don't be so ungrateful! And show a bit of humility! Don't forget it was you who made me go to see the vaivode. And made me come on this journey in the first place! We should never have left Gibelet!"

I'd spoken to him in Genoese rather than Arabic, as I do instinctively whenever I come up against typically Oriental difficulties.

I have to admit that as the hours, and then the days, went by, my thoughts took much the same tone as Boumeh's, though I'd suspected him of facetiousness and taxed him with ingratitude. Sometimes, at least. At other times I thanked my lucky stars for having sent Morched Agha my way. I wavered between the two points of view. At one moment I'd see him as a wise and mature dignitary, concerned about our fate and well-being, apologising every time, in spite of himself, he caused us any inconvenience. At others, all I could think of was that black mouthful of shark's teeth. When the time hung heavy and the dangers threatening us seemed far away, I'd sometimes ask myself if it wasn't ridiculous for us to be shut up in a house belonging to someone we didn't know and who was neither an official responsible for law and order nor a friend. Why was he doing this for us? Why should he get on the wrong side of the locals, and even of the authorities, to whom he ought to have handed us over from the start? Then he started having the door of the cell opened and summoning us up into the house, usually during the night, inviting us to share a meal with him and his men, installing us in the place of honour and giving us the choicest morsels of chicken or lamb before bringing us up to date on how our case was getting on.

"Alas," he would say, "you are in mortal danger. The local people keep watch over my door – they're sure I'm still hiding you here. The whole city is looking for whoever started the fire, and the authorities promise they'll make an example of the guilty parties."

If we were caught we couldn't even expect a proper trial. We'd be impaled the very same day, and our bodies exposed in the public squares.

So long as we remained hidden in the house of our benefactor, we were safe. But we couldn't stay there indefinitely. Every secret eventually got out. And the judge had sent his clerk on a visit of inspection. So he must suspect something.

My hand no longer trembles as I write. But for nine days and nights my life was a nightmare, and the presence of my wretched nephew did nothing to alleviate my distress.

The situation wasn't resolved till yesterday. After letting me think that the judge might have the premises officially searched at any moment, and that it was growing more and more risky for him to shelter me, my host at last brought me good news.

"The judge sent for me this morning, and I said my prayers as I went! When he began by saying he knew you were hidden here – the janissaries had confessed as much – I threw myself at his feet and begged him to spare my life. He told me to get up, and said he approved of my noble attitude, defending two innocent people. For he believes that you're innocent, and if feelings weren't running so high he'd let you go free straight away without a stain on your characters. But we need to be careful, he said. Before you leave you ought to be provided with a safe-conduct. 'Only your excellency,' I said, 'can supply them with that.' He said he needed to think it over, and told me to come back again this afternoon. What do you think?"

I told him I was delighted: it was the best possible news.

"We'll have to make the judge a suitable present."

"Of course. How much do you suggest?"

"Think it over carefully. He's an important person. And a proud one – he won't want to haggle. He'll just see what you offer, and if he thinks it's enough he'll issue the safe-conduct. If he thinks it isn't enough, he'll throw it back in my face and it'll be goodnight for ever for all three of us!"

He drew his hand across his throat, and I automatically copied him.

So how much money ought I to offer to save my life? How can anyone possibly answer such a question? Is there a figure beyond which I'd prefer to lose my own life and that of my nephew?

"All I've got on me," I said, "is four piastres and sixty aspres. I know that's not enough . . ."

"Four and a half piastres is what we need to give my men to thank them for protecting and looking after us for ten days."

"That's what I intended to do. But I also meant, as soon I get home, to send a magnificent present to you, our host and benefactor."

"Don't bother about me – I don't want anything. You've been here in my house day and night and it hasn't cost you anything. And I haven't been risking my life in order to be given presents. I took you and your nephew in because I believed from the start that you were innocent. For no other reason. And I shan't sleep easy until I know you're safe. But the judge has to have a suitable present, and woe betide us if we get it wrong."

"How does he have to be paid?"

"He has a brother who's a wealthy and respected merchant. You write him an IOU for goods worth a certain sum that he's supplied you with and that you promise to pay within a week. If you haven't got that much in ready cash, you can borrow it."

"Provided someone will lend it."

"Listen, my friend! Take the advice of a man of experience! Start by getting yourself out of the hole you're in with your head still on your shoulders. You can think about where to get the money from later on. We mustn't waste any more time. I'll draft the IOU. Bring me some paper and a pen!"

He asked me for my full name, usual place of residence, address in Constantinople, religion, origins and exact profession, and started smartly writing it all down, leaving one line blank.

"How much shall I put?"

I hesitated.

"What do you think?"

"I can't help you. I don't know how much you've got."

How much have I got? Perhaps, including everything, 250,000 maidins – that is, about 3,000 piastres. But is that really the question? Shouldn't I really know how much the judge usually charges for such services?

Every time a figure occurred to me, it stuck in my throat. Supposing my host said it wasn't enough? Should I add another piastre? Another three? Another twelve?

"So how much?"

"Fifty piastres!"

He didn't look very pleased.

"I'll put 150!"

He started to write it down, and I didn't protest. Then my nephew and I signed the document and he got two of his men to witness it.

"Now pray that all goes well," he said. "Otherwise we're all dead men."

We left Morched Agha's house early yesterday morning, when the streets were still deserted, after his men had made sure no one was watching. We were armed with a rather sketchy safe-conduct allowing us to travel all over the Empire without let or hindrance. The only part of the signature that was legible was the word "cadi", meaning judge.

We slunk back to our house in Galata, dirty, penniless – if not like beggars, at least like travellers who'd been on the road for a long time and had many a brush with death. Despite our safe-conduct we were afraid of being stopped and questioned by some patrol, or, worse still, coming face to face with people from the neighbourhood of the fire.

Only when we reached home did we learn the truth: the very next day after the fire we had been cleared of suspicion. Although he was unwell, and shattered by the loss of his house and his books, the noble vaivode had gathered all his neighbours together and told them we'd been wrongly accused. The fire had been started when a maid dropped some embers from a hookah on a woollen rug. A few people had suffered superficial burns, but no one had been killed, apart from the crazy youth cut down by the janissaries.

Marta, Habib and Hatem, worried by our absence, had come to the vaivode's palace the following day to ask what had happened to us, and of course they were directed to Morched Agha's house. He told them he'd put us up for one night to save us from the mob, but we had left immediately afterwards. Perhaps we'd decided to leave the city for a while, he said, to avoid being apprehended. Our supposed benefactor was warmly thanked by my people, who agreed to let him know what had become of us as soon as they could, seeing that he and we had become, according to him, such great friends. While they were having this courtly conversation, Boumeh and I were stuck in a dungeon under their feet, fondly imagining that our host was doing his best to save us from the clutches of the mob.

"I'll make him pay for this," I said, "as sure as my name's Embriaco! He'll give me my money back, and then he'll be the one to rot in a dungeon, if he escapes impaling."

No one objected to this at the time, but when I was alone with my clerk he begged me not to pursue the matter.

"No question of that!" I replied. "Even if I have to take it as far as the Grand Vizier!"

"If a crooked minor official manages to steal your purse and make you sign an IOU for 150 piastres before he sets you free, how much do you think you'll have to pay the Grand Vizier and his people to get satisfaction?"

"I'll pay whatever it takes, but I want to see that scoundrel impaled!"

Hatem left it at that. He wiped the table, collected an empty cup and left the room, eyes downcast. He knows I must be handled with care when my pride is involved. But he also knows that I take in whatever is said to me, however I react on the spur of the moment.

So by this morning my mood had changed. I no longer want revenge – I just want to get away from this city, taking my nearest and dearest with me. Nor do I wish to have anything more to do with that accursed book: it seems to me that if ever I go near it again something awful will happen. First it was Idriss, then Marmontel. And then the fire. The book brings not salvation but disaster. Death, shipwreck, conflagration. I want no more of it. I'm off.

Marta too begs me to leave the city without more ado. She says she'll never set foot in the Sultan's palace again; she's sure it would get her nowhere. Smyrna is where she wants to go now – somebody once told her her husband had gone to live thereabouts, and she's sure it's there she can get the document that will give her back her freedom. Very well. I'll take her to Smyrna. If she gets what she wants there, we'll go back to Gibelet together. And there I'll marry her and take her to live in my house. I don't feel like promising her that just now – there are too many obstacles still in the way. But I like to think that next year, said to be the year of the Beast and of a thousand predicted calamities, will be the year of our wedding. Not the end of the world, but another beginning.

NOTEBOOK II

The Voice of Sabbataï

The harbour, Sunday 29 November 1665

There were still quite a lot of empty pages left in my other notebook, but I'm now beginning another that I've just bought in the harbour. I don't have the other one any more, and I think if I didn't get it back again, after all I've set down in it since August, I'd lose the inclination to write at all, and with it something of my will to live. But it isn't lost – I simply had to leave it behind when I left Barinelli's house in a hurry this morning. I hope to have it back by tonight, God willing. Hateb has gone to fetch it and a few other things, and I trust him to manage . . .

Meanwhile I'll deal with the events of this long day and the setbacks it has inflicted on me. Some of them I expected. Others not.

This morning, then, while I was getting ready to go to church in Pera with all my people, a Turkish official arrived in state. He didn't dismount from his horse, but sent one of his entourage to find me. All the local people saluted him very deferentially, some doffing their hats; then they vanished down the nearest alley.

When I presented myself he greeted me in Arabic from amid his elaborate trappings. He spoke as if we'd known one another for years, and called me his friend and brother. But his knitted brows told quite a different tale. He invited me to honour him with a visit some time, and I politely answered that the honour would be mine, wondering all the time who he was and what he wanted of me. Then he pointed to one of his men and said he'd send him to escort me to see him next

129

Thursday. I was suspicious after all that's happened to me lately, and had no wish to go to the house of a stranger. So I replied that unfortunately I had to leave the city on urgent business before Thursday, but that I gladly accepted his generous invitation for the next time I was in this delightful capital. Not if I can help it! I thought.

Then he suddenly took from his pocket the document my jailer had got me to sign by trickery and under duress. He unfolded it, pretending his name was on it and claiming to be surprised that I should think of leaving Constantinople without discharging my debt. He must be the judge's brother, thought I. But he could be any powerful person in league with my jailer, and the latter could have meant to pass my IOU to him all along. The alleged judge was probably a mere invention.

"Oh, you must be the cadi's brother!" I said, to give myself time to think and indicate to everyone else that I didn't really know who he was.

His tone grew curt now.

"Never mind whose brother I am! I'm certainly not the brother of a dog from Genoa! When are you going to pay me what you owe me?"

The time for pleasantries was clearly past.

"May I see the document?"

"You know very well what's in it!" he replied, feigning impatience.

But he held it out towards me, and I moved closer to read it.

"The money's not due for another five days," I said.

"Thursday – next Thursday. And be sure you bring me the whole amount – not an aspre less. And if you try to slip away before then, I'll see to it that you spend the rest of your days in prison. My people will watch you day and night from now on. Where are you going?"

"It's Sunday. I was going to church."

"That's right – go to church! Pray for your life! Pray for your soul! And hurry up and find a good moneylender!"

He ordered two of his men to stand guard at the door of the house, and went off with the rest of his entourage, his leave-taking much less ceremonious than his arrival.

"What are we going to do now?" Marta asked.

It didn't take me long to reply.

"What we were going to do anyway. Go to church."

I don't often pray when I'm in church. I go there to be soothed by the singing, the incense, the pictures, the statues, the vaults and the stained-glass windows; I like to lose myself in meditation, reveries, daydreams that have nothing to do with religion and are sometimes even rather daring.

I gave up praying, as I remember very well, when I was thirteen. I lost my ardour when I stopped believing in miracles. I ought to explain how that happened – and I shall do, but later. Too many worrying things happened today; I'm not in the mood for long digressions. I just wanted to say that this morning I did pray. I prayed for a miracle. And I expected my prayer to be answered. I even – God forgive me! – felt I deserved it. I've always been an honest merchant, and also a decent man. I've often given a helping hand to poor people whom the Almighty Himself had abandoned – God forgive me again! I've never taken advantage of the weak, or humiliated anybody who's dependent upon me. So why should He let anyone persecute me, ruin me, threaten my liberty and my life?

So, standing there in the church at Pera, I wasn't ashamed to gaze at the image of the Creator above the altar, radiating beams of gold like the Zeus of the Ancients, and ask him for a miracle. As I write this, I don't yet know if my prayer has been answered. I shan't know until tomorrow – until dawn tomorrow. But it seems to me there has been a preliminary sign.

I listened with only half an ear to Father Thomas's sermon. It was on the subject of Advent, and the sacrifices we ought to make to thank God for having sent us the Messiah. I started paying attention towards the end, when the preacher asked his congregation to pray for those among them who were due to go to sea tomorrow, that they might be granted fair winds and a safe voyage. At this, eyes turned towards a gentleman in the front row holding a captain's hat under his arm, who bowed in acknowledgement of the priest's recommendation.

Suddenly I was struck by a solution to my dilemma: we should leave straight away, without returning to Barinelli's house. Go straight to the ship, spend the night on board, and put some distance between us and our pursuers as fast as possible. What times we live in, when an innocent man's only resource is flight! But Hatem's right – if I make the mistake of appealing to the authorities, I risk losing both my money and my life. These rascals seem so sure of themselves, they must have accomplices among the powers-that-be. And I'm just a foreigner, an "infidel", a "dog from Genoa" – I'll never get any justice trying to fight against them. That would only endanger the lives of my nearest and dearest as well as my own.

On leaving the church I went to see the captain, whose name is Beauvoisin, and asked him if by any chance he intended to put in at Smyrna. To tell the truth, in the state I'd been in since that interview with my persecutor this morning, I was ready to go anywhere. But I might have scared the captain off if I'd let him suspect I was a runaway. I was glad to learn that the ship was indeed due to call in at Smyrna to take on cargo and to put ashore Master Roboly, the French merchant who'd been acting as temporary ambassador and whom I'd met with Father Thomas. We agreed on a price to cover both transport and board: ten French écus – the equivalent of 350 maidins – payable half on embarkation and the other half on arrival. The captain emphasised that we mustn't be late coming on board: he meant to sail at daybreak. I suggested that to make sure of being on time we should embark this evening.

And so we did. First I sold the mules we had left, and sent Hatem to Barinelli's to explain our hasty departure and collect my notebook and a few other things. Then Marta and my nephews and I went on board. That's where we are now. Hatem isn't back yet, but I expect him at any minute. He intended to enter the inn through a back door so as to elude our persecutors. I know he'll manage, but I can't help being anxious.

All I've had to eat is a piece of bread and some dates and dried fruit. They say that's the best way to prevent sea-sickness.

But it's not sea-sickness I'm worried about at the moment. It was probably best to board the ship right away, without going back to Barinelli's place, but I can't help thinking somebody might have started looking for us. And if they have contacts everywhere, and it occurs to them to search the port, we might be arrested. Perhaps I should have told the captain why I was in such a hurry, so that he wouldn't spread it abroad that we were on his ship, and would know what to say if any dubious person came looking for us. But I didn't like to tell him all my misfortunes in case he changed his mind about taking us.

It's going to be a long night. Until we get safely out of the port tomorrow morning, I'll jump out of my skin at the slightest sound. Lord, how did I sink from being an honest and respectable merchant to being an outlaw, without doing anything wrong?

Talking of which, when I was introducing myself to Captain Beauvoisin outside the church, I heard myself saying I was travelling with my clerk, my nephews and "my wife". Yes, despite the fact that I decided to put an end to such duplicity when I got to Constantinople, there I was, on the eve of my departure, putting the same false coin back into circulation. And so thoughtlessly too: my fellow-passengers on the ship won't be like the anonymous members of the Aleppo caravan – they'll include gentlemen who know my name and with whom I might have to deal in the future.

The captain may already have told Father Thomas he's agreed to take me and my wife as passengers. I can just see the priest's face. He wouldn't say anything because of the secrecy of the confessional, but I can guess what he'd think.

What on earth makes me behave like that? Simple souls say love makes people act irrationally. No doubt that's true, but there are other things involved beside love. There's the approach of the fateful year; the feeling that our actions will have no consequences; that causes are no longer followed by effects; that crime won't necessarily be punished;

that good and evil, what is acceptable and what is unacceptable, will soon all be merged together in the same deluge, and hunters die at the same time as their prey.

But it's time I shut my notebook. It's the waiting, the anxiety, that have made me write like this tonight. Perhaps I'll write quite differently tomorrow.

Monday 30 November 1665

If I thought dawn would bring me salvation I've been very disappointed, and it's difficult to hide my anxiety from my companions.

We've been hanging about the whole day, and I find it hard to explain why I remain on board when all the other passengers and the crew take advantage of the delay to go ashore and browse around the market. The only excuse I could think of is that I've spent more than I expected to in Constantinople and find myself short of money, so I don't want to give my nephews and "my wife" the chance to make me spend still more.

The reason for the delay is that during the night the captain heard that Monsieur de la Haye, the French ambassador, had at last arrived in Constantinople to take up his duties – five years after he was appointed to succeed his father. It's an important event for all the French people here: they hope it will restore better relations between the French crown and the Grand Vizier. There's talk of renewing the Capitulations signed last century between François I and Soliman the Great. Captain Beauvoisin and Master Roboly wanted to go to welcome the ambassador and pay him their respects.

This evening I gather that because of certain complications the ambassador hasn't yet gone ashore: negotiations with the Ottoman authorities haven't been completed, and his ship, *Le Grand César*, is at anchor at the entrance to the harbour. So it looks as if we shan't leave until tomorrow evening at the earliest, perhaps not until the day after tomorrow.

Meanwhile, mightn't it occur to our enemies to come and look for us in the port? But with luck they'll think we're going back to Gibelet overland, and more likely to be found in the direction of Scutari or on the road to Izmit.

It's also possible that the scoundrels were just bluffing all along, to scare me into paying up, and that they're as anxious as I am to avoid the repercussions of an incident in the port. As foreigners, their victims could count on protection from their ambassadors and consuls.

Hatem is back safe and sound, but empty-handed. He couldn't get into Barinelli's place: the house was under surveillance, back and front. He did manage to send a message to our host, though, asking him to hold on to our things until we could reclaim them.

It upsets me to be parted from my notebook and think vulgar eyes might be gloating over my secrets. Does the disguise I use really protect them? But it's no good thinking about it all the time, getting worked up and wondering if I ought to have acted differently. Better to trust in Providence, my lucky star, and above all Barinelli. I'm very fond of him, and I'm sure he wouldn't do anything unseemly.

At sea, 1 December 1665

I awoke to a delightful surprise. We were no longer in port. I'd spent the night feeling queasy and unable to sleep. I didn't close my eyes till just before dawn. But when I opened them it was the middle of the morning and we were sailing across the Sea of Marmara.

We'd left unexpectedly because, instead of coming with us, Master Roboly had decided to spend some time with the ambassador to bring him up to date on his own stewardship. So Captain Beauvoisin, who'd planned to go and see Monsieur de la Haye only to keep Master Roboly company, saw no reason for further delay.

As soon as I realised we were under way my sea-sickness abated, though usually the further you are from shore the worse it gets.

I gather that if the winds are favourable and the sea remains calm we'll reach Smyrna in less than a week. But it's December, so it won't be surprising if we encounter a bit of rough weather.

Now that I'm feeling more peaceful I'll keep my promise and tell the story of how I lost interest in religion, and in particular stopped believing in miracles.

As I said before, I was thirteen when it happened. Until then I was always to be found on my knees, with a rosary in my hand and surrounded by women in black. I knew the virtues of all the saints by heart. I'd been more than once to the chapel at Ephrem, a modest cell hewn out of the rock, once inhabited by a pious anchorite still revered in the region round Gibelet for the many wonders he performed.

So one day when I was about thirteen and had just returned home after one such pilgrimage, a litany of miracles still ringing in my ears, I couldn't help telling my father about the paralytic who'd been able to walk back unaided down the mountainside, and the madwoman from the village of Ibrine whose reason was restored the moment she rested her forehead against the chill stone wall of the shrine. I used to be very upset by my father's indifference to things concerning the Faith, especially after a devout lady from Gibelet hinted that my mother's early death – I was only four at the time, and she herself scarcely twenty – was due to her not having been prayed over properly. I held this against my father, and wanted to bring him back to the straight and narrow.

He listened to my edifying anecdotes without showing either scepticism or astonishment. He just kept nodding impassively. When I'd finished he stood up, tapped me on the shoulder to tell me to wait, then brought from his bedroom a book I'd often seen him reading.

Laying it down on the table, close to the lamp, he began to read out, in Greek, a number of stories about miraculous cures. He didn't say which saint had performed them; he wanted me to guess. I liked this idea. I considered myself quite capable of identifying a miracle-worker's style. Was it Saint Arsenius? Or Bartholomew? Or Simeon Stylites? Or Proserpina, perhaps?

The most fascinating story – it elicited great ecstasies from me – told of a man whose lung was pierced by an arrow that remained lodged there. He slept for a night in the saint's room, and dreamed the holy man had touched him. When he awoke he was cured, and the head of the arrow that had wounded him was clutched in his own right hand. The arrow made me think the saint in question might be Sebastian. No, not him, said my father. I wanted to go on guessing, but my father demurred, and told me flatly that the person who had performed the miraculous cures was Asclepius. Yes, Asclepius, the Greek god of medicine, in his shrine at Epidaurus, where countless pilgrims have gone for centuries. The book containing the stories was the famous *Description of Greece*, written by Pausanius in the second century AD.

When my father told me all this, I was shattered to the depths of my piety.

"It was all lies, then?"

"I don't know. Perhaps. But people believed in it enough to go to the temple of Asclepius year after year to be cured."

"But false gods can't perform miracles!"

"I suppose not. You're probably right."

"Do *you* believe it's true?"

"I haven't the slightest idea."

And he went and put the book back on its shelf.

From that day on I've made no more pilgrimages to the chapel at Ephrem. Nor have I prayed very often. Though I haven't actually become a unbeliever. I now take the same view as my father of all praying and kneeling and prostration – a view that's sceptical, distant, neither respectful nor contemptuous, sometimes intrigued, but always free of any certainty. And I like to think that out of all His creatures the ones the Creator likes best are those who have managed to be free. Doesn't a father like to see his sons grow out of infancy into manhood, even if their young claws wound a little? And why should God be a less benevolent father than the rest?

At sea, Wednesday 2 December

We've passed the Dardanelles and are heading due south. The sea is calm and I often stroll on the deck with Marta on my arm. She looks like a lady from France, and the crew eye her surreptitiously – just obviously enough for me to realise how much they envy me, but at the same time most respectfully. So I manage to be proud without being jealous.

Day after day, almost imperceptibly, I've got used to her presence. So much so that I hardly ever call her "the widow" now – it's as if the word were no longer good enough – though in fact the reason we're on our way to Smyrna is to get proof of her widowhood. She's sure she'll get it. I am more sceptical. I'm afraid we might fall among venal officials again, who'll try to drain us piastre by piastre of all the money we've got left. If that happens we'd do best to take Hatem's advice and get a false death certificate. I still don't care for the idea, but we may be reduced to it if all the honest solutions fail. But come what may I won't abandon the woman I love and go back to Gibelet without her, and plainly we can't go back there together without a document, genuine or otherwise, that will let us live under the same roof.

Perhaps I haven't yet made it quite clear that I'm deeper in love now than ever I was in my youth. I don't want to open old wounds – they are deep, and still unhealed despite the passage of time. I just want to explain that my first marriage was a marriage of reason, while the marriage I envisage with Marta is one of passion. A marriage of reason at nineteen, and a marriage of passion at forty? Well, that's how my life will have been. I don't complain – I have too much reverence for the person I'd have to complain of, and I can't blame him for wanting me to marry a Genoese wife. It's because my forbears always married Genoese wives that they managed to preserve their own language and customs, and remained attached to their original country. As far as all that is concerned, my father was in the right, and anyhow I wouldn't have opposed him for anything. It was just unfortunate that the girl who came our way was Elvira.

She was the daughter of a Genoese merchant from Cyprus. She was sixteen, and both her father and mine believed she was fated to be my wife. I was about the only young Genoese in our part of the world, and our marriage seemed to be in the order of things. But Elvira had promised herself to a young man from Cyprus, a Greek whom she loved to distraction. Her parents wanted to separate them at all costs. So from the first she saw me as a persecutor, or at least an accomplice of her persecutors, whereas in fact I was as much forced into the marriage as she was. I was more docile, though, and more naive; curious to find out about what everyone said were the most wondrous of pleasures; amused by the rituals involved; and as obedient to my father and his commands as she was to hers.

Too proud to submit, too smitten with the other youth to listen to or look at or smile at me, Elvira was a sad episode in my life cut short only by her early death. I don't like to say it came as a relief. Nothing concerning her makes me think of relief or serenity or peace. The whole misadventure left me with nothing but a lasting prejudice against marriage and its ceremonies, and against women too. I've been a widower since I was twenty, and was resigned to remaining one. If I'd been more inclined to prayer I might have gone to live in a monastery. Only the circumstances of this journey have made me question my deep-rooted doubts. I may be able to go through the same motions as believers, but in that area too I remain a doubter.

I find it very painful to rake over that old story. Whenever I think of it I start to suffer again. Time has hardly healed the wound at all.

Three days of storm, fog, creaking timbers, driving rain, nausea and dizziness. My legs will scarcely carry me. I try to hang on to wooden walls, passing ghosts. I trip over a bucket, two unknown arms help me up, I immediately fall down again on the same spot. Why didn't I stay at home in my nice quiet shop, peacefully writing out columns of figures in my ledger? What madness made me set out on my travels? Above all, what possessed me to go to sea?

It wasn't by eating forbidden fruit that man annoyed the Creator – it was by going to sea! How presumptuous it is to risk life and property on this seething immensity, to try to mark out paths over the abyss, grazing with our oars the backs of buried monsters like Behemoth, Rahab, Leviathan and Abaddon – serpents, beasts, dragons! That's where the insatiable pride of man lies, the sin he commits over and over again in the face of repeated punishments.

One day, says the Apocalypse, long after the end of the world, when Evil is at last overcome, the sea will no longer be liquid. Instead it will be like glass, a surface that can be walked over dry-shod. No more storms, no more drownings, no more sea-sickness. Just one vast blue crystal.

Meanwhile the sea is still the sea. This Sunday morning there isn't a moment's respite. I put on clean clothes and have been able to write these few lines. But the sun is going dark again, time has ceased to exist, and the passengers and crew of our fine carrack are hurrying about in all directions.

Yesterday, when the storm was at its height, Marta came and clung to me. Her head on my chest and her hips against mine. Fear had become an accomplice, a friend. And the fog a tolerant innkeeper. We held one another, desired one another, our lips met – and people roamed around us without seeing us.

Tuesday the 8th

After Sunday's brief lull we're in the midst of bad weather again. I don't know that "bad weather" really describes it – it's all so strange. The captain tells me he's never seen anything like it in twenty-six years' experience all over the world – certainly not in the Aegean, anyhow. A kind of sticky fog lowering over everything, unmoved by the wind. The air is dense, heavy, ashen.

The ship is buffeted about all the time but doesn't make any progress. As if it were impaled on a fork. I suddenly feel I'm nowhere and going nowhere. All the people around me keep crossing themselves and muttering. I shouldn't be frightened, but I am – like a child alone at night in a wooden house, when the last candle goes out and the floorboards start to creak. I look around for Marta. She's sitting with her back to the sea, waiting for me to finish writing. I can't wait to put my desk away and go over and hold her hand – and go on holding it as I did that night in the tailor's village where we slept in the same bed. She was a foreign element, an intruder, in my journey then. And now she's its compass. Love is always an intrusion. And by it chance is made flesh, passion becomes reason.

The fog is getting denser. My head is throbbing.

Wednesday the 9th

Darkness at noon, but the sea has stopped tossing us about. The ship is quiet – people have given up shouting at one another, and when they do speak it's in hushed voices, apprehensively, as if in the presence of royalty. Some albatrosses are flying overhead, and other birds with black plumage that I don't know the name of, screeching horribly.

I found Marta weeping. She didn't want to tell me why, and said it

141

was just because of the fatigues and concerns of the journey. When I pressed her she eventually confessed.

"Ever since we put to sea I've had the feeling we'll never reach Smyrna."

Was it a premonition? Or just the effect of her anxiety and all her previous misfortunes?

At any rate, I clapped my hand over her mouth to stop her words flying up to Heaven. I begged her never to speak like that again on board ship. I should never have forced her to speak at all. But, Lord, how was I to know she set so little store by superstition? I don't know if I should admire her for it or be frightened.

Hatem and Habib keep whispering together, sometimes laughing and sometimes serious. But they stop whenever I come near.

As for Boumeh, he walks back and forth on the deck from morning till night, deep in unfathomable meditations. Silent, absorbed, wearing that distant smile that isn't a smile at all. The down on his cheeks is as light as ever, though his younger brother has been shaving for three years now. Perhaps he ought to be more interested in women. But he doesn't really take an interest in anything, whether men or horses or finery. The only thing he knows is books. The only skin he admires is parchment. Several times he's walked past me without even seeing me.

But this evening he came and asked me a riddle.

"Do you know the names of the seven Churches in the Apocalypse?"

"I've read about them. Let's see . . . there's Ephesus, and Philadelphia, and Pergamos, I think, and Sardis, and Thyatira . . ."

"That's it . . . Thyatira! That's the one I'd forgotten."

"Wait . . . that's only five of them!"

But my nephew went on, as if reciting to himself:

"'I, John, who also am your brother, and companion in tribulation, and in the kingdom and patience of Jesus Christ, was in the isle that is called Patmos, for the word of God, and for the testimony of Jesus Christ. I was in the Spirit on the Lord's day, and heard behind me a great voice, as of a trumpet, saying, What thou seest, write in a book, and send it unto the seven churches which are in Asia; unto Ephesus, and unto Smyrna, and unto Pergamos, and unto Thyatira, and unto Sardis, and unto Philadelphia, and unto Laodicea.'"

God! Why had I forgotten Smyrna?

Friday the 11th

Marta's presentiment was wrong. We have arrived in Smyrna.

Now I'm on terra firma again I can write it down without my hand trembling: I felt the same as she did throughout the crossing. It was more than a feeling, though – it was a horrible conviction. It caused me physical pangs, though I did my best to hide them from the others. I really did feel this was my last voyage. And so it may be, after all, even if it won't have ended before we get to Smyrna. The only question I asked myself was how the end would come. At first, when the storm began, I was sure we were going to be shipwrecked. Then, as the sea and the sky grew calmer but at the same time darker, my fears became more ambiguous and less admissible. My fears were no longer those that afflict all who go to sea: I didn't scan the horizon for pirates or storms or fabled monsters; I wasn't worried about fire or epidemics or treacherous currents or falling overboard. There wasn't any horizon, there wasn't any deck to fall from. Only the endless gloom, the clinging fog, the low apocalyptic cloud.

I'm sure all my fellow-passengers felt the same. I could tell from the look on their faces – like people suddenly and inexplicably condemned to death. And from the way they muttered to themselves. Not to mention the haste with which they eventually disembarked.

We are now ashore in Smyrna, thank God. Admittedly it's still dark, but that's because it's nearly nightfall. The sky started to clear as soon as we entered the bay. Tomorrow we shall see the sun.

Smyrna, Saturday 12 December 1665

We slept in the Capuchin monastery and I dreamed about being shipwrecked. All the time I was at sea I was afraid during the day, but at night I dreamed I was on dry land, in my house in Gibelet.

The monks received us politely, but without enthusiasm, even though I'd told them – rather improperly, it's true – that I'd been recommended to them by Father Thomas of Paris. If I'd asked him for a letter of introduction I'm sure he'd have obliged, but things happened so fast I didn't know I'd be leaving so soon. And I didn't want my pursuers in Constantinople to go to the church and learn from him where I'd gone to. I suppose I could have asked him not to tell them anything, but then I'd have had to explain why I was being pursued, and to ask him to lie to protect me. To cut a long story short, I came without a recommendation but acted as if I had one. I even referred to Father Thomas as "my confessor", which was not actually untrue but slightly inaccurate and rather boastful.

But that's not really what I meant to talk about today. I just wanted to write up my notes in chronological order, starting with last night and my dream, before getting on to my main preoccupation: the strange things that everyone tells me are taking place here in Smyrna. I have many different sources of information. The first is an elderly Capuchin monk, Father Jean-Baptiste of Douai, who has lived in the Levant for twenty years. Before that he spent fifteen years in Genoa, which he misses and loves as if it were his birthplace. He says it's an honour for him to talk to a descendant of the famous Embriaci, and he opens his heart to me as if he'd known me from childhood. But I've also heard evidence about what's going on from other foreigners whom I've met today, as well as from some of the local people.

They all say that a man living here in Smyrna, a Jew called Sabbataï, or Shabtai, or Shabetai, has proclaimed that he is the Messiah and predicted that the world will end in 1666 – in June of that year, I believe, to be precise. The strangest thing about it is that most of the people in Smyrna, even the Christians and the Turks, and even those who make fun of the man himself, seem to believe his prophecy will come true. Father Jean-Baptiste himself maintains that the appearance of false Messiahs is a sign that the end of the world is at hand.

People say the Jews are no longer willing to work, and spend all day in prayer and ritual fasting. Their shops are shut, and travellers are unable to find a money-changer. I haven't been able to check that this is true, because yesterday evening and today have been the Jewish Sabbath, but I'll be able to do so tomorrow, which is the Lord's Day for us but not for the Jews and the Turks. I shall go to the Jewish quarter, which is on the hillside near the old castle. The foreigners here – mostly English and Dutch – live by the sea, on either side of the avenue skirting the harbour. Then I'll see with my own eyes whether what people tell me is true.

13 December 1665

The Jews say it's a wonder, and I, who've always lived in Ottoman territory, agree with them. Their so-called Messiah is safe and sound – I've seen him with my own eyes, walking freely through the street and singing at the top of his voice! And yet this morning everyone had given him up for dead.

He'd been summoned to appear before the cadi, the judge who rules the roost in Smyrna and who deals extremely harshly with anyone who is a threat to law and order. And, in the eyes of the authorities, what is going on now in Smyrna is more than a threat – it's an extraordinary challenge, an insult even. No one is working. It's not only the Jews. In a city that has almost as many foreign merchants as there are anywhere, nothing is being bought or sold. The dockers in the harbour won't load or unload cargoes. Stalls and workshops are shut, and the people just gather in the squares, talking about the end of the world and the destruction of empires. It's reported that delegations are beginning to arrive from faraway countries to prostrate themselves before this Sabbataï, whose supporters call him not only the Messiah, but also the king of kings.

I say "his supporters" and not "the Jews" because the latter are very divided in their opinions about him. Most of them believe he is the Anointed One heralded by the prophets, but some of the rabbis see him as an impostor, a blasphemer, because he dares to utter the name of God – a thing that is prohibited among the Jews. But his supporters say nothing may be forbidden to the Messiah, and that this breaking of the rules is a sure sign that Sabbataï is not just an ordinary believer. The battles between the two factions apparently went on for months without anything becoming known of the matter outside the contenders' own community. Then a few days ago the controversy took a new turn. Various incidents took place in the streets, and some Jews accused other Jews of being infidels in front of a crowd of mystified Christians and Turks.

And yesterday something serious happened at prayer time in a large meeting place known as the Portuguese synagogue. It was full of Sabbataï's enemies, who did not want him to be admitted. But he arrived, surrounded by his supporters, and proceeded to hack down the door with an axe. It was because of this that the cadi decided to send for him, as I learned early this morning from Father Jean-Baptiste, who takes a close interest in all this. It was he who encouraged me to go to the cadi's house to watch Sabbataï's arrival and tell him all about it. I needed no persuading. I've grown more and more curious about this affair every day, and consider it a privilege to witness such portentous events. A privilege, and also – why should I go on being afraid of the word? – a sign. Yes, a sign. What else can I call what's happening? I left Gibelet because of all the rumours about the year of the Beast, and was overtaken on the way by a woman whom people were always talking to about Smyrna because it was there that her husband was supposed to have been seen for the last time! For love of her I find myself in that very town, and now I discover that it's precisely here and now that the end of the world is announced. We're only a few days away from 1666, and I'm in the process of losing my doubts in the same way as other people lose their faith. Just because of a false Messiah? someone may ask. No, because of what I have seen today, and what my reason can no longer comprehend.

The cadi's residence can hardly be compared to the palaces in Constantinople, but it's by far the most imposing house in Smyrna. Three storeys of delicate arcades, a gate that visitors must stoop to pass through, and a huge garden where the horses of the guards browse. For the cadi is the governor as well as a judge, and if the Sultan is God's shadow on earth, then the cadi is the Sultan's shadow in the city. It is his job to make the Sultan's subjects live in fear, whether they are Turks, Armenians, Jews or Greeks, or even strangers. Not a week goes by that someone isn't tortured, hanged, impaled or beheaded, or if the person concerned is of high rank and the Porte has so decided, respectfully strangled. So people never hang around too close to the cadi's residence.

Even this morning, though there was a crowd of onlookers there-abouts, they were scatterered through the alleys, ready to disperse at the first sign of trouble. Among them were many Jews in red caps, whispering feverishly together, and also numbers of foreign merchants there, like me, to see what happened.

Suddenly a shout went up. "There he is!" said Hatem, pointing to a man with a red beard, wearing a long coat and a head-dress set with precious stones. He was accompanied by a dozen or so of his entourage; about a hundred more followed at a distance. He walked slowly but steadily, as becomes a dignitary, then suddenly started to sing loudly, waving his hands as though haranguing the crowd. Some of his followers went through the motions of singing too, but his was the only voice that could be heard. Around us, other Jews were smiling with approval, looking askance at a small group of janissaries who were mounting guard. Sabbataï walked right past them without so much as a glance, and still singing regardless. I was sure they'd grab him and beat him up, but all they did was smile broadly, as if to say, "We'll soon see what song you sing when the cadi delivers his sentence!"

We had a long wait before he emerged again. Meanwhile many of the Jews prayed, swaying from side to side; some were already weeping. As for the European merchants, some of them looked worried, others mocking or contemptuous, according to their nature. There were varying attitudes even in our small group. Boumeh was radiant, proud to see events confirming his forecasts about next year – as if his perspicacity will win him special treatment when the end of the world came! His brother, meanwhile, had forgotten all about the false Messiah and the apocalypse, and was busy ogling a young Jewess leaning nonchalantly against a wall nearby to fasten her shoe. From time to time she glanced at my nephew, covering the lower part of her face to hide a smile. Standing in front of her was a man who might have been her husband or her father. He turned round now and then as if he suspected something, but he saw nothing. Only Hatem and I were watching the romantic manoeuvres – the kind that each of the parties concerned knows will come to nothing, though it seems the human heart often feeds off its own desires, and may even grow empty again once they are satisfied.

As for Marta, she felt sorry for the man about to be sentenced to death. Then she leaned towards me and asked if it wasn't before this same judge, in this same house, that her husband was brought a few years ago, before he was hanged. "God have mercy on him!" she whispered. She ought, like me, to have been thinking, "Let's hope we can get proof of it!"

Then up went another shout. The condemned man had emerged! But he hadn't been condemned at all. He was free, and attended by all his followers, and when those who'd been waiting for him saw him smiling and waving to them, they started shouting, "The law of the Most High has shown forth its power!" Sabbataï replied with something similar, then started singing as before. This time many other voices were loud enough to be heard, though not loud enough to drown his: he sang himself hoarse, and his face was red.

The janissaries on sentry duty didn't know what to do. In normal circumstances they'd already have drawn their sabres, ready to intervene. But the judge had let this man go free – they themselves would be guilty of disobedience if they arrested him. So they decided not to do anything, and on an order from their officer went in and took refuge in the palace garden. Their withdrawal had an instant effect on the crowd, who started calling out "Long live King Sabbataï!" in Hebrew and Spanish. Then they formed a procession and set out for the Jewish quarter, singing louder and louder as they went. Ever since then the whole town has been in a state of ferment.

A wonder, did I say? What else can I call it? In this country, people have had their heads cut off for crimes thirty times less serious than what I saw today! Until nightfall, processions went through the town in all directions, calling citizens of all religions to rejoice, to repent, or to fast! Hailing the advent of a new age, the age of the Resurrection. They call next year not "the year of the Beast" but "the year of the Jubilee". Why? I don't know. But what does seem evident is that they're glad to see the end of an age that brought them, they say, nothing but humiliation, persecution and suffering. But what will the future bring? What will the world be like after the end of the world? Shall we all have to die in some cataclysm in order to make way for the Resurrection? Or will it just be the beginning of a new era, a new kingdom, the Kingdom of God restored on earth, after all human governments have shown through the ages how unjust and corrupt they are?

This evening everyone in Smyrna feels that this Kingdom is at hand, and that all the others, including that of the Sultan, will be swept away. Is that why the cadi let Sabbataï go free? Was he trying to manipulate the ruler of tomorrow, as the powers-that-be do so often when they sense that the wind is changing? Today an English merchant told me, with a knowing look, that the Jews had paid the judge a large sum of money to let "their king" go safe and sound. I find that hard to believe. If the

Sublime Porte heard such a thing had happened today in Smyrna, it's the cadi's own head that would fall! No sensible man would take such a risk. So should I believe what I was told by a Jewish merchant newly arrived from Ancona? He said that in Sabbataï's presence the Turkish judge, having at first greeted the accused without rising and spoken to him contemptuously, was suddenly dazzled by a mysterious light and started to tremble with awe. He saw the Jew to the door with great deference, begging forgiveness for his previous behaviour. But I find that hard to believe too. I'm confused, and none of the accounts I hear is satisfactory.

Perhaps I'll see things more clearly tomorrow.

Monday, 14 December 1665

Today I'm still tempted to talk of wonders, but I don't want to debase the word by using it in its popular sense. I'd rather speak of something unexpected, amazing, a happy coincidence. I've just met, in a street in Smyrna, the man I most longed to talk to.

I didn't get much sleep last night. I'm extremely disturbed by what's happening, and keep tossing and turning in my mind as well as in my bed, wondering what to believe, who to believe, and how to prepare myself for the upheavals that are imminent.

I remember writing, before I set out, that I was afraid I was losing my mind. How the devil could it be otherwise? Yet I keep trying to unravel the mystery as serenely as I can. But I can't go on shutting myself up night and day in the citadel of my reason, with my eyes shut and my hands over my ears, telling myself it's all untrue, the whole world has got it wrong, and signs only become signs because you're watching out for them.

I have to admit that between my leaving Gibelet and the end of my stay in Constantinople, nothing out of the ordinary happened to me –

nothing that can't be explained in terms of life's usual ups and downs. What about old Idriss's death, followed by that of Marmontel? I was shaken by both events at the time, but it's in the order of things that an old man should die and a ship be wrecked. The same thing applies to the fire in the Walachian collector's palace. In a big city with so many wooden buildings, such incidents are commonplace. It's true that in every one of these cases Mazandarani's book was involved. In normal times I'd have found that intriguing, fascinating. But I'd have recited a few apposite proverbs, then returned to my usual commercial concerns.

It was during my sea voyage that the citadel of my reason was undermined – I'm quite lucid when I say this. And I'm quite lucid when I say nothing special happened that might be regarded as the cause of such a development. Nothing but the vaguest of impressions. Those abnormally gloomy days. That sudden storm, as suddenly dying out. And all those people moving about silently in the fog, as if they were already lost souls.

Then I set foot on the ladder of Smyrna. Uncertainly, but hoping I'd gradually recover my composure and, in the city that so many European merchants love to visit, become once more the Genoese merchant I am and always have been.

But alas, so much has been happening since I got here, I've had no time to recover. I can no longer speak of accidental circumstances and act as if, at the end of a journey instigated by fear of the coming year, it was pure chance that brought me to the very place where the end of the world was going to be announced. Smyrna! – whereas when I left Gibelet I hadn't the slightest intention of coming here! I had to change my route because of a woman who wasn't supposed to come on the journey at all. As if Marta was meant to lead me to the place where my fate awaited me. Where suddenly the meaning of all that happened on the journey was revealed at last.

Now each of the events that contributed to my being here can be seen if not as a sign, then at least as a milestone on the winding path that was traced for me by Providence, though I went through all its stages believing I was my own guide. Should I go on pretending to decide things for myself? Or, in the name of reason and free will, claim that I came to Smyrna of my own volition, and that it was by chance that I landed here at the very moment the end of the world was announced? But may I not be describing as lucidity what is really just blindness? I've asked myself that question before, and it seems to me I'll have to go on asking it, without any hope of an answer.

Why am I saying all this? Why am I arguing with myself? Probably because the friend with whom I was reunited today told me what I ought to have told myself months ago. I was ashamed to disagree with him face to face and thus reveal my own feeble-mindedness.

But perhaps, before dealing with this encounter at more length, I should set down today's events in general.

Today, as yesterday and the day before yesterday, most people in Smyrna did very little work. In the morning the rumour was already circulating that Sabbataï had proclaimed Monday a new Sabbath, to be observed in the same way as the usual one. No one could tell me if he meant just today or all future Mondays. An English merchant whom I met in the street remarked that what with the Turks' Friday, the Jews' Saturday, our own Sunday, and now Sabbataï's Monday, a full week's work wasn't going to amount to much. For the moment, as I've already said, no one dreams of working at all, apart from the sellers of sweetmeats, for whom these days of unexpected rejoicings are a godsend. People just wander about – not only the Jews, but especially them – from party to party, from one procession to another, arguing fiercely.

Strolling this afternoon near the Portuguese synagogue, I witnessed a strange scene taking place in a little square. A crowd had gathered round a young woman lying on the ground outside a house and apparently suffering from convulsions. She was speaking in broken phrases: all I could make out was the odd word, like "the Anointed One", "captives", and "Thy kingdom". But the onlookers seemed to be listening closely, and someone behind me told his neighbour, "She's Eliakim Haber's daughter. She's prophesying. She can see King Sabbataï sitting on his throne." I walked on, leaving the young woman still prophesying. I felt uncomfortable. As if I'd gone into a house where someone was dying, without being a member of the family or even a neighbour. And indeed it seems fate was awaiting me elsewhere. When I left the square I plunged straight into a series of alleys, as if I knew where I was going and whom I was going to meet.

I came out into a wider street where a crowd of people were all looking in the same direction. A procession was just arriving, led by Sabbataï: this was the second time I'd seen him in two days. Today, too, he was singing loudly. Not a psalm or a prayer or a hymn of praise, but strangely enough a love song, an old Spanish ballad. "I met Meliselda, the king's daughter, radiant and beautiful." His face was red, like his beard, and his eyes shone like those of a young man in love.

People from the houses lining the street had brought out their most valuable carpets and spread them before him, so that his feet never had to touch the sand or gravel. Although it's December, the weather was neither cold nor wet: a lightly veiled sun bathed the city and its inhabitants in a spring-like glow. The scene I witnessed couldn't have taken place if it had been raining. The carpets would have been soggy with mud, and the Spanish ballad would have called forth only tears and longing. As it was, on this mild winter's day the thought of the end of the world brought with it no sadness or regret. For a moment I saw it as the beginning of a long, festive eternity. Yes, I began to wonder – I, an intruder, but there were many other intruders besides me in the Jewish quarter today – if I hadn't been wrong to fear the approach of the fateful year. I realised that the period I'd got used to associating with terror had in fact taught me what love is, and caused me to live more intensely than at any other time in my life. I even went so far as to tell myself I felt younger today than when I was twenty, and to fancy that feeling would last indefinitely. And then a friend appeared, and put me at odds with the apocalypse again.

Maïmoun. Curse him. Bless him.

The last ally of my failing reason. The destroyer of my illusions.

We fell into one another's arms. I was happy to embrace my best Jewish friend; he was glad to get away from all the Jews on earth and take refuge in the bosom of a Gentile.

He'd been walking at the end of the procession, looking preoccupied and depressed. As soon as he saw me he stepped out of line at once and drew me aside.

"Let's get out of here! I have to talk to you!"

We hurried down the hill towards the road round the harbour where the foreign merchants live.

"A French caterer has just opened a shop near the customs house," said Maïmoun. "Let's go and have supper there and drink some of his wine."

On the way he started to tell me his troubles. His father, overcome with religious fervour, had suddenly decided to sell everything he possessed for a song, in order to come to Smyrna.

"Forgive me, Balthasar my friend – there are things I didn't tell you during our long conversations. They were still secret then, and I didn't want to betray my family's trust. But now, unfortunately, everything has come out. You won't have heard of Sabbataï Tsevi before you came to Smyrna. Except perhaps in Constantinople . . ."

"No," I said. "Not until I got here."

"I met him last summer in Aleppo. He stayed there for a few weeks, and my father even asked him to visit us. He was very different then from the character you see today. He was reserved, modestly spoken, didn't call himself king or Messiah, and didn't strut round the streets singing. So his visit to Aleppo didn't cause any stir, except in our community. With us it was the beginning of a debate that's still going on. Because members of Sabbataï's entourage were already whispering that he was the expected Messiah; that a prophet from Gaza called Nathan Ashkenazi had recognised him as such, and that before long he would manifest himself. People were and still are divided about him.

We had three letters from Egypt saying there was no doubt that he was the Messiah, but a highly respected hakham wrote from Jerusalem to tell us he was an impostor, and we must beware of everything he said and did. Every family was split over him – ours worse than the rest. From the moment he first heard of him, my father lived only for his coming. Whereas I, his only son, flesh of his flesh, didn't believe in Sabbataï for a single second. It will all end very badly. Our people, who for centuries have lived quietly and moderately, never raising their voices, have suddenly started shouting that their king will soon rule over the whole world, and the Ottoman Sultan will kneel down before him and offer him his throne. Yes, they say such crazy things out loud, heedless of the fact that they may be unleashing the Sultan's wrath on us. Stop being afraid of the Sultan, my father tells me – and he's spent his whole life quaking at the shadow of the lowliest official sent by the Sublime Porte! Why be afraid of the Sultan? His day is done. The age of the Resurrection is about to begin!

"My father was determined to go to Constantinople, as I told you, but I went instead, for fear he wouldn't be able to bear the hardships of the journey. He promised to wait for me, and I promised to bring back the opinions of the most eminent hakhams, those who are universally respected by all our people.

"I kept my promise, but my father didn't keep his. As soon as I got to the capital I set out to visit all the most learned men, one after the other, carefully noting down what each of them said. But my father was too impatient to wait. One day I heard that he'd left Aleppo with two rabbis and a few other worthies. Their caravan passed through Tarsus two weeks after ours, then followed the coast road to Smyrna.

"Before leaving home my father had sold all we possessed. 'Why did you do that?' I asked him. He answered, 'What use to us are a few stones in Aleppo if the age of the Resurrection has already begun?' I said, 'But what if this man wasn't the Messiah? And if the time of the Resurrection hadn't already come?' My father answered, 'If you won't share my happiness, you're no longer my son!'

"Yes, he sold everything, then came and laid the money at Sabbataï's feet. And Sabbataï, to show his gratitude, has just made him a king. Yes, Balthasar, we must celebrate – my father's been made a king. I'm not the son of Isaac the jeweller any more – I'm the son of King Asa! You must treat me with great respect." And he poured himself a good swig of French wine.

I felt rather at a loss, not knowing how far I ought to join in his sarcastic remarks.

"Perhaps I should point out," added my friend, "that Sabbataï appointed no fewer than seven kings today, and yesterday it was a dozen. No other city has ever entertained so many kings at once!"

Presented like this, the strange events I've just witnessed do look like a lamentable piece of tomfoolery. But should I believe what Maïmoun tells me? Or ought I to contradict him and tell him why I myself am troubled, though I haven't believed in miracles for a long time, and for a long time have silently scorned anyone who does?

But I didn't argue with him. I'd have been ashamed to admit that though I'm not a Jew and though I don't expect what they expect, I am troubled by all these inexplicable coincidences, all these signs. I'd have been ashamed to see from his expression that he was disappointed with and contemptuous of my present "feeble-mindedness". And as I didn't want to say the opposite of what I think, either, I just listened to what he said.

I hope he's right. I hope with my whole being that 1666 will be an ordinary year, with ordinary joys and sorrows, and that I and my nearest and dearest will get right through it just as I've got through forty or so other years. But I can't convince myself. None of those other years presented itself like this. None of them was introduced by signs and portents. The closer it gets, the more the fabric of the world seems to unravel, as if the threads were going to be woven again into something different.

Forgive me, Maïmoun my friend, if it's I who am wrong, as I forgive you if it's you. And forgive me, too, for seeming to agree with you as we sat drinking French wine and then answering you back now, in these pages, unbeknown to you. What else was I to do? The words we speak leave marks in people's hearts; the words we write lie buried and cold in their leather tomb. Especially mine, which no one will ever read.

15 December 1665

There are only seventeen days of this year left, and from the customs house to the old citadel, Smyrna is swept with rumours. Some are alarmist: the Sultan was supposed to have ordered Sabbataï to be put in irons and taken under guard to Constantinople; but the so-called Messiah was still here that same evening, honoured by his followers, and said to have appointed seven more kings, among them one of the town's beggars called Red Abraham. Other rumours speak of a mysterious character who is supposed to have appeared at the door of a synagogue – an old man with a long silky beard whom no one had ever set eyes on before. Asked who he was, he claimed to be the prophet Elijah, and told the Jews to rally round Sabbataï.

Sabbataï, according to Maïmoun, still has many detractors among the rabbis, and also among the wealthy merchants of the community, but they don't dare attack him in public now, and instead shut themselves up at home for fear of being dubbed infidels and unbelievers by the mob. It's said some of them have even left Smyrna altogether, heading for Magnesia.

Today at noon I invited Maïmoun to eat with me at the French caterer's. (He paid for everything yesterday evening, though as his father has lost the family fortune he must be hard up, or soon will be. But I didn't want to annoy him by mentioning it, so I let him treat me.) The cooking there is the best in the whole of the Empire, and I'm delighted to have found the place. There are two other French eating-houses in Smyrna, but this one is the most popular. And the Frenchman doesn't hesitate to sing the praises of his wine. Nor do the Turks hesitate to drink it. On the other hand, he doesn't serve ham, and pretends not to like it much himself. I'm not sorry I went back there, and shall continue to do so all the time I'm here.

It was a mistake, though, to tell Father Jean-Baptiste of my discovery. He rebuked me for setting foot under the roof of a Huguenot and drinking the wine of heresy. But we weren't alone when he produced this ridiculous phrase, and I suspect he was only saying what the other people wanted to hear. He himself has lived in the Levant long enough to know that good wine has no colour and no spirit but its own.

16 December

I invited Marta to Master Ezekiel Moineau's at midday today. That's the name of the French caterer. I'm not sure she liked the food, but she was pleased with the invitation, and did a bit more than justice to the wine. I managed to stop her halfway between gaiety and tipsiness.

Back at the monastery we found ourselves alone when everyone was due to take a siesta. We were longing to fall into one another's arms, and without any attempt at prudence, that's what we did. I was listening all the time in case my nephews or one of the monks should catch us unawares. I didn't worry about my clerk – he knows how to see and hear nothing when necessary. But the anxiety didn't spoil our pleasure – on the contrary. It was as if every second might be the last, and had to be worth its weight in pleasure even more than the second before. So our love-making grew ever more vigorous, intense and abandoned. Our bodies were redolent of warm wine, and we promised each other years of happiness, whether the world lives or dies.

We were exhausted long before anyone turned up. She fell asleep, and I'd have liked to do the same, but it would have been too risky. I gently adjusted her gown, then covered her up to the neck with a modest blanket. Then I wrote these lines in my journal.

My nephews didn't come back until the middle of the night. And I haven't seen Father Jean-Baptiste again: he had visitors yesterday, and probably spent the whole day with them. Much good may it have done them all. They'll have collected a lot of fresh rumours. All I collected was wine-like dew from a pair of willing lips. If only the world would always pass us by as it did today! If only we could live and love each other in the half-light day after day, forgetting all about prophecies! Getting drunk on heretical wine and forbidden love!

Lord! Only Thou can arrange for Thy will not to be done!

17 December

I left the Capuchin monastery today and went to stay in the house of an English merchant I'd never met before. Yet another of the strange things that happen to me these days as if to remind me we're not living in ordinary times. So here I am installed in someone else's house as if it were my own, and this evening I'm writing these pages on a cherrywood desk, shiny with new red lacquer, in the light shed from a solid silver candlestick. Marta's waiting for me. She has a room of her own here, opening off mine, and tonight and all the nights that follow I shall be sleeping with her in her bed.

It all happened very quickly, as if the business had been settled beforehand in Heaven, and all we humans had to do was meet here below and shake hands on it. The meeting place was of course the Huguenot's eating-house, where I now go every day, sometimes more than once. This morning I'd only dropped in for a glass of wine and some olives before having lunch at the monastery. Two men were already sitting at a table there, and the Frenchman introduced us.

One was English and the other Dutch, but they seemed good friends despite the fact that their countries don't get on too well. I'd had occasion to tell Master Moineau my profession, and it so happens that my Englishman, Cornelius Wheeler by name, is also a dealer in curios. The other, the Dutchman, is a Protestant pastor called Coenen – very tall and thin, with the knobbly, bald skull typical of certain old men.

I soon learned that my colleague was getting ready to leave Smyrna late in the day for England; his ship was already waiting alongside. His departure had been decided on in haste, for family reasons I wasn't told about, so no arrangements has been made about the house. We'd been sitting together for barely a quarter of an hour, and I was conversing politely with the pastor about the Embriaci's past, Gibelet, Sabbataï, and current events, while Wheeler said little and seemed scarcely to hear what we said, so deeply was he absorbed in his own worries. Then he suddenly emerged from his torpor and asked me point-blank if I'd care to stay at his place for a while.

"If we're soon to find ourselves living in the reign of chaos," he said, "I'd like to know my house is being looked after by a noble spirit."

Not wanting to seem too eager, I explained that I was only in Smyrna for a short time, to settle some urgent business, so I too might have to leave from one day to the next. But I couldn't have sounded very convincing, for he didn't bother to answer my objection and just asked if I'd mind taking a stroll with him and the pastor so that he could show me my "new home".

I think I've already mentioned that the foreigners' quarter is a long avenue running along by the beach. It's lined on both sides with shops, warehouses, workrooms, a hundred or so houses, a few well-reputed caterers and four churches, including that of the Capuchins. The houses overlooking the sea are more sought after than those giving on to the hill, the old citadel and the districts inhabited by the local people – Turks, Greeks, Armenians and Jews. Wheeler's place is neither the biggest nor the safest of the houses: it's at the end of the avenue, and the sea practically knocks at the door. Even when it's calm, as it was today, you can hear the roar of the waves. When there's a swell the noise must be deafening.

The most attractive thing about the place is the huge room I'm in at the moment. It's surrounded by the bedrooms, and full of statues, statuettes, fragments of ancient columns and bits of mosaic, all excavated by Wheeler himself, who does a good trade in such articles.

What I can see all round me, and what makes me feel as if I'm living on the site of some Greek temple or antique villa, must be the remains of the remains – nothing but items that are cracked or broken or have bits broken off them, or of which there are three or four examples. The best pieces have no doubt been dispatched to London, where my host will have sold them at a handsome profit. Good luck to him! I know from experience that the people round here will never buy such things. Those who have the means to acquire them don't appreciate them, and most Turks, if they don't regard them as meaningless, are eager to deface or destroy them on religious grounds.

When he embarked yesterday, Wheeler took a number of packing cases with him, despite the fact that he was leaving at short notice. The largest and heaviest crate, as he told me himself, contained a magnificent sarcophagus ornamented with bas-reliefs that had been found in Philadelphia. Having accepted his invitation about the house, I obviously couldn't but join the pastor and see my host off on his journey. This turned out to be fortunate for him, as we found when we reached the harbour that the dockers were refusing to load any cargoes, no matter how much money they were offered. I couldn't discover the reason for this, but their attitude fits in with the general atmosphere of confusion, demoralisation, touchiness and irresponsibility. I enlisted the help of Hatem and my nephews, so we had the help of seven pairs of arms, including those of the pastor and of Wheeler's own clerk, to get the crates safely on board. Only the sarcophagus was too much for us, and we had to bribe some sailors to haul it up on ropes.

After thanking the Capuchins for their hospitality and leaving a generous contribution towards the repair of their church (damaged in the last earthquake), I came and settled in here with all my travelling companions.

Wheeler has left us a young servant maid with an evasive expression who hasn't been with him long and whom he suspected of pilfering food and crockery. Perhaps money and clothes as well – he wasn't sure. If I should decide to dismiss her I wasn't to hesitate. Why hadn't he done so himself? I didn't ask. I haven't seen much of her yet. She's been through the house a couple of times, barefoot, with eyes downcast, and wrapped in a red and black check shawl.

We've shared out the bedrooms. There are six altogether, not counting the maid's, which is on the roof and reached by a ladder. Hatem has taken the room usually occupied by our host's own clerk; each of my nephews has a room to himself; and so do Marta and I, to keep up appearances, though I have no intention of sleeping in a different room from her.

I'm going to join her now.

18 December

There's still one bedroom free in Wheeler's house, and this morning I offered it to Maïmoun.

Ever since he's been in Smyrna he's lived with his father in the house of a man from Aleppo called Issac Laniado, an ardent supporter of Sabbataï and next-door neighbour to the "Messiah's" family. This has been forcing my friend to conceal his true feelings, and he told me, sighing, that he didn't know if he could bear another long Sabbath in their company.

But he declined my invitation. "It's when our nearest and dearest lose their way that we ought to stay close to them," he said. I didn't insist.

In the town itself a quiet chaos still reigns. People have lost their fear of the law, as if the Kingdom that is to come will be one of mercy and forgiveness, not of discipline and order. But this sense of impunity doesn't lead to unbridled violence; there are no riots, no bloodshed or looting. The wolf lies down with the lamb without trying to eat it, as it says somewhere in the Scriptures. This evening a score of Jews, men and women, went down from their own quarter to the harbour singing "Meliselda, the king's daughter" and waving torches, thus breaking both their own law, which forbids them to kindle a fire on Friday evening, and the law of the country, which allows only foreign merchants to use torches when they go out at night. Not far from here the Jews met a patrol of janissaries marching behind their officer. The singing wavered for a moment, then went on again louder than before, each group going on its way without taking any notice of the other.

How much longer will this exaltation last? One more day? Three? Forty? Those who believe in Sabbataï say for ever and ever. A new era will soon begin, they declare, and it will never end. Once the Resurrection has begun it will never stop. Resurrection will not be followed by death. What will end is humiliation, subservience, captivity, exile, diaspora.

And where do I come in in all this? What ought I to be hoping for? Maïmoun blames his father for abandoning everything to follow his king-cum-Messiah. But haven't I done something much worse? Haven't I left my home town, my occupation and my quiet life just because of rumours of an apocalypse, and without even hoping for salvation?

Aren't I just as crazy as these misguided folk walking about brandishing torches on the night of the Sabbath? I am defying the laws of religion and of the country by sleeping with a woman who's not my wife, and may still be the wife of another, with the knowledge of all my entourage. How much longer can I go on living this lie? And above all, how long shall I escape unpunished?

But if the prospect of punishment does occasionally occur to me, it doesn't turn me away from my desires. The thought that God can see me bothers me less than the thought that other people do. Last night, for the first time, I took Marta in my arms without having to check the windows and doors, without having to listen for footsteps. Slowly I undressed her, slowly undid the ribbons and buttons and let her clothes fall on the floor, then blew out the candle. She raised her arm and hid her eyes; only her eyes. I took her hand and led her over to the bed. Laid her down, and lay down beside her. Her body smelled of the scent we bought together in the Genoese merchant's shop in Constantinople. I whispered that I loved her and always would. As I breathed into her ear she put her arms round me and drew me to her warm body, murmuring words of joy, eagerness, consent, abandon.

I made love to her with the fire of a lover and the serenity of a husband. Could I have done so if everything around us, in the city and in the world, hadn't been in this supreme state of exaltation, of unreality?

19 December

The Dutch pastor paid me a visit early this morning, saying he just wanted to make sure I was comfortable in his friend's house. When I answered with some enthusiasm that I was already living there as if the place was my own, he saw fit to reply that I must never forget that it was not. I was annoyed at this unnecessary remark, and pointed out shortly that I'd merely been trying to express my gratitude. I'd agreed to come here only in order to be of service, I told him. I'd been quite happy at the monastery and could easily go back there. I thought he'd put on his hat then and leave, or perhaps ask *me* to go and take all my tribe with me. But after a moment's hesitation he gave a little laugh, apologised, coughed, and said there must have been a misunderstanding – his Italian wasn't very good. In fact he speaks it as well as I do! In short, he tried so hard to put matters right that when he got up to go five minutes later I laid my hand on his arm and asked him to stay for a cup of coffee. "My wife" was just getting it ready, I said.

After this somewhat awkward start, our conversation took a more agreeable turn, and I soon found I was talking to a sensible fellow and a scholar. He told me that for several months a number of European cities had been buzzing with rumours about the lost tribes of Israel, which were said to have appeared in Persia and raised a huge army. They are said to have seized Arabia, defeated the Ottoman forces, and even advanced as far as Morocco. People say that this year the caravan of pilgrims which should have set out from Tunis to Mecca gave up the idea for fear of meeting the lost tribes on the way. Coenen himself doesn't believe these rumours, and thinks they're put about by Vienna, which is being besieged by the troops of the Sultan, and by Venice, which has been at war with the Sublime Porte for thirty years, and is trying to get up its courage with the thought of unexpected allies preparing to attack the Muslims from the rear.

The Dutch minister says that every month travellers passing through Smyrna bring him letters to this effect from Holland, France, Sweden and especially England, where many people are on the look-out for strange events that might herald the end of the world and Christ's Second Coming. What's happening in Smyrna can only sharpen their expectations.

I told Coenen that I myself had been following these events with great interest, had seen the so-called Messiah twice with my own eyes, and was very troubled by it all. When I added that a Jewish friend of mine was highly sceptical, Coenen was anxious to meet him, and I promised to pass his invitation on to Maïmoun as soon as possible.

Going over the things that had worried me most in the last few days, I mentioned the to me inexplicable fact that the cadi had let Sabbataï go free last Sunday, and further that the authorities had so far done nothing to cut the current excesses short and get the people back to work. The pastor replied that according to reliable sources the judge had been given a large sum of money by certain wealthy Jewish merchants, supporters of Sabbataï, to leave the self-proclaimed Messiah alone.

"I don't know," said I, "how corrupt the Ottoman officials may be, nor how much they are motivated by sheer greed. But what we see at present is utter chaos. And as soon as Constantinople finds out what's going on here, heads are going to roll. Do you really think the cadi would risk his own head for a handful of gold?"

"My young friend," he answered, "if you think men always act sensibly it shows you have no idea how the world wags. Irrationality is the creative principle of History."

In his opinion, he went on, the reason why the cadi had let Sabbataï go free was not only that he himself had been bribed, but also because he must have concluded that a man who came before him singing psalms must be a mere madman, a danger perhaps to his own community but no threat whatsoever to the power of the Sultan. Coenen must have been told this by a janissary responsible for the security of the Dutch merchants. And it's probably what the cadi himself hints at to his janissaries, to excuse his tolerance.

On a completely different plane, I saw today that my nephew Boumeh had let his hair and beard grow. I wouldn't have noticed if he hadn't been wearing a loose white shirt that makes him look like a certain kind of dervish. He's out all day, and hardly opens his mouth when he comes back in the evening. Perhaps I ought to ask him why he's dressing up like that.

Maïmoun has come and sought refuge here. I welcomed him with open arms and put him in the last spare bedroom, which I'd intended for him all along. Though he declined my invitation before, something happened this morning to make him change his mind. He's still very shaken.

His father asked him to go with him to see Sabbataï. It wasn't the first time he'd been, but before he'd always managed to stay in the background, mingling with the crowd and observing from a distance the manifestations of allegiance and enthusiasm. But this time his father, now a "king", insisted that he approach their benefactor and ask for his blessing. My friend did as he was asked, went forward with his eyes downcast, hurriedly kissed the "Messiah's" hand, and as soon as he could tried to step back to make way for others. But Sabbataï, holding him back by the sleeve and forcing him to look up, spoke to him in a friendly manner and asked him two or three questions. Then, suddenly, he raised his voice louder and asked Maïmoun, his father, and a couple of rabbis from Aleppo who were with them, to utter the Ineffable Name of God. The others obeyed, but Maïmoun, though he was the most pious of them all, hesitated. He might not invariably follow the precepts of the Faith to the letter, and sometimes, in the synagogue, he would mutter the prayers half-heartedly, as if his heart was not quite in harmony with what his lips professed. But between such backslidings and committing the sin now being asked of him there was an insuperable difference. So Maïmoun remained silent, hoping Sabbataï would be satisfied with being obeyed by the other three. Little did he know! The self-styled Messiah went on holding him by the sleeve, and started explaining to the assembled company that in this new age what was formerly forbidden is forbidden no longer, that those who believe in the emergence of the new era shouldn't be afraid of transgressing, and those who have faith in him, Sabbataï, should know he wouldn't ask them to do anything incompatible with the true will of the Most High, especially if it appears to contradict what only seems to be His will.

By now all eyes were on my friend, including those of his own father, who bade him trust "our king and Messiah" and do as he asked.

"I'd never have thought I'd live to see the day," Maïmoun told me, "when my father, who'd brought me up to respect our law, would ask me to break it in the worst possible manner. For such a thing to happen, for piety to be confused with impiety in that way, the end of the world really must be at hand."

He lapsed into thought and melancholy. I had to interrupt his reverie to make him finish the story.

"So what did you do?"

"I told Sabbataï that what he was asking of me was a serious matter, and I needed to pray first. Then, without asking leave, I withdrew. And as soon as got outside I came straight here."

He swore that until "this madness" is over he won't set foot in the Jewish quarter again. I told him he was quite right, and that I was delighted to welcome him under my roof.

I went on to tell him about the visit of the Dutch pastor and Coenen's desire to meet him. He didn't refuse, but indicated that he'd rather put it off for a few days: for the moment he didn't feel like talking to a stranger about what had happened.

"My mind's still in a whirl. I'm confused. I don't want to say something I'll regret next day."

I said there wasn't any hurry, and it would be best if we both distanced ourselves from all this bother.

Monday, 21 December 1665

Are there really some honest officials in the Ottoman Empire? I hardly dare say so. It's strange enough that I can even ask the question!

For some days Marta's been saying we ought to take up here the approaches we made in Constantinople, in the hope that they might meet with more success in Smyrna. So I went to see Abdellatif, the clerk at the local prison, who I'd been told kept a record of all the sentences passed in this part of Asia Minor and the Aegean islands. He let me set out my request, took notes, asked for a few more details, then said it would take him a week to look into the matter before he could give me a satisfactory answer. This, of course, brought back an unpleasant memory of the clerk in the Armoury of the Sultan's palace, who'd got one sum of money after another out of us on the pretext of having to consult a series of different ledgers. But I'd decided in advance that I'd pay up without making too much fuss, if only to show Marta I'd do anything for her. So I asked the man the usual question about "how much his informants would have to be paid". My hand was already in my purse. But the man plainly signed to me to take it out again.

"Why should your honour pay?" he asked. "You haven't got anything yet."

Not wanting to annoy him by insisting, I withdrew, saying I'd come back in a week, and that I prayed Heaven would reward him as he deserved. No honest man could object to that.

Marta and Hatem had been waiting for me outside in the shade of a walnut tree. I told them what had happened, word for word. Marta said she was sure everything would be all right: perhaps Providence was about to look favourably on her cause at last. My clerk was more sceptical: in his view, when the powers-that-be are kind it's only a sign that some worse disaster is on the way.

We shall see. Normally I'd agree with him, but today I'm not entirely without hope. So many incredible things are happening. A wind of strangeness is sweeping through the world. I don't think anything will ever surprise me again.

23 December 1665

I'm trembling. I can hardly speak.

Shall I be able to tell what happened as if it had happened to someone else, without shrieking at every line and talking all the time about signs and wonders?

Perhaps I ought to have waited for my emotions to settle down inside me, in the depths of my soul, like grounds in a cup of coffee. To have let a couple of days go by, or even a week. But when today's events have cooled, others will have come along, still boiling hot.

So as long as I can I'd better stick to my decision to write down every day the evil thereof. To every date its own self-contained account. Without reading over what I've written; just turning each last page as I finish it so that the one that follows is ready to record the next batch of astonishments. Until the day comes when the page will remain blank – the end, my own end, or the end of the world.

But let me go back to the beginning as far as today is concerned.

This afternoon, having managed to overcome Maïmoun's reservations, I took him to see Pastor Coenen. He welcomed us warmly, served us some delicious Turkish sweetmeats with our coffee, then started talking in moderate terms about Sabbataï, observing my friend's reactions out of the corner of his eye. First he repeated some highly laudatory references to Jesus on the part of the alleged Messiah: Christ's soul, he said, was indissolubly linked to his own. "I'll see that he now takes his place among the prophets," he's supposed to have said before witnesses. Maïmoun confirmed that Sabbataï always referred to Jesus in respectful and affectionate terms, and often spoke sadly of the sufferings inflicted upon him.

The pastor said he was both surprised and delighted to hear this, but regretted that Sabbataï was not equally exemplary when speaking of women.

"Has he not promised to make them equal to their husbands and free them from the curse of Eve? That's what I've heard from a reliable source. According to him, women ought in future to live just as they please, without having to obey any man."

He looked inquiringly at Maïmoun, who with some reluctance confirmed that this was so.

"He's even supposed to have said," the pastor went on, "that men and women ought not to be kept separate any more, either at home or in the synagogue, and that soon, in the kingdom he wants to create, everyone will be able to go with anyone he desires, without restriction or shame."

"I've never heard *that*," said Maïmoun firmly, "or anything like it."

He shot me a glance that seemed to ask why on earth I'd got him into this.

I stood up.

"You have some splendid things here," I said. "Would you allow me, as a colleague, to have a look round?"

"Of course!"

I was hoping my friend would stand up too, and make use of the diversion I'd created to change an embarrassing subject and interrupt what was turning into a cross-examination. But to avoid offending our host he stayed where he was. Admittedly, if we'd both leaped up at the same time our attempt at evasion would have been obvious and rather uncouth. So the conversation went on without me, though I listened to every word and took in very little of the furniture, books and curios I was supposed to be inspecting.

Behind me, Maïmoun was explaining to Coenen that most rabbis didn't believe in Sabbataï, but they didn't dare say so openly because the whole populace was on his side. Anyone who refused to recognise him as king and Messiah had to hide or even leave the city, or risk being attacked in the street.

"Is it true Sabbataï said he was going to Constantinople in a few days' time to take possession of the Sultan's crown and sit in his place on the throne?"

Maïmoun sounded horrified at this, and his voice rose.

"Do you set much store by what *I* tell you?" he asked.

"Of course!" The pastor seemed rather taken aback. "Of all the good people I've questioned, you're the most sensible, the most accurate and the most observant . . ."

"Believe me, then, when I tell you Sabbataï has never at any time made any such claims."

"Yet the person who told about them is very close to him."

Coenen lowered his voice and spoke a name I couldn't catch. I did hear Maïmoun's angry reply.

"That rabbi's crazy! Anyone who says such things is crazy, whether they're Sabbataï's supporters, who think the world belongs to them already, or his enemies, who'd do anything to destroy him. If such foolishness ever comes to the ears of the Sultan, all the Jews will be slaughtered, together with all the other inhabitants of Smyrna!"

Coenen agreed, and started on another tack.

"Is is true that there was a letter from Egypt . . . ?"

But I didn't hear what followed. I was gazing at something on a low shelf, half-hidden behind a table from Zealand. A statuette that looked familiar. *My* statuette! My statuette of the two lovers, miraculously preserved! I bent down, then crouched to take hold of it, stroking it and turning it this way and that in my hands. No doubt about it! Those two conical heads covered with gold leaf, the strange kind of rust joining the two hands together, uniting them beyond death. There's nothing else like it in the whole world!

I waited a few seconds, swallowing two or three times lest my voice betray me.

"Your honour, where did this come from?"

"Those statuettes? Wheeler gave them to me."

"Did he tell you if he dug them up himself?" I asked disingenuously.

"No. I was visiting him one day and a man came knocking at the door trying to sell him some things from a cart. Cornelius bought almost everything he had, and as I'd shown an interest in those votive statuettes, which probably come from some ancient temple, he insisted on making me a present of them. But for an important dealer in curios like you, such things must be two a penny."

"Yes, some *have* passed through my hands. But this one is different from all the others."

"You must have a better eye than I have for this sort of thing. What's special about it?"

The pastor didn't seem particularly interested in what I was saying. He listened to me and asked a few questions out of politeness, no doubt thinking my reactions were quite commonplace in a man really devoted to his profession, and just waiting for me to resume my tour of inspection so that he could get back to the only subject that concerned him today: Sabbataï. So I went over to him, carefully carrying "the two lovers".

"What's special about this statuette is that it consists, as you see, of two figures accidentally rusted together. It's a very rare phenomenon, and I'd recognise it anywhere. And I can tell you with absolute certainty that four months ago it was in my own shop in Gibelet. I gave it for nothing to the Chevalier de Marmontel, the envoy of the King of France, who'd just bought a rare book from me for a very large sum of money. He set sail from Tripoli, taking the statuette with him, but was shipwrecked before reaching Constantinople. And now I find my statuette here on this shelf."

Coenen could remain seated no longer. He was as pale as if I'd accused him of theft or murder.

"I warned Wheeler against those bandits disguised as beggars who go round peddling valuable objects. They're out-and-out scoundrels, all of them. And now I feel as if I were their accomplice, a receiver of stolen goods! My house is defiled! May God punish you, Wheeler!"

I did my best to reassure him, saying neither he nor the Englishman was to blame: they didn't know where the things had come from. At the same time I questioned him discreetly about what else the peddler had with him besides my "lovers". Of course I was anxious to find out if *The Hundredth Name* had survived too. Hadn't it been taken on the same ship, among the same baggage? I know a book is more perishable than a metal statuette, and the wreckers who caused the loss of the ship and murdered the men on it to get hold of its cargo, are likely to have kept statuettes covered in gold leaf and tossed a mere book overboard.

"Cornelius bought a lot of things from that fellow."

"Any books?"

"Yes, one."

I didn't dream I'd get such a plain answer!

"A book in Arabic that seemed to astonish him."

As long as the peddler was still there, Coenen told me, his friend hadn't seemed to attach any importance to the book. But as soon as he left, very pleased with himself at having got rid of so many of his wares, the Englishman's enthusiasm knew no bounds. He kept examining the book from every angle and reading and re-reading the first page.

"He seemed so pleased with it that when I asked him a question about the age of the statuettes, he gave them to me there and then. He would take no denial, and told his clerk to wrap them up and deliver them to my house."

"Did he say anything about the book?"

"Not much. That it was rare, and that for years a lot of his customers had been asking him to find them a copy, imagining it would put them in possession of some kind of magic power and afford them divine protection. It was a sort of talisman. I remember telling him a true believer didn't need such devices: to win Heaven's favour it was enough to do good and say the prayers Our Saviour taught us. Wheeler agreed, and said he didn't believe in such nonsense himself, but as a dealer he was glad to have acquired a much sought-after item that he could sell at a good price."

Coenen then resumed his lamentations, wondering if God would forgive him for having in an unguarded moment accepted a present he suspected of being of doubtful provenance. As for me, I found – and still find – myself back in a number of dilemmas I'd thought were things of the past. If *The Hundredth Name* still exists, shouldn't I start looking for it again? The book's a kind of siren – no one who's heard her song can ever forget her. And I've done more than hear the song. I've held the siren in my arms, stroked her, possessed her briefly, before she escaped and headed for the open sea. She sank beneath the waves, and I thought she was swallowed up for ever, but a siren cannot drown. And scarcely had I begun to forget her than she rises up before me to remind me of my duties as a bewitched lover.

"So where is the book now?"

"Wheeler's never mentioned it to me again. I don't know if he took it with him to England or left it in his house in Smyrna."

In Smyrna? In his house? In other words, in mine?

Can anyone blame me if I'm trembling and can hardly speak?

24 December

Nothing I did today was a crime, but no doubt I *am* guilty of abusing Mr Wheeler's hospitality. Searching from top to bottom a house I've been lent, as if it were the den of a receiver of stolen goods! I trust my Englishman will forgive me. I had no choice. I had to try to find the book that made me set out on my travels. Not with any very high hopes of success. I'd have been greatly surprised if my colleague, knowing how important the book is, had left it behind. I wouldn't go so far as to suppose it's because of *The Hundredth Name* that he suddenly decided to go away, leaving his house and possessions to be looked after by a stranger. But I can't rule out the possibility altogether.

Coenen says Cornelius Wheeler belongs to a family of booksellers who for a long time have had a shop in the old St Paul's market in London. I've never actually been either to London or to the market, but both must seem familiar to anyone who trades in antique books. Just as the name of the house of Embriaco, in Gibelet, must be familiar to some booksellers and collectors in London and Oxford – or so I like to think. It's as if all those who love the same things were linked together across the seas by an invisible thread. And in my merchant's heart I believe the world would be a better and more cordial place if there were many such threads, woven into an ever thicker and stronger fabric.

At present, however, it gives me no pleasure to know that someone on the other side of the world wants to get hold of the same book as I do, and that the book itself is on a ship bound for England. Will he be shipwrecked, like the unfortunate Marmontel? I don't wish that, as God's my witness. But I would have liked the book, through some inexplicable spell, to be still in this house. But it hasn't turned up yet, and though I can't say I've looked in every single nook and cranny, I'm sure I shan't find it.

All my people took part in the treasure hunt except Boumeh, who has been out all day. He's often been out lately, but I was careful not to criticise him for it today. I was glad he didn't know we were looking for Mazandarani's book, and I especially didn't want him to learn the present whereabouts of something he wants more than any of us. He's quite capable of dragging us to England after it! I made all the rest of the household promise not to breathe a word to him about it all, threatening dire punishment if they disobeyed.

In the afternoon, while we were all slumped in the sitting room, as worn out with disappointment as with effort, Habib said: "Well, there's one Christmas present we shan't be getting!" We laughed, and

I thought that it really would have been a wonderful present for us all on this Christmas Eve.

We were still laughing when there was a knock on the door. It was Coenen's servant, bringing us the statuette of the two lovers, wrapped in a crimson scarf. There was a note with it, saying, "After what I learned yesterday I couldn't keep it under my roof."

The pastor wasn't intending to give us a Christmas present, I presume, but that's what it seemed like to us. Nothing could have given me greater pleasure, except *The Hundredth Name*.

But I had to hide the statuette straight away, and make the others keep quiet about that too. If my nephew saw it he'd guess everything.

How long shall I be able to keep the truth from him? Wouldn't it be better if I just learned to say no to him? I ought to have done that at the beginning, when he wanted me to come on this journey. Instead of setting out on this slippery slope with nothing to stop me sliding further and further. Except perhaps the buffer of the calendar. In a week's time the fateful Year will have begun.

27 December

A rather sordid incident has just occurred. I'm writing it down just to soothe my nerves, and then shall say no more about it.

I'd retired to my room early to do some accounts, and at one point got up to go and see if Boumeh was back: he's been out too much lately, and it's worrying, given his mood and that of the city.

Not finding him in his room, I thought he might have gone out into the garden to answer some nocturnal call of nature, so I went out too and started to stroll back and forth near the door. The night was mild, amazingly so for December, and you had to strain your ears to hear the waves, near as they were.

Suddenly there was a curious sound, like a groan or a stifled cry. It came from the direction of the roof, where the maid's room is. I went over, making no noise, and slowly climbed up the ladder. The groans continued.

"Who's there?" I asked.

No answer, and the sounds stopped.

I called out the maid's name: "Nasmé! Nasmé!"

But it was Habib's voice that answered.

"It's me, Uncle. It's all right. You can go back to bed!"

Go back to bed? If he'd put it differently I might have been more sympathetic. I might have turned a blind eye, not having been beyond reproach myself lately. But when he spoke to me like that, as if I were senile or simple-minded . . .

I rushed into the room. It was very small and dark, but I could make out the two shapes and gradually recognise them.

"You dare to tell *me* to go back to bed . . . !"

I treated him to a volley of Genoese oaths and gave him a good box on the ear. The ill-mannered lout! As for the maid, I've given her till the morning to pack up her things and go.

I've calmed down a bit now, and it strikes me it's my nephew who deserved to be punished rather than the wretched girl. I know how attractive he can be. But one hands out chastisement as one can, not as one would like. I know it's unfair to sack the maid and merely tell my nephew off. But what else can I do? Give the maid a box on the ear and turn my nephew out?

Too many things are happening in my house that wouldn't have happened if I'd behaved differently. It pains me to write this down, but perhaps it would hurt me more if I didn't. If I hadn't allowed myself to live as I pleased with a woman who isn't my wife, if I hadn't taken so many liberties with the laws of Heaven and of man, my nephew wouldn't have behaved as he did, and I wouldn't have had to hand out punishments.

*   *   *

What I've just written is true. But it's also true that if those laws hadn't been so harsh neither Marta nor I would have needed to get round them. In a world where everything is ruled by chance, why should I be the only one to feel guilty of sin? And why should I be the only one to suffer from remorse?

One day I must learn how to act unfairly and simply not worry about it.

Monday 28 December 1665

I went back to see Abdellatif, the Ottoman official, the scribe in the prison in Smyrna, and I now see I wasn't mistaken when I said he was honest. He's more honest than I could have imagined. I only hope the next few days won't prove me wrong!

I took Marta and Hatem with me, and a purse full enough to deal with the usual demands. He received me politely in the gloomy office he shares with three other officials, who were receiving their own "clients" when I arrived. He signed to me to come close, then told me very quietly that he'd looked in all the available records but been unable to find out anything about the man we were interested in. I thanked him for his trouble and asked him, with my hand on my purse, how much his researches had cost him. He raised his voice to answer.

"That'll be 200 aspres!"

That struck me as a pretty large sum, though neither completely unreasonable nor unexpected. In any case, I had no intention of arguing, and just put the coins into his hand. He thanked me in the usual phrases, and got up to show me out. That did surprise me. He hadn't bothered to stand when I came in, or asked me to sit down, so why should he now be taking me by the arm as if I were an old friend or a benefactor?

Once we were outside he handed back the money I'd just given him, folding my fingers round the coins and saying: "You don't owe me anything. I only consulted a ledger, and that's part of the work I'm paid for. Farewell, and may God protect you and help you find what you're looking for."

I was dumbstruck. I wondered whether he was genuinely repentant or just playing another Turkish trick to try to get even more money out of me. Should I press him to take something, or merely leave with a word of thanks, as he seemed to be suggesting? But Marta and Hatem, who'd been watching all this, starting singing the man's praises as if they'd just witnessed a miracle.

"God bless you! You're a good man – the best of all our master the Sultan's servants! May the Almighty watch over you and yours!"

"Stop!" he cried. "Do you want to be the death of me? Be off, and don't let me ever set eyes on you again!"

So we did go, taking our unspoken questions with us.

29 December 1665

Today, despite the scribe's objurgations, I went to see him again. Alone, this time. I wanted to understand why he'd acted as he did. I had no idea how he'd react when he saw me, and as I made my way from the merchants' quarter to the citadel I had a presentiment that I'd find his place empty. One doesn't usually remember presentiments, nor mention them unless they come true. In this case my presentiment was wrong. Abdellatif was there. An oldish woman was talking to him, and he signed to me to wait until he'd finished dealing with her. When she left he jotted down a few words in his notebook, then stood up and led me outside.

"If you're here to give back that 200 aspres you're wasting your time," he said.

"No," I replied. "I came just to thank you again for your kindness. Yesterday my friends made such a to-do I couldn't tell you how grateful I am. I've been trying for months to get somewhere in this business, and every time I've gone away cursing. But thanks to you I went away from here thanking God and the Porte, even though I wasn't much nearer my goal. It's very unusual these days to come across a man of integrity. I can understand my friends' exuberance, but it offended your modesty, and you asked them to stop."

I hadn't actually asked the question that was on the tip of my tongue. The man smiled, sighed, and laid a hand on my shoulder.

"I wasn't being modest. I was being careful," he said.

He paused, and seemed to be searching for words. Then he glanced round to make sure no one was watching.

"In a place where most people will take money improperly, anyone who refuses it is seen by the others as a threat, a possible informer. And they'll do anything they can to get rid of him. I've actually been warned: 'If you want to keep a head on your shoulders, do as we do and don't act as if you're either better or worse than the rest of us.' So as I've no wish to die, though I don't want to sin and go to perdition either, I prefer to act as I did with you yesterday. Inside this place I sell myself, and outside it I redeem myself."

What strange times we live in, when good must disguise itself in the tawdry rags of evil!

Maybe it's time the world came to an end.

30 December 1665

This morning Sabbataï left for Constantinople and an unknown fate. I'm told he sailed on a galley, together with three rabbis – one from Aleppo, one from Jerusalem, and one from Poland. There were three other people with them, including Maïmoun's father. My friend would have liked to go too, to be with his father, but the self-styled Messiah was against it.

The sea looks stormy, and there are dark clouds on the horizon, but all the passengers sang as they went on board, as if the presence of their leader did away with such things as storms and swells.

Even before they left, rumour was rife. Maïmoun told me of all the stories circulating in the upper part of the city, so that I might share in his anxiety and bewilderment. Sabbataï's supporters claim he's going to Constantinople to meet the Sultan, tell him the new era of Resurrection and Deliverance is come, and urge him to submit without offering any resistance. They also say that in the course of this interview the Almighty will manifest His will in the form of some great marvel, causing the terrified Sultan to fall on his knees and hand over his crown to the one who is to replace him as God's representative on earth.

Sabbataï's opponents, on the other hand, say he did not set out as a conqueror: it was the Ottoman authorities, through the cadi, who ordered him, within three days, to leave Smyrna for Constantinople, where he would be apprehended on landing. This is a plausible explanation – the only plausible one, in fact. What sane man could believe in a miraculous interview during which the most powerful monarch in the world would lay his crown at the feet of a caterwauling nobody with a red face? No, I don't believe that's possible, and Maïmoun is even more sceptical than I am. But this evening most people in the Jewish quarter do believe that version of what's happening. Those who have doubts hide them, and pretend to be preparing for the rejoicings.

Boumeh too seems to believe the world is on the point of collapse. I'd be surprised if he didn't. Whenever a choice is possible, he always opts for the most stupid alternative. But he can still argue and make us think; even give us pause.

"If the authorities mean to arrest Sabbataï as soon as he lands," he says, "why did they let him leave freely, on the ship of his choice, instead of sending him straight to prison under escort? How can they be sure where he'll go ashore?"

"What are you trying to tell us, Boumeh? That the Sultan is going to give in without more ado as soon as this fellow tells him to? You must have lost your reason too."

"Reason has only another day to live. The new year is about to begin, the new era. What used to seem reasonable will soon seem ridiculous; what once seemed unreasonable will appear self-evident. Those who have left it till the last moment to open their eyes will be blinded by the light."

Habib laughed, and I shrugged my shoulders and turned to Maïmoun, expecting him to share my opinion. But his thoughts seemed to be elsewhere – no doubt with his father, aged, ailing and misled. In his mind's eye he could see the old man going aboard the galley without a backward glance or a wave of farewell, and heading perhaps for humiliation or death. My friend didn't know what to think any more, or what to hope for. Or rather he did know, but it was not much comfort.

Since we've been living together I've talked to Maïmoun often enough to know exactly the dilemma he's in. If his father turned out to be right; if Sabbataï turned out to be the king and Messiah; if the expected miracle occurred; if the Sultan fell on his knees and recognised that former times are past, the kingdoms of this world are no more, that the powerful will be powerful no longer, the proud no longer proud, the meek no longer humiliated – if the whole mad dream could, by the will of Heaven, come true, how could Maïmoun fail to weep for joy? But that's not what is going to happen, he tells me. In my friend, Sabbataï inspires no trust; no reverence, no expectation, no joy whatsoever.

"We're still a long way from the Amsterdam of our hopes," he says. Laughing so as not to weep.

31 December 1665

God – the last day!

I've been going round in circles since this morning, unable to eat, talk or think. I do nothing but mull over the reasons why I'm so nervous. Whether you believe in Sabbataï or not, there's no doubt that his appearing at this precise moment, on the eve of the fateful year, and in the city named by the apostle John as one of the seven churches primarily concerned by the message of the Apocalypse, can't be wholly due to a bunch of coincidences. Nor can what has happened to me in recent months be explained without reference to the approach of the new age – whether it's the age of the Beast or of Redemption – and to the signs that herald it. Do I need to go through these portents again?

While the rest of my household was taking a siesta, I sat down at my desk to write down the thoughts inspired in me by the events of the day. I thought I'd produce quite a long screed, but when I came to that question mark I found my hand pausing before beginning to list yet again the signs that have punctuated my life and the lives of my companions for the last few months. In the end I put away my writing things, wondering if I'd ever have a chance to dip my pen in the ink again. I went out and walked through the almost empty streets, then along the beach, which was just as deserted, and where I was soothed and even lulled by the sound of the waves and the wind.

Back home I lay down on my bed for a few minutes – almost sitting, really, because my head was propped up on so many pillows. I got up again in an excellent humour, resolved not to let my last day – if that's what it was – be frittered away in melancholy and fear.

I'd decided to take my whole family out to dinner at the French eating-house. But Maïmoun excused himself, saying he had to go to the Jewish quarter to meet a rabbi just arrived from Constantinople, who might be able to tell him what kind of a reception awaited Sabbataï and his crew. Boumeh said he was going to stay in his room, meditating until daybreak, as we all ought to do. And Habib, either mourning his loss or merely sulking, didn't want to go out either. I didn't let all these refusals get me down: I told Marta I hoped she'd come with me, and she didn't say no. She even seemed highly delighted, as if today's date didn't affect her in the least.

I asked Master Moineau to serve us quite simply the best he had – the dish he was most proud of as a cook, and the best wine in his cellar. As if it were our last dinner, I thought, though I didn't say so and wasn't unduly perturbed at the prospect. I think I've come to terms with it.

As everyone seemed to have gone to bed by the time we got home, I went straight to Marta's room and latched the door from inside. Then we vowed to sleep in one another's arms until the morning – or at least, thought I, half joking and half terrified, until whatever it was that took the place of morning in the year of the Beast. But after we'd made love, my companion went to sleep and I couldn't. I went on holding her close for a while, an hour perhaps, then laid her gently aside, got up, put on some clothes, and went back to my writing things.

Again I intended to sum up the events of the last few months, listing the various signs and portents in the hope that the act of setting them down on paper would suddenly reveal their hidden meaning. But for the second time today I gave up. I just recorded the run-of-the-mill things I'd done this afternoon and evening, and now I shan't write anything more.

I wonder what time it is? I don't know. I shall slip back into bed beside Marta, taking care not to wake her, and hoping my thoughts will calm down enough to let me sleep.

Friday, 1 January 1666

The year of the Beast has begun, and it's a morning just like any other. The same light outside the shutters, the same noises. And I heard a cock crow not far away.

But Boumeh is not put out. He claims he never said the world was going to end from one day to the next. It's true he never said it in so many words, but even yesterday he was still behaving as if the gates of hell were on the point of opening up. He'd be well advised to drop that disdainful expression of his and admit he knows as little as the rest of us. But that wouldn't occur to him. He's still prophesying, in his own peculiar way.

"The new era will come in at its own pace," proclaims my nephew the oracle.

It could take a day, or a week, or a month, or even the whole year: but what's certain, he says, is that it has started, the transformation of the world has begun, and everything will have been completed by the end of 1666. He and his brother now maintain that unlike me, their uncle, they were never afraid. Whereas in fact they could scarcely draw breath all day yesterday, and kept going round in circles looking as if devils were after them.

Maïmoun, who spent yesterday evening and today in the Jewish quarter, tells me that for the past few weeks their community in Constantinople has been hanging on the news from Smyrna, and that all of them, rich and poor, learned and ignorant, saints and sinners alike, with the exception of a few wiser heads, are awaiting Sabbataï's arrival with infinite hope. Houses and streets are being swept and garnished as if for a wedding, and rumour has it there, as in Smyrna and many other places apparently, that the Sultan is preparing to lay his turban and diadem at the feet of the Messiah-king in exchange for his life and a place in the coming Kingdom, the Kingdom of God upon Earth.

Sunday, 3 January 1666

In the Capuchins' church the preacher attacks those who predict the end of the world, those who juggle with figures, and anyone who is taken in by such mystifications. He says this new year will be just like any other, and he scorns the Messiah of Smyrna. The congregation smile at his sarcasms, but cross themselves in terror whenever he mentions the Beast or the Apocalypse.

4 January

At noon something happened because of me that might have led to the direst consequences. But I had the presence of mind, thank God, to right the boat before it sank.

I'd gone for a walk with Marta and Hatem, and we ended up near the new mosque, in the quarter where a number of booksellers ply their trade. As I looked at their stacks of volumes I suddenly felt the urge to question them about *The Hundredth Name.* My previous misadventures in Tripoli and Constantinople should have made me more careful, but my desire to own the book got the better of my prudence. I told myself that in the atmosphere currently reigning in Smyrna, even though things had been quieter since Sabbataï left, some things that were hitherto suspect or banned might now be tolerated. I further convinced myself that in any case my fears were exaggerated and probably even unnecessary.

I now know this was not the case. Scarcely had I uttered Mazandarani's name and the title of his book than the expressions of most of the people I spoke to became evasive, suspicious, or even downright threatening. No one said, still less did, anything definite: everything was veiled, elusive, impossible to pin down. But I'm certain now that the authorities have clearly warned the booksellers against the book and against anyone looking for it, in Smyrna, Constantinople, Tripoli, Aleppo, and all the other cities in the Empire.

I hastily changed my approach, for fear of being accused of belonging to some secret fraternity planning to overthrow the Sultan. I embarked on a minute and fanciful description of the binding of the book "as it had been described to me", saying that it was merely this that interested me. I doubt if my interlocutors were taken in by my ruse. Nonetheless, one of them was a keen enough man of business to hurry to his stall and fetch me a tome with a binding not dissimilar to what I'd described. It was of damascened wood, with the title inlaid in mother-of-pearl and fine hinges like those used for boxes and caskets. I'd once had a book bound in this very unusual manner in my own shop, but of course it wasn't *The Hundredth Name*.

The subject of the work the bookseller brought me today is the Turkish poet, Yunus Emre, who died in the eighth century of the Hegira, the fourteenth century of our own era. I just skimmed through some pages, enough to see it wasn't simply a collection of poems but a mixture of poems, commentaries and biographical anecdotes. I looked especially closely at the binding, and passed my hand over it several times to make sure it had been damascened properly and the surface was quite smooth. And of course I bought it. After all I'd said, and with all those people watching, I had no alternative. The man who sold it to me for six piastres made a good bargain. But so did I. For six piastres I learned a lesson worth my own weight in gold: never to mention *The Hundredth Name* in Ottoman country again!

Tuesday, 5 January 1666

Yesterday evening, just before going to sleep, I read a few passages from the book I bought yesterday. I'd occasionally heard Yunus Emre spoken of before, but never read anything by him until now. For decades I've been reading the works of poets from all over the world, sometimes learning their verses by heart, but I've never read anything like this before. I wouldn't like to say it's the greatest I've come across, but for me it's the most surprising.

> *A fly undid an eagle*
> *And made it bite the dust*
> *And that's the truth*
> *I saw the dust myself.*
> *The fish climbed the poplar tree*
> *To eat some pickled pitch*
> *The stork gave birth to a baby ass*
> *What language did it speak?*

While I was glad, when I awoke, to have discovered this book, it had come to me during the night that I oughtn't to keep it, but instead to make a present of it to someone who deserved it and would enjoy the language it was written in better than I: Abdellatif, the honest scribe. I had a debt to him that I'd be glad to pay off, without quite knowing how to manage it. I couldn't give him jewellery or some expensive fabric – his principles would have made him refuse them. And a Muslim wouldn't care to accept an illuminated Koran from a Genoese. But what could be better, thought I, than a secular book that made pleasurable reading and that would remind him of my gratitude whenever he dipped into it?

So in the morning I set off for the citadel, my gift under my arm. At first he looked astonished. I even sensed that he was somewhat suspicious, as if he were afraid I might ask for some favour in return that would trouble his conscience. He scrutinised me at such length that I began to regret my impulse. But then he relaxed, embraced me and called me his friend, telling a fellow sitting by the door to bring us some coffee.

When, after some minutes, I rose to leave, he took my arm and led me out. He still seemed quite overcome by my completely unexpected gesture. Before I left him he asked me for the first time where I usually lived, where I was staying in Smyrna, and why I was interested in the fate of Marta's husband. I explained straight out that he'd abandoned her years ago, that she'd had no news of him, and so didn't know whether she was still married to him or not. This made him regret all the more that he'd been able to do nothing to remove her uncertainty.

On my way home I started reconsidering the suggestion Hateb made a few weeks ago – to get Marta a false death certificate for her husband. But if ever I did have to resort to such methods, I thought, I couldn't go to this new and upright friend of mine for help.

Up till now I've tried to explore less hazardous approaches. But how much longer must we wait? How many more scribes and judges and janissaries must I question and bribe utterly in vain? It's not the expense that bothers me: God has provided amply for me. But I'm going to have to return to Gibelet before too long, and then I'm going to need some document or other that will give "the widow" back her liberty. There's no question of her putting herself at the mercy of her in-laws again!

Back "home", my head still buzzing, and finding everyone waiting for me to arrive before they sat down to dinner, I was tempted for a moment to ask each of them if he or she thought the time had come for us to go back to Gibelet. But looking around at them, I decided to remain silent. Maïmoun sat on my right, Marta on my left. If I suggested going home to her, it would be as if I were deserting her, or worse – handing her over defenceless to her persecutors. And how could I say to him, who was now living under my roof, that the time had come for me to leave Smyrna? It would be as if I was tired of being his host and wanted to turn him out.

I was just thinking that I was right to say nothing, and that if I'd spoken unthinkingly I'd have regretted it to my dying day, when Boumeh turned to me and said suddenly:

"It's London we ought to go to – that's where the book we're looking for is."

I was startled. First, because my nephew had looked at me as if he'd heard, and was answering, the question I'd bitten back. It was only a feeling, I know – a false and far-fetched impression. There was no way that crazy youth could have divined my thoughts! But there was a mixture of assurance and irony in his voice and expression that made me uneasy. There was also a second reason for my surprise: I'd made all the others promise to say nothing to Boumeh about the finding of the statuette and the fact that Wheeler might have the book by Mazandarani. Who could have told the secret? Habib, of course. I looked at him, and he looked straight back at me, impudently, defiantly. I should have been prepared for it. After what happened the day after Christmas, when I boxed his ears and dismissed the maid, I ought to have expected him to seek revenge!

Turning to Boumeh, I told him angrily that I had no intention of following his advice again, and that when I left Smyrna it would be to go back home to Gibelet and nowhere else. "Not to London, nor Venice, nor Peru, nor China, nor to the land of the Bulgars!" I thundered.

No one around the table risked contradicting me. Everyone, Habib included, sat with their eyes meekly cast down. But it would have been a mistake to conclude that the discussion was closed. Now he knows where the book is, Boumeh will go on harassing me as only he knows how.

7 January

It has been raining all day – tiny cold drops that sting like pin-pricks. I didn't venture outside once, and indoors I stayed close to the fire. I have a pain in my chest, perhaps because of the cold, though it went away when I got a bit warmer. I haven't mentioned it to anyone, not even Marta. No point in worrying her.

Since Tuesday nothing more has been said about going home, nor about where else we might go from here. But Boumeh brought the subject up again this evening. He said that since we came on this long journey to find *The Hundredth Name*, it would not make sense to go back to Gibelet without it and spend the rest of the year of calamities moping and trembling. I almost replied as angrily as the day before yesterday, but this evening the atmosphere was more relaxed, and not suited to laying down the law. So instead I asked everyone else what they thought.

I started with Maïmoun, who at first didn't want to interfere in what was really a family matter. But when I pressed him he politely advised my nephews to trust to my age and judgement. Could a respectful guest do otherwise? But Boumeh retorted: "Sometimes the son in a family behaves more sensibly than the father!" Maïmoun was taken aback for a moment, then burst out laughing. He patted my nephew on the shoulder, as if to show he understood the allusion, appreciated Boumeh's quick-wittedness, and wasn't offended. But he didn't say another word the whole evening.

I took advantage of this exchange to avoid another argument with Boumeh about England. The more so as the pain in my chest had come back, and I didn't want to lose my temper. Marta didn't express an opinion either. But when Habib told his brother, "If there's anything to be found, I somehow have a feeling it's here in Smyrna that we'll find it – we just need to be patient!", she smiled her approval and commented, "God preserve you – you've said all that needed to be said!"

As for me, I grow more suspicious every day, and it seemed to me that Habib's attitude, as usual, was dictated by sentimental considerations. He was out all day today, and yesterday. He's stopped sulking. He must be hanging around some girl.

8 January

What I found out today will change the whole course of my life. Some people say that your life only changes course in order to take the path it was always fated for. No doubt . . .

I haven't said anything to anyone yet, and especially not to Marta, the person mainly concerned. I'll tell her about it in due course, naturally, but first I want to think it over on my own, and decide what ought to be done without being influenced.

When I was getting up this afternoon after my siesta, Hatem came and told me a young boy wanted to see me. He brought me a note from Abdellatif the scribe, asking if I could honour him with a visit: his son would show me the way to his house.

He lives not far from the Citadel, in a house less modest than I would have expected, but which I gather he shares with three of his brothers and their families. The place is full of children fighting, barefoot women running after them, and men shouting orders.

Once the courtesies were over, Abdellatif took me to a quieter room on the first floor, and invited me to sit on the floor beside him.

"I think I know where the man you're looking for is," he said.

One of his nieces brought us cool drinks. He paused, and didn't go on until she'd left, shutting the door behind her.

He told me Sayyaf had indeed been arrested in Smyrna, for theft, five or six years ago, but was only in prison for a year. After that he went to live on the island of Chios in the Cyclades, where he's supposed to have managed to prosper, by some dubious means.

"If he hasn't been bothered by the police, it's because someone's protecting him. The local people are even said to be afraid of him."

My friend was silent for a few moments, as if pausing for breath.

"I hesitated for a while before sending for you. I'm not supposed to give such information to a Genoese merchant. But I couldn't let a good man go on wasting more of his time and money looking for a scoundrel."

I told him how grateful I was in all the Arabic and Turkish phrases I could think of, embraced him, and kissed his beard as if we were brothers. Then I bade him farewell without giving any sign of the disarray I was in because of his revelations.

So what am I to do now? And what ought Marta to do? She embarked on this journey with the sole object of obtaining proof that her husband was dead. And now we find out that the opposite is the case. The fellow's still alive, and she's no longer a widow. Can we go on living under the same roof? Can we ever go back to Gibelet together? My head's in a whirl.

I came back from Abdellatif's about two hours ago, and pretended to the others, who were anxiously awaiting me, that he just wanted to show me a gold ewer that was in his family. Marta didn't look convinced by this explanation, but I don't yet feel ready to tell her the truth. I'll do so tomorrow, probably, or the day after tomorrow at the latest. Because she's sure to ask my opinion about what she should do, and at present I feel incapable of advising her. If she was tempted to go to Chios, ought I to dissuade her? And if she insisted on going there, ought I to go with her?

I wish Maïmoun had been here this evening: I'd have asked him for his advice, as I did in Tarsus and on many other occasions. But he promised to spend the Sabbath with the rabbi from Constantinople, and won't be back till late Saturday, or Sunday.

Hatem too is a sensible fellow and gives sound advice. I can see him pottering about on the other side of the room, waiting for me to finish writing so that he can speak to me. But he's my clerk and I'm his master, and I don't want him to see how undecided and distraught I am.

9 January

In the end I told Marta sooner than I'd meant to.

We'd gone to bed yesterday evening and I'd taken her in my arms. But when she snuggled up close to me from head to toe, I suddenly felt as if

I was taking advantage of her. So I sat up, leaned back against the wall, got her to sit up too, and clasped her hands in mine.

"I found out something today, when I went to see the scribe, and I was waiting until we were alone to tell you about it."

I tried to speak as neutrally as possible, in tones associated neither with good news nor condolences. It would have been unseemly to sound regretful when announcing that a man was not dead. A man whom she'd learned to hate, but who nonetheless was still her husband, who'd once been the love of her life, and who'd held her in his arms long before I did.

Marta showed neither surprise nor delight, neither disappointment nor confusion; nothing. She just sat absolutely still, like a pillar of salt. Silent. Scarcely breathing. Her hands were still in mine, but only because she'd forgotten them.

I too was motionless and speechless. Looking at her. Until she said, without emerging from her lethargy:

"What could I say to him?"

Instead of answering what was not a real question, I advised her to leave it for a night before taking any decision. She seemed not to hear, turned her back on me, and said no more until the morning.

When I woke up she was no longer in the bed. I was worried for a moment, but as soon as I went out of the bedroom I saw she was in the drawing-room, polishing the door handles and dusting the shelves. Some people haven't the strength to stand up when they're anxious; others have to keep busy and rush about until they drop. I'd thought last night that Marta must be one of the first group. Evidently I was wrong, and her torpor had been merely temporary.

Has she already made up her mind? I still don't know as I write this. I didn't ask her, for fear she might feel committed by what she'd said during the night. It seems to me that if she'd really decided to go she'd have started packing her things. She must still be hesitating.

I won't press her. I'll let her go on hesitating.

10 January

How delightful those first nights were, when we lay side by side pretending to fall in with the whims of Providence, she acting as if she were mine and me feigning to believe that was so. Now that we love one another we are no longer playing, and the sheets themselves are sad.

If I seem disillusioned it's because Marta has made up her mind and there's nothing I can say to dissuade her. What could I say? That it would be a mistake for her to go and see her husband, when he's living quite nearby and she came on this journey expressly to settle this matter and end her doubts? Yet I'm convinced no good will come of their meeting. If the fellow decided to insist on his rights over his lawful wife no one could gainsay him, not she herself and especially not me.

"What do you mean to say to him?"

"I'll ask him why he went away, why he sent me no news, and if he intends to come back."

"And if he makes you stay with him?"

"If he was as keen on me as that he wouldn't have left me."

What sort of answer is that! I shrugged, moved to the other side of the bed, turned my back, and said nothing.

May God's will be done! That's what I keep saying to myself. May His will be done! But I also pray that His will may not be too cruel. It sometimes *is* harsh.

13 January

I roam the streets and the beaches, sometimes alone, often with Maïmoun. We talk about this and that – Sabbataï, the Pope, Amsterdam,

Genoa, Venice, the Ottomans. Everything except her. But as soon as I'm back home I forget all our fine words, and don't write anything down. I haven't written a line for three days. A travel journal needs to cover all kinds of preoccupation, and now I've only one. I'm trying to get used to the idea of losing Marta.

She hasn't said anything more since she told me of her decision to go and see her husband. She hasn't mentioned any date, or talked about how she means to get to Chios. Is she still undecided? I don't ask any questions. I don't want her to feel under pressure. Sometimes I talk to her about her father, or Gibelet, or pleasant memories such as our unexpected meeting at the gates of Tripoli, or the night we spent in the house of Abbas the tailor, God bless him!

I no longer take her in my arms at night. Not because *I* think of her as another man's wife again, but because I don't want *her* to feel guilty. I've even thought of going back to sleeping in my own room; I haven't used it for some time. But after thinking it over for a day, I changed my mind. It would have been unforgivably tactless – not the considerate act of a chivalrous lover, but a sort of desertion, which Marta might have seen as an incitement to go back to her "husband" right away.

So I still sleep by her side. I kiss her on the forehead and sometimes hold her hand, but without getting too close to her. I desire her more than ever, but I shan't do anything that might frighten her. I can understand that she should want to see her husband and ask him the questions she's been revolving in her mind for so long. But there's no reason why she should go immediately. He's been living in Chios for years; he's not going to leave there tomorrow. Nor the next day, nor next week, nor next month. So there's no hurry. There are still a few crumbs left on our table before it's cleared.

17 January

Marta spent the evening in her room, weeping and weeping. I went several times and stroked her hair, her brow and the backs of her hands. She didn't say anything, but she didn't draw away.

When we went to bed she was still weeping. I didn't know what to do. Just for something to say I murmured clichés that couldn't possibly be of any comfort, such as "Everything will turn out all right – you'll see!" What else could I say?

Then suddenly she turned to me and cried in a voice that was both angry and piteous:

"Why don't you ask me what I'm crying *for*?"

There was no reason why I should. I knew why. Or thought I did.

"I'm late!" she said.

Her cheeks were pale as wax, and her eyes round with fright.

It took me endless seconds to grasp what she was trying to tell me.

"You're pregnant?"

I must now look as cadaverous as she did.

"I think so. I'm already a week late."

"That's too soon to be sure."

She put her hand on her flat stomach.

"*I* am sure. The child is there."

"But you said you couldn't have children."

"That's what I've always been told."

She stopped crying but was still dazed. Her hand went on feeling her belly. I dried her eyes with my handkerchief, then sat down beside her on the edge of the bed with my arm round her shoulders.

I tried to console her, but I was as distraught as she was. And just as guilty. We'd broken the laws of God and man by living as husband and wife, believing our love-making would have no consequences. Marta's barrenness, which we should have regarded as a misfortune, we saw as a blessing, a promise of impunity.

But the promise wasn't kept. The child is there.

The child. My child. Our child.

I've always dreamed of having an heir, and now Heaven is giving me one, conceived in the womb of the woman I love!

We should both be deliriously happy; this should be the best moment in our whole lives. Shouldn't it? But the world won't let us see it like that. We're supposed to regard the child as a curse, a punishment. To mourn its coming, to look back with regret to the blissful days of infertility.

Well, if that's the world, the sooner it ends the better – that's what I say! May it be destroyed by fire or flood, or the breath of the Beast! Let it be annihilated, engulfed, destroyed!

When Marta, riding beside me last summer in the mountains of Anatolia, told me that not only did she not fear the end of the world, but she was waiting and hoping for it, I didn't understand. Now I understand her rage, and share it.

She's the one that's weakening.

"I must go and find my husband on his island as soon as possible."

"So that he thinks the child is his?"

She nodded miserably, and stroked my forehead and face.

"But it's mine!"

"Do you want people to call him a bastard?"

"Do you want people to call him the son of a scoundrel?"

"You know it has to be like that. There's nothing we can do about it."

I'd admired Marta for rebelling against her fate, and couldn't hide my disappointment.

"Expectant mothers are said to draw courage from their unborn children, but yours makes you timid."

She moved away from me.

"I'm not brave enough for you? I'm going back to a man who no longer loves me, who'll insult me and beat me and keep me shut up for the rest of my life, and all so that my child shouldn't be called a bastard – and you call *me* timid?"

*　　*　　*

Perhaps I shouldn't have criticised her, but I meant every word I said. She says she's about to sacrifice herself? Self-sacrifice can have as much to do with cowardice as with courage. Pure courage consists of confronting the world, defending oneself inch by inch against attack, and dying on one's feet. The best that can be said of just exposing oneself to blows is that it's an honourable rout.

Why should I accept that the woman I've started to love should go and live with a scoundrel, taking with her the child we've engendered together, a child that she'd given up hoping for and that I have given her? Why? Because a drunken priest in Gibelet once laid his hands on her head and mumbled three ritual sentences?

To hell with men's laws, their mumbo-jumbo, their chasubles and their ceremonies!

Monday, 18 January 1666

I've just told Maïmoun everything, and he agrees with Marta and thinks I'm wrong. He listens to what I say, but he doesn't really take it in. All he can say is, "That's the way things are!"

He says it would be madness to let her carry the child and give birth anywhere else but in her husband's house: according to him she might die of anguish and shame. She'll grow more frantic every day; I mustn't try to hold her back any longer.

To make it less painful for me, he says he's sure she'll come back to me one day, before long. "Heaven often sends misfortunes to those who don't deserve them, but sometimes, too, it sends them to those who do," he promises, screwing up his eyes as if to make out the real meaning of things. By this he means that Marta's husband might suffer the fate that brigands deserve, that reality might catch up with rumour, and that then the future mother of my child would be a widow again . . . But I know all that. Of course anything may happen. But wouldn't it be despicable to live in hopes of a rival's death, praying to Heaven every day to have him drowned or hanged? A man younger than I am, what's more! No, that's not how I aim to spend my future.

I argue and struggle, but I know the battle is lost in advance. Marta won't dare let her pregnancy grow obvious under my roof; her only thought is to go and conceal her wrongdoing in the bed of a husband she hates; and I can't make her stay with me against her will. She never stops weeping, and seems to get thinner and more wasted by the hour.

So what is there for me to hope for? That when she meets her husband she'll decide for some reason or other not to stay with him? Or that he won't want her? I suppose I could offer him money to have their marriage annulled, alleging that it was never consummated. He's keen on money. If I offered him enough we could all come away from his house together – Marta, our child and myself.

There I go – making up fairy stories, just to give myself some reason, however flimsy, to go on living. Lying to yourself is sometimes the only way to get through your troubles.

19 January

During the night Marta told me she was leaving tomorrow for Chios. I said I'd go with her, and promised not to interfere in any way between her and her husband: I'd just hang around so that she could call upon me if necessary. She agreed to this, though she made me promise again, twice, not to do anything unless she expressly asked me to. If her husband suspected what has happened between us, she said, he'd cut her throat before she had time to cross the threshold.

There are two ways of getting to Chios from here. By road to the end of the peninsula, after which it's scarcely an hour's trip by barge to the town of Chios. Or by sea all the way. Hatem, after making extensive inquiries at Marta's request, advises the latter route. You have to allow a day for the voyage if there's a fair wind; otherwise two.

My clerk will come with us, and I even thought of taking my nephews along too. Didn't I promise my sister Patience I'd keep them with me all the time? But after weighing the pros and cons I decided they'd better stay on in Smyrna. The matter we have to settle in Chios is a delicate one, and I'm afraid one or the other of them might charge in and spoil everything if they were there. Perhaps I'd have changed my mind if they'd insisted. But neither of them made any objection, which I must say surprised and rather worried me. I've asked Maïmoun to watch over them like a father until I'm back.

How long I'll stay on the island I don't know. A few days? Two or three weeks? We'll see. Will Marta come back with me? I still hope so. To return with her to "our" house in Smyrna already seems to me the most wonderful thing that could happen to me, while I'm still there now, and can still look around at the walls and doors, the carpets and furniture as I write.

Maïmoun told me that when I get back he plans to set out on a long journey that will take him to Rome, Paris and of course Amsterdam, among other places. He looks forward to telling me more about it when I'm more in the mood to listen. But shall I really be so when I get back from Chios?

He'd like me to go with him on his journey. I'll see. For the moment I haven't the heart to contemplate any such project. My only dream at present is to go to Chios with Marta, and to come back from there with her.

22 January

To approach Chios from the sea and watch the coast-line, the mountains beyond, and the innumerable mills in between gradually emerge, ought to lighten a traveller's heart like some gradually bestowed reward. For most people the island is a promised land, a foretaste of Heaven. But

I'm travelling out of necessity, not for pleasure, and all I can think of is getting away again as soon as possible.

Marta was silent throughout the crossing, and deliberately avoided catching my eye. Hatem tried to cheer me up by telling me a tale he'd heard the day before yesterday in the harbour at Smyrna. Apparently there's a convent some way inland on the island of Chios inhabited by some very strange nuns. Travellers may be accommodated there as guests, as in many religious houses, but here the hospitality is of a very special kind. It's said that during the night the nuns slip into the visitors' beds and bestow on them favours far in excess of what is required by the precept of loving one's neighbour.

I lost no time in destroying my clerk's illusions by telling him curtly that I'd read and heard similar stories about many other places. But when I saw that he believed me and the gleam had gone out of his eye, I was rather sorry to have put paid to his dream. I expect I'd have been more tolerant if I'd been my usual self.

Chios, 23 January 1666

Ever since we got here, Hatem has spent all his time in the shops, taverns and alleys of the old port, asking after the man we're looking for. But strangely enough, no one seems to know him.

Could Abdellatif have misled me? I don't see why he should have. Was he himself lied to by his informants? Perhaps *they* got the island wrong and confused Chios with Patmos or Samos or Castro, which was once called Mytilene.

Anyhow, I'm not displeased by this turn of events. A few more days' investigations and we'll go back to Smyrna. Marta will weep and protest, but resign herself to it in the end.

And she'll fling her arms round my neck when I bring her a firman certifying that her husband really is dead – and I'll get one, even if it costs me a third of my fortune! Then we'll be married, and if Heaven isn't too hard on lovers, the former husband will have the goodness never to set foot in Gibelet again.

And in our old age, surrounded by our children and grandchildren, we'll remember this expedition to Chios with a shudder, and thank God for having made it so fruitless.

24 January

How charming I'd have found this island if I'd come here in other circumstances! Everything is so pleasing to my heart whenever I can forget for a moment what brought me here. The houses are attractive, the streets clean and well paved, the women are elegant as they stroll about, with a smile in their eyes for strangers. Everything reminds me of the past splendour of Genoa: the citadel is Genoese, so are the people's clothes and all the best souvenirs. Even the Greeks, when they hear my name and discover my origins, clasp me to their bosom and curse Venice. I know they curse the Turks too, but they never do so aloud. Ever since the Genoese left a hundred years ago, the island has never had a sympathetic government, and all the people I've met in the last few days admit as much, each in his own way.

This morning I took Marta to mass. One more time – I only hope it's not the last! – she's gone to church on my arm. My head was proud, but my heart was miserable. We went to St Anthony's, which belongs to the Jesuit fathers. The church bells here ring as they do in a Christian country, and on feast days there are street processions, with the copes and canopies and lamps and gold of the Holy Sacrament. It was the King of France who years ago got the Grand Turk to allow the Latin rite to be practised publicly here, and the Porte still respects this privilege.

All around me, ordinary people were murmuring with more pride than envy such illustrious names as those of the Giustiniani, the Burghesi and the Castelli. I'd have thought I was in Italy had it not been for the two janissaries on sentry duty on a small hill not far from the church.

After mass, Marta went and talked for a long time to a priest. I waited for her outside, and when she emerged I didn't ask her anything and she didn't tell me anything. Perhaps she only went to confession. You're bound to take a strange view of people who confess their sins when you yourself are the sin.

25 January

Hatem is still doing his best to find our man. Marta begs him to leave no stone unturned. Meanwhile I pray to all the saints that he won't find anything.

This evening my clerk told me he might have a lead. When he was in a tavern in the Greek quarter a sailor came up and told him he knew Sayyaf, who according to him lives not in the town of Chios but further south, near a village called Katarraktis, on the road that leads to the Cabo Mastico peninsula. The man is charging a gold sultanin to take us there. I consider this exorbitant, but I've agreed to the arrangement. I don't want Marta to blame me later on for not having done everything I could to fulfil her wishes. She says she's certain now that she's with child, and she wants to find her husband again as soon as possible, whatever life he may lead her. "After that, God will do with us as He wills!"

So I agreed to pay the go-between, a certain Drago, the amount required, and I asked Hatem to bring him here tomorrow so that I can see and hear and size him up for myself.

Deep down I still hope he's a common swindler who'll pocket his money and disappear as suddenly as he came. This must be the first time a merchant like me has prayed to be robbed, lied to and taken advantage of!

During the night I tried to take Marta in my arms for what might well be the last time. But she pushed me away, weeping, and didn't speak to me once. Perhaps she wants me to get used to not having her near me any more, and to get used herself to no longer sleeping with her head on my shoulder.

Her absence has already begun.

26 January

At this moment I'm tempted to write that I'm the happiest man in Genoa and the world, as my late father used to say. But it's still too soon. So I'll just say I have high hopes. Very high hopes. Of getting Marta back, and taking her back first to Smyrna and then to my house in Gibelet, where our child will be born. Heaven grant that my exultation doesn't desert me as quickly as it came!

The reason I'm so jovial is that the man who's supposed to take us to Marta's husband called in today with excellent news. Although I'd been hoping he'd disappear without trace, I'm not sorry now to have met and talked to him. I haven't any illusions about him – he's just a haunter of low taverns, and I'm well aware he told me what he did with the sole object of getting another gold piece out of me. No doubt I whetted his appetite by forking out the first one so easily.

But to get to what's made me so pleased: Drago told me that Sayyaf got married again last year and is soon to be the father of a child. His new wife is said to be the daughter of a rich and powerful local dignitary, who of course doesn't know his son-in-law is already married. I presume his parents-in-law will one day find out about many other hidden facets of this rogue, and be sorry they let their daughter get mixed up with him, but – God forgive me! – *I* shan't try to remove the scales from their eyes. Let everyone pay for his own sins and bear his own cross – mine is heavy enough already. Just let me be relieved of that burden and I'll quit Chios without a backward glance.

I'm delighted with this news because it could completely change the attitude Marta's husband is likely to take. Instead of trying to get her back, he'll see her as a threat to the new life he's made for himself on the island. Drago, who knows him well, is sure he'll agree to any arrangement to save his present situation. He might even sign in the presence of witnesses a document certifying that his first marriage was never consummated and is therefore null and void. If that's so, Marta will soon be free! Free to marry again, free to marry me, free to give her child a father's name.

We're not there yet, I know. The "widow's" husband hasn't signed or even promised anything so far. But what Drago says makes perfect sense. So yes, I have high hopes, and even Marta, in the midst of her tears and morning sickness and prayers, risks a smile.

27 January

It's tomorrow that Drago's to take us to see Sayyaf. I say "us" because I'd like it to *be* us, but Marta prefers to go alone. She says she'll get what she wants more easily if she talks to her husband by herself. She's afraid he might jib if he sees her surrounded with men, and might suspect there's something between her and me. She's probably right, but I can't help being uneasy at the thought that she's going to put herself, even for an hour, at the mercy of such a rascal.

In the end we came to what strikes me as a sensible compromise. We'll all go together as far as the village of Katarraktis. I'm told there's a small Greek monastery there where travellers often break their journey: it provides good Phyta wine and excellent food, and is close to Sayyaf's house. We'll be able to wait there in comfort for Marta's return.

So here we are in the monastery, and I'm working away at writing to make the time pass more quickly. I dip my reed pen in the ink the way other people sigh or protest or pray. Then I set down words in a hand that's as assured as my stride was when I was young.

Marta slipped away more than an hour ago. I saw her go into an alley. My heart turned over, I held my breath and murmured her name, but she didn't turn round. She walked steadily forward, like a condemned man resigned to his fate. Drago, who was walking ahead of her, pointed to a door. She went through it and it closed behind her. I caught only a glimpse of the brigand's house, because it's hidden behind a surrounding wall and tall trees.

A monk came and suggested I should eat something, but I prefer to wait until Marta's back, so that we can have a meal together. In any case, I couldn't swallow or digest a thing till she's with me again: my throat seems to have shrunk, and my stomach has seized up. I'm on tenter-hooks. I keep telling myself I ought not to have let her go, should have stopped her by force if necessary. But damn it, I couldn't lock her up, could I? Heaven grant my misgivings fade and she'll come back safe and sound – if not I'll spend the rest of my life consumed with remorse.

How long has she been gone? My mind is so clouded I doubt if I can tell the time. Yet I'm a patient man. Like all antique dealers I sometimes wait weeks and weeks for a wealthy customer who said he'd come back and never will. But today I haven't a scrap of patience. Time started being interminable for me as soon as she vanished from my sight. She, and the child she's carrying.

I took Hatem with me and went for a stroll through the streets, despite the fact that it had started to drizzle. We walked through the alley Marta had entered, as far as the door at Sayyaf's place. Once there we couldn't hear a sound, nor see anything but bits of yellow wall just glimpsed through the branches of pines. The alley ends in a cul-de-sac, so we turned back and retraced our steps.

I was tempted to knock at the gate, but I've promised Marta not to interfere and to let her solve her problem in her own way. And I shan't let her down.

It's almost dusk already. Marta isn't back yet, and I haven't seen anything more of Drago either. I still refuse to eat a morsel until she's with me again. I've re-read what I've just written, where I said "I shan't let her down", and I wonder if it's by interfering or by not interfering that I'd be letting her down.

It's beginning to get dark, and I agreed to have a bowl of soup with a dash of wine in it. They added so much wine that the soup was as red as a beetroot, with a decided twang to it – their idea was to calm me down, keep my fingers from shaking, and stop me pacing up and down. Everyone's looking after and making a fuss of me as if I were seriously ill or a grieving widower.

I'm a widower who was never the husband. An unknown father. A deceived lover. It's night now, and between cravenness and misgivings I'm all pale and wan. But at daybreak my Genoese blood will flood back into my veins, and I shall rebel.

The sun is rising, I haven't slept, and Marta still isn't back. But I've got a grip on myself and can still think straight. I'm not as furious as I might be. Am I already resigned to what's happening? So much the better if that's what people think: *I* know what I'm capable of in order to get her back.

Hatem sat up with me all night for fear I might do something rash. It was only when I relit the candle, undid my writing case, put out the ink-well, smoothed the paper and started writing this that I saw his head fall back, mouth open.

All around me, everyone's asleep. But where is Marta sleeping? Wherever she is, in a man's bed or in a dungeon, I'm sure she hasn't closed her eyes, and that at this very minute she's thinking of me just as I'm thinking of her.

Her face is as clear and constant in my mind's eye as if I were seeing it by the light of this candle. But I don't see anything else. I can't imagine the place she's in, the people with her, the clothes she's wearing or wearing no longer. I talk of beds and dungeons; I might just as well talk of whips, coshes, blows and swollen faces.

My fears go much further than that. I sometimes think her brigand of a husband might consider getting rid of her altogether in order to save his new marriage. The idea did come into my head yesterday, but I dismissed it. There are too many witnesses, and Sayyaf knows it: myself, Hatem, Drago, and even the monks, who saw Marta arrive with us, before we went with her as far as that gate. If I'm anxious again on that score, it's because sleepless nights revive one's fears. And also because I can't work out where Marta can have spent the night.

In fact, anything is possible. Anything. Including an affectionate reunion between the couple, who might suddenly have remembered their former love and embraced one another with all the more ardour because each needs the other's forgiveness for so many things. Because of her condition, Marta's best hope must be to be made love to the very first night. Then, by cheating the dates a bit, she could make Sayyaf think the child is his.

Of course, there's still the other wife and the parents-in-law. Their existence rules out such a happy solution. For Marta's sake I ought to regret this; for my own I ought perhaps to be glad of it. But no – I can't. Because of the extreme measures a man like Sayyaf might resort to. Ever since this cursed business began, I can't be glad about anything, and nothing can comfort me. Especially this early in the morning, or late at night, when my mind's so weary it looks on the black side of everything. And can't even see that clearly.

I'm nearly at the end of the page, and I might as well take advantage of that to lie down for a bit and let the ink dry by itself.

NOTEBOOK III

A Starless Sky

Genoa, 3 April 1666

Almost every day for five months I recorded the events of my journey, and now I don't possess the slightest trace of what I wrote. One notebook is still at Barinelli's place in Constantinople, and the other is in the monastery in Chios – I left it in my room there at daybreak, still open at the last page for the ink to dry. I intended to go back to it before the evening to set down what happened in the course of that crucial day. But I never did get back to it.

Alas, the day turned out to be even more decisive than I expected, and in a way quite different to what I'd hoped. I'm now separated from all the people I love, away from all my family, and ill. But thank God, though Fortune abandoned me with one hand she picked me up again with the other.

I may be stripped of everything, but if I'm naked it's in the way a newborn infant is naked on its mother's bosom. For I'm reunited with my mother-land, my mother-shore, my mother-city.

Genoa.

Every day since I got here I've meant to start writing again, to tell the story of my journey and to describe my feelings, which alternate all the time between despondency and optimism. If I haven't written anything before today it's mainly because of having lost my notebooks. I know my words are bound to end up in oblivion. Our whole existence borders on oblivion. But we need at least a semblance, an illusion of permanence if we are to do anything at all. How can I fill these pages, how can I go on searching for the right words to describe events and emotions, if I can't come back in ten or twenty years to revisit my past? And yet I still am writing, and shall go on doing so. Perhaps the honour of mortals resides in their inconsistency.

But to get back to my story. That morning in Chios, after a night of waiting, I resolved to go and find Marta at all costs. As I write that, I feel as if I'm talking of a previous life: since the woman I love went away, I've drifted into a kind of tainted after-life. Her pregnancy must have developed, I suppose, but I wonder if I shall ever see the child that will be born of my seed. But I must stop complaining and pull myself together. I want the words I write to cure my melancholy, not make it worse, so that I can tell my tale calmly, as I've vowed I would.

Well then, after dozing for less than an hour in the guest-house run by the monks in Katarraktis, I woke with a start and decided to go to Marta's husband's place. Hateb saw it was no use arguing with me, so he came too.

A guard opened the door when I knocked – a huge fellow with a shaven head but a bushy beard and moustache, who asked us what we wanted without letting us in. He spoke to us in a kind of pirate's Greek, without any of the usual politenesses, unsmiling, and fingering the handle of a curved dagger. A few paces behind him stood two other characters cast in the same mould, not so tall as he but with equally fierce expressions. I thundered at them in no uncertain manner, while Hatem remained cool in the background. Then with, in my opinion, more smiling and bowing and scraping than such louts deserved, he explained that we were from Gibelet, in their master's native country, and that he would no doubt be glad to know we were visiting his island.

"He's not here!" growled the one who'd opened the door, getting ready to shut it again. But Hatem persisted.

"If he's away, perhaps we could pay our respects to his wife, who's a relation of ours –" he began.

"His wife doesn't see anyone when he's not here!"

And this time the door slammed shut. We just had time to jump out of the way.

Brutish behaviour, but in the eyes of the law it was I, the respectable merchant, who was in a false position, and the guard and his henchmen who were acting within their rights. Marta married this man, and as he hadn't been obliging enough to make her a widow, she was still his wife. I had no right to take her away from him, nor even to see her again if he didn't want me to. I should never have let her go and put herself in his power. But I still felt guilty however often I told myself she was only doing as she wished, and there was nothing I could say to stop her. Even if I had made an error of judgement, though, and did feel I had to expiate it, that didn't mean I was resigned. I was prepared to pay for my mistake, but the price must be a reasonable one! There was never any question of abandoning Marta to that scoundrel's tender mercies for ever. I'd got her into this trouble, and I must find a way to get her out of it.

But how? With my thinking blurred by an almost sleepless night, I could see only one chink in my enemy's armour: his second marriage. That had been my first idea. Scare Sayyaf with the threat that his rich and influential father-in-law might learn the truth, and so force him to come to terms.

I could spend whole pages describing all the possible solutions I dreamed up, only to conclude that nothing would work. But I'm still too weak, and I'm afraid of depressing myself again.

As we approached the monastery guest-house after our brief expedition, we caught sight in the distance of Drago's green shirt. He seemed to be waiting for us, hidden in the shadow of a wall. But when Hatem beckoned him over, he turned round and took to his heels. We were so surprised we made no attempt to follow him. We'd never have found him in the maze of village streets, anyway.

Suddenly everything became clear to me. There'd never been any second wife or influential father-in-law; Marta's husband had been manipulating us all the time. As soon as he found out we were looking for him he'd sent Drago, one of his followers, to bait the hook, lulling our suspicions by hinting at the possibility of an arrangement that would suit our purposes perfectly. So I'd let Marta go to see him, believing it wouldn't take her too long to get him to agree to her claiming that their marriage was never consummated, and asking for it to be annulled.

When he heard about this, one of the monks in the guest-house, to whom we'd said nothing before so that our plans should't leak out, roared with laughter. It was public knowledge that his neighbour from Gibelet lived with a trollop he'd picked up in some port in Candia. No resemblance whatever to any daughter of a local worthy in Chios.

Now what could I do? I remember spending the rest of that cursed day and part of the night not moving or eating, pretending to cudgel my Genoese merchant's brain for some supreme challenge to misfortune, while all I was really doing was mope and torture myself with self-reproach.

At one point, towards dusk, my clerk came to me and said in a voice at once apologetic and firm that it was time I faced the facts. There was nothing more to be done. Any fresh move would only make Marta's situation and our own more awkward and dangerous still.

"Hatem," I said, not even looking up, "have I ever beaten you?"

"My master has always been too kind!"

"Well, if you dare advise me just one more time to go away and leave Marta to her fate, I'll give you such a beating you'll forget I was ever kind!"

"In that case my master had better beat me here and now, for until he stops defying Providence I shan't stop trying to caution him."

"Get out of my sight!"

Anger sometimes acts as midwife to ideas. While I was huffing and puffing at Hatem and trying to silence him, a spark was suddenly kindled in my mind. Before long it would confirm my clerk's worst prophecies, but at the time it struck me as very ingenious.

My plan was to go and see the commanding officer of the janissaries and tell him I was worried about certain matters. Sayyaf's wife was my cousin, I'd say, and I'd heard rumours that he'd strangled her. I know that was piling it on a bit, but murder was the only thing that would make the authorities intervene. And my fears weren't feigned, either. I really was afraid Marta might have come to some harm. Otherwise, why weren't we allowed to enter the house?

The officer listened to my explanations, which were all the more convoluted for being expressed in a mixture of bad Greek and bad Turkish, with a few words of Italian and Arabic thrown in. When I mentioned murder he asked if it was only a rumour or if I was sure of what I alleged. I said I wouldn't have come and disturbed him unless I was sure. Then he asked if I'd be ready to stake my head on it. That scared me, of course. But I was determined to carry the thing through. So instead of answering his dangerous question, I opened my purse, took out three hefty coins, and put them down on the table in front of him. He pocketed them with a practised hand, put on his plumed hat, and ordered two of his men to accompany him.

"May I come too?" I asked.

I'd hesitated before asking. On the one hand I didn't want to show Sayyaf how interested I was in what might happen to his wife, lest he find out what already had happened between her and me. But on the other hand the officer didn't know Marta, and they could have shown him any woman and told him that it was her and that she was perfectly well. And Marta wouldn't dare say anything if I wasn't there.

"I oughtn't to take you with me," said the officer. "It might get me into trouble."

He hadn't said no. And he was smiling meaningly, and eyeing the spot on the table where I'd put the crucial coins. I undid my purse-strings again, and passed the additional present straight into his hand. His men, looking on, seemed neither surprised nor perturbed.

The squad – three soldiers and me – set off. On the way, I saw Hatem making signs at me from behind a wall, but I pretended I hadn't noticed him. As we passed the guest-house I thought I saw a couple of the monks, together with their elderly maidservant, standing at one of the windows and apparently enjoying the show.

We had no trouble entering Sayyaf's house. The officer hammered on the door and shouted an order. The bald giant opened the door and stood aside silently to let him in. After a moment Sayyaf rushed up, all smiles and as anxious to please as if his dearest friends were paying him an unexpected visit. Instead of asking why we'd come, he lavished words of welcome on us – first on the Turk and then on me. He said he was delighted to see me again and called me friend and cousin and brother, showing nothing of any anger he might feel towards me.

Since I'd last seen him, in Gibelet, he'd put on weight without acquiring dignity. He was a now a gross bewhiskered pig in Turkish slippers – I'd never have recognised, beneath his greasy fat, his ample robes and his gold jewellery, the barefoot urchin who used to roam the streets in Gibelet.

Partly out of politeness and partly to carry off my role satisfactorily, I pretended to enjoy the reunion, submitting to his embraces and even ostentatiously reciprocating his cousinly greetings. This allowed me, as soon as we were installed in the sitting room, to ask for news of "our cousin and his wife, Marta khanum". I'd made the effort to speak in Turkish so that the officer would understand our conversation. Sayyaf answered that she was well despite the fatigues of the journey – explaining to the Turk that as a devoted wife she'd crossed seas and mountains to be with the husband on whom Heaven had bestowed her.

"I hope she's not too tired," said I, "to come and say hallo to her cousin."

The husband looked embarrassed, and I could see in his eyes that he'd done something wrong. This impression was confirmed when he said, "If she feels better now, she'll get up and come to see you – yesterday evening she couldn't hold up her head."

I was so furious, anxious and desperate that I leapt up, ready to seize the wretch by the throat. Only the sight of the official, the representative of law and order, held me back. But if it restrained my actions it didn't moderate my words: I told Sayyaf and his crew just what I thought of them. I called the fellow himself all the names he deserved: lout, criminal, brigand, pirate, highwayman, cut-purse, cut-throat, runaway husband unworthy to dust the shoes of the woman who'd entrusted herself to him. And I hoped he'd die impaled.

He let me have my say, without answering or protesting his innocence. But while I was working myself up I saw him sign to one of his henchmen, who then disappeared. At the time I paid no attention and went on even more loudly with my diatribe, mixing up the various languages and eventually getting so heated that the officer lost patience and told me to stop. He waited for me to obey and sit down again, then said to Sayyaf:

"Where is your wife? I want to see her. Call her!"

"Here she is," replied the other.

And Marta made her entrance, followed by the man who'd just left the room. It was then that I realised that her husband had tricked me yet again. He hadn't wanted her to appear until it suited *him* – that is, after I'd made a fool of myself and given myself away.

Of all the mistakes I've made, that's the one I still regret the most today; I think I'll rue it for the rest of my life. To tell the truth, I don't really know how far I gave myself away – myself, her, our love and our relationship. I don't remember all I may have said in my wrath. I was sure that this villain had killed her, everything about his behaviour seemed to prove it, and I no longer even heard the words streaming out of my mouth. He on the other hand listened to them calmly and haughtily, like a judge listening to the confessions of an adulteress.

Forgive me, Marta, for all the harm I've done you! I'll never forgive myself. I can see you now, your eyes lowered, not daring to look either at your husband or at the man who'd been your lover. Penitent, distant, resigned, sacrificed. No longer thinking, I imagine, of the child you are carrying, just wishing this masquerade would end and your husband would take you back into his bed as soon as possible so that in a few months' time you can persuade him the child is his. I'll have been in your life for only one fatal moment, a moment of illusion and deceit and shame, but by God, woman, I loved you and I shall go on loving you until my dying day. And I'll find no peace in this world or the next until I've atoned for the sins I've committed. At the time, in that house, that trap I'd gone to as a dispenser of justice only to find I was a culprit myself, I'd have liked to take back what I'd said somehow, so that you, Marta, wouldn't have to pay for my ranting. But I didn't say any more. I was afraid that if I tried to vindicate you I'd only make matters worse. So I stood up and tottered out like an automaton, without saying a word to you, without a farewell glance.

As I was going back to the monastery, I caught a distant glimpse of the minaret in the Turkish quarter, and had a fleeting impulse to go there, rush up the stairs to the top, and jump off. But you don't kill yourself on a fleeting impulse. I'm neither a soldier nor a murderer, and I've never got used to the idea of death. I've never had that kind of courage. I'm afraid. Afraid of the unknown, afraid of being afraid when I'm about to jump, afraid of the pain when my head hits the ground and my bones break. And I wouldn't have wanted my family to be humiliated while Sayyaf was celebrating, drinking, dancing and making Marta clap in time to the music.

No, I shan't kill myself, I muttered. My life's not over yet. But my journey is. *The Hundredth Name* is lost and so is Marta. I've no longer any reason, nor have I the strength, to go on roving round the world. I'll go and pick up my nephews in Smyrna and then go straight home to Gibelet and wait there patiently, in my dear old curiosity shop, for this cursed year to end.

I told my clerk, who'd come out of the guest-house to meet me, of my intentions, and asked him to be ready to leave before the end of the day. We'd spend the night in Chios town and set sail for Smyrna tomorrow. There, after saying goodbye to Maïmoun, pastor Coenen and a few others, we'd embark on the first ship leaving for Tripoli.

Hatem ought to have been delighted, instead of which he looked absolutely terrified. I didn't have time to ask why.

"Hey, you, the Genoese!" a voice cried out behind me.

Turning round, I saw the officer and his men. He beckoned me over. I went.

"Down on your knees!" he yelled.

There? In the middle of the street? With all those people already gathering behind walls and tree-trunks and in windows so as not to miss the show?

"You've made me lose face, you dog of a Genoese, and now it's my turn to humiliate you! You lied to me, and made use of me and my men!"

"I believed every word I said to you, I swear!"

"Silence! You and your like think you can do anything you please and get away with it, because at the last minute your consul will come and save you. Well, not this time! No consul in the world is going to save you from me! When will you people realise this island doesn't belong to you any more? It belongs, now and for ever, to the Sultan Padishah, our master. Take off your shoes, sling them over your shoulders, and follow me!"

The road was lined with sniggering beggars and loafers. Our wretched procession set off in a circus atmosphere that seemed to entertain everyone including the janissaries, though not Hatem. Quips, ululations, more laughter. I tried to console myself by thinking I was lucky all this wasn't taking place in the streets of Gibelet: no one here knew me, and I'd never have to meet the eyes of somebody who'd seen me being humiliated in this way.

When we reached the janissaries' headquarters my hands were tied behind my back and I was put into a sort of shallow pit hollowed out in the floor. It was so small I couldn't have moved even if they hadn't tied me up.

After an hour or two I was sent for, my hands were untied, and I was taken before the officer. He seemed to have calmed down by now, though he was still pleased at the trick he'd played on me. He lost no time in hinting that we might strike a bargain.

"I'm not sure what I ought to do with you," he said. "I should really have you charged with false accusation of murder. That would mean flogging, prison, and even worse if we add adultery."

He paused, and I was silent too. My protestations of innocence wouldn't have convinced anyone, even my own sister. I *was* guilty of false accusation of murder, and of adultery. But the officer had said he hadn't yet made up his mind what to do with me. I waited for him to go on.

"I *could* have pity on you, turn a blind eye to all you've done, and just deport you to your own country . . ."

"I'd be very grateful."

I really meant I was prepared to do a deal. The officer was venal, but I needed to behave as if I myself were the goods for which the price had to be assessed. I won't deny that I felt better when things reached this stage. Confronted with the law, whether of men or of Heaven, I was helpless. But when it came to fixing a price I had words and to spare. God had made me wealthy in a land of injustice: if I made the powerful envious, I also had the wherewithal to satisfy their greed.

We agreed on a price, though I'm not sure "agreed" is the word. In fact, the officer asked me to put my purse on the table. I did so without demur, and held out my hand as merchants usually do when they want to seal a bargain. He hesitated for a moment, then shook my hand, wearing a lofty smile. Immediately afterwards he left the room, and his men came in, tied me up again, and took me back to my cell.

It was daybreak, though I hadn't slept, when they came and blind-folded me, wrapped me up in a sort of canvas shroud, loaded me into a wheelbarrow, and pushed it and me along what felt like steep paths to a place where they unceremoniously tipped me out on to the ground. I guessed I must be on the beach because the ground was soft and I could hear the sound of waves. Then I was hoisted on to a man's back and put on a boat, as if I were a bale or a trunk.

Genoa, 4 April

I'm preparing to take up the thread of my story again, sitting on the terrace of a friendly house, breathing in the scents of spring, lending an ear to the gentle noises of the city, and to the honeyed tongue that is the language of my heart. And yet in the midst of this paradise I weep when I think of her, far away, a prisoner, heavy with child, guilty of having wanted to be free and of having loved me.

It wasn't until some time after I was on board the ship that I found out where I was going. I'd been laid down deep in the hold, and the captain had been ordered to keep me blindfolded until the coast of Chios was out of sight. He obeyed his orders to the letter, or almost, for when he allowed me up on deck you could still make out the tops of the mountains. Some sailors even pointed out to me the outline of a castle in the distance, saying it was called Polienou or Apolienou. Anyhow, we were a long way away from Katarraktis, and heading west.

Strangely enough, the way in which the authorities had deported me won me the sympathy of the captain, a Calabrian of about sixty with long white hair, whose name was Domenico. He was as thin as a stray dog and always swearing ("By my ancestors!") or threatening to hang his crew or throw them to the fishes. But he took such a fancy to me that he told me about his misdeeds.

His ship – a brigantine – is called the *Charybdis*. He'd put in at Katarraktis, where the creek is used mainly by fishing boats, because he's engaged in a highly lucrative form of smuggling. I guessed straight away that what was involved was mastic: Chios is the only place in the world where it's produced, and the Turkish authorities allow it to be used only in the Sultan's harem, where it's fashionable for the noble ladies to chew it from morn till night to whiten their teeth and perfume their breath. The farmers on the island who grow the precious tree (*Pistacia lentiscus*), which is very like the pistachio tree we have in Aleppo, have to hand the mastic over to the authorities for a fixed price, but those who produce a surplus try to sell it on their own account, though if they're found out they may spend a long time in prison or in the galleys or even be put to death. Despite this, the desire for profit has led to a flourishing contraband trade, in which customs officers and other representatives of the law often dabble.

Captain Domenico boasted to me that that he was the wiliest and boldest of all the smugglers. In the course of the last ten years, he said, he'd been to Chios no fewer than thirty times to take on the forbidden cargo, and never once been caught. He told me plainly that he rewarded the janissaries generously for looking the other way, which didn't surprise me after the way they'd deported me.

For the Calabrian, to defy the Sultan in his own territory and deprive him of the dainties intended for his favourites was not only a source of income but also an act of bravura, almost a sacred duty. In the course of our long evenings at sea he regaled me with detailed accounts of all his adventures, especially those during which he had almost been caught – these made him laugh more than the others. As he spoke he took sips of brandy to help him remember how frightened he'd been. I was amused by the way he drank: straight out of a skin flask that he kept within arm's reach, first holding it poised high in the air with his mouth clamped to the opening, like someone about to play the oboe.

Sometimes, as when he spoke of the countless tricks the farmers got up to evade the Ottoman laws, he taught me something I didn't know before. At other times he told me nothing I didn't know already. I forget if I mentioned earlier that our family, before going back to Gibelet, had settled in Chios and gone in for the mastic trade. All that ended in my great-great-grandfather's time, but the memory of it has survived. The Embriaci forget nothing and deny nothing: their lives, made up variously of military exploits and trade, distinctions and misfortunes, add up as the rings do year by year in the trunk of an oak tree. The leaves die every autumn, and occasionally a branch is broken, but the oak remains itself. My grandfather used to tell me about the mastic in the same way as he told me about the crusades, explaining how the bark of the mastic tree is tapped to extract the precious drops, and reproducing for my benefit, though he had never seen a *Pistacia lentiscus* himself, the motions his own grandfather had taught him.

But to return to my smuggler captain and his dangerous trade, his best customers were the ladies of Genoa. Not that they were more concerned about the sweetness of their breath or the whiteness of their teeth than the ladies of Venice, Pisa or Paris. But Chios belonged to Genoa for a long time, habits tend to persist, and although the Turks took the island a hundred years ago, our ladies have never been willing to give up their mastic. Nor have their husbands: it's a point of honour for them to get hold of the stuff, as a sort of revenge on fate and on the Sultan who embodies it. Has moving your jaws up and down really become a demonstration of pride? Given the price the ladies pay for their gum, their munching reveals their rank more surely than the most costly jewels.

How ungrateful of me to be so flippant! When it's because of the ladies and their precious mastic that I'm back on this terrace in Genoa instead of wasting away in a Turkish dungeon. Munch on, ladies; munch on!

The captain didn't want to call in at any of the Greek islands in case the Turkish customs men should take it into their heads to come on board. He made straight for Calabria and an inlet near Catanzaro, his native town, where he told me he'd sworn to make an offering to his patron saint every time he returned from the Levant safe and sound. I went with him to San Domenico's, having even more reason to pray than he. Kneeling there in the dim, cold church amid the smell of incense, I muttered a half-hearted and not too generous prayer: if I got Marta back, together with the child she is carrying, I would name it Domenico if it was a boy and Domenica if it was a girl.

As we sailed up the boot of Italy to Genoa we put in at three more ports, to shelter from storms and to take on water, wine and provisions.

I'd always thought I'd weep when I first saw Genoa, but the circumstances in which I arrived there were very different from what I'd imagined. I was really born in this city long before I actually came into the world, and the fact that I'd never seen it only made it dearer to me, as if I'd deserted it and must love it better in order to be forgiven.

No one else belongs to Genoa as the Genoese from the East do. No one else can love it as they can. Even if it has fallen, for them it still stands. Even if it has grown ugly, for them it's still beautiful. Even though it be ruined and mocked, they still see it as prosperous and proud. Nothing remains of its empire but Corsica, Corsica and the small coastal republic where every neighbourhood turns its back on the rest, where every family calls down a plague on the others, and where the whole population curses the Catholic king while besieging the ante-rooms of his representatives in search of favour or influence. Yet in the sky above the Genoese in exile such names as Caffa, Tana and Yalta still shine, together with Mavocastro, Famagusta, Tenedos, Phocea, Pera and Galata, Samothrace and Kassandreia, Lesbos, Lemnos, Samos, Ikaria, Chios and Gibelet – like so many stars and galaxies and Milky Ways!

My father always told me our mother country wasn't the Genoa of today but the Genoa of all time. But he quickly added that in the name of the Genoa of all time I must cherish the Genoa of today, no matter how far it had declined. I must even love it in proportion to its distress, like a mother grown old and infirm. Above all he told me not to resent it if when I visited our home city it didn't recognise me. I was still very young then, and didn't really understand what he meant. How could Genoa either recognise or not recognise me? Yet when, at dawn on our last day at sea, I saw the city in the distance amid its hills, its lofty steeples, pointed roofs, narrow windows and most of all its crenellated towers, square or round, one of which I knew still bore our family name, I couldn't help thinking that Genoa was looking back at me. And I did wonder whether it was going to recognise me.

Captain Domenico hadn't recognised me. When I told him my name he showed no reaction. Obviously he'd never heard of the Embriaci, or of the part they played in the Crusades, or of their seigniory in Gibelet. If he trusted me enough to tell me about his smuggling exploits, it's because I'm from Genoa and got myself deported from Chios, where he thinks I'll be careful never to set foot again. But it was different with his Genoese partner, Master Gregorio Mangiavacca, who'd come to take delivery of the cargo. He was a huge red-bearded man dressed in yellow, green and feathers like a parrot, and I'll never forget his reaction when he heard my name.

My hands shake and my eyes fill with tears even now, when I think of it.

We hadn't yet gone ashore, and Mangiavacca had come aboard with a couple of customs men. I'd just introduced myself as "Baldassare Embriaco, from Gibelet", and was about to explain how I came to be on the ship, when he interrupted me, grabbing me by the shoulders and shaking me as if trying to pick a quarrel.

"Baldassare Embriaco – son of whom?"

"Son of Tommaso Embriaco."

"Tommaso Embriaco, son of whom?"

"Son of Bartolomeo," I said quietly, trying not to laugh.

"Son of Bartolomeo Embriaco, son of Ugo, son of Bartolomeo, son of Ansaldo, son of Pietro, son of . . ."

And he went on reciting from memory my whole genealogy back to the ninth generation. I couldn't have done it myself.

"How do you come to know all my ancestors?" I asked.

By way of answer, he just took me by the arm and said:

"Will you do me the honour of living under my roof?"

As I had nowhere to go, and no money at all, either Genoese or Ottoman, I could only see this invitation as the work of Providence. So I forgot conventional politeness and expressions of reluctance and embarrassment; it was clear I was a welcome guest in Master Gregorio's house. I even had a strange feeling that he'd been on that quay in Genoa for centuries, awaiting my return.

He called two of his men and introduced me to them, laying great emphasis on my name. They doffed their caps and bowed low, then asked me to be good enough to point out my luggage so that they could take charge of it. Captain Domenico, who'd been looking on, proud of having such a noble personage for a passenger but somewhat ashamed that my name hadn't meant anything to *him*, explained in a low voice that as I'd been forcibly deported by the Turkish janissaries I hadn't any luggage.

Master Gregorio, interpreting this in his own fashion, felt all the more admiration for the distinguished blood that ran in my veins. He told his men – and everyone else within a radius of a couple of hundred paces – that I was a hero who'd defied the laws of the infidel Sultan and forced the heavy gates of his jails. Heroes like me didn't sail the seas with luggage, like ordinary antique dealers!

It was touching, and I'm rather ashamed of myself for making fun of his enthusiasm. He's memory and fidelity personified, and I wouldn't hurt him for the world. He installed me in his house as if it was my own, and as if he owed all he has and all he has achieved to my ancestors. Of course that's not so. The truth is that the Mangiavaccas used to belong to the clan led by my ancestors. They were a client family, allies, and traditionally the most devoted of all our followers. Then, unfortunately, the Embriaci clan – my father and grandfather called it simply the "albergo", as if it was one huge shared house – fell on hard times. My forbears, impoverished, scattered among the trading posts abroad, decimated by wars, shipwrecks and plagues, cut off from their own family and rivalled by newer ones, gradually lost their influence. Their voice was no longer heard, their name no longer revered, and all the client families abandoned them and followed other masters, in particular the Dorias. *Almost* all the client families, said my host: the

Mangiavaccas had handed down the memory of the good old days from
father to son for generations.

Today Master Gregorio is one of the richest men in Genoa. Partly
because of the mastic he imports from Chios; he's the only man in
Christendom who sells it. He's the owner of the palace I'm in now,
near Santa Maddalena church on the heights overlooking the harbour.
As well as of another, apparently even larger, on the banks of the River
Varenna, where his wife and three daughters live. The ships he charters
range the seven seas, the nearest and the most dangerous ones alike,
as far as the Malabar Coast and the Americas. He doesn't owe any of
his fortune to the Embriaci, but he insists on honouring the memory
of my ancestors as if they were his benefactors. I wonder whether in
this he's not obeying a kind of superstition that makes him think he'd
forfeit divine protection if he neglected the past.

Be that as it may, the tables have been turned, and now it's he who
bestows benefits on us. I arrived here like the Prodigal Son, ruined, lost
and desperate, and he welcomed me like a father and killed the fatted
calf. I live in his house as if it were my own, I walk in his garden, sit on
his shady terrace, drink his wine, give orders to his servants, dip my pens
in his ink. And he thinks I'm behaving like a stranger because yesterday
he saw me go and smell an early rose without picking it. I had to swear to
him that I wouldn't have picked it in my own garden in Gibelet, either.

But while Gregorio's hospitality has made my distress more bearable, it
hasn't made me forget it. Ever since that cursed night in the janissaries'
cell in Chios, not a day has gone by when I haven't had that pain in
my chest again which I felt before in Smyrna. Yet that's the least of my
sufferings, and I don't think about it except when it's there. But the pain
I suffer over Marta never leaves me day or night.

She who came on that journey to get the proof that would set her free
is now a prisoner. She put herself under my protection, and I failed to
protect her.

And my sister Pleasance, who entrusted her two sons to me, making me promise to keep them with me all the time – haven't I betrayed her too?

Then there's Hatem, my faithful clerk – haven't I abandoned him too, in a way? It's true I don't worry so much about him: I sometimes think of him as one of those agile fishes that, even after they're caught in the fishermen's nets, find the strength to wriggle out and jump overboard back into the sea. I have confidence in him, and it reassures me to know he's in Chios. If he can't do anything for Marta on the island, he'll go back to Smyrna and wait for me there with my nephews, or else return with them to Gibelet.

But what about Marta? In her condition, she can never escape!

6 April

I've spent all today writing, but not in this new notebook. I've written a long letter to my sister Pleasance, and a shorter one to my nephews and Maïmoun in case they're still in Smyrna. I don't yet know how to get these missives to the people they're addressed to, but merchants and other travellers are always passing through Genoa, and with Gregorio's help I'm sure to find a way.

I've asked my sister to write as soon as she can to set my mind at rest about what has become of her sons and Hatem; I gave her a brief account of my own misadventures, without saying too much about Marta. At least half the letter to Pleasance dealt with Genoa, my arrival here, the welcome I received from my host, and all the nice things he said about our family.

My letter to my nephews instructs them to go back to Gibelet as soon as possible, if they haven't done so already.

I asked all my correspondents for detailed replies. But shall I still be here when their answers arrive?

7 April

I've been in Genoa for ten days now, yet until today I hadn't left my host's house and the garden surrounding it. I was exhausted, sometimes obliged to stay in bed, and at best could only drag myself from one chair or bench to another. It was when I made the effort to start writing again that I began to come back to life. Words became words again, roses roses.

Master Mangiavacca, so forceful aboard the ship the day we met, has proved a most tactful and considerate host. Realising I needed a period of convalescence after all my trials and tribulations, he was careful not to hurry me. But today, sensing that I felt better, he suggested for the first time that I should go with him on his daily business visit to the harbour. He asked his coachman to drive us through the Piazza San Matteo, where the Dorias' palace is, then past the tall square tower of the Embriaci, before taking the coast road to the port itself, where a crowd of clerks was waiting. Before leaving me in order to attend to his affairs, my host ordered the coachman to drive me back home via several places of interest, one of which was the via Balbi, where you can still see how magnificent Genoa must have been in its heyday. Every time we stopped, the coachman would turn and tell me about the memorable building or monument before us. He had the same smile as his master, and talked to me with the same enthusiasm about our past glories.

I duly nodded and smiled back. In a way I envy him. I envy both him and his master for being able to contemplate this whole scene with pride. I myself can feel only longing. How I'd have loved to live when Genoa was the most splendid of cities, and mine the most splendid of its families. I can't get over not having been born till now. Lord, how late it is! How insipid the world seems! I feel as if I'd been born in the twilight of time, unable to imagine what the midday sun was like.

Today I borrowed 300 livres of good money from my host. He didn't want me to make out an IOU, but I wrote out, dated and signed one in due form. When the repayment date comes round, I know I'll have to argue with him about reimbursing him. That will be in April 1667. The year of the Beast will be over, and we'll have had time to see if it kept its terrifying promises. What will have become of our debts by then? Yes, how will it be with our debts when the world, together with all its men and all its wealth, is extinct? Will they just be forgotten? Or will they be taken into account in deciding each man's ultimate fate? Will bad debtors be punished? Will those who pay up on time get into Heaven more easily? Will bad debtors who keep Lent be treated more kindly than good payers who don't? Just like a merchant to bother his head with such questions, you'll say! Perhaps. Perhaps. But I have the right to ask them because it's my own fate that's at stake. Perhaps the fact that I've been an honest merchant all my life will earn me the right to some of Heaven's mercy? Or shall I be judged more severely than someone who was always cheating his customers and colleagues, but never lusted after another man's wife?

May the Almighty forgive me, but I regret my mistakes and my follies, but not my sins. It's not having possessed Marta that torments me; it's having lost her.

How far I've strayed from what I was meaning to say! I started talking about my debt, but one idea led to another and I found myself talking of Marta and my passionate remorse. Forgetfulness is one grace I shan't be granted. And I don't ask for it. I ask for redress, I think all the time of making things right again. I keep mulling over the wretched episode that got me deported from Chios, trying to think what I should have done to get the better of all those tricks and deceits. Like an admiral after a defeat, I can't stop moving the various ships about in my head to find the strategy that might have brought me victory.

I shan't say any more now about my plans, except that they're there inside me and keep me alive.

Towards the end of the morning I took the money order to the Baliani brothers in the Piazza Banchi – Gregorio had recommended them highly – and opened an account. I deposited most of the money I'd borrowed, keeping just twenty or so florins for small necessities and for tips to my host's domestics, who serve me so willingly.

As I walked back to the house I had a strange feeling that I was starting a new life. I was in another country, surrounded by people I'd never set eyes on till a few days ago, and with new coins jingling in my pocket. But it's a life lived on credit, in which I can command anything but own nothing.

9 April

I couldn't understand why Gregorio's family didn't live with him. There was nothing surprising about his owning two palaces, or even three or four – that's long been quite usual among the wealthiest citizens of Genoa. But I was intrigued by his living apart from his wife. He's just told me the reason. Not without some stammering and stuttering, though he's not shy by nature and isn't one of those people who blush for nothing. His lady, whose name is Orietina, is very pious, he said, and stays away from him every year during Lent lest he be tempted to forget his duty to remain chaste during the fast.

I suspect he forgets it anyway, for he comes back from certain day-time as well as night-time visits with a tell-tale sparkle in his eye. Nor does he try to deny it. "Abstinence doesn't suit me," he says, "but it's best not to sin under one's own roof, in the house consecrated by matrimony."

I can't help admiring this way of coming to terms with the rigours of the Faith. I myself pretend to ignore its precepts, but I always hesitate before breaking them in a big way.

10 April

Today I heard some amazing news about Sabbataï and his visit to Constantinople. The stories sound as if they were made up, but I'm quite willing to believe them.

My source is a monk from Lerici, who spent the last two years in a monastery in Galata. He's a close cousin of my host's, and Gregorio invited him to supper so that I could meet him and hear his account.

"The most reverend, holy and learned Brother Egidio", was how Gregorio introduced him. I've met all kinds of "Brothers" and "Fathers" and such-like in my time: sometimes they've been saints and often they've been rogues, sometimes fountains of knowledge and often ignoramuses. So I learned long ago to judge them on the evidence. I therefore listened to this one, observed him, asked him some straight questions, and finally was convinced he was genuine. He doesn't pass on anything he hasn't seen with his own eyes or been told by unimpeachable witnesses. He was in Constantinople last January, when the whole population was in a state of excitement, not only the Jews but also the Turks and the various Christians, whether foreigners or Ottoman subjects – all expecting the most extraordinary events.

The account Brother Egidio gave us may be summarised as follows. When Sabbataï reached the Sea of Marmara aboard the caïque bringing him from Smyrna, he was arrested by the Turks even before he could go ashore, and those of his followers who'd gathered to greet him were distressed to see him manhandled by two officers like a criminal. But he himself seemed quite unaffected, and called to those who were lamenting to have no fear, for they would soon hear that which they'd never heard before.

This restored the confidence of the waverers. They forgot what they were seeing and clung on to what they were hoping, which seemed all the more foolish because the Grand Vizier intended to deal with this grave business himself. He'd been told what was being said among Sabbataï's disciples – that he'd come to Constantinople to have himself proclaimed king, and that the Sultan was going to prostrate himself before him. He'd also been told that the Jews had stopped working, the money-changers were treating every day as the Sabbath, and that all this was doing great harm to trade in the Empire. No one doubted that in the absence of the Sultan himself, who was in Adrianople, the Grand Vizier was going to take extremely harsh measures: the head of the so-called Messiah would be detached from his body without delay and exposed on a tall column, so that no one would ever dare to challenge the Ottoman dynasty again, and business could go on as usual.

But what had happened in Smyrna – I had witnessed it myself – now happened again in Constantinople. Sabbataï, brought before the most powerful person in the Empire after the Sultan himself, was not met with blows or remonstrances or threats of punishment. Make what you can of it, the Grand Vizier greeted him warmly, told the guards to loosen his bonds, offered him a seat, and conversed with him at length on various subjects. Some people swore they saw them laugh together, and heard them address one another as "my honoured friend".

When the time came for sentence to be pronounced, it was neither death nor flogging, but a punishment so light it seemed almost a tribute: Sabbataï is currently held in a citadel where he's allowed to receive visits from his followers from morning till night, to pray and chant with them, preach sermons and give advice, and all without any let or hindrance from the guards. More incredible still, said Brother Egidio, the false Messiah sometimes asks the soldiers to take him to the seashore to perform his ritual ablutions, and they obey as if they were under his orders, take him wherever he chooses to go, and wait for him to finish before they bring him back. The Grand Vizier is even supposed to make him an allowance of fifty aspres, handed over to him every day in the prison, so that he shan't lack for anything.

What more can I say? Isn't this a great wonder, one that defies common sense? Wouldn't any sensible person be sceptical about such a tale? I myself would certainly have railed against human credulity if I hadn't been present at similar happenings in Smyrna last December. This time it's the Grand Vizier who's involved instead of a provincial judge, but that only makes the whole thing more incredible. But the wonder itself is the same, and I can't doubt it.

This evening, as I write in my bedroom by the light of a candle, I think of Maïmoun and wonder how he'd have reacted if he'd heard this story. Would he have ended up agreeing with his father and, like him, joining those who call themselves "believers" and other Jews "infidels"? No, I don't think so. He sees himself as a man of reason, and for him a wonder cannot take the place of a sound argument. If he'd been with us this evening, I imagine he'd have curled his lip and looked away, as I've often seen him do when the conversation made him uncomfortable.

I hope with all my being that he's right and I'm wrong! If only all these prodigies could turn out to be false! all these signs misleading! this year a year like any other and neither the end of past time nor the beginning of an unknown future! May Heaven not confound men of good sense, but grant that intelligence triumph over superstition!

I sometimes wonder what the Creator thinks of what men say. How I'd love to know whose side He in His benevolence would take! That of the people who predict that the world will come to a sudden end, or that of those who think it still has a long road to travel? Is He with those who rely on reason, or those who despise and demean it?

Before I shut this notebook for the night I ought to record under today's date that I've given Brother Egidio my two letters. He's soon leaving for the East, and he's promised to deliver them, if not in person then at least through another churchman.

11 April

Could Gregorio, my host and benefactor, be thinking of marrying me to his daughter?

She's the oldest of the three girls; her name's Giacominetta and she's thirteen. This evening, as we were walking in his garden, he spoke to me about her, saying she was very beautiful, and her soul was still even purer than her skin. Then he suddenly added that if I wanted to ask for her hand I'd do well not to wait too long, as such requests would soon be pouring in. He laughed heartily as he spoke, but I can tell the difference between what's a real laugh and what isn't. I'm sure he must have thought it over for a long while, and like any clever dealer he's already got a plan in mind. I'm not the young handsome match girls dream about, and my fortune is nothing in comparison with his. But I'm an Embriaco, and I'm sure he'd be very happy for his daughter to marry into that name. I suppose that for him it would be the culmination of a lifetime's effort to rise in society.

For me too such a marriage could only be attractive – if it weren't for Marta and the child she's carrying!

So do I forbid myself to marry out of fidelity to a woman from whom life has already parted me, and who is still the wife of another before God and man?

Put like that, my attitude is unreasonable, I know. But I also know that this is what my heart tells me, and it would be unreasonable to go against that.

All day Gregorio was unusually gloomy, depressed and taciturn. So much so that I was afraid I'd annoyed him by the lack of enthusiasm with which I'd reacted when he spoke to me yesterday evening about his daughter. But it wasn't that at all. What was worrying him were rumours originating in Marseilles that a huge battle was imminent between the French and Dutch fleets on the one hand and the British navy on the other.

I'd learned when I got to Genoa that in January the King of France had declared war on England, but it was said he'd done so reluctantly, in obedience to a treaty, and no one here seemed to think it would really come to a confrontation. But now the auguries are different, and there's talk of a real war and dozens of ships converging on the North Sea with thousands of soldiers on board. No one is more worried about it than Gregorio: he thinks that seven or eight of his ships must be thereabouts – some of them had even left Lisbon and were on the way to Bruges, Antwerp, Amsterdam or London – and that all of them could be stopped for inspection or destroyed. He broached the subject this evening, and I watched as he scribbled down dates and names and figures, as downcast as in other circumstances he might have been exultant.

At one point in the evening he asked me, without looking up:

"Do you think God is punishing me for not keeping Lent?"

"Do you mean to say the King of France might have sent his fleet against England because Signor Gregorio Mangiavacca hasn't mortified the flesh for Lent? I should think the greatest historians of the future will ponder over that crucial question."

He was taken aback for a moment, then burst out laughing.

"You Embriaci have never been very religious, yet Heaven hasn't abandoned you!"

My host was more cheerful now, but not reassured. If he were really to lose his ships and their cargoes it would mean his lucky star had deserted him.

13 April

Rumour is mixed up with news, tidings of war with reports about the expected apocalypse. Genoa goes about its business glumly, half-heartedly, as in a time of plague. Spring is at the gates of the city, waiting for Lent to be over. Flowers are still few and far between, the nights are clammy, laughter is stifled. Am I seeing my own anxiety reflected back at me in the mirror of the world? Or is it the other way round?

Gregorio has spoken to me again about his daughter. To say that, for him, whoever marries her will be a son rather than a son-in-law. The son that Heaven never granted him. Even if he had had a son, muscle and boldness would have been the only advantages the youth had over his sisters. For subtlety of mind and moral courage, not to mention filial affection and piety, Giacominetta left him no room for regret. All in all, he was quite satisfied with what Providence had decreed, provided that the lack of a son was made up to him when his daughters got married.

I listened in a friendly manner, filling each pause with conventional good wishes, not saying anything that might commit me in any way, but not betraying any reluctance or embarrassment either. While he didn't press me further about my intentions, I've no doubt he'll revert to the subject.

Should I consider running away?

I know that sounds disagreeable and ungrateful. Gregorio is my benefactor. I was in dire straits when he came into my life, and he transformed everything by turning humiliation into honour and exile into homecoming. If I believe at all in signs sent by Providence, Gregorio must be one of them. Heaven sent him my way not only to snatch me out of the clutches of the world but also to save me from my own vagaries. Yes, that's what he did, and that's what I'm blaming him for. He wants to lead me out of a blind alley, a pointless quest. In short, he offers me a chance to discard the tattered old clothes of my former life and put on a set of fine new ones. A new house, a spotless young wife, a position in my new-found mother country, where I should no longer be a foreigner and an infidel. It's the most sensible and generous proposition a man could hope to have. I ought to rush to the nearest church and give thanks to God. And while I'm kneeling in prayer, whisper to my father, whose soul is never far away, that I'm finally going to marry a girl from Genoa as he always wanted me to. Instead of which I jib, I feel persecuted, I claim I'm embarrassed, I plan to run away. Where to, and to do what? To try to get a criminal to give me his own lawful wife?

But she's the one I love!

May God and Gregorio and my father forgive me, she's the only one I love!

Marta. If only I could lie down beside her now and hold her in my arms, console her, and slowly stroke the belly that's carrying my child.

15 April

My host grows a little more insistent every day, and my stay in his house, which began under such favourable auspices, is beginning to be irksome.

Today's news from the north was bad, and Gregorio was feeling sorry for himself. He'd been told that the English had stopped and inspected ships bound to or from Dutch ports, and that the Dutch and the French were now doing the same to ships that frequented English ports.

"If it's true, I'm going to lose everything," he said. "I should never have got involved in so many projects all at once. I'll never forgive myself – I was warned about the risks of war, but I wouldn't listen!"

I told him that if he wept over mere rumours he wouldn't have enough tears left when genuine bad news arrived. That was my way of cheering him up, and it elicited a brief smile and a word of affectionate admiration for the Embriaci's composure.

But he soon went back to his lamentations.

"If I was ruined, completely ruined," he said, "would you withdraw your request for Giacominetta's hand?"

Now he was going too far. I don't know whether he was distracted with anxiety or taking advantage of the situation to extract a promise from me. Anyhow, he was talking as if my marrying his daughter was an understood thing, so that if I hesitated it would seem like a withdrawal, and that at the worst possible moment, like a rat leaving a sinking ship. I was outraged. Yes, I was seething inwardly. But what could I do? I'm living under his roof and indebted to him in other ways too, and he's in trouble. How could I do anything that would humiliate him? Moreover, he's not asking a favour – he's making me a present, or so he thinks, and my lack of enthusiasm so far is already almost an insult.

I responded with an attempt to comfort him a little without compromising myself.

"I'm sure that in a few days' time we'll have news that will blow all these clouds away."

He evidently saw this as an evasion, and saw fit to counter it by sighing through those ginger nostrils and delivering what seemed to me an uncalled-for remark: "I wonder how many friends I'd have left if I really was ruined."

I retorted with a sigh of my own.

"Do you want me to pray for the opportunity to demonstrate my gratitude?"

He didn't hesitate. "No need for that," he said apologetically, taking my arm and heading for the garden, where we started to talk like friends again.

But I'm still annoyed, and it's probably time I thought about leaving. But where am I to go? To Smyrna, in case my people are still there? No, Gibelet would be better. Though in Smyrna, with the help of Abdellatif the scribe, I might try to do something for Marta. I think about it from time to time, and get some ideas . . .

I'm probably deluding myself. Deep down I know it's too late to save her. But isn't it also too soon to give up?

17 April

This morning I made inquiries about ships going to Smyrna. I found one that sails ten days from now, on the Tuesday after Easter. The date suits me. It will allow me to meet Gregorio's wife and children briefly, without getting drawn too far into the family reunion.

I haven't said anything to my host yet. I'll tell him tomorrow or the next day. There's no hurry, but it would be uncouth to leave it till just before my "desertion".

18 April

Today is Palm Sunday, when people, without admitting it, start celebrating the approaching end of Lent, and my host is slightly more optimistic about the fate of his ships and their cargoes. He hasn't had better news – but he got up in a more cheerful mood this morning.

I seized the opportunity. Before broaching the subject of my departure, I gave him an account of my journey, with details I'd hitherto omitted or dressed up a bit. Of course, what happened to me could be revealed only to someone really close to me. What's more, whenever we were together, Gregorio monopolised the conversation and rarely let me get a word in. I now knew almost all there was to know about him, about his ancestors as well as mine, about his wife and daughters, and about his business. Sometimes his conversation was cheerful, sometimes gloomy, but it rarely stopped: if he asked me a question I'd scarcely begun to answer before he was in full spate again. I made no effort to restore the balance, still less to complain. I've never been very talkative. I've always preferred to listen and reflect, or rather pretend to, for to tell the truth I'm usually daydreaming, not thinking.

But today I overrode both my habits and his. I used all kinds of wiles to stop him from interrupting, and told him everything, or at least all that was essential as well as a good deal that was not. *The Hundredth Name,* the Chevalier de Marmontel and his shipwreck, my nephews and their shortcomings, Marta the false widow, the child she's expecting – yes, it was necessary to tell him even that – as well as my wretched adventures in Anatolia, in Constantinople, at sea, in Smyrna and then on Chios. Right up to my present regrets and vestiges of hope.

The further I got in my story the more downcast my host looked, though I couldn't tell whether this was out of sympathy with my misfortunes or because of their consequences for his own plans. For on this subject he caught my drift. I hadn't yet said I intended to leave; I'd just explained the reasons why I couldn't marry his daughter or stay on in Genoa indefinitely, when he said, succinctly for him:

"So when are you leaving us?"

This was put without rudeness or any sign of annoyance – he wasn't turning me out. If I'd had any doubt on that score I'd have left his house forthwith. No, his question was a simple acknowledgement of the facts: sad, hurt, disappointed.

"In the next few days," I answered vaguely, meaning to go on to tell him how grateful I was and how much in his debt. But he just patted me on the shoulder and went out to wander round the garden alone.

Do I feel more relieved than ashamed? Or the other way round?

19 April

Dawn is breaking and I haven't slept a wink. All night I've been mulling over useless ideas that exhausted me without getting anywhere: I ought to have said this rather than that to Gregorio, or that rather than this; and I was ashamed that I'd hurt him. I'd already forgotten his insistence and his crude attempts at manipulation, and could think of nothing but my own qualms.

Did I really betray his trust? I'd never promised him anything. But he managed to make me feel I'd been ungrateful.

I've been thinking so much about Gregorio's reactions and how he'll remember me that I haven't asked myself the questions that really matter. Have I made the right decision? Should I really go away instead of accepting the new life he offered me? What am I going to do in Smyrna? What mirage will I follow? How can I possibly believe I'm going to get Marta back, and my child? If I'm not rushing towards a precipice, I'm heading for the foot of a cliff that will bar my path.

Today I'm upset at having offended my host. Tomorrow I'll regret not having done as he wished.

20 April

I seem to be in the grip of an irresistible impulse to confide in people, like a girl in love for the first time. I'm usually quiet, and have a reputation for taciturnity; I'm sparing of speech, and let myself go only in this journal. Yet recently I've told the story of my life twice – on Sunday to my host, in order to justify my attitude, and today to a perfect stranger.

When I got up this morning I had only one thought in my head – to give Gregorio such a splendid present he'd forget our differences and we'd be able to part as friends. I had nothing particular in mind, but I'd noticed a very large curio shop in an alley near the harbour, and had promised myself to visit it as a colleague practising the same trade. I was sure I'd find exactly what I wanted there – perhaps an imposing antique statue that would look just right in the Mangiavacca family garden and be a permanent memento of my visit.

I felt at home in the shop as soon as I entered it. The goods were set out in almost the same way as in my own place. Old books stacked on shelves. Stuffed birds above them. In various nooks and crannies on the floor, imposing but damaged vases that couldn't quite be thrown away and were kept year after year though clearly no one would ever buy them. Even the owner of the premises was quite like me – a middle-aged Genoese of about forty, clean-shaven and rather stout.

I introduced myself and was greeted very cordially. The man had heard of me – not just of the Embriaci, but also of me personally, for some of his own customers had been to Gibelet. Even before I said what I was looking for, he invited me to take a seat in a cool and shady little courtyard, sent a maid for iced cordials, and came and sat down facing me. His family too, he told me, had lived for a long time in various cities abroad. But they'd come back to Genoa some seventy years ago, and he himself had never left it.

When I said I'd recently been in Aleppo, Constantinople, Smyrna and Chios, his eyes filled with tears. He told me he envied me for having been "everywhere"; he dreamed all the time of faraway places but had never plucked up the courage to travel.

"I go to the harbour twice a day and watch the ships arriving and departing. I talk to the sailors and the owners, drink with them in the taverns so as to hear the names of the places they've put in to. They all know me now, and when my back is turned must say I'm crazy, because it intoxicates me just to hear those strange names. But I've never had the wit to go abroad myself."

"The folly, you mean!"

"No – people tend to forget that one of the ingredients of true wisdom is a dash of folly."

He looked so sad that I pointed out:

"You'd like to be in my place and I'd like to be in yours!"

I said this to allay his regrets, but by all the saints I thought it too, and still do! At that moment I'd have liked to be sitting in my own shop with a cool drink in my hand, never having dreamed of setting out on this journey, never having met the woman on whom I brought misfortune and who brought misfortune on me, and never having heard of *The Hundredth Name*.

"Why do you say that?" he asked, to get me to tell him of my travels. So I began to talk. Of what made me set out, my brief pleasures, my misadventures, my regrets. The only thing I left out was my difference with Gregorio: I just described how kindly he'd taken me in when I arrived, and said that before I went away I wanted to show my gratitude with a gift worthy of his generosity.

At this point my colleague – his name was Melchione Baldi – ought, as a good businessman, to have asked me what I had in mind. But apparently he was too absorbed in our conversation about my travels. He kept asking questions about the things I'd seen in various places, then wanted to know more about Mazandarani's book, which he'd never heard of before. After this had gone on for some time, he asked where I planned to go now.

"I don't know yet whether to return to Gibelet directly or go back to Smyrna first."

"Didn't you say the book that made you undertake the journey is in London now?"

"Does that mean I have to follow it there?"

"Oh no! And what right have I, who've never left dry land, to urge you to make such a journey? But if you should decide to go, do come and tell me about it when you get back!"

We then went into another courtyard on the other side of the shop, to look at a collection of statues, some of them antiques and some more modern. It seemed to me that one of them, which had been found near Ravenna, would be very suitable for my host's garden. It represents Bacchus, or perhaps a feasting emperor, holding a cup of wine and surrounded by all the fruits of the earth. If I don't see anything I like better, I shall buy it.

There was a spring in my step as I walked back to Gregorio's, and I resolved to go back and see my amiable colleague again. I'd have to anyway, for the statue.

Should I give it to Gregorio as it is, or have in mounted on a plinth? I'd better ask Baldi. He'll know what's usually done.

22 April

Gregorio's wife and his three daughters arrived home today after visiting seven churches on the way, as is the custom on Maundy Thursday. Dame Orietina is thin and curt and dressed all in black. I don't know if this is for Lent, but it looks to me as if it's Lent all the year round for her.

She wasn't supposed to come back until Saturday, the day before Easter, but she chose to risk her husband's impetuosity two days early. If I was her husband – God forbid – she'd have nothing to fear from my ardours, in Lent or at any other time.

Why do I speak of her so harshly? Because as soon as she got here and I joined her husband and the rest of the household to greet her return, she gave me a look that meant I was not welcome in her house, and I shouldn't really have been allowed over the threshold.

Did she take me for Gregorio's companion in vice? Or was it that she'd heard of his plans for me and their daughter and was trying to show her disapproval of the idea? Or perhaps she'd taken offence at my lack of enthusiasm? At all events, ever since she got here I've felt like a stranger in the house. I've even thought of leaving without more ado, but I didn't want to affront Gregorio, who has treated me like a brother. So I pretended to think his wife's demeanour was to be set down to fatigue, to Lent, and to the thought of the sufferings endured by Our Lord during this Holy Week – a consideration not likely to make anyone bubble over with joy. But I shan't stay on too long. This evening I didn't join the others for dinner, either. I said I had to go and see a colleague.

As for the famous Giacominetta, whom her father praised to me so, I haven't really seen her. She rushed to her room without speaking to anyone. I suspect her mother's hiding her deliberately.

It's time I was off. High time.

I'm passing a very uncomfortable night, though there's nothing wrong with me. Yes, there is – it upsets me to think I'm no longer welcome in this house. I can't get to sleep. It's as if my very sleep had been stolen or begged for from my hosts. The expression I remember seeing on Dame Orietina's face has grown uglier and more intense as the night wears on. I can't stay here any longer. Not till Christmas, not even till Easter, which is only two days away. Not even till tomorrow morning. I shall leave a polite note and creep out. I'll sleep in an inn near the port and embark on the first boat that leaves.

For the East or for London? I still can't make up my mind. Should I try to find the book first? Or forget the book and try to save Marta? But how? Or forget all my crazy ideas and go back to my people in Gibelet? I find it harder than ever to decide.

23 April, Good Friday

I'm in my new room in an inn called The Maltese Cross. From my window I can see the harbour, and dozens of ships with their sails furled. Perhaps I'm looking now at the one that I'll travel on. I'm still in Genoa, but I've already left it. I expect that's why I miss it already, and feel like an emigrant again.

I did what I said I'd do and left Gregorio's place, despite some unforeseen incidents that cropped up at the last minute. Early, very early in the morning I got together my few belongings and left a short note thanking my host for his hospitality. I didn't say anything unkind or even ambiguous; just expressions of gratitude and friendship. I didn't even mention the 300 livres I owe him – that would have offended him. I left the letter in a prominent place, weighted down by some coins for the servants. I tidied the room and left it as neat as if I'd never lived in it. Then I went.

Outside it was beginning to get light, but the house was still dark. And silent. If the servants were up, they were being careful to make no noise. The room where I'd slept is on the first floor, up a flight of wooden stairs that I meant to go down cautiously so that the planks wouldn't creak.

I was still on the top step, clutching the banister so as not to trip up in the dark, when I saw a light. A girl appeared from somewhere, who could only be Giacominetta. She was carrying a two-branched candlestick which suddenly lit up the stairs as well as her face. She was smiling. An amused, knowing smile. There was no question of my retreating: she'd seen me, carrying my luggage, and I had no choice but to go on. So I smiled too, and winked as if to share my secret with her. She was as radiant as her mother was dowdy, and I couldn't help wondering if her character was different too. Perhaps she'd acquired some of her father's cheerfulness. Or perhaps each woman's attitude was determined by her age.

When I reached the bottom of the stairs I nodded silently in her direction and made for the door, which I softly opened and closed behind me. She had followed me with the light, but had said nothing, asked nothing, and made no attempt to stop me. I went along the path to the gate leading into the street. The gardener opened the gate for me, I slipped a coin into his hand, and walked away.

In case Gregorio, alerted by his daughter, might try to catch up with me, I made my way swiftly and through the darkest alleys to the port and the inn. I'd noticed its sign last week.

Now I've written these lines I shall draw the curtains, take off my shoes and stretch out on the bed. It will do me good to sleep, even if it's only for a few minutes. There's a smell of dried lavender, and the sheets seem clean.

It was midday and I'd slept for a good two or three hours when I was wakened by the most infernal din. It was Gregorio hammering on my door. He said he'd been to all the inns in Genoa trying to find me. He was weeping. According to him I'd betrayed him, stabbed him in the back, humiliated him. For thirty-three generations the Mangiavaccas had been as close to the Embriaci as the hand to the arm, and in a moment of annoyance I'd slashed right through bones, veins and sinews. I told him to sit down and keep calm. There'd been no treachery and no slashing or anything like it. Not even any bad feeling. At first I refrained from telling him what I really felt. The truth has to be deserved, and he didn't deserve it, behaving like this. So I pretended I wanted to leave him in peace with his reunited family, and was leaving his house with the best possible memories. He said that wasn't true: his wife's coldness had driven me away. Tired of pretence, I finally admitted that it was true – his wife's attitude hadn't encouraged me to stay. Then he sat down on the bed and wept as I'd never seen a man weep before.

"She's like that with all my friends," he said eventually, "but it's only a question of appearances. When you've got to know her better . . ."

He kept pressing me to go back, but I stuck to my guns. After leaving as I had I couldn't crawl meekly back without forfeiting everyone's respect. But I promised to go and share the Easter meal with them. An honourable compromise.

24 April, Holy Saturday

I called on Melchione Baldi again today, to confirm that I was going to buy the Bacchus statue and ask if he could have it delivered to Gregorio's house. He invited me to sit down, but there was a person of rank in the shop – a Dame Fieschi, I believe – together with her numerous entourage, so I preferred to leave, promising to come back another time. I left my colleague the name of my inn, which is only a stone's throw from his place, in case he feels like paying me a visit.

I'd have liked my present to reach my host and hostess late tomorrow afternoon, by way of thanks after the Easter meal I'll have had with them by then. But Baldi isn't sure he can get anyone to deliver it on Easter Sunday, and has asked me to wait till Monday.

25 April, Easter Day

Melchione Baldi, meaning to do me a favour, has instead made me feel extremely embarrassed and ashamed.

I'd originally asked him to have the statue delivered to my host and hostess late on Sunday afternoon, hoping they'd receive this token of my gratitude when I'd already left their house after sharing their Easter meal at midday. But when Baldi doubted if he could find men prepared to work on a holiday, I decided it would be perfectly all right if the present arrived the next day. It might even be better. Courtesies should not be too rushed.

But Baldi didn't want to disappoint me, so he managed to find four young porters, and they came and knocked at Gregorio's door while we were still in the middle of the meal. Everyone got up from the table and started rushing to and fro, and there was such a hullabaloo . . . I didn't know where to hide my face, especially when the young men, all inexperienced and perhaps slightly tipsy, overturned a stone bench in the garden and broke it in two, and started trampling over the flower beds like a pack of wild boars.

I can't describe how I felt.

Gregorio went purple with stifled fury, his wife made sarcastic remarks, and their daughters laughed. What was intended as an elegant gesture had been turned into a crude farce!

And that wasn't the first of the day's surprises.

Towards noon, when I arrived at the Mangiavacca house – perhaps for the last time – Gregorio welcomed me at the door like a brother and took me into his study to chat until his wife and daughters were ready. He asked if I'd made up my mind about leaving, and I told him I still meant to sail some time during the next few days, probably for Gibelet, though I was still uncertain about my destination.

He told me again how much my departure would grieve him, that I'd always be welcome in his house, and that if in spite of everything I decided to stay in Genoa he would see that I never regretted it. Then he asked if I'd given up the idea of going to London. Not yet, I told him, but although I was still attracted by *The Hundredth Name*, it would probably be wisest to return to the East to take my too long neglected business in hand again and to make sure my sister was safely reunited with her children.

Gregorio, who seemed to be listening with only half an ear, started singing the praises of the cities I'd go through if I went by sea to England – Nice, Marseilles, Agde, Barcelona, Valencia, and above all Lisbon.

Then he asked, his hand lying heavy on my shoulder:

"Could you do something for me if you change your mind?"

I said truthfully that nothing would give me greater pleasure than to repay a little of my moral debt for all he'd done for me. He explained that the effects of the war between England and Holland had recently rather interfered with his business, and he needed to get an important message to his agent in Lisbon, a certain Cristoforo Gabbiano. Then he took from a drawer a letter already written and closed with his own seal.

"Take this," he said, "and take good care of it. If you decide to go to London by sea you'll have to go through Lisbon. In that case I'd be eternally grateful if you'd deliver this letter to Gabbiano himself. You'd be doing me a great favour! On the other hand, if you should decide to go somewhere else and can't manage to give the letter back to me, promise me you'll burn it unopened and unread!"

I promised.

It was another and this time quite pleasant surprise when just before we sat down to table Gregorio asked his eldest daughter to show me round the garden. The few minutes that followed confirmed my excellent impressions of the girl. She was still smiling, had a very graceful walk, and knew the names of all the flowers. As I listened I thought to myself that if my life had turned out differently and I hadn't met Marta; if I didn't have a house, a business and a sister over the sea, I might have been happy with Gregorio's daughter. But it's too late for that, and I hope she'll be happy without me.

I'm not sure whether I should end this list of the pointless incidents of my Easter Day by noting that my friend's wife, the virtuous Dame Orietina, welcomed me this afternoon with a smile and some other indications of pleasure. I suppose it's because she knows I'm leaving, never to return.

Monday, 26 April 1666

I was sitting in my room, gazing out of the window, when suddenly the door burst open. I turned round to see a very youthful sailor standing breathless in the doorway, his hand still on the latch. Did I want to go to London? he asked. I was so struck by what seemed like a call of fate that I immediately said yes. He then told me to make haste, because the ship would soon be setting sail. I hurriedly tied up my few things into a couple of bundles, which stuck out like angels' wings when he picked them up and stowed one under each arm. His long fair hair was tucked roughly into a woollen cap. I followed him down the stairs and across the hallway, stopping just long enough to say a brief farewell to the innkeeper's wife and throw down a handful of coins.

Then we ran through the narrow streets to the quay, where I hurtled up the gangway with my tongue hanging out.

"So here you are at last!" said the captain. "We were going to leave without you."

I was too breathless to ask any questions. All I could do was stare in astonishment. But no one noticed.

I'm writing this aboard the *Sanctus Dionisius*. Yes, I'm already at sea.

I arrived in Genoa unexpectedly, and a month later I'm leaving there in much the same way. I was still weighing up the pros and cons of, on the one hand, going straight back to Gibelet, and, on the other, making a detour to Smyrna or Chios or somewhere else first, when all the time Providence, unbeknown to me, had chosen my path for me.

Sitting slumped on a crate to get my breath back, I kept asking myself whether it was really me who was expected on board. Mightn't the young sailor have been sent to The Maltese Cross to fetch some other traveller? I stood up and looked down along the quay, expecting to see someone running towards the ship, shouting and waving his arms. But there was no one there but tired porters, unoccupied customs men, clerks, holiday-makers out for a walk in their best clothes, and ordinary citizens come to watch the comings and goings in the harbour.

Among the latter I recognised a familiar face. It was Melchione Baldi, whom I'd cursed so heartily yesterday at Gregorio's. He was leaning against a wall and waving to catch my eye. His face glowed with sweat and satisfaction. He'd told me he spent all his Sundays, holidays and other idle hours in the harbour watching the ships arrive and depart and getting the sailors to talk to him. He was a dreamer as well as a merchant

– a stealer, or rather a receiver, of voyages. After the embarrassment he'd caused me yesterday I felt more like reproaching than smiling at him, and I almost averted my eyes. But I was about to leave Genoa for ever, and it would have been unkind to snub him. He'd only been trying to please me, and must still think the statue was delivered safely as and when I'd wished, and that I was grateful to him. So I forgot my resentment and waved back at him in as pleased and friendly a manner as if I'd just caught sight of him. Whereupon he jumped up and down excitedly, clearly delighted with our final encounter. I too – I've often reproached myself for this sort of thing – welcomed the silent reconciliation with relief.

Slowly the ship began to move away from the quay. Baldi was still waving a white handkerchief at me, and from time to time I waved my hand back at him. At the same time I looked around me, still trying to understand how on earth I came to be here. I felt, and still feel, neither glad nor sorry about it. Simply intrigued.

Perhaps it would be wise to end this page with the words "His will be done!" It will be, anyway.

At sea, 27 April

Yesterday I mentioned Providence, because I know that's what poets and famous travellers do. But I'm not fooled. No doubt all of us, strong or weak, wily or naive, are the blind instruments of Providence. But Providence has nothing to do with this voyage! I know perfectly well what hand has traced my route and led me to the sea, to the west, to London.

At the time, in the breathlessness, the surprise and the general hubbub of departure, I didn't understand. But this morning I see it all. When I say "all" I'm only exaggerating a little. I know who impelled me in this direction, I can guess the means by which Gregorio manoeuvred me into accepting the idea of going to England – but I still can't make out all his calculations. I suppose he's trying to get me to marry his daughter, and wanted to prevent me from returning to Gibelet because I'd probably never come back again. This voyage of a few months to the other side of the world probably makes him feel he's still got some hold on me.

But I don't blame Gregorio or anyone else. No one forced me to go. I could just have said no to the fair-haired messenger and I'd still be in Genoa or else on my way back east. But I ran to catch this ship!

If Gregorio is guilty then I'm one of his accomplices, along with Providence, the year of the Beast, and *The Hundredth Name*.

At sea, 28 April

Yesterday evening, after I'd written those few lines expressing resignation, I saw the fair young sailor going along the deck – the boy they sent to fetch me from the inn. I signed to him to come over to me; I wanted to ask him a few urgent questions. But there was such a childlike look of fear in his eyes I just slipped a silver gros into his hand and didn't say anything.

The sea has been calm ever since we set sail, but I've been ill all the same. It's as if it were vexation rather than the waves that upsets me when I'm on board a ship.

Now, for instance, neither my head nor my stomach is churning. But I daren't go on writing much longer. The smell of ink, which usually I'm not even aware of, makes me feel ill.

I'd better stop straight away.

3 May

It's Monday, and this morning, when for the first time in a week I was able to take a turn round the deck, the ship's surgeon came and asked me if it was true that I was Master Gregorio Mangiavacca's future son-in-law. Amused by this inaccurate and, to say the least, premature description, I said I was one of that gentleman's friends, but no relation. How, I asked the surgeon, had he learned that we knew each other? He suddenly looked embarrassed, as if he wished he hadn't spoken, and then hurried away, saying the captain had sent for him.

The incident made me think people were talking about me behind my back. Perhaps they make fun of me when they gather together for meals. I ought to be angry, but I think, "What does it matter? Let them laugh! It doesn't cost anything to mock the worthy, portly Baldassare Embriaco, dealer in curios. Whereas they might be flogged for making fun of the captain, though God knows he probably deserves it, and worse!"

Judge for yourself. Instead of taking the usual route and calling in either at Nice or Marseilles or both, he's decided to make straight for Valencia in Spain, on the pretext that the north-east wind will get us there in five days. But the wind keeps changing. After carrying us as far as the open sea, it blew itself out; and since then it has changed direction every night. With the result that on the eighth day of the voyage we're still nowhere! We can't see either the Spanish or the French coast, nor even Corsica or Sardinia or the Balearics! Where *are* we? Who knows! The captain says he does, and no one dares to contradict him. We shall see. Some of the passengers have run out of food, and most have almost no water left. We haven't reached disaster yet, but we're heading towards it with all sails spread!

5 May

On the *Sanctus Dionisius*, whenever two people whisper together they're talking about the captain. Some roll their eyes up to heaven, others now dare to laugh. But how long can we go on just laughing and whispering at his rashness?

I'm quite well again. I walk about, have a hearty appetite, talk to all and sundry, and look down on those of my fellow-passengers that are still sea-sick.

I didn't make any arrangements beforehand about meals, apart from expecting to buy what food might be available on the ship. I'm sorry I didn't engage a cook or bring some provisions on board with me, but it all happened so fast! Most of all I wish I still had Hatem with me. I only hope nothing has happened to him, and that he's safe and sound in Gibelet.

Where, incidentally, I ought to have gone myself. That's what I think now, though I didn't start doing so until I'd set out in the opposite direction. Ah well, there it is. I shrug my shoulders. I don't complain. I defy the sea by humming a Genoese song. I record in my notebook the various decrees of fate, interspersed with my own passionate shilly-shallyings. Yes, there it is, I'm resigned to my fate. Everything ends underground, so what does it matter how it gets there? Why should I take short cuts rather than detours?

6 May

"A good captain turns the Atlantic into the Mediterranean. A bad captain turns the Mediterranean into the Atlantic."

That's what one of the passengers, a Venetian, had the audacity to say aloud today. He didn't say it to me, but to all the people gathered near the ship's rail. I didn't answer him, but I memorised what he'd said, intending to write it down here.

It's true that we all feel as if we were lost in the midst of a vast ocean, and long for the moment when someone shouts "Land!" And yet we're in the most familiar waters, and at the best time of the year.

The latest rumour has it that we should berth tomorrow evening in either Barcelona or Valencia. We're so disorientated that if we'd been told "It'll be Marseilles", or Aigues-Mortes, or Mahon, or Algiers, we'd have believed it.

Somewhere in the Mediterranean, 7 May 1666

Today I exchanged a few sentences with the captain. He's forty years old and his name is Centurione, and quite literally he's mad!

I don't mean he's bold, or reckless, or capricious, or eccentric. I mean he's crazy. He believes he's being pursued by winged demons, and thinks he can escape them by following winding routes!

If another passenger had talked to me like that, or a sailor, or the surgeon, or the carpenter, I'd have gone straight to the captain so that he could clap him in irons and put him ashore at our next port of call. But what are you to do if it's the captain himself who is crazy?

If he was obviously insane, raving, shrieking and foaming at the mouth, we'd have got together and overpowered him. And we'd have notified the authorities in the port where we called next.

But it's not like that at all! What we have here is a quiet madman, who walks about in a fitting manner, talks, jokes and gives orders as to the manner born.

Until today I'd practically never spoken to him. Just a couple of words that last day in Genoa, when I rushed up and he told me the ship had nearly left without me. But this morning, when he was strolling round the deck, he passed quite close to me. I greeted him politely and he replied conventionally. As is the custom in Genoa in respectable society, we spoke first about our families, and he courteously referred to the Embriaci's renown and the history of the city.

I was beginning to think the satirical comments about him were unfair, when a bird swooped low over our heads, its cry making us both look up. I noticed that the captain was looking uneasy.

"What kind of bird is it?" I asked. "A common gull? A herring gull? An albatross?"

"It's a demon!" he replied with some agitation.

At first I thought this was just a way of objecting to the nuisance birds can cause, then I wondered whether it wasn't a seaman's name for a particular species.

Meanwhile the captain went on, becoming more and more disturbed.

"They're after me! Wherever I go they find me! They'll never leave me in peace!"

One flap of the creature's wings had been enough to set him off.

"They've been after me for years, everywhere I go . . ."

He wasn't talking to me any longer: he was just taking me to witness his incomprehensible conversation with himself or his demons.

After a few moments he left me, muttering that he was going to give orders for us to change course to throw off our pursuers.

Good God, where is he taking us?

I've decided not to tell anyone about this, at least for the time being. Anyhow, who would I confide in, and what should I say? And with what object? Did I want to stir up a mutiny? Fill the ship with fear, suspicion and revolt, and be responsible for the bloodshed that might ensue? Too dangerous. Keeping quiet might not be the most courageous solution, but I really think the best thing to do is just watch and wait and be on the alert.

It's a good thing I can tell this journal what I can't tell anyone else.

8 May

This morning I had a conversation with my Venetian fellow-passenger, Girolamo Durrazzi. Our talk was brief, but courteous. If my late lamented father could read these lines I'd have said "courteous, but brief".

Another passenger is a Persian whom the crew refer to under their breath as "the prince". I don't know if he really is a prince, but he carries himself like one, and two sturdy fellows follow him closely everywhere looking around in all directions as if they feared for his life. He has a short beard and wears a turban that's so narrow it looks almost like a band of black silk. He never speaks to anyone, even his two guards; he just looks straight in front of him as he walks along, stopping now and then to gaze at the horizon or the sky.

Sunday, 9 May 1666

We've dropped anchor at last. Not in Barcelona or Valencia, though: we're at the island of Minorca in the Balearics, more precisely in the port of Mahon. Re-reading my last few pages, I see it's one of the many places rumoured to be our destination. Rather as if the name were written on the face of the dice thrown for us by Providence.

Instead of trying to find a last vestige of sanity in the heart of madness, why don't I leave this crazy ship? In other words, let them all go to perdition without me – the captain, the surgeon, the Venetian, the Persian "prince" and all! But I shan't go. I shan't run away. Do I still care what happens to these strangers? Or is it that I no longer care about my own survival? Am I acting out of supreme courage or supreme resignation? I don't know. But I'm staying.

At the last moment, seeing how many people were flocking round the boats, I even decided not to go ashore, but to call the young sailor with fair hair and get him to buy some things for me. His name's Maurizio, and he feels he owes me something because of the trick he played on me. To tell the truth, I don't hold it against him at all: I find the sight of his yellow locks rather a comfort – but it's better he shouldn't know that.

I wrote him a list of the things I need, but I could see from his embarrassment that he'd never been taught to read. So I made him memorise the shopping list, and gave him more than enough money to cover the cost. When he got back I let him keep the change, and he seemed overjoyed. I expect he'll come and ask me every day if there's anything he can do for me. He can't take Hatem's place, but like him he looks bright and honest. And what more can one ask of an employee?

One day I shall get Maurizio to tell me who it was that sent him to find me at The Maltese Cross. But is there any point? I know exactly what he'll say. Yes, on reflection, there is a point – I want to hear with my own ears that Gregorio Mangiavacca paid him to come to fetch me that day and make me run to catch the ship now carrying me to England! To England, or God knows where . . .

But I'm not in any hurry. We'll both still be on this ship for weeks, and if I'm patient and ingenious the lad will tell all in the end.

11 May

Well, I'd never have thought I'd be friends with a Venetian!

It's true that when two merchants meet on a long sea voyage they're bound to get into conversation. But it went beyond that. We found we had so many interests in common that I soon forgot all the prejudices instilled in me by my father.

No doubt it helped that Durrazzi, though born in Venice, had lived since he was a child in various places in the East. In Candia to begin with, then in Tsaritsin on the River Volga. He recently settled in Moscow itself, where he seems to enjoy a distinguished reputation. He lives in the Foreign Quarter, which he tells me is becoming a city within a city. It contains French caterers, Viennese pastry-cooks, Italian and Polish painters, Danish and Scottish soldiers, and of course dealers and adventurers from all over the place. Some of them have even set up a pitch outside the city where they play a sort of English game that involves kicking a ball. The Earl of Carlisle, King Charles's ambassador, sometimes goes to watch.

12 May

My Venetian friend asked me to sup with him in his quarters yesterday. (I still hesitate and feel embarrassed when I call him that: I suppose one day I'll get used to it.) He's brought a cook with him, as well as a valet and one other servant. I ought to have done the same, instead of coming on board alone like a vagabond or an exile!

In the course of the meal my friend told me why he is going to London. His object is to recruit some English artisans to go and ply their trades in Moscow. He hasn't actually been commissioned to do so by the Tsar Alexis, but he travels with the Russian ruler's approval and under his protection. Any skilled craftsmen will be welcome, whatever their speciality, on condition that they don't try to convert anyone to their own religion. The Tsar is a sensible man, and doesn't want Moscow to become a den of fanatical Christian republicans. It's said that England is full of them, but since the return of King Charles six years ago many of them have gone into hiding or exile.

Girolamo tried to persuade me to go and live in Moscow. He treated me to another pleasing description of life in the Foreign Quarter there. Out of politeness and to encourage him to go on, I said "perhaps", but I'm not tempted. I'm forty now, and too old to start a new life in a country where I know neither the language nor the customs. I have two homelands already, Genoa and Gibelet, and if I had to leave one it would be to go to the other.

Moreover, I'm used to being able to see the sea, and I'd miss it if I had to be away from it. Admittedly, I don't feel comfortable aboard ship; I prefer to have both feet on dry land. But it has to be near the sea! I need to smell the ozone! I need to hear the waves dying and being reborn and dying again! I need to be able to lose myself gazing at its vastness!

Some people might be able to make do with the vastness of the desert or of snow-covered plains. But not someone born where I was born, and with Genoese blood in his veins.

That said, I can easily understand people who leave their home and their loved ones, and even change their name, to go and start a new life in another country without any boundaries. The Americas or Russia. Didn't my ancestors do the same thing? And not only my ancestors, but everyone's ancestors. All the towns in the world, and all the villages too, were founded and populated by people from elsewhere. The whole earth has been filled by migration after migration. If I were still light-hearted and fleet of foot, I might let myself be drawn away from my native Mediterranean and go and live in that Foreign Quarter whose very name I find tempting.

13 May

Is it true that the King of France intends to invade the lands of the Ottoman Sultan, and has even ordered his ministers to draw a detailed plan of attack? Girolamo says so, and backs up his assertion with various pieces of evidence that I have no reason to doubt. He even maintains that the French king has sounded the Sophy of Persia about the possibility that the latter, a great enemy of the Sultan, might at a given moment stir up trouble and lure the Turkish armies to Georgia, Armenia and Atropatene. Meanwhile, with the help of the Venetians, King Louis would seize Candia, the Aegean Islands, the Bosphorus Straits and perhaps even the Holy Land.

Although this doesn't strike me as at all impossible, I'm surprised that my Venetian should speak of it so openly to someone he's only just met. He's certainly rather talkative, but I can hardly blame him when I learn so much from him, and when his indiscretion is due solely to our friendship and the fact that he trusts me.

I spent all night mulling over the King of France's plans, and I can't say I like the sound of them. Of course, if things went his way and he could get a lasting grip on the islands, the Straits and the Levant as a whole, I wouldn't complain. But if he and the Venetians embarked on some rash enterprise that came to nothing, the vengeance of the Sultan would fall on me and my colleagues – yes, on all the European merchants living and working in the Ports of the Levant. The more I think about it the more I'm convinced that such a war would from the very outset be a disaster for me and mine. Heaven grant that it never happens!

I've just re-read the last few lines, and those before them, and I suddenly wonder if it isn't dangerous to write such things and express such wishes. Naturally, I set everything down in my usual gibberish, which nobody but myself can decipher. But that applies only to personal matters, which I want to conceal from my family and possible snoopers. But if the authorities were ever to take an interest in my papers, if some Ottoman official, some wali or pasha or cadi were to take it into his head to look into them, and threatened me with impalement or torture to make me hand over the key to the code, how could I hold out? I'd reveal the secret, and then they'd see that I'd be pleased to see the King of France lay hold of the Levant.

Perhaps I should tear this page up and throw it away when I go back east. And even avoid mentioning such things in future. I'm probably being over-cautious – no wali or pasha is really going to come and pry among my notes. But for anyone in my position, whose family has lived abroad for generations and who's at the mercy of every kind of snub and denunciation, prudence is not just an attitude. It's absolutely essential to survival.

14 May

Today I exchanged a few words with the Persian nicknamed "the prince". I still don't know if he's a prince or a merchant. He hasn't said.

He came across me when he was taking his usual walk round the deck. He smiled, and I took this as an invitation to join him. As soon as I moved towards him his guards took fright, but he signed to them to do nothing, then made me a slight bow. I greeted him in Arabic, and he made a suitable reply.

Apart from the usual courtesies that all Muslims know, he has difficulty speaking Arabic. But we succeeded in introducing ourselves, and I think we could manage a conversation if the occasion arose. He said his name was Ali Esfahani, and he was travelling on business. I doubt if that's his real name. Ali is the commonest name among his people, and Isfahan is their capital. In fact, the "prince" told me very little about himself. But at least we're acquainted now, and we'll be talking again.

As for Girolamo, my Venetian friend, he keeps singing the praises of Moscow and the Tsar Alexis, whom he seems to admire very much. He says he's very concerned about the good of his subjects and anxious to attract merchants, artisans and educated men to Muscovy. But not everyone there is so well-disposed towards foreigners. While the Tsar himself seems delighted with what's happening in his capital, which hitherto was only a huge dreary village, and though he poses for painters, keeps up with the latest novelties, and wants to have his own company of actors, there are thousands of cantankerous priests who see all these newfangled notions as the mark of the Antichrist. They regard what goes on in the Foreign Quarter as debauchery, corruption, impiety and blasphemy, harbingers of the imminent reign of the Beast.

Girolamo told me of a significant incident in this connection. Last summer a troupe of Neapolitans went and performed in Moscow at the invitation of one of the Tsar's cousins. Their number included actors, musicians, jugglers, ventriloquists and so on. At one point a man called Percivale Grasso presented a very striking show in which a marionette with the head of a wolf, which had been lying on the ground, stood up and began talking and singing, then strutted about and started dancing – and all the time it was impossible to detect that the puppet was being manipulated by a man standing on a ladder behind a curtain. The whole audience was captivated. Then suddenly a priest got up and shouted that what they were all staring at was the Devil himself. He quoted the Apocalypse: "And he had power to give life unto the image of the beast, that the image of the beast should speak." Then he took a stone out of his pocket and threw it at the stage, and some of the people with him did the same. Then they all started cursing the Neapolitans and foreigners in general, and everyone involved in any way with what they considered profanities and the works of Satan. They declared that the end of the world and the Day of Judgement were at hand. The audience began to trickle away. Even the Tsar's cousin dared not oppose such fanatics. And the troupe of entertainers had to leave Moscow at dawn the next day.

While my friend was telling me all this, I remembered the visitor who'd come to see me in Gibelet a few years before with a book prophesying that the world would end in 1666. This year. His name was Evdokim. I told Girolamo about him. The name means nothing to him, but he's familiar with *The Book of the One True Orthodox Faith*, and every day has to listen to someone referring to the prediction. He himself refuses to take it seriously, I was relieved to hear, and puts it down to sheer stupidity, ignorance and superstition. But in Muscovy, he says, most people really believe in it. Some even claim to know the exact date: according to some calculation or other, the world won't last beyond St Simeon's Day, September 1, which they regard as the beginning of the New Year.

15 May 66

I think I gained the confidence of the "prince" from Isfahan today; or more probably awakened his interest.

We met, as before, when we were both taking a stroll, and as we went on together a little way I told him about all the towns I'd been to in the last few months. He nodded politely at each fresh name, but when I mentioned Smyrna his expression changed. To encourage me to continue, he said, "Izmir, Izmir", the Turkish name for the place.

I'd spent forty days there, I said, and on two occasions had seen with my own eyes the Jew who claims to be the Messiah. The Persian then seized my arm, called me his honoured friend, and said he'd heard many contradictory stories about "Sabb ataï Levi".

"I heard the Jews call him Sabbataï Zevi or Tsevi," I said.

He thanked me for the correction, and asked me to tell him exactly what I'd seen, so that he could distinguish the true from the false in what was being said about this character.

I told him some things, and promised him more in due course.

16 May

Yesterday I revised what I'd said about gaining the "prince's" confidence, and said, rightly then, that it was rather that I'd aroused his curiosity. Now I really can speak of trust, for today, instead of just listening to me, he talked about himself.

He didn't tell me any secrets – why should he? But for someone who's a foreigner and evidently likes to keep himself to himself, the little he did communicate is a token of esteem and a mark of confidence.

He said he wasn't really travelling on business in the usual sense, but to see the world and find out at first hand about the strange things that are happening in it. Though he didn't say so, I'm sure he's someone of importance, perhaps a brother or cousin of the Grand Sophy.

I've thought of introducing him to Girolamo, but my Venetian friend is rather garrulous and might scare him. Then, instead of opening out gradually like some shy rose, the Persian might just close up again.

So I mean to see them separately, unless they should happen to meet one another without me.

17 May

Today the prince invited me to his "palace". The word is not excessive, relatively speaking. The sailors sleep in a barn, I sleep in a shed, Girolamo and his entourage have a house, and Ali Esfahani, who has a whole suite of rooms which he's decorated with rugs and cushions in the Persian style, lives in the equivalent of a palace. His staff includes a butler, a translator, a cook and his scullion, a valet, and four general manservants in addition to the two guards, whom he calls "my wild animals".

The translator is a French ecclesiastic from Toulouse who calls himself "Father Angel". I was surprised when I first saw him with Ali, especially as they spoke to one another in Persian. I haven't been able to find out anything more: the translator disappeared when his master said he and I could make ourselves understood to one another in Arabic.

In the course of the evening my host told me a very strange thing: it's said that every night since the beginning of this year several stars have vanished from the sky. You have only to look up at the part of the sky where the stars are most densely concentrated to see that some of them suddenly go out, never to reappear. Ali seems to believe that as the year goes by the night sky will gradually empty, until at last it's completely dark.

To check whether this is true I prepared to spend most of the night sitting on deck with my head flung back, watching the sky. I tried to focus on fixed points, but my eyes kept blurring. After an hour I felt so cold I gave up and went to bed without having proved anything.

18 May

I told my Venetian friend the tale about the stars, and he burst out laughing before I'd even finished. Luckily I hadn't said where I'd heard it. And luckily I haven't introduced the two men to one another.

Though he goes on making fun of rumours about the end of the world, Girolamo has told me some things I find disturbing. When I'm with him I feel the same as I used to with Maïmoun. On the one hand I wish I could share his serenity and his scorn for all superstition, and this makes me seem to agree with what he says. But at the same time I can't prevent these same superstitions, even the most extravagant of them, from lodging in my mind. "What if these people were right?" "What if their prophecies came true?" "Supposing the world really was less than four months away from extinction?" Questions like these flit about in my head in spite of me. I know they're foolish, but I can't manage to get rid of them. This depresses me and makes me doubly ashamed: in the first place for sharing the apprehensions of the ignorant, and in the second for being so deceitful with my friend – nodding my head at what he says, and all the time disagreeing with it in my heart.

I felt like this again yesterday, when Girolamo was telling me about some Muscovites known as Capitons, who want to die, he says, "because they believe Christ will soon come into the world again to set up His kingdom, and they want to come back in His train rather than be among the multitude of sinners who will endure His wrath. The Capitons live in small groups scattered throughout Muscovy, out of reach of the authorities. In their view the whole world is now ruled by the Antichrist and inhabited by the damned – even Muscovy, and even its church, whose prayers and rituals they reject. Their leader exhorts them to let themselves die of hunger and thus avoid being guilty of suicide. But some of them are in such a hurry they do not shrink from breaking God's law in the most atrocious manner. Not a week goes by without terrible reports coming in from one region or another of the vast country. Groups of people gather in churches or even mere barns, block up the windows and deliberately set the building on fire, so that whole families burn themselves alive amid prayers and the shrieks of children."

Ever since Girolamo told me of these things, their images have haunted me. I think of them day and night, and keep wondering if it's possible that all these people are dying for nothing. Can anyone really be so mistaken, and sacrifice his life so cruelly just through an error of judgement? I can't help feeling some respect for them, though my Venetian friend says I am wrong. He compares them with ignorant beasts, and thinks their behaviour is stupid, criminal and impious. At most he feels some pity for them, but below his pity lies scorn. And when I say I find his attitude cruel, he answers that he could never be as cruel to these people as they are to themselves and their wives and children.

19 May

It may be difficult to check whether the stars are really disappearing, but my Persian friend's story shows without a shadow of doubt that he is concerned as I am with all that's said about this cursed year.

No, he's much *more* concerned than I am. My thoughts are divided between my love, my business, and my trivial dreams and worries, and every day I have to do violence to my natural apathy if I'm not to abandon my pursuit of *The Hundredth Name.* I think of the Apocalypse now and again, I half believe in things, but my father brought me up in such a way that the sceptic in me saves me from any great religious outbursts – or perhaps I should say precludes any kind of constancy, whether in the exercise of reason or in the quest for chimeras.

But to return to my "prince" and friend, he listed for me today the various predictions he's heard of concerning this year. There are many of them, and they come from every corner of the globe. Some I'm familiar with already, others not or only partly. He's collected many more examples than I have, but I know some things he doesn't.

Above all, of course, there are the predictions of the Muscovites and the Jews. Then those of the sectaries of Aleppo and the English fanatics. And the quite recent prophecies of a Portuguese Jesuit. In Ali's view the most disturbing prognostications are those of the four greatest Persian astrologers, who usually disagree and compete for the favours of their ruler, but who apparently declare unanimously that this year men will call God by His Hebrew name, as Noah did, and that things will happen that have never been seen since Noah's own day.

"Another Flood?" I asked.

"Yes, but a deluge of fire this time!"

The way he said this reminded me of my nephew Boumeh – that triumphal tone to announce the most awful calamities! As if the Creator, by letting them know what was in store, was implicitly promising them immunity.

20 May

During the night I thought again about the predictions of the Persian astrologers. Not so much the threat of another flood – you find that in all prophecies about the end of the world – but rather the allusion to the name of God, and in particular His Hebrew name. I suppose that's the sacred Tetragrammaton that must not be uttered – if I've read the Bible correctly – by anyone except the high priest once a year, in the Holy of Holies, on the Day of Atonement. So what would happen if, at the behest of Sabbataï, thousands of people all over the world were to speak the ineffable name aloud? Wouldn't Heaven be angry enough to annihilate the world and everyone in it?

I discussed all this at length today with Esfahani, who takes quite a different view. He says that if men do utter the unspeakable name they won't be intending to defy the will of the Almighty, but on the contrary to hasten its fulfilment in the form of the end of the world and deliverance. He doesn't seem at all put out by the fact that the so-called Messiah of Smyrna advocates this general transgression.

I asked if he thought that the Tetragrammaton revealed to Moses might be the same as the hundredth name of Allah sought by some commentators on the Koran. He was so pleased by this question that he threw an arm round my shoulders and walked me along with him for a few paces. This kind of familiarity, coming from him, rather embarrassed me.

"What a pleasure it is," he said warmly, "to find one has a scholar as a fellow-passenger!"

I said nothing to disillusion him, though it seems to me that a real scholar, instead of having to ask such a question, would be able to provide the answer.

"Come with me!" he went on, leading the way to a little room he calls "the cubby-hole where I keep my secrets". I suppose that before he came on board the place didn't have a name – it was just a small space used for storing bits of damaged cargo. Now, however, the shelves are curtained, the floor is fitted with a little carpet, and the air is heavy with incense. We sat down facing one another on a couple of plump cushions. An oil-lamp hung from the ceiling. A servant brought in coffee and sweetmeats and left them on a chest to my right. On the other side was a big irregular window opening on to the blue horizon. I had a pleasant impression of being back in the bedroom I used to sleep in as a child, in Gibelet.

"Has God got a hidden hundredth name in addition to the ninety-nine we already know of?" asked Ali. "If so, what is it? Is it a Hebrew name? Or a Syriac or an Arabic one? How would we recognise it if we read it in a book or heard it? Who has known it in the past? And what powers does it confer on those who have found it out?"

He asked his questions without haste, sometimes glancing at me but more often looking out to sea, so that I was able to study his aquiline profile and painted eyebrows.

"Ever since the dawn of Islam, scholars have argued over a verse that occurs three times in similar terms in the Koran and lends itself to various interpretations."

He quoted the phrase carefully: "Fa sabbih bismi rabbika-l-azim," which may be translated as "Glorify the name of your Lord, the Most High".

The ambiguity arises from the fact in Arabic the epithet "l-azim", "the Most High", may refer either to the Lord or to His name. In the first case, the verse is merely a normal exhortation to glorify the name of the Lord. But if the second interpretation is correct, the verse might mean "Glorify your Lord by His highest name", which would suggest that among the names of God there is a major one which is superior to all the others, and the invoking of which produces special results.

"The argument had gone on for centuries, with the advocates of each interpretation finding, or thinking they find, proof of their own and disproof of their opponents' case in the Koran itself, or in the various pronouncements attributed to the Prophet. And then a new and powerful argument was put forward by a scholar in Baghdad known as Mazandarani. I don't say he managed to convince everybody. Some people still hold to their previous positions, especially as Mazandarani himself had rather a dubious reputation – he was said to practise alchemy, to use magic alphabets, and to study various occult sciences. But he had many disciples, and his house was always full of visitors. So clearly his argument undermined some certainties, and whetted the appetite of scholars and laymen alike."

According to "the prince", Mazandarani's argument, in brief, was that if it has been possible for the verse in question to be understood in two different ways, that is because God – who for Muslims is the author of the Koran – intended the ambiguity.

"Indeed," said Esfahani, continuing his commentary, though without making it clear whether he actually agreed with Mazandarani, "if God put it that way rather than another, and used the same form of words almost identically three times, it's unthinkable that He could have done so by mistake, or incompetence, or accident, or ignorance of the language. If He did it, He must have done it deliberately!

"Having thus so to speak changed doubt into certainty and darkness into light, Mazandarani asked himself *why* God wanted to create this ambiguity. Why didn't He tell his creatures plainly that the supreme name doesn't exist? And Mazandarani answered his own question: if He expressed Himself equivocally it was not to deceive or mislead us – that too would be unthinkable! He couldn't have let us believe the supreme name might exist if it didn't. Therefore it necessarily does exist. And if the Most High doesn't tell us so more explicitly it's because His infinite wisdom commands Him to show the way only to those who deserve it. When they read the verse in question, as when they read many others in the Koran, most people will go on thinking they've understood all there was to understand. But the elect, the initiates, will be able to slip through the subtle door He has left ajar for their benefit.

"Judging that he'd established beyond all possible doubt that the hundredth name exists, and that God doesn't forbid us to try to find it, Mazandarani promised his followers to say in a book what it is not and what it is."

"And did he write the book?" I asked, not very comfortably.

"There again opinions differ. Some people say he never did write it. Others say he did, and that it's called *The Book of the Hundredth Name*, or *A Treatise on the Hundredth Name*, or *The Unveiling of the Hidden Name*."

"I had a book through my shop once with that title, but I don't know if it was by Mazandarani." Again, I couldn't be more truthful without giving myself away.

"Have you still got it?"

"No. Before I could read it an emissary from the King of France asked for it and I gave it to him."

"If I'd been you I wouldn't have given it away before I'd read it. But don't worry – no doubt it was a forgery."

I think I've reproduced what Esfahani said pretty faithfully, at least in the main, for our conversation lasted three whole hours.

I think he was speaking frankly, and I intend to be as sincere myself in our future exchanges. I shall go on asking questions, though, because I'm sure he knows much more than he's told me so far.

21 May

A really hopeless sort of day.

While yesterday brought me pleasure and information, today produced nothing but disappointment and vexation.

As soon as I woke up I felt queasy. Perhaps it was a recurrence of sea-sickness, brought on by the bumping of the ship. Or perhaps I ate too many of those Persian sweetmeats yesterday evening, cooked with pine kernels, pistachio nuts, chick peas and cardamum.

I felt so out of sorts I decided to spend the day fasting and reading in my cramped quarters.

I'd have liked to continue my conversation with "the prince", but I wasn't fit for any kind of company. To console myself, I reflected that it might be best not to seem too eager. He might be put off if he thought I was trying to pump him for information.

Early in the afternoon, when everyone else would be taking a siesta, I decided to take a turn round the deck; it was, as I'd hoped, deserted. Then suddenly I saw the captain a few paces away, leaning back against the rail and apparently deep in thought. I didn't want to have to talk to him, but neither did I want to look as if I was avoiding him. So I walked steadily on, bowing politely as I passed him. He bowed back, but rather absent-mindedly. To fill the silence, I asked him when we were going to put in at a port, and where.

It seemed to me a perfectly natural question, the most obvious one for a passenger to put to a captain. But Centurione turned on me suspiciously.

"Why do you ask? What are you after?"

Why does a passenger ever want to know where his ship is bound? But I smiled as I explained, almost apologetically:

"I didn't buy enough provisions at our last port of call, and I'm starting to run short of some things."

"It's your own fault! Passengers ought to have a bit of foresight."

He seemed almost ready to give me a box on the ear. I mustered such patience and politeness as I had left, took leave of him and walked away.

An hour later he sent Maurizio to me with some soup.

Even if I'd been in perfect health I wouldn't have gone near it. Today, with my upset stomach . . .

I asked the young sailor to convey my thanks, but at the same time launched a few well-chosen sarcasms in the captain's direction. But Maurizio pretended not to hear, so I had to act as if I hadn't said anything.

* * *

So much for my day, and now I'm just sitting here with my pen in my hand and tears in my eyes. All of a sudden I feel bereft of everything. Dry land, Gibelet, Smyrna, Genoa, Marta, even Gregorio.

A really hopeless sort of day.

24 May

We're anchored in Tangiers, beyond Gibraltar and the Pillars of Hercules. It's recently come under the English crown – though I admit I didn't know that until this morning. For a couple of centuries it belonged to Portugal, which acquired it by force, but when the Infanta Catherine of Braganza married King Charles four or five years ago she brought him two fortresses in her dowry – Tangiers was one, the other was Bombay in India. I'm told the English officers who've been sent here dislike the place, which they cry down and dismiss as a worthless acquisition.

But the town itself struck me as charming, with its broad straight streets lined with well-built houses. There are also fields of orange and lemon trees which give off a wonderful heady perfume. Tangiers' mildness derives from its singular situation at the crossroads between four different climates, close to both the Mediterranean and the Atlantic, both the Atlas mountains and the desert. In my opinion, any king would be glad to possess such a place. Walking round, I met an elderly Portuguese burgess who was born here and refused to leave when his king's soldiers went. His name is Sebastiao Magalhaes – I wonder if he's a descendant of the famous navigator? No, he would have told me. It was he who told me what people were whispering, adding that he was sure the English officers' mockery is entirely due to the fact that their king's wife is a "Papist": some of them think the Pope himself secretly promoted the marriage in an attempt to win England back to Rome.

But according to my interlocutor there's another explanation for the marriage: Portugal is constantly at war with Spain, and Spain still hopes to reconquer Portugal, so Portugal is always trying to strengthen its links with its enemy's enemies.

I'd promised myself that as I couldn't do so aboard ship, I'd entertain my Persian and Venetian friends royally when we reached our first port of call. I meant to find out beforehand what were the best places to go to, so I took advantage of my meeting with Master Magalhaes to ask his advice. He said at once that I'd be welcome at his house. I thanked him, but told him I had several invitations to return and would feel awkward to set sail again without having repaid my debts to my friends. But he wouldn't listen.

"If you'd had a brother here, wouldn't you have invited them to his place? Well, consider that to be the case, and you may be sure you and your friends will be much better off chatting in my library than in some tavern in the harbour."

25 May

I couldn't add anything to my journal yesterday evening. It was dark by the time I got back from Magalhaes' house, and I'd eaten and drunk too much to be able to write.

Our host had even pressed us to stay the night, which would have made a pleasant change from all the nights we've spent in beds being bumped up and down all the time. But I was afraid the captain might take it into his head to sail before dawn, so I preferred to decline the invitation.

It's midnight now, and the ship is still moored to the quay. Everything is quiet. I don't think we can be about to leave.

Yesterday evening passed pleasantly enough, but the fact that we had no language in common rather spoiled things. Of course, Father Angel was there to act as interpreter for his master, but he didn't over-exert himself. Some of the time he was busy eating. At other times he hadn't been listening and was obliged to ask us to repeat what we'd said. At other times again he would translate a long speech by just a couple of words, either because he couldn't remember it all or because he disapproved of some of it.

For instance, at one point Esfahani, who was very interested in Muscovy and what the Venetian had to say about its people and their customs, wanted to know what religious differences there were between Orthodox and Catholic believers. Girolamo started to explain the Patriarch of Moscow's arguments against the Pope, but Father Angel didn't like having to repeat that kind of thing, and when Durrazzi said that the Muscovites, like the English, referred to the Pope as the Antichrist, the priest went red in the face, dropped his knife with a clatter, and said to the Venetian, his voice trembling:

"You'd do better to learn Persian and say such things for yourself. I don't propose to soil my lips or the prince's ear with them."

Father Angel was so furious he'd spoken in French, but everyone present had understood the word "prince", and though he tried to mend matters the damage was done. Perhaps it was a similar incident that gave rise to the old saying that a translator is the same thing as a traitor.

Anyhow, after a month as his fellow-passenger, I now know for sure that Esfahani really is a prince. Perhaps by the time we land in London I'll have found out exactly who he is and why he's on this journey.

Yesterday evening, when we'd been talking again about Tangiers being handed over by the Portuguese, he leaned over and asked me if one day I'd explain to him in detail both the similarities between the various Christian countries and the things that divided them from one another. I promised I'd tell him what little I knew. And by way of preamble I told him half jokingly that if anyone wanted to understand anything of what is going on around him he should bear in mind that the English hate the Spaniards, the Spaniards hate the English, the Dutch hate both the English and the Spaniards, and the French cordially detest all of them.

Then suddenly, Girolamo, who, heaven knows how, had understood what I'd just said in an aside and in Arabic too, intervened.

"And tell him too that the Sienese curse the Florentines, and the Genoese prefer the Turks to the Venetians!"

I translated this faithfully, and then protested, hypocritically:

"The proof that we Genoese no longer bear a grudge against Venice is the fact that you and I are talking together like friends!"

"Yes, now!" he answered. "But to begin with you always looked round first to make sure there wasn't any other Genoese watching!"

Once more I contradicted him. But he may be right. Except that I wasn't so much looking round as looking up to Heaven, where my ancestors are supposed to be, God rest their souls.

I translated our exchange to "His Highness", but I don't know if he understood. I suppose he must have done. Hasn't Persia got places of its own like Genoa and Venice, Florence and Siena, all full of schismatics and fanatics, as well as kingdoms and peoples squabbling all the time like our Englishmen and Spaniards and Portuguese?

The *Sanctus Dionisius* didn't sail till nightfall. If we'd known we could have spent last night between the comfortable sheets that Magalhaes offered us. What a lot of good that would have done us! But instead of speaking of regrets as I leave Tangiers, I should be thanking God for the unexpected meeting that made my stay there so significant. I only hope we gave our host as much pleasure as he gave us, and that our visit did something to lighten his melancholy. When the Portuguese owned Tangiers he was a highly respected citizen, but since the English took possession, he feels he's gone down in the world. But what could he do? he asked. At over sixty years old, he can't leave his house and land and go and start a new life somewhere else. And after all, the English are allies, not enemies – their queen is Catherine of Braganza.

"So I've become an exile without ever leaving my country."

That's something a Genoese living abroad can understand, isn't it? God bless you, Sebastiao Magalhaes, and give you patience!

26 May

Perhaps after all there's some method in the captain's madness.

According to Girolamo, the reason why Centurione chose to avoid the ports on the Spanish coast and stop in Tangiers is that he's taking an important cargo to England and is afraid it might be seized. That's why he's making for Lisbon now instead of Cadiz or Seville.

I still haven't told Durrazzi – or anyone else – about the flying demons episode, but I suppose the captain could be pretending to be crazy in order to explain his erratic route.

I can't quite believe that, but I do hope it's true. I'd rather the ship was commanded by a schemer than by a raving lunatic.

Prince Ali invited Girolamo and me to eat with him today. I expected Father Angel to be there too, but our host explained that his intermediary had vowed to fast all day and devote himself to silent meditation. In my opinion he wants to avoid having to translate anything irreligious. So it fell to me to convert Italian into Arabic and vice versa. Of course I know both languages and have no trouble switching from one to the other, but I'd never before had to translate every word of a conversation lasting through a whole meal, and I found it exhausting. I couldn't enjoy either the cooking or the conversation.

On top of the effort of translating I had, like Father Angel, to cope with the embarrassment that Durrazzi does his best to cause.

He's the sort of person who must say whatever comes into his head. So he couldn't help bringing up the subject of the King of France's plans for making war on the Sultan, and the Sophy's alleged undertaking to take the Ottomans from the rear. He wanted our host to tell him if such an alliance really had been concluded. I tried to stop him from asking such a delicate question, but he insisted almost rudely on my translating it word for word. Out of politeness or weakness I did so and, as I expected, the prince curtly declined to answer. Worse still, he said he suddenly felt tired, so we were obliged to get up from the table too.

I feel humiliated, and as if I'd lost two friends with one stone.

This evening I wonder if my father wasn't right after all to hate the Venetians. He used to say they were arrogant and deceitful, adding – especially when he had other Italian guests – that it was when they wore their masks that they dissembled least!

27 May

When I opened my eyes this morning, one of Prince Ali's "wild beasts" was standing over me. I must have gasped with fright, but he didn't move. Just waited for me to sit up and rub my eyes, and then handed me a note from his master, asking me to go and have coffee with him.

I hoped he'd talk about *The Hundredth Name* again, but soon realised he only wanted to do away with the impression I might have been given yesterday when he practically threw us out.

By inviting me on my own, without Girolamo, he wanted to show he differentiated between us.

I shan't try to bring them together any more.

1 June

I've just remembered Sabbataï's prediction that the age of Resurrection would begin in the month of June, which starts this morning. But which day? I don't know. It was Brother Egidio who told me about the prophecy and I don't think he specified the date.

I've just re-read the page in question, dated the 10th of April, and I see I didn't mention the prediction. But I remember hearing about it. Perhaps it was on another day, though.

Now I remember that it was in Smyrna, soon after I got there. Yes, that was it, I'm sure. Even if I haven't got that notebook any more and can't check.

Durrazzi hasn't heard anything about the end of the world starting in June. He laughs at that idea, just as he does as the Muscovite fanatics and their 1st of September.

"For me the end of the world will be if I fall into the sea," he says irreverently.

Again I wonder if it's wisdom or blindness.

Lisbon, 3 June

After a week at sea the *Sanctus Dionisius* dropped anchor at noon today in Lisbon harbour. And hardly had we arrived than I had to deal with a serious disappointment that nearly turned into a disaster. I hadn't done anything wrong – I was merely unaware of something that other people knew. But ignorance is no excuse.

Just before we were due to go ashore, while I was thinking that the first thing I must do was deliver to Master Cristoforo Gabbiano the letter

Gregorio asked me to bring him, Esfahani sent me a note in his beautiful writing asking me to go and see him in his apartments. He was angry with Father Angel, accusing him of being disrespectful, narrow-minded and ungrateful. Not long afterwards, I saw the priest coming out of his own quarters, carrying his belongings and looking equally cross. The two men had quarrelled because the prince wanted to go and see a Portuguese Jesuit, Father Vieira, whom Esfahani had told me about in the course of the voyage: he's said to have made certain prophecies about the end of the world, and others foretelling the imminent collapse of the Ottoman Empire. Ever since hearing of this priest a few months ago, the prince had vowed to meet him and ask him for more details about his predictions if ever he himself was in Lisbon. But when he asked Father Angel to go with him as his interpreter, he refused, saying that the Jesuit was a blasphemous heretic who'd committed the sin of pride when he claimed to know the future. He, Father Angel, did not wish to meet him. He wouldn't change his mind, and the prince hoped I might replace him. I saw no reason why not. On the contrary, I was as interested as the prince in what the Jesuit might say, both about the end of the world and about the fate of the empire where I live. So I agreed, and took advantage of Esfahani's delight to make him promise not to be too hard on Father Angel, who had to obey the laws of his religion and keep his vows. His attitude should be seen as proof of fidelity rather than as treachery.

As soon as we were ashore, the prince, his "wild animals" and I made our way to a large church near the harbour. Outside it, I asked a young seminarist if by any chance he knew Father Vieira and could tell me where he lived. His face fell slightly, but he asked me to go with him to the presbytery. I did so, leaving the prince and his men waiting outside.

Once in the house, the seminarist asked me to sit down while he went to find a superior who might be able to give me more information. After a few minutes he came back and told me "the vicar" was on his way. I waited and waited, and then I started getting impatient, the more so as the prince was still there outside. At one point I got up and opened the door through which the young man had left the room. And there he was, spying on me through the crack, and when he saw me he nearly jumped out of his skin.

"Perhaps I've come at an inconvenient moment," I said politely. "I can come back tomorrow if you wish. Our ship has just got in, and we'll be in Lisbon until Sunday."

"Are you friends of Father Vieira's?"

"No – we haven't met him yet, but we've heard of his writings."

"Have you read them?"

"Not yet, unfortunately."

"Do you know where he's living at the moment?"

I was starting to get annoyed, and to think I must be saddled with a simpleton.

"If I knew that I wouldn't have come and asked you!"

"He's in prison, on the orders of the Holy Office!"

He started telling me why the Jesuit had been incarcerated by the Inquisition, but I said I was in a hurry and left as fast as I could, collecting the prince and his men and telling them to walk fast and not look back. I couldn't say exactly what I was afraid of. I knew I'd done nothing wrong, but I still didn't want, on the very day I arrived here, to be hauled before some vicar or bishop or judge, or any other representative of authority. Especially not the Holy Office!

Back on board, I told Durrazzi what had happened to us, and he said he knew all along that Vieira had been tried by the Inquisition and had been in prison since last year.

"You should have told me you wanted to meet him. I'd have warned you. If you talked as freely to me as I do to you, you'd have spared yourself the disappointment!"

No doubt he's right. But I'd probably have let myself in for other troubles.

Anyhow – to look on the brighter side of things for a moment – I found out this evening about where to eat in Lisbon, so that, after being unable to do so properly in Tangiers, I can invite my friends to dinner tomorrow evening. I've been told of a very good tavern where they cook fish dishes with spices from all corners of the globe. I had decided not to bring the Persian and the Venetian together again, but now the prince can tell the difference between Girolamo and me, and I shouldn't take any notice of my own whims and fancies. There aren't so many of us on board who are capable of carrying on a gentlemanly conversation!

At sea, 4 June 1666

This morning early I went to see Master Gabbiano. The visit should have been short, polite and perfectly ordinary. But in fact it has changed the whole course of my journey, and that of my fellow-travellers too.

I located him without any difficulty: his offices are quite near the harbour. His father was Milanese and his mother Portuguese, and he has lived in Lisbon for thirty years. As well as running his own business, he represents the interests of a number of other merchants from various different countries. Gregorio had conveyed the impression that Gabbiano was his agent, almost his clerk; but perhaps I misunderstood him. The man himself seems like a prosperous ship-owner, and his offices occupy the whole of a four-storey building and employ about sixty people. Despite the earliness of the hour the heat was stifling, and Gabbiano was being fanned by a mulatto woman standing behind him. This apparently wasn't enough, for every so often he fanned himself with one of the sheets of paper he was reading.

Although he was already trying to deal with five other visitors, all talking at once, he seemed impressed when he heard my and Mangiavacca's names. He took the letter immediately, broke the seal, and read it in silence, frowning. Then he called his secretary, whispered something in his ear, and apologised to me for having to spend a moment dealing with the other people. The secretary returned after a few minutes, bringing with him about 2,000 florins.

I looked surprised. Gabbiano showed me the letter. Apart from the usual salutations, Gregorio just asked him to hand over the sum in question to me personally. I would pay him back in Genoa.

What was my would-be "father-in-law" up to? Was he trying to force me to go and see him again on my way back from London? I expect so. Just like him!

I tried to tell Gabbiano that I hesitated to carry so much money about with me, especially as I had no intention of passing through Genoa again. But he wouldn't listen. He owed Gregorio that amount, and since Gregorio was now asking for it back he couldn't do otherwise than send it. Anyhow, it was entirely up to me whether I went back to Genoa or had the money conveyed to Gregorio by some other means.

"But I haven't got a safe place to keep it in on the ship –"

He remained perfectly polite, but his smile betrayed a certain impatience as he indicated his petitioners, now growing rather insistent. He couldn't take on my problems as well as his own!

I stowed the heavy purse away in my canvas bag and stood up. As I did so I said, as if to myself, in a voice at once worried and resigned:

"To think I'll have to try to get it safely all the way to London!"

This last shaft, shot blindly, found its mark.

"London, did you say?" he cried. "You mustn't dream of such a thing! I've just heard on the best possible authority that several ships bound for England have been stopped by the Dutch. And there's a big naval battle taking place on your route. It would be sheer madness to sail now."

"The captain intends to leave the day after tomorrow. Sunday."

"That's much too soon! Tell him from me he shouldn't go. He'd be putting his ship in danger. Better still, tell him to come and see me this afternoon without fail, and I'll explain the situation to him. Who is he?"

"I think his name's Centurione. Captain Centurione."

Gabbiano pursed his lips to show he didn't know him. I almost took him aside to tell him about the captain's strange behaviour, but decided against it. The other people were glaring at me and getting restive. It was too delicate a matter to explain in a hurry. And anyhow, if Gabbiano spoke to Centurione face to face he'd see the situation for himself.

So I hastened back to the ship and went straight to the captain's quarters. He was alone and deep in thought, or in silent conversation with his demons. After politely asking me to sit down, he looked up and said ponderously:

"Well, what's the matter?"

But when he heard that Gabbiano wanted to tell him about the alleged dangers of trying to sail to London, he started to listen intently. Then he looked at me wide-eyed, stood up, and patted me on the shoulder. He'd just leave me a moment and give some orders, then we'd go and talk to to Master Gabbiano together.

As I was waiting, the captain returned for a moment, saying he was arranging for us to leave. I took him to mean for Gabbiano's house, but either I misunderstood or else he was deliberately misleading me, for he was soon back again to tell me, without any ambiguity this time, that he'd just ordered his men to hoist sail and cast off in order to leave Lisbon as fast as possible.

"We're heading out to sea already!" he announced.

I bounded up in amazement. He told me to sit down while he explained.

"Didn't you notice anything at that person's house?"

I'd noticed lots of things, but I couldn't tell which he meant, nor why he referred to Gabbiano as "that person".

"That Gabbiano's?" he prompted me.

Then I understood, and was appalled. If, as I knew from experience, the madman in front of me went into a frenzy just when he saw a gull, what state was he likely to be in when he heard that the name of the man asking him to postpone his voyage was the same, in Italian, as the bird's! I was lucky he regarded me as a friend come to warn him of the plot, rather than a demon disguised as a Genoese traveller. It's a good thing my name's Embriaco, and not Marangone, like a colleague of my father's from Amalfi. His name means "cormorant"!

So we'd already left Lisbon!

My first thought was not for myself and the others on board, my companions in misfortune, who were going to having to run the gauntlet of warring gunships and perhaps be killed or taken captive. No, strangely enough the people I felt sorry for were those we'd left behind in Lisbon. The captain had absolutely no right not to wait for them to rejoin the ship before it left, though I realised that his culpable negligence would probably save their lives and spare them all the woes those on board would inevitably encounter.

I knew that Durrazzi and Esfahani, the two friends I'd made during the voyage, were still ashore. They'd left the ship at the same time as I did this morning, and were to remain in town in order to be my guests for dinner this evening.

But all that has been overtaken by events. I'm heading for the unknown in the power of a madman, and my friends are probably standing on the quayside wringing their hands as they watch the *Sanctus Dionisius* vanish inexplicably in the distance.

I'm not the only person on board who feels helpless and distraught this evening. The few passengers and all the crew are in the position of hostages whom no one will ever ransom. Whether we're hostages to the captain or to the demons that pursue him, or to fate, as future victims of war, we all, merchants and mariners alike, rich and poor, aristocrats or servants, feel like a pack of lost souls.

At sea, 7 June 1666

Instead of sailing northward along the Portuguese coast, the *Sanctus Dionisius* has for the last three days been heading west, due west, as if it were making for the New World. We are now in the middle of the vast Atlantic, the sea's getting rough, and every time a wave hits the ship I can hear shouting and yelling.

I ought to be frightened, but I'm not. I ought to be angry, but I'm not. I ought to be rushing about in all directions and bombarding the crazy captain with questions, but I'm sitting cross-legged in my room on a blanket folded in four, as mild as a flock of sheep. As mild as old people dying.

At the moment I'm not afraid of being shipwrecked or being taken captive. I just dread being sea-sick.

8 June

Now, on the evening of the fourth day, the captain, perhaps thinking he's thrown his demons off the scent, has just changed direction and is steering north.

I still can't shake off my queasiness and dizzy spells. So I keep to my cabin and don't write much.

Maurizio brought me the same supper as the sailors. I couldn't touch it.

12 June

Today is the ninth day of our voyage to London, and the *Sanctus Dionisius* has stood still for three hours on the open sea – though I couldn't say what our position is or which is the nearest coast.

We'd just passed another Genoese ship, the *Alegrancia*, which made signs to us and sent us a messenger, whom we hoisted on board. Rumours immediately started to circulate confirming that a fierce battle was taking place between the Dutch and the English, making our route dangerous.

The messenger stayed only a few minutes in the captain's quarters. Then Centurione shut himself up alone for some time, issuing no orders to the crew, while the ship was buffeted about where it lay, sails furled. He was probably trying to make up his mind. Should he turn back? Take shelter somewhere and wait for more news? Or try to steer round the combat zone?

According to Maurizio when I asked him this evening, we're now still on much the same course as before, but slightly more to the north-east. I told him frankly that I thought it rash of the captain to take such risks, but again the young man pretended not to hear. I didn't press the matter, not wanting to weigh down his young shoulders with such anxieties.

22 June

Last night, unable to sleep and feeling queasy again, I went for a walk round the deck, and in the distance, on our left, I noticed a curious light that looked to me like a ship on fire.

Today it was clear no one else had seen it. I was beginning to think my eyes had deceived me when, in the evening, I heard the sound of gunfire in the distance. This time everyone on board is in a flutter, and we're heading blithely for the scene of the battle. No one dreams of arguing with the captain or challenging his authority.

Am I the only one who knows he's out of his mind?

23 June

The din of war grows louder before and behind us, but we still sail imperturbably on toward our destination – and our destiny.

I'll be very surprised if we ever arrive in London safe and sound. But I'm not an astrologer or a seer, thank God, and I'm often wrong. I only hope I'm wrong this time. I've never asked Heaven to save me from error – only from misfortune.

I'd like my path through life to go on for a long while yet and be full of wrong turnings. Yes, I want to live for some years still, and make a lot more mistakes, even commit a few more sins worth remembering.

It's fear that makes me write such nonsense. I shall now dry my ink, put my notebook away, and listen calmly, like a man, to the sounds of war nearby.

Saturday, 26 June 1666

I'm still free, and at the same time I'm a prisoner.

This morning, at dawn, a Dutch gunboat approached us and ordered us to stow our sails and hoist the white flag. We did so.

Some soldiers came on board and seized the ship, and now, according to Maurizio, they're taking us to Amsterdam.

And who knows what will happen to us there?

I suppose all the cargo will be confiscated, but I don't care about that.

I suppose we'll all be taken prisoner too, and our belongings seized. So I shall lose the money Gabbiano gave me, as well as my own, and as well as this book and all my writing things.

It puts me off trying to write.

In captivity, 28 June 1666

The Dutch threw two sailors into the sea. One was English but the other was a Sicilian. I'd heard shouts of terror and a great uproar. I rushed to see what was the matter, but when I saw the crowd, and the armed soldiers gesticulating and shouting and bawling in their own language, I turned back. It was Maurizio who told me what had happened, a bit later. He was shaking in every limb, and I tried to comfort him, though I'm far from easy in my own mind.

Up till now, everything had gone fairly calmly. We were all resigned to being diverted to Amsterdam: we were sure the captain couldn't have got away with his weird behaviour for ever. But today's carnage has brought it home to us that we are prisoners and likely to remain so indefinitely, and that the most reckless and the most unlucky among us may come to a sticky end.

The English sailor was reckless – and probably tipsy – enough to tell the Dutch their navy would be defeated in the end. And the Sicilian was unlucky enough to be standing by and anxious to intercede on his comrade's behalf.

In captivity, 29 June

I don't leave my room any more, and I'm not the only one. Maurizio tells me the decks are deserted. Only the Dutch are to be seen; the crew only leave their quarters to carry out orders. The captain is now supervised constantly by a Dutch officer who issues commands through him. I have no complaints about that.

2 July

Last night, after blowing out my lamp, I suddenly felt cold, although I was just as warmly dressed as I had been recently, and the day had been quite mild. Perhaps the sensation was due to fear rather than cold. And I dreamed I was seized by the Dutch sailors, dragged along the ground, then stripped and flogged till I bled. I believe I cried out with the pain, and this was what woke me up. I couldn't get back to sleep afterwards. I tried, but my head was like a fruit that wouldn't ripen, and my eyes wouldn't stay shut.

4 July

Today a Dutch sailor pushed my cabin door open, looked round, then went away. A quarter of an hour later one of his colleagues did exactly the same, but this one did mutter something meant to convey "Good-day". It seemed to me they were looking for someone rather than something.

We can't be far from our Dutch destination now, and I keep wondering what attitude I should adopt when we get there. Above all, what ought I to do with the money that was entrusted to me in Lisbon, with my own money, and with this notebook?

I have two alternatives.

Either I assume I'm to be treated as a foreign trader, with consideration and perhaps even permission to enter the United Provinces, in which case I ought to take all my "treasure" with me when I go ashore.

Or I assume that the *Sanctus Dionisius* is to be regarded as a prize, in which case its cargo will be confiscated and everyone on board, including me, held for a while, then sent away, together with their ship. In which case it would be best to leave my "treasure" in some safe hiding-place, pray that nobody finds it, and try to recover it when the present ordeal is over.

After hesitating for a couple of hours, I've decided on the second alternative. I only hope I shan't regret it!

Now I'm going to put my notebook and my writing things away in the same hiding-place where Gregorio's money is already – behind a loose plank in the wall. I shall stow half the money I have left there too, though I ought to keep a reasonable amount on me: otherwise they'll smell a rat and make me produce the lot.

I'm tempted to keep my notebook with me. Money comes and goes, but these pages are my own flesh, my own last companion. I can hardly bear to part with them. But I suppose I must.

14 August 1666

I haven't written a line for more than forty days. I've been ashore, in confinement, while my notebook was still in its hiding-place on the ship. But now we're both safe, thank God! and reunited at last.

I'm too shaken up to write today. Tomorrow I'll have my joy more under control, and I'll tell all then.

*   *   *

I still find it difficult to write, but it's even more difficult not to. So though I shall set down the misadventure that now finds a happy ending, I'll skip most of the details, like someone leaping from stone to stone to cross a stream.

On Wednesday, 8 July, the *Sanctus Dionisius* crawled into Amsterdam harbour like a captured beast on a leash. I was on deck, my canvas bag over my shoulder, my hands on the rail, my eyes on the pink walls, the brown roofs, and the black hats on the quay – though all my thoughts were elsewhere.

As soon as we'd berthed, we were ordered – without violence but without ceremony either – to leave the ship and proceed to a building at the end of the quay. And there we were shut up. It wasn't really a prison – just a space with a roof over it, with sentries on duty at the two doors to prevent us from leaving. We were divided into two or three groups: the one I was in included the few remaining passengers and part of the crew, but not Maurizio or the captain.

On the third day a dignitary from the town came and inspected the premises. When he saw me, he said a few reassuring words, but he still wore a stern expression and he didn't make any definite promises.

A week after that the captain arrived, with various other people I didn't know. He picked out by name the sturdiest of the sailors – clearly to unload the cargo from the ship. They were brought back to the shed at the end of the day, and sent for again the next day, and the day after that.

One question was on the tip of my tongue: when they unloaded the cargo, had they searched the passengers' cabins too? I tried for some time to think of a way of asking that would satisfy my curiosity without arousing suspicion, but in the end I gave up. In the situation I was in, it was dangerous to be too impatient.

How often, in those long days of anxiety and inaction, I thought of Maïmoun, of all he'd told me about Amsterdam, and of all I used to say about it myself. The faraway city had become for us a kind of shared dream, a distant hope. We sometimes talked of going and living there together for a while. And it may even be that Maïmoun is here now, as he planned. As for me, I regret ever having set foot in the place. I regret having come to the country of free men as a prisoner, and having spent so many days and nights in Amsterdam without seeing anything but the wrong side of its walls.

Two weeks went by before they let us back on the *Sanctus Dionisius.* But we weren't allowed to set sail. We might be aboard our ship, but we were still not free, and there were soldiers on patrol all the time.

In order to keep a better watch on us, they confined us all to one part of the ship. My cabin was in the other part, and to avoid giving away my secret I made a point of not going there.

Even when the ship was under way at last, I still waited a while before going back to my former quarters: a squad of Dutchmen stayed on board until we left the Zuider Zee behind and emerged into the North Sea.

Not until today was I able to check that my treasure was still intact in its hiding-place. I've left it there, taking only my notebook and writing materials.

15 August

All the sailors on board are getting tipsy, and I myself have drunk a little.

Strangely enough I didn't get sea-sick this time after we'd left the harbour. And in spite of all my potations, I can walk about the deck quite steadily.

Maurizio, who's just as drunk as his elders, told me that when our ship was seized the captain said that only a third of our cargo was bound for London and the other two-thirds were going to a merchant in Amsterdam. Once ashore, he sent for this man, whom he knew very well, but as the friend was out of town he had to wait for his return. Then things moved fast. The merchant sized up the situation, saw his advantage, confirmed what Centurione had said, and took delivery of the goods. The Dutch authorities confiscated the other third of the cargo, then released the ship and the people on it.

Well, our captain seems sharp enough, though I still maintain he's crazy! Unless he's two different people alternately.

17 August

According to Maurizio, our captain has fooled the Dutch again. He made them think he was going back to Genoa, whereas in fact he's heading straight for London!

19 August

We're sailing up the Thames estuary, and I haven't any companions left on board – I mean anyone with whom I can have a proper conversation. Given that there's nothing else to do, I should get down to some writing. But my mind's a blank, and my hand is reluctant.

London. I never dreamed I'd see it, yet I'll soon be there.

Monday, 23 August 1666

We reached the landing-stage of the port of London at first light today. The English are so wary after their recent confrontations with the Dutch that we were intercepted three times as we came up the estuary.

As soon as we arrived, I left my meagre belongings at an inn by the river near the docks, and went in search of Cornelius Wheeler. I knew from what Pastor Coenen had said that his shop was near St Paul's Cathedral, and found my way to it by making inquiries of some other merchants.

Having asked to see Master Wheeler, I was shown upstairs by a young clerk and greeted by a very old man with a thin, sad countenance, who turned out to be Cornelius's father. His son was in Bristol, he told me, and wouldn't be back for two or three weeks. But if I needed a book or any information in the meantime, the old gentleman would be happy to help me.

I'd already introduced myself, but as my name didn't seem to mean anything to him, I explained that I was the Genoese friend to whom Cornelius had lent his house in Smyrna.

"I hope nothing went wrong?" said the old man anxiously.

No, he needn't worry, the house was quite all right. I hadn't come to London on that account, but to attend to business of my own. I chatted to him about it for a while, telling him of the books that sell well in my part of the world and those that are no longer in demand. He was bound to be interested since we're both in the same trade.

At one point I mentioned *The Hundredth Name*, hinting that I knew Cornelius had brought it back from Smyrna. The old man didn't actually start, but I caught a gleam of curiosity, perhaps not unmingled with mistrust, in his eye.

"Unfortunately I don't read Arabic. I can tell you exactly what we have on our shelves in Italian, French, Latin and Greek, but for Arabic and Turkish you'll have to wait for Cornelius."

I told him in detail what the book looked like – its dimensions, the concentric gold patterns on the green leather binding. Then the young clerk, who was hanging about listening to us, chipped in.

"Isn't that the book the chaplain came for?"

The old man looked daggers at him, but the damage was done and it was too late to try to cover it up.

"Yes, it must be. We sold it a few days ago. But look around – I'm sure you'll find something that interests you.

He asked the lad to bring various volumes, but I didn't even try to register their names. I didn't intend to let myself be thrown off the scent.

"I've come a long way to get that book," I said, "and I'd be grateful if you'd tell me where I can find that chaplain so that I can try to buy it from him."

"Excuse me – I'm not supposed to tell you who buys what, and especially not to reveal a customer's address."

"But if your son trusts me enough to lend me his house and everything in it –"

I didn't have to go on.

"Very well," said the old gentleman. "Jonas will take you there."

On the way, no doubt misled by having heard me attempt a few words in English, the lad bestowed on me a flood of all but incomprehensible confidences. I just nodded from time to time as I observed the crush in the narrow streets. I did manage to make out that the man we were going to see had once been a chaplain in Cromwell's army. Jonas couldn't tell me his real name, and seemed not even to understand my question. He'd never heard him called anything but "chaplain".

As the man who'd bought the book was a churchman, I thought we must be on the way to the nearby cathedral, or some church or presbytery. What was my surprise, then, when we stopped at a dubious, ramshackle place defined by a sign outside as an ale-house. Inside, we felt the glazed stare of a dozen pairs of eyes. The room was dark as twilight, though it wasn't yet noon. Conversation had dropped to a murmur, though I could tell I was its subject. They can't often see Genoese finery there. I gave a little nod, and Jonas asked the landlady – a tall plump woman with shiny hair and a half-naked bosom – if the chaplain was there. She merely pointed upwards. We went along a passage to a flight of creaky stairs, at the top of which the lad knocked on a closed door and, without waiting for an answer, opened it, calling out:

"Chaplain!"

He didn't look at all like a cleric to me. Well, perhaps I exaggerate. He did have a kind of natural solemnity. He was tall, too, and had a bushy beard, though this made him look more like an Orthodox priest than an English clergyman. Wearing a mitre and a chasuble and holding a crozier, he might have resembled a bishop addressing his congregation. As it was, he radiated neither piety, nor odour of sanctity, nor any kind of temperance. On the contrary, he struck me straight away as a heathen roisterer. There were three mugs of beer on the low table in front of him, two of them empty and one two-thirds full. He'd probably just taken a swig: there was some white froth on his moustache.

He smiled broadly and asked us to sit down. But Jonas said he had to go back to his master. I gave him a coin, and the chaplain asked him to order us a couple of pints as he went out. The landlady, very eager and respectful, soon brought them up to us, and the man of God thanked her with a slap on the behind – not a discreet tap, but a hearty, obvious one that seemed intended to shock me. I didn't try to hide the fact that I was embarrassed – I think they'd both have been very annoyed otherwise.

Before the landlady appeared, I'd introduced myself to the chaplain and told him I'd just arrived in London. I made a painful attempt to speak English, but to spare me further suffering my host answered me in Latin – a scholarly Latin that sounded very strange in those surroundings. I imagine he was trying to paraphrase Virgil or some other classical poet when he said:

"So, you have left a land watered by Grace to come to this country harrowed by Malediction!"

"What little I've seen of England so far hasn't given me that impression," I replied. "On the contrary, I've noticed that the people here have a very liberal attitude and are strikingly cheerful."

"That's what I said – a cursed place! You have to shut yourself away and drink all day if you want to feel free. If a jealous neighbour accuses you of blasphemy, you're publicly flogged. And if you look too healthy for your age you're suspected of witchcraft. I'd rather be taken prisoner by the Turks."

"That only shows you've never seen the inside of the Sultan's jails!"

"Perhaps," he admitted.

But the atmosphere relaxed after the landlady had come and gone, and despite my earlier moment of discomfiture, I felt sufficiently at ease to tell my host straight out why I'd come to see him. As soon as I mentioned *The Hundredth Name*, his face lit up and his lips twitched. Thinking he was going to tell me something about the book, I paused, my heart thumping. But he merely smiled more broadly and waved his wooden mug to encourage me to go on. So I went on, and told him exactly why I was interested. This was a risky thing to do. If the book really did contain the saving name, how could I ask him, a priest, to sell it to me, and for how much? A better bargainer would have spoken of the book and its contents in more moderate terms, but I felt instinctively that it would be wrong to try to outsmart him. I was seeking the book of salvation; how could I, under the eye of God, obtain it by deceit? Could I ever outwit Providence?

So I made myself tell the chaplain quite plainly how much the text in question is worth. I told him all that the booksellers say about it, about the doubts entertained as to its authenticity, and the various speculations rife about its alleged virtues.

"And you?" he said. "What do you think about it?"

He always wore the same unvarying smile. I couldn't make it out, and was starting to find it annoying. But I tried not to let on.

"I've never quite decided. One day I think it's the most valuable thing

303

in the world, and the next I'm ashamed of having been so gullible and superstitious."

His smile had vanished. He raised his mug towards me like a censer, then emptied it in a single draught. This, said he, was as a tribute to my sincerity, which he had never expected.

"I thought you would tell me some typical merchant's tale and say you were trying to find the book for a collector, or that your father had told you about it on his deathbed. I don't know if you were being honest by nature or out of supreme cunning – I don't know you well enough to say – but I like your attitude."

He paused, picked up his empty mug, put it down on the table again, then burst out:

"Open the curtain behind you! The book's there!"

I sat there for a moment, stunned, wondering if I'd understood aright. I'd got so used to traps, disappointments and unpleasant surprises that to be told quite simply that the book was there behind me took my breath away. I even wondered whether it mightn't be due to the beer I'd swallowed so thirstily.

Anyhow, I stood up and ceremoniously drew aside the dark and dusty curtain my host had indicated. The book was there. *The Hundredth Name.* I'd have expected to find it in some sort of casket with a candle on either side, or open on a lectern. But no, it was just lying on a shelf with a few other books, together with some pens, a couple of ink-wells, a stack of blank paper, a packet of pins, and a jumble of other odds and ends. I picked it up very gingerly and opened it at the title page, doing all I could to make sure it was the book which old Idriss had given me last year and which I'd thought lost for ever in the depths of the sea.

Was I surprised? Of course I was surprised. And understandably shaken. It was like a miracle! On my very first day in London, when I've scarcely got used to being on dry land, the book I've been trying to track down for a year has fallen into my hands! My host waited for me to recover, to drift slowly back to my chair clasping the book to my beating heart. Then he said – it wasn't a question:

"That's the one you were looking for . . ."

I said it was. To tell the truth, the room was so dark I could scarcely see. But I'd glimpsed the title, and before that I'd recognised the title on the cover. I hadn't any doubt whatsoever.

"I suppose you can read Arabic perfectly."

Yes, I said again.

"In that case I'd like to propose a bargain."

I looked up, still clutching my new-found treasure. The chaplain looked extremely thoughtful: his head seemed more imposing than ever, and more massive, even without his greying beard and hair.

"Yes, a bargain," he repeated, as if to gain a little more time for reflection. "You want to own this book, and I just want to understand what's in it. Read it to me from end to end, and then you can have it."

Again, without a shadow of hesitation, I agreed.

How right I was to come to London! My lucky star was waiting for me here! My persistence has paid off! The obstinacy I inherited from my ancestors has served its purpose! I'm proud to be of their blood, and to have lived up to it!

London, Tuesday 24 August 1666

I know it's not going to be easy.

It'll take me a good number of sessions to get through those 200-odd pages, translating them from Arabic into Latin, not to mention explaining what they mean when the author never intended them to be explicit. But the chaplain's unexpected suggestion immediately struck me as an opportunity, if not a sign. He's offering me an opportunity not only to get Mazandarani's book back, but also to study it as I never would have done for myself. To have to read every sentence and translate every word so as to make it intelligible to a demanding listener is no doubt the best way of finding out once and for all if the book really does contain some great secret truth.

The more I think about it, the more excited I feel, but I'm puzzled too. I've had to follow this book from Gibelet to Constantinople, and from Genoa to London, and then to that tavern and the lair of that peculiar chaplain, in order to start on this necessary labour at last. It's almost as if everything that's happened to me this last year has been merely a prelude, a series of tests that God wanted me to go through so that I might be worthy of discovering His hidden name.

I said "this last year", and indeed it's exactly a year ago to the day that my long journey began: it was on Monday, 24 August 1665 that I left Gibelet. The entry I wrote in my journal on that occasion isn't to hand – I do hope Barinelli found that notebook and kept it and can send it back to me one day!

But I'm straying from the point. I was saying that if I could re-read the pages I wrote at the beginning of my journey, I wouldn't find much resemblance between my original plan and the route I eventually followed. I didn't expect to go any further than Constantinople – certainly not to England. Nor did I expect to find myself all alone like this, without any of the people with whom I set out, and not knowing what has become of them all. In the course of the year everything has changed around me, and inside me too. Sometimes I think the only thing that hasn't changed is my desire to go back home to Gibelet. But no – if I consider the question at more length, I'm not so sure. Since my visit to Genoa, I sometimes feel that's the place I ought to go back to. That's where I'm from – my family, if not I myself. Despite the fact that Bartolomeo, my distant forbear, came down in the world when he tried to go back there and make a fresh start, I believe it's only in Genoa that an Embriaco can really feel at home. In Gibelet I shall always be a foreigner. And yet my sister lives in the Levant, and it's there that my parents are buried. My house is there, and so is the shop that makes me reasonably well off. I nearly added that the woman I've learned to love lives there too. My mind must be playing me tricks. Marta isn't in Gibelet any more. I don't know if she'll ever be able to go back there. I don't even know if she's still alive.

Perhaps that's enough for this evening.

25 August

I'm beginning again in order to go into the question of dates. I was meaning to do so yesterday evening, but the thought of Marta made me forget. Here in London there's a muddle about dates that I never suspected. For us, as I've noted at the head of the page, it's the 25th of August, but for the people who live here it's only the 15th! Out of hatred for the Pope, whom everyone here is supposed to regard as the "Antichrist", the English, like the Muscovites, refuse to follow the Gregorian calendar, which we adopted more than eighty years ago.

There are several comments I could make about this, but I'm expected at the ale-house. That's where our readings are to take place, and that's where I shall be staying from now on. I objected to this arrangement at first, wishing to keep my distance: they're very hospitable folk, but I don't know them well enough to want to be with them all day and all night. But yesterday evening after dinner, when I left to go back to my inn, I had a feeling I was being watched. It was more than a feeling; I was sure of it. Was it thieves? Government agents? In either case, I had no desire to repeat the experience every evening.

I know it's unwise to have so much to do with a man like the chaplain, who was once an influential character and whom the authorities still regard with suspicion. If all I was concerned with was my own safety, I'd have kept my distance. But my first concern is not prudence – if it were, I wouldn't have come to London looking for *The Hundredth Name*, and there are a lot of other things I wouldn't have done. No, my object now is to get the book back, and leave as soon as possible with it under my arm. And it's by living near this man and keeping my contract with him that I can achieve my object fastest.

After settling me in a top-floor room just over the chaplain's and away from the din that usually prevailed in the main part of the ale-house, Bess, the landlady, came upstairs three times to make sure I had everything I needed.

These people are easy to get on with – hospitable, kind, fond of laughter and good food. Living here will probably be very pleasant. But I shan't stay too long.

26 August

This morning I was due to start reading *The Hundredth Name* aloud. But I soon had to stop, for a strange and highly disturbing reason.

There were four of us there in the chaplain's room: he'd invited a couple of young men, apparently followers of his, to act as scribes. One of them, whose name was Magnus, was to write down the Latin translation of the text, and the other, Calvin, was to record the comments.

I said I "was due" to start the readings, because things didn't turn out out as we'd expected. I'd begun by reading and translating the overall title, *The Unveiling of the Hidden Name of the Master of Creatures,* then Mazandarani's full name – Abu-Maher Abbas son of So-and-so, son of So-and-so, son of So-and-so . . . But I had scarcely turned the first page when the room went dark, as if the sun had been covered by a cloud of soot and its rays could no longer reach us. Could no longer reach me, I should say, for none of the other people in the room seemed to have noticed anything.

At the same moment, the door opened and Bess brought us in some beer. This gave me a brief respite, but soon all eyes were on me again, and the chaplain, puzzled by my silence, asked me what was the matter, why didn't I go on reading? I told him I had a splitting headache and couldn't see properly, and he said I'd better go and rest so that we could go on with the reading tomorrow.

I closed the book, and immediately felt I was back in the light again. A great sense of well-being swept over me, but I was careful to conceal it lest the others think my brief illness had been assumed.

Now, as I write this account, it's almost as if I only imagined that passing darkness. But I know without a shadow of doubt that I wasn't dreaming. Something happened to me, but I don't know what to think or say about it. That's why I didn't tell the chaplain the truth when he asked me why I'd stopped reading. Whatever it was, it brought back the memory of something that had happened more than a year before and hadn't seemed at all mysterious at the time. I'd come back from old Idriss's house with the book he'd given me, and as I leafed through it in my shop I couldn't manage to read it, although the light there was quite adequate. The same thing had happened the previous day, in Idriss's shack, though I'd taken even less notice then. Of course, his place was very poorly lit, but not so badly as to make the pages of the book itself illegible: I'd had no trouble reading the title page, where the characters were not much larger.

All very inexplicable and alarming.

Could there be a curse on the text itself?

Or was the strange happening due to my own terror at being about to see the supreme name there, written down, before my very eyes?

I wonder whether the same thing hasn't happened to everyone who has tried to approach *The Hundredth Name.* Perhaps the text is protected by some magic spell, some amulet or talisman?

If that's so, I'll never get anywhere. Unless the curse or spell is lifted somehow.

But doesn't its very existence prove that the book is unique, and contains the most precious, unspeakable, formidable and forbidden of truths?

27 August 1666

Yesterday evening, as I was still writing my travel journal by daylight – it gets dark very late here – I was surprised to see Bess enter my room. She had knocked, but the door was ajar, so she came straight in. Without undue haste, I put my notebook away under the bed, meaning to get it out again when she'd gone. But she stayed for a long while, and afterwards I'd forgotten what I meant to write.

She said she was worried about my headache, and said she'd get rid of it for me. She talked about "undoing the knot" in my shoulders or the nape of my neck, and the phrase awakened my curiosity. She made me sit on a low chair, then stood behind me and patiently kneaded me, flesh and bones alike, with her fingers and the palms of her hands. As I didn't have the pain I'd laid claim to, just a vague unidentifiable discomfort, I couldn't judge whether her treatment was effective or not. But I was touched by the trouble she'd gone to, and, so as not to hurt her feelings, said I suddenly felt a lot better. She then offered her services during the readings. I hastily declined, and as soon as she'd left the room, burst out laughing. I could just see myself solemnly reading and translating for the benefit of the chaplain and his two disciples while the buxom landlady massaged my neck and back and shoulders. Some of those present might feel rather disturbed, I imagine.

Be that as it may, I'm going to have to find some solution, or my readings will soon come to a halt. Today there was a short bright interval, during which I was able to read a few lines from Mazandarani's introduction, then the darkness returned. I moved a bit closer to the window and thought the text looked more legible there, but that didn't last long, and soon I could see nothing. I and my eyes alike were shrouded in shadow. The chaplain and the two young men looked annoyed and disappointed, but didn't utter any reproaches and agreed to put the reading off till tomorrow.

I'm sure now that some powerful will protects this text from eager eyes. Mine included. I'm not a holy person, I'm no more deserving than the next man, and if I were sitting in the seat of the Most High, I certainly wouldn't reveal my most precious secret to someone like me! Me, Baldassare Embriaco, dealer in curios, honest enough but not pious or saintly, without any sufferings or sacrifices or poverty to put forward – why the devil should God choose me as the repository of His supreme name? Why should He befriend me as He did Noah, Abraham, Moses and Job? I'd have to be very proud and very blind to think for a moment that God might see me as someone exceptional. Some of His creatures are remarkable for their beauty, intelligence, piety, devotion or character – He could be proud of having created them. But about having created me, He can be neither very glad nor very sorry. He must look down on me from His heavenly throne with disdain, or at best with indifference.

And yet here I am in London having crossed half the world in pursuit of this book, and having, contrary to all expectations, found it again! Is it too crazy to think that, despite all I've just said, the Most High is watching me, and guiding me along paths I would never have trod without Him? Every day I hold *The Hundredth Name* in my hands; I've already made a beginning on some pages; I'm advancing step by step through the labyrinth. All that holds me back is this strange blindness, but perhaps that's only one more obstacle, one more test that I'll get past in the end. Because of my own perseverance or obstinacy, or through the unfathomable will of the Master of Greatness.

28 August 1666

There was another bright interval today, and it lasted a bit longer than yesterday's. Perhaps my perseverance is bearing fruit. There was a kind of veil over my eyes all the time, or over the book, but it didn't completely blot out the words. I was able to read three whole pages before the shadow got too dark and the lines too blurred for me to go on.

. In those pages Mazandarani endeavours to refute the widespread view that the supreme name, if it exists, must not be uttered by man because those beings and things which may be named are those over which some authority may be exercised, whereas it is evident that God cannot be subject to any domination. To counter this objection, Mazandarani makes a comparison between Islam and Judaism. While the religion of Moses punishes anyone who utters the unspeakable name, and tries to avoid all direct mention of the Creator, the religion of Mahomet adopts a diametrically opposite attitude, exhorting the faithful to speak the name of God day and night.

In fact, I told the chaplain and his disciples, in Islamic countries the name of Allah crops up ten times in every conversation. Both parties to every bargain swear by Him all the time as "wallah", "billah", or "bismillah". There isn't a phrase of welcome, farewell, threat or exhortation, or even of exhaustion, that doesn't explicitly invoke Him.

This encouragement to keep repeating the name of God applies not only to Allah but also to the ninety-nine names attributed to Him, together with a hundredth name in the case of those who know it. Mazandarani quotes the verse from which all the debates about the supreme name derive – "Glorify the name of your Lord, the most high" – pointing out that the Koran not only tells us there is a name consisting of the phrase "most high", but also clearly calls on us to glorify God by that name.

As I read this passage, I remembered what Prince Ali Esfahani told me when we were at sea together. And I now felt convinced, despite his denials, that he had had occasion to read Mazandarani's book; and so I wondered whether as he did so he had experienced the same temporary blindness as I did. It was while I was revolving all this in my mind that everything went dark again, and I had to stop reading. I clutched my head as if struck by a very bad headache, and my companions sympathised and suggested remedies. Magnus, who is also subject to such attacks, said the best thing was to remain in complete darkness. If only he knew!

*

Although today's session was cut short, my colleagues seemed less disappointed than before. I had managed to read to them, and translate, and expound the text, and if I could go on like that the book would soon hold no more secrets for them – or for me.

We're to skip tomorrow and continue on Monday. I only hope I can perform then as well as I did today. I don't ask God to remove the veil from my eyes once and for all. All I beg is that He should lift a bit more of it every day. Is that still too much to ask?

Sunday, 29 August

All the others went to mass early this morning. It's compulsory here, and people who don't go are often denounced by their neighbours and imprisoned or flogged or subjected to other harassments. I, as a foreigner and a "Papist", am let off. But I've been told I'd be wise not to flaunt my impious face in the streets. So I stayed out of sight in my room, relaxing, reading and writing. I don't often get the chance.

My room is like a little tower overlooking the city; to the right there's an expanse of roofs, and to the left is St Paul's Cathedral, so huge that it seems quite close. The bed takes up most of the space in my room, but if I clamber on a few crates and climb up through the rafters I can find a cool spot. I sat up there in the shade for some time. If there were bugs and rats, I didn't see any. All morning I felt perfectly peaceful, glad that everyone had forgotten me and hoping they'd go on doing so even if it meant I didn't get anything to eat till the evening.

30 August

We were supposed to go on with the readings today, but the chaplain, without giving me any warning, failed to turn up. So did his young men. Bess says they'll be back in three or four days. She looked worried, but didn't tell me anything.

So this was another idle day. I didn't mind. But instead of doing nothing in my room, I decided to take a stroll round London.

I feel such a stranger here! It seems to me that people are looking at me all the time, looking at me in an unfriendly way. I've never seen travellers regarded with such hostility. Is it because of the war still going on with the Dutch and the French? Or because of the old civil wars that have set brother against brother, son against father, and filled everyone with bitterness and suspicion? Or is it because of the fanatics, who are still very numerous, and are hanged as fast as possible when they are found? Perhaps it's all these things, because enemies, real and imaginary, are so thick on the ground.

I wanted to go and see St Paul's Cathedral, but I gave up the idea, fearing some sexton might take against and denounce me. All "Papists" are suspect here, especially if they're from Italy – at least that was the impression I got while I was walking about. I had to struggle all the time to overcome my uneasiness.

The only place I felt safe was in the bookshops near St Paul's Churchyard. There, instead of being a foreigner and a Papist, I was a customer and a colleague.

I've always thought, and now I'm convinced of it, that trade is the only respectable activity and those engaged in it the only people who are civilised. The scoundrels Jesus drove out of the Temple must have been not merchants, but soldiers and priests!

31 August

I was getting ready to go out to browse round the bookshops again, when Bess invited me to have a beer with her. We sat down at a table in a corner of the tavern as if we were customers, and though she got up from time to time to serve drinks or chat with the regulars, on the whole there weren't more than the usual number of people about, and the place was neither so quiet that we had to whisper, nor so noisy that we had to shout.

I couldn't catch every single word she said, but I think I understood most of it, and it was the same for her. Even when I got carried away and spoke more in Italian than in English, she nodded vigorously to show she'd followed. I was ready to believe her. Anyone endowed with reason and goodwill must be able to understand a bit of Italian!

We each had two or three pints – she slightly more perhaps – but we weren't there just for the drink. Nor because we hadn't anything better to do, or out of curiosity, or just to have someone to talk to. We both needed a friendly ear and a friendly hand. I think of it with wonder: for I've just discovered, after forty years of existence, how fulfilling it can be just to spend a few hours in close yet blameless contact with a woman you don't know.

Our long conversation started with a kind of childish game. We were sitting with our mugs in our hands: we'd just clinked them and wished one another good health in the usual way. She was smiling, and I was wondering if we'd be able to find anything else to say, when she took a penknife out of her apron pocket and marked a rectangle on the board in front of us.

"That's our table," she said.

Then she drew one little circle on my side and another on her side.

"That's me and that's you."

I'd guessed, and waited for what followed.

She reached out and boldly carved a wandering line from one side of

the table to the little circle that stood for me; then, from the other side
of the table, an even more tortuous line leading to the little circle that
stood for her.

"I came from here, you came from there. And now we're both sitting
at the same table. I'll tell you how I got here – will you tell me how
you did?"

I shall never be able to remember exactly all Bess told me today, about
herself and about London and England in recent years – the wars, the
revolutions, the executions, the massacres, the fanatics, the plague . . .
I thought I knew something about this country before, but now I see I
knew nothing.

How much of all that should I write down here? Well, to begin with
I'll record what she says about the people I've been mixing with since
I got here. Then whatever has to do with the object of my journey,
and the rumours and beliefs predicting the end of the world. But
nothing else.

And what I do mean to write about I shan't deal with tonight. All
of a sudden, my head feels heavy, and I find it hard to find words
or sort out my thoughts. So I shall go to bed without waiting for
it to get dark. I'll get up early in the morning and start again with
a clear head.

Wednesday, 1 September 1666

This morning I woke with a start. I'd just remembered something my
Venetian friend said on the ship taking us to Genoa – I must have
written it down in the missing notebook. Didn't he say the Muscovites
expected the end of the world to take place today, the 1st of September,
the beginning of their New Year? It was only after I'd splashed my face
with cold water that it struck me that in both Moscow and London today
is Wednesday, 22 August. So it was a false alarm. There are still ten more

days till the end of the world. I still have time to lounge about, chat with Bess, and visit the booksellers.

I only hope I'll take it all as lightly in ten days' time!

But that's enough bluster. I must write down what Bess told me before I forget. After a day and a night, some parts of it are getting vague already.

She told me first about the plague. A very young man had just come into the main room of the tavern, and she said, with a lift of her chin in his direction, that he was the last surviving member of his family. She herself had lost several relations. When was it? Last summer. She lowered her voice and whispered in my ear: "People are still dying of the plague, but you get into trouble if you talk about it." The king had had masses said to thank God for ending the epidemic, so anyone who said it wasn't over was more or less accusing God and the king of lying! But the truth is that plague still lurks on in the city of London, and it kills – a score of people a week, sometimes two or three times as many. Admittedly, that's not many when you think that a year ago the plague was killing more than a thousand Londoners every day! At first, the victims were buried at night so as not to frighten the rest of the population, but when the situation worsened even that precaution had to be abandoned. Then they started collecting up corpses by day as well as night. Carts went through the street, and people threw the bodies of their parents, their children and their neighbours on them as if they were old mattresses!

"At first," said Bess, "you are afraid for your nearest and dearest. But as more and more people die, you have only one thought in your head – to escape, to escape, even if the rest of the world should perish! I didn't weep for my sister or my five nephews and nieces, or for my husband, God forgive me! I had no tears left! I must have gone through it all like a sleepwalker, only wondering if it would ever end."

The rich and powerful, beginning with the king and the heads of the church, had fled the city. The poor had stayed behind because they had nowhere to go; those who'd tried to wander the roads were dying of hunger. But there were some noble souls – some doctors, some men of religion – who kept endeavouring to fight the evil, or at least to allay the sufferings of others. Our chaplain was one of these. He could have left too, said Bess. He's not destitute, and one of his brothers has a house in Oxford, one of the towns least affected by the epidemic. But he didn't want to run away. He stayed here in this neighbourhood, persisting in visiting the sick, consoling them. He told them the world was about to end, and they were just departing a little while before the others. In a while, when they were living in the gardens of Paradise, surrounded by the delicious fruits of Eden, they would watch the rest of mankind arrive, and it would be their turn to be the comforters.

"I saw him at my sister's bedside," Bess told me. "He held her hand and managed to comfort her as she was dying – so much so that she gave what looked like a blissful smile. It was the same with all those he went to see. He disregarded his friends' advice and disregarded quarantine. You should have seen him striding through the streets, when everyone else was hiding away – that great white figure, with its white robes, long grey hair and long grey beard – just like God the Father! When other people saw a red cross drawn on the door of a house, they crossed themselves and went another way round to avoid it. He walked straight up to it. One day God will give him his reward."

But the authorities didn't show any gratitude for all that devotion, and the populace showed still less. At the end of last summer, when the plague was beginning to weaken, he was arrested by a halberdier for spreading the disease through his visits to the sick. And when he was released a week later, he found his house had been burned to the ground. Someone had spread a rumour that he possessed a secret potion that allowed him to survive, but that he wouldn't share with others. While he was in prison, a gang of ragamuffins broke into his house looking for the potion. They wrecked the place, took away everything they could carry, and set fire to the rest, partly in a rage at not finding what they were looking for, partly to cover up their traces.

Everyone wanted to force him out of the city, said Bess. But she, out of gratitude, offered to put him up. And she was proud of it. Why was everyone against the old man? I asked. Because of his past activities, Bess said. She went into it all at length, quoting dozens of names, most of which I'd never heard of. So I don't remember much of it. But I do recall that our man, who'd been a chaplain in Cromwell's army, had later quarrelled with him and tried to raise a revolt against him. This is why, at the restoration of the monarchy six years ago, when the leaders of Cromwell's revolution were persecuted or sent into exile, and the body of the Protector himself was dug up and publicly hanged and burned, the chaplain was let off comparatively lightly. But he wasn't pardoned. No one who rebelled against the crown or was implicated in any way in the execution of King Charles will ever be pardoned. So – according to Bess – the chaplain is and always will be, until he dies and even after that, an outcast.

There's one last thing I want to mention briefly in case it slips my memory, though I mean to come back to it later at more length. It's this. England's misfortunes began – like others' – in 1648. The date keeps cropping up: the end of the German wars; the advent of the Jewish year of the Resurrection and the beginning of the great persecutions that Maïmoun told me about; the publication of the Russian book of the Faith, which fixed the present year as the date when the world would end. And of course, in England, the beheading of the king, for which the whole country is still accursed, took place, according to the calendar used here, at the end of 1648. And for me that was the year of the visit by the pilgrim from Muscovy, which was the cause of my own misfortunes as well as the year of my father's death, in July.

It's as if a door opened that year, an unlucky door that let through various disasters for the world and for me. I remember Boumeh speaking of the three last steps, three times six years, that would lead from the year of the prologue to the year of the epilogue.

Reason tells me that juggling with figures like that only suggests all kinds of things without proving anything. And for the moment, for this evening at least, I'm still trying to listen to the voice of reason.

The day before yesterday, when I was describing my long conversation with Bess, I spoke of our "close but blameless contact". Since last night it has become a little more close and considerably less blameless.

I'd spent the whole day writing, making very slow progress. Because of the method I use, it's always a laborious business. I write in my own language, Italian, but in Arabic characters and in my own special code, and that means going through several stages before setting down every word. When, on top of all that, I have to try to remember what Bess told me in English . . .

But I did get somewhere, witness all the text I managed to produce yesterday morning and evening. I didn't cover all I'd have liked to, but I have unburdened my memory of some things that might otherwise have been lost.

Bess came up twice to bring me food and drink, and lingered a while to watch me producing all those mysterious characters running from right to left. I don't hide my notebook any more when I hear her coming: she knows all my secrets now, and I trust her. But I do let her think I'm writing in ordinary Arabic. I'll never tell her – or anyone else! – that I'm using a special code of my own.

When the tavern had closed for the evening, Bess came and suggested we dine and chat together as we had yesterday. I said I'd join her downstairs, at the same table as before, as soon as I'd finished my paragraph.

But the paragraph spun itself out, and I didn't want to stop in case, if a further conversation intervened, I should forget something. I forgot my promise and wrote on regardless. Meanwhile, my landlady had time to tidy the room downstairs and then come up again to see what was keeping me.

Instead of being annoyed at my remissness, she tiptoed out and came back a few minutes later with a tray, which she left on the bed. I said I had only a few lines to finish and then we'd dine together. She signed to me to take my time, and went out again.

But I got absorbed in my work again, forgetting both the woman and the dinner once more, and assuming she had forgotten me. But when at last I did call her, she came straight in as though she'd been waiting outside the door – smiling still and showing no impatience. I was surprised and touched by such considerate behaviour, and thanked her for it. She blushed. Bess, who didn't blush at a hearty slap on the backside, was blushing at a word of thanks!

The tray held some smoked meat cut into fine slices, a cheese, some white bread, and a mug of what she calls "buttered" beer, though it's very spicy. I asked if she'd like to eat with me, but she said she was never hungry at mealtimes – she nibbled at bits and pieces all day as she waited on her customers. She'd just brought herself a mug of buttered beer so that we could toast each other. So, after watching me write, she now watched me eat. She looked at me exactly as my sister Pleasance used to look at me, and before that my poor mother – with a gaze that takes in both the eater and the food, hanging on every mouthful and turning the object of this concentration into a child again. I felt suddenly at home in this stranger's house. I couldn't help thinking of the words of Jesus: "I was an hungred, and ye gave me meat." Not that I was in danger of starving. All my life, excess has been more of a threat than deprivation. But there was something maternal in the way this woman had fed me. I suddenly felt for her – for her bread, her buttered beer, her presence, her watchful smile, her patience, her dirty apron, her awkward figure – a great surge of affection.

She stood there barefoot, leaning against the wall with her mug in her hand. I stood up, holding my own beer to clink mugs with her, but instead took her gently by the shoulders and thanked her again, softly, then dropped a kiss on her forehead, between her eyebrows.

Drawing away, I saw that her eyes were full of tears, and her lips, still trying to smile, were trembling with expectation. She gripped my fingers awkwardly in her plump hand, and I drew her towards me, slowly stroking her hair and her gown. She didn't resist, but clung to me as to a blanket in freezing weather. I held and touched her lightly all over, as if gently exploring the limits of her body, of her quivering face, of the eyelids hiding her tears, even of her hips.

She had changed her dress since her first visit to my room, and was now wearing a shimmering dark green gown that felt like silk. I was tempted to lie down with her on the bed, which was close by, but decided to remain standing. Things were proceeding at a pace of their own, and I didn't want to precipitate matters. It was still almost light outside, and there was no reason why we should shorten our pleasures; one longs to shorten one's sufferings often enough.

Even when she herself wanted to lie down, I still held her upright. I think she was surprised, and puzzled, but she let me take the lead. Lovers lose half the pleasure by lying down too soon. The first phase of love takes place standing up, when you sway about holding one another, dazed, unseeing, unsteady. Isn't it best to draw this stage of things out, to whisper to one another, brush lips, undress one another gradually, and all this still standing up, embracing one another passionately as each garment falls to the floor?

So we stayed like that for some while, drifting round the room exchanging slow murmurs, slow caresses. My hands unclothed, then held her, and on her trembling form my lips patiently sought where to alight to gather nectar, then where else to alight to gather more, from the lids hiding her eyes, to the hands covering her breasts, to her broad bare white hips. The woman, a field of flowers; my fingers and lips, a swarm of bees.

One Wednesday, in Smyrna, in the Capuchin monastery, I had a moment of intense pleasure when Marta and I made love expecting all the time to be interrupted by my nephews, or Hatem, or one of the monks. The taste of this other Wednesday of love, here in London, was just as enchanting, but in a completely different way. There, haste and urgency lent every second a furious intensity. Here, the fact that time was unlimited gave every movement a resonance, a length, and echoes that enriched and deepened it. There, we were like hunted animals, pursued by others and by the feeling that we were doing something forbidden. Here, on the contrary, the city knew nothing about us, the world knew nothing about us, and we didn't feel we were doing wrong. We were living outside good and evil, far away from bans and prohibitions. Out of time, too. The sun was on our side, setting slowly; the night too, promising to be long. We'd be able to drain one another little by little, down to the last drop of delight.

7 September

The chaplain is back, and so are his disciples. There were already in the house when I got up. He didn't tell me why he went away, and I didn't ask. He just muttered an excuse.

I might as well say it at once – something seems to have upset my relationship with these people. I'm sorry about it, but I don't think I could have prevented it.

The chaplain was cross and irritable when he came back, and gave vent at once to his impatience.

"We must buckle down to it today," he announced, "and get something out of this text – if there's anything in it. We'll keep at it day and night as long as necessary, and anyone who falls by the wayside is no friend of mine."

Both his words and his tone surprised me, and so did all the grim faces around me. I said I'd do my best, but the illness that had delayed my readings was not my fault. At this, I thought I detected some sceptical smiles, but didn't feel I had the right to object. I hadn't actually lied: I couldn't help the attacks of blindness. But I'd misrepresented the symptoms and feigned some headaches. Perhaps I ought to have admitted, at the outset, to my strange illness, inexplicable though it was. But it's too late for that now: if I confessed I'd lied, and started describing those extraordinary symptoms, it would only confirm their worst suspicions. So I decided to say nothing, and just try to read as best I could.

But Heaven was not on my side today. In fact, instead of helping it hindered me. The darkness descended as soon as I opened the book. And it wasn't only the book that I couldn't see: the whole room, the people in it, the walls, the table, even the window – all were black as ink.

For a moment I thought I'd gone blind, and told myself that God, after giving me several warnings which I'd obstinately ignored, had decided to punish me as I deserved.

I slammed the book shut. And immediately I could see again. Not completely clearly, as I'd have expected to do at noon, but as if it were evening and the room was lit by candles. There was a thin veil over everything, and it's still there now, as I write. It's as if there were a cloud in the sky just for me. The pages of this notebook have gone a brownish colour, as if they'd aged a hundred years in a day. The more I talk about it the more it worries me. I can hardly go on writing.

But I must.

"What's the matter now?" said the chaplain when I shut the book.

I had the presence of mind to reply:

"I have a suggestion. Why don't I go up to my room, and read and take notes on the book in my own time? Then I'll come back tomorrow morning with the Latin text. If I can avoid headaches by following this method, we can adopt it permanently. And then we'll be able to make regular progress."

I managed to convince them, though the old man accepted my proposal without enthusiasm and made me promise to translate at least twenty pages of text by tomorrow.

So I went upstairs, followed, I suspected, by one or other of the two disciples – I could hear someone pacing back and forth outside my door.

But, as I didn't want to have to object, I pretended not to notice.

Once sitting down at my desk, I opened *The Hundredth Name* in the middle and placed it face down in front of me. Then I picked up this notebook and leafed through it till I found the entry for 20 May – my account of what my Persian friend told me about the debate on the hidden name of God and about Mazandarani's views on the subject. Using this journal entry as a basis for the content, I wrote out what I shall put forward tomorrow as a translation of Mazandarani's own text. For the style, I used my recollections of what little I'd been able to read from the beginning of the cursed tome.

Why do I call it "cursed"? Is it really accursed? Or is it blessed? Or bewitched? I still don't know. All I do know is that it's protected. Protected from me, anyhow.

8 September

All went well. I read out my Latin translation, and Magnus copied it down word for word. The chaplain said that's how we ought to have set about it from the beginning, and urged me to work faster.

I hope that's only a sign of renewed enthusiasm, and that he'll moderate his expectations. Otherwise, I fear the worst. The subterfuge I've resorted to so far can't be kept up indefinitely. Today I called partly on what Esfahani told me and partly on my memory. I might still summon up things I've heard about *The Hundredth Name*, but, again, that wouldn't last long. Sooner or later I'm going to have to get through the book itself and quote the name they're all waiting for, whether it's really the Creator's secret name or only what Mazandarani supposes that to be.

Perhaps, in the next few days, I ought to make another attempt at reading . . .

* * *

I started this page full of hope, but my confidence in the future waned in the course of a few lines, just as the light does whenever I open the forbidden volume.

9 September

I spent yesterday evening filling pages with Latin supposed to be a translation of Mazandarani's text. Because of that I have neither the time nor the energy to go on with my own writing, and shall have to be satisfied with brief notes.

The chaplain asked me how many pages I'd managed to translate so far, and I told him forty-three. I might just as easily have said seventeen or seventy. He asked how many were left, and I said 130. He repeated that he hoped I'd finish the reading in a few days now, certainly before the end of next week.

I said I would, but I can feel the trap closing in on me. Perhaps I ought to run away.

10 September

Bess came to me during the night. It was dark, and she slipped into bed beside me. She hadn't been back since the chaplain's return. She left again before dawn.

If I decided to flee, ought I to warn her?

I finished my text for the day this morning. I'm running out of knowledge, and had to fill in the gaps with my imagination. But the others listened to me more intently than ever. Admittedly I quoted Mazandarani as saying that when he reveals the supreme name of God it will fill all who thought they knew it with fear and amazement.

I've probably gained time and a certain amount of credit with my three auditors. But increasing the stake doesn't necessarily bring good luck!

11 September

This is the first day of the Russian New Year. I thought about it all night long. I even dreamed that Evdokim the pilgrim threatened me with retribution and exhorted me to repent.

We met towards noon in the chaplain's room, and I tried to create a diversion by referring to this date. I told them, with only a little exaggeration, what I'd learned from my friend Girolamo on board the *Sanctus Dionisius:* that lots of people in Muscovy believe that today, the feast of St Simeon and the beginning of their New Year, will this year see the end of the world in a deluge of fire.

Despite his disciples' questioning glances, the chaplain remained silent as I spoke, listening abstractedly, almost with indifference. And although he didn't challenge what I'd said, he took advantage of a moment's silence to bring us back to the subject in hand. I grudgingly shuffled my papers together and started on the day's fabrications.

Sunday, 12 September 1666

My God! My God!
  What else can I say?
  My God!
  Can it really have happened?

                    *   *   *

London caught fire in the middle of the night. And now I'm told it's all starting to burn, one district after the other. From my window I can see the flaming apocalypse and hear the shrieks of the terrified people. There's not a star in the sky.

My God! Can the end of the world be like this? Not a sudden void, but a gradually approaching fire, like a rising flood that may eventually swallow me up?

Is it my own end I see approaching as I look out of the window, and that I try to describe as I bend over the page?

The all-devouring fire draws closer and closer, and I sit here at this wooden table, in this wooden room, committing my last thoughts to a sheaf of pages that will ignite at the smallest spark! It's madness, madness! But isn't that just an image of my mortal condition? I dream of eternity when my grave is already dug, piously commending my soul to the One who's about to snatch it away from me. When I was born I was a few years away from death. Now it may be no more than a few hours. But what's a year anyway in comparison with eternity? what's a day? an hour? a second? Such measures have meaning only for a heart that's still beating.

Bess came to sleep with me. We were still in one another's arms when we started to hear shouting nearby. From the window, looking towards the Thames, you could see in the distance, though not all that far away, the monstrous red glow, with tongues of flame shooting up every so often and then subsiding.

Even worse than the flames and the glare was the sinister crackling noise, as if some gigantic beast were crunching up in its jaws the wood all the houses were built of, crushing, grinding, chewing the timbers and then spitting them out.

Bess rushed to her room for some clothes, for she'd come to my room with very little on. When she returned she was soon joined by the chaplain and his two disciples, who had stayed in the tavern overnight. By daybreak they were all gathered together in my room: my window was the highest in the house and had the best view of the fire. Amid all the lamentations, tears and prayers, someone would mention a street or tall building that had been spared by or caught up in the conflagration. As I wasn't familiar with the places in question, I wasn't sure when I should be worried and when relieved. And I didn't want to bother the others with my outsider's questions. So I stayed in the background, away from the window, leaving it to their more experienced observation, while I just stood apart and took in their comments, alarms and other reactions.

After a few minutes we all, one after the other, went down the rickety wooden stairs to the main room of the tavern, where we could no longer hear the noise of the fire but caught echoes of the cries of the ever-increasing and angry-sounding crowd.

If I live long enough to remember anything, I shall remember some quite trivial scenes. Magnus, who'd gone out for a moment, came back in tears because the church of his patron saint, St Magnus's near London Bridge, was on fire. We were to have this kind of news hundreds of times that wretched day, but I'll never forget the distress of that young man, so devoted to his religion, silently accusing Heaven of having betrayed him.

No customers came through the ale-house door the whole morning. Whenever Magnus or Calvin or Bess went outside to see what was happening, we just opened the door a crack to let them out, and the same to let them back in again. The chaplain didn't once get up out of the armchair he'd collapsed into. As for me, I took care not to be seen in the street: rumours had been circulating since dawn that the fire had been lit by "Papists".

I just said the story started at dawn, but that's not quite right. I hope to be accurate until my last breath, and the order of events was in fact slightly different. The rumour that was going round first thing in the morning was that the fire had started in a bakery in the City: an oven hadn't been put out properly, or a maid had fallen asleep, so that the flames had begun by spreading along the neighbouring street. The street in question is Pudding Lane, which is close to the inn where I spent my first two nights in London.

An hour later, someone in our own street told Calvin that the French and Dutch fleets had sailed in and set fire to the town, and intended to use the resulting confusion to make an all-out attack on the capital. We could only expect the worst.

After another hour had gone by, the talk was no longer of foreign fleets, but of agents of the Pope, the "Antichrist", who were trying "yet again" to destroy this good Christian country. I even heard of people being seized by the mob just because they were strangers. It's not a good idea to be a foreigner when London's on fire, so I prudently lay low all day. At first I took refuge in the main room of the tavern, then, when neighbours started coming in there – we could hardly shut the door in their faces – I retreated upstairs to my room, my wooden "observatory".

It was to distract myself from my anxiety that I wrote these few paragraphs, in between long periods spent looking out of the window.

The sun has gone down and still the fire is raging. The air is all red, and the sky seems empty.

Could all the other towns be on fire too? With each one, like London, thinking it's the only Gomorrha?

Could Genoa be burning today too? And Constantinople? And Smyrna? And Tripoli? And even Gibelet?

It's getting dark, but tonight I shan't light any candles. I'll lie down in the darkness, breathe in the wintry smells of burning wood, and pray God to give me the courage to go to sleep one more time.

Monday, 13 September 1666

The apocalypse is not over. It's still going on. And so is my ordeal by fire.

London continues to burn, and I'm hiding from the flames in a nest of dry tinder.

When I woke up, however, I went downstairs and there in the main room of the tavern I found Bess, the chaplain and his disciples slumped in their chairs; they hadn't stirred all night. Bess opened her eyes only to beg me to go back to my hiding-place before anyone saw or heard me. Several foreigners had been apprehended during the night, including two natives of Genoa. She didn't know their names, but she was sure of the facts. She said she'd bring me something to eat, and in her eyes I could see a promise of love as well. But how could we make love with a city burning all round us?

As I was about to slink upstairs, the chaplain caught me by the sleeve.

"It seems your prediction is coming true," he said with a forced smile.

I pointed out with some fervour that it was the Muscovites' prediction, not mine; I'd only passed on what a Venetian friend had first passed on to me. In present circumstances I don't want to be seen as a prophet of doom – harmless gossips have been burned for less! The chaplain saw why I was exercised, and apologised for speaking so thoughtlessly.

When Bess joined me a little while later she relayed further apologies from him: he hadn't spoken to anyone else about the prediction, he'd insisted, and realised he might put me in danger by spreading such stories.

That incident being closed, I asked her for news of the fire. After a brief lull, it had started to spread again, driven by an east wind. The flames had now reached a dozen new streets; I can't remember their names. The one piece of good news was that the fire was advancing only slowly in our own street, even though it's called Wood Street. So there's no plan to evacuate yet. On the contrary, some of Bess's cousins have come and left some of their furniture here: their house is nearer the river, and they're afraid it may soon be consumed by the flames.

But it's only a respite. We may be safe here today, but not tomorrow, and certainly not the day after tomorrow. And if the wind should shift a little to the south we could be trapped and unable to escape. But I haven't mentioned this to Bess. I don't want to look like a Cassandra to her too.

Tuesday, 14 September 1666

I've had to withdraw to the attic. In a state of temporary reprieve, like the house itself, and the city, and the world.

Watching London burn, I ought to be able to write just as Nero fiddled, but I can only manage a few disjointed phrases.

Bess says I should just wait. I mustn't make any noise. I needn't be afraid.

So I'm waiting. I don't stir, I've given up watching the flames, and I expect I'll soon stop writing.

In order to write I need some sense of urgency, but also some peace of mind. Too much peace and my hand gets lazy; too much urgency and it's paralysed.

It seems the mob is searching houses now for those who are supposed to have caused the fire. The guilty parties.

Everywhere I've been this year I've felt guilty. Even in Amsterdam! Yes, Maïmoun, my friend, my brother, can you hear me? Even in Amsterdam!

How am I going to die? By fire? At the hands of the mob?

I'm not writing any more. I'm waiting.

NOTEBOOK IV

Temptation in Genoa

Genoa, Saturday, 23 October 1666

I hesitated for a long time before I started writing again. But finally, this morning, I got myself a new bound notebook, and now, with some delectation, I'm writing the very first page. But I'm not sure I'll go on.

I've already started three other notebooks, meaning to set down my plans, my wishes, my worries, my impressions of cities and men, a few touches of humour or wisdom – like so many travellers and chroniclers before me. But I haven't their talent, and my pages can't equal the ones I used to dust on my shelves. Still, I did my best to record everything that happened to me, even when prudence or pride might have kept me silent, even when I felt tired. Except when I was ill or shut up somewhere, I've written something every evening, or almost. I've filled hundreds of pages in three different notebooks, but not one of them is left. I've written just for the flames.

The first notebook, which told the beginning of my travels, was lost when I had to leave Constantinople in haste. The second was left behind when I was deported from Chios. The third probably got burned in the Great Fire of London. And yet here I am smoothing the pages of the fourth, a mortal oblivious of death, a pitiful Sisyphus forever pushing a rock to the top of a hill only for it to fall down again.

When, in my shop in Gibelet, I had to throw the occasional decrepit old tome on the fire, I could never help sparing an affectionate thought for the poor fellow who wrote it. Sometimes it was the only book he'd written in his whole life – his sole hope of leaving some trace of his passage. But his fame would turn into smoke, just as his body would turn into dust.

I'm describing the death of a stranger. But I'm really talking about myself.

Death. My own death. What can it matter, what can books matter, or fame, if the whole world is about to go up in flames, like London?

My mind's so confused this morning! But I must write. My pen must get up and move over the paper in spite of everything. Whether this notebook survives or burns, I shall write, I shall go on writing.

First, how I got away from the inferno in London.

When the fire broke out, I had to hide to escape the fury of the mob – they wanted to cut the Papists' throats. With no other proof of guilt than the fact that I was a foreigner and from the same country as the "Antichrist", ordinary citizens would have seized, manhandled and tortured me, and then thrown my remains into the flames, feeling that they'd advanced the good of their souls. But I've already spoken of this madness in the notebook that was lost, and I haven't the strength to go over it again. What I do want to say something more about is my fear. Fears, rather. For I had two fears, and then one more. I was afraid of the raging flames and of the raging mob, but also of what this whole sinister episode might mean, happening as it did on the very day the Muscovites had indicated as that of the apocalypse. I don't want to speculate any more about "signs". But how can one fail to be terrified by such a coincidence? All day long on that accursed 11th of September – the 1st of September according to the English calendar – I mulled over that wretched prophecy. I'd discussed it at length with the chaplain. I don't say we were expecting the world to explode from one minute to the next in the vast commotion announced in the Scriptures, but we were on the alert. And it was towards midnight at the end of that very day that the fateful clamour burst out. I could watch the progress of the flames, and hear the cries of the people, from my bedroom.

I had one comfort in my woe, in the devotion of the people round me. They'd become a family to me, whereas three weeks earlier they didn't even know I existed, any more than I knew they did: Bess, the chaplain and his young disciples.

Let no one think my gratitude to Bess was just that of a lonely man who found consolation in the naked arms of a sympathetic innkeeper! What her presence satisfied in me was not the carnal hunger of a traveller: it was my original, fundamental distress. I was born a foreigner, I have lived as a foreigner, and I shall die more of a foreigner still. I'm too proud to talk of hostility, humiliation, resentment, suffering – but I know how to recognise looks and gestures. Some women's arms are places of exile; others are a native land.

After having hidden, protected, fed and reassured me, on the third day of the fire Bess came and told me we must try to make a get-away. The fire was getting inexorably nearer, which meant that the mob was getting farther away. We could attempt to make our way between the two, aiming at London Bridge; there we'd board the first boat available to take us away from the conflagration.

Bess said the chaplain approved of this course of action, though he himself preferred to stay on a while longer in the ale-house. If it escaped the flames, he could protect it from looters. His two disciples would stay on with him to keep watch, and to help him if, after all, he had to flee.

When the time came to leave, I wasn't thinking only of saving my life: I was also concerned about *The Hundredth Name*. The book had been on my mind during all those days and nights, and the clearer it became that my stay in London was approaching its end, the more I wondered if I'd be able to persuade the chaplain to let me take *The Hundredth Name* with me. I even thought of taking it against his will. Yes, of stealing it! I'd never have been capable of such a thing in other circumstances, during an ordinary year. In any case, I'm not sure I'd have gone through with such a despicable thing. Fortunately I didn't have to. I didn't even have to use the arguments I'd prepared. When I knocked at the door of his room to take my leave, the old man asked me to wait for a moment before asking me in. I found him sitting in his usual place, holding the book out towards me with both hands like a kind of offering. The gesture left both of us silent and motionless.

Then he said in Latin, with some solemnity:

"Take it. It's yours. You've deserved it. I promised it to you in return for your undertaking to translate it, and I know quite a lot now about what it says. Without you, I shan't be able to find out any more. Anyway, it's too late."

I was moved. I thanked him, and embraced him. Then we promised each other, without much conviction, that we'd meet again, if not in this world then in the next. "That'll be very soon, as far as I'm concerned," he said. "As far as all of us are concerned!" I answered, indicating all that was going on around us. We'd have embarked on yet another discussion about the fate of the world if Bess hadn't begged me to hurry. She wanted us to set out at once!

Just before we left the house, she turned round one last time to check up on whether I'd pass muster as an Englishman. She made me promise never to open my mouth, never to look people straight in the eye, but just to look sad and exhausted.

It was a quarter of an hour's walk as the crow flies from the ale-house to the river, but we had to take a roundabout route to avoid the fire. Bess sensibly opted for skirting the whole of the area affected. She even started off along an alley on our left that seemed to lead in the opposite direction. I didn't argue. Then came another alley, and a third, and perhaps fifteen or twenty others. I didn't count. I didn't even try to make out where we were. It was all I could do to avoid falling into holes, walking into debris, and stepping in dirt. I followed Bess's mop of red hair as a soldier on the battlefield follows a plume or a standard. I trusted her with my life as a child puts its hand in its mother's. And I had no reason to regret it.

We had only one scare. Emerging into a little square at a place called

Houndsditch, near the city wall, we came on a crowd of about sixty people manhandling someone. Not wanting to show we were running away, Bess went up and asked a young woman what was going on. She was told that another fire had just broken out in the neighbourhood, and the foreigner under attack – a Frenchman – had been found lurking nearby.

I wish I could say I intervened to stop the mob from doing their worst. Or at least that I tried, but Bess prevented me. The sad truth is that I walked on as fast as I could, only too glad to escape notice and not be in the victim's shoes, as I easily might have been. I didn't even look at the crowd, lest our eyes meet. And as soon as my lady friend had, without undue haste, turned into a nearly empty alley, I followed her. Smoke was rising from a half-timbered house. Strangely enough, it was the top storey that was being licked by tongues of flame. But Bess walked on, neither turning back nor hurrying forward, and I did the same. On the whole, if I had the choice, I preferred to die in the fire rather than at the hands of the mob.

We completed the rest of our journey more or less without incident. We were almost choking on the acrid smell, the sky was veiled in smoke, and we were both stiff and short of breath, but Bess had chosen the safest route. We reached the Thames beyond the Tower of London, then turned back to the nearby landing-stage, by Irongate Stairs.

About forty other people were waiting there, some of them women in tears. They were surrounded with piles of chests, bundles large and small, and pieces of furniture; you wondered how they could have got them there. Bess and I must have been travelling lighter than any of them: all I had with me was a canvas bag Bess had lent me. We must have looked very poor, but less unfortunate than the rest. All of them had obviously either lost their houses already or expected to, like most of the city's inhabitants. But in my meagre baggage I had the book for which I'd travelled across half the world, and I was leaving the great disaster unscathed.

At the sight of all the melancholy faces surrounding us, we resigned ourselves to a long wait. But a boat arrived after a few minutes and moored nearby. It was half-full of Londoners fleeing the city; the rest of the space was taken up with piles of casks. There were a few places left for passengers, but two strapping fellows barred the way on board – tall, bearded, brawny-armed rascals with wet scarves wound round their heads.

"A guinea each – man, woman or child!" one of them shouted forbiddingly. "Paid on the nail! No money, no room!"

I signed to Bess, and she said curtly:

"All right – we'll pay."

The man held out a hand. I took it and jumped into the boat, which was placed at an angle so that only one person could board it at once. But when I turned and stretched out a hand to help Bess jump too, she just touched my fingers and then drew back, shaking her head.

"Come on!" I urged.

She shook her head again, and waved a hand in farewell. There was a sad smile on her face, but also, I think, a trace of regret or uncertainty.

Someone pulled me back by my shirt so that others could get on to the boat. Then one of the sailors came to claim the fare. I got two guineas out of my purse, but gave him only one.

I still feel a pang as I write about it. Our farewells were too hasty, too sketchy. I ought to have talked to Bess before the boat arrived and found out what she really wanted. I behaved all the time as if it was understood that she'd come with me, even if it was only for part of the way. But I ought to have seen that she wouldn't be coming with me, that there was no reason why she should leave her tavern and her friends to come with me. Anyway, I'd never asked her to; never even thought of doing so. So why do I always have a sense of guilt whenever I mention her or London? Probably because I left her as I might have left a stranger, while in just a few days she gave me what people much closer to me will never give me in a lifetime. Because I owe her a debt that I can never repay. Because I escaped the inferno of London, and she returned to it without my making sufficient effort to stop her. Because I left her there on the quay without a word of thanks or a sign of affection. Because it seemed to me that at the last moment she was hesitating, and a firm word from me might have made her jump into the boat. And there are other reasons too. I'm sure she doesn't blame me. But it will be a long time before I stop blaming myself.

I can hear Gregorio's voice. He's just back from the harbour. I must go and sit with him and have something to eat. I'll write some more this afternoon, while he's having his siesta.

Over our meal my host talked to me about various matters concerning both our futures. He's still trying to persuade me to stay in Genoa. Sometimes I beg him to desist, and sometimes I give him some hope. The fact is I don't know my own mind. I have a feeling that it's late, time is getting short on the battlefield; and he's asking me to stop rushing about, to settle down and take my place beside him, like a son. It's a great temptation, but I have other temptations. As well as other obligations, other matters of urgency. I already blame myself for having left Bess in too cavalier a manner; how would I feel if I just abandoned Marta to her fate? Marta, who's carrying my child, and who wouldn't be a prisoner today if I'd looked after her better.

I want to spend what little time is left to me wiping out my debts and putting right my mistakes. And Gregorio wants me to forget the past, forget my home and my sister and my sister's sons and my former loves, and start a new life in Genoa.

We are now in the last few weeks of the fateful year. Is this the right moment to begin a new life?

All these questions have exhausted me. I must dismiss them from my mind and get on with my story.

I'd got to where I was on the boat, leaving London. The passengers were muttering that the rogues who were conveying us would end on the gallows. The sailors themselves were singing and laughing, delighted with their spoils. They must have made more money in the last few days than they usually made in a year, and must be praying for God to stoke up the fire indefinitely.

Not content with having extorted all those guineas for the fare, they made haste to land again as soon as we were out of the city, and then drove us off the boat like a herd of cattle. We hadn't been on board for more than about twenty minutes. They told anyone who protested that they'd saved our lives by taking us away from the fire, and we ought to thank them on our bended knees instead of complaining about how much they'd charged. I didn't protest – I was afraid my accent might give me away. And while our "benefactors" made their way back to London to collect more guineas, and most of my companions in misfortune, after a moment's hesitation, set off together for the nearest village, I decided to wait for another boat to come along. One other person did the same – a tall, fair, sturdy fellow, who didn't speak and avoided catching my eye. I hadn't paid much attention to him among the crowd, but now we were alone it was going to be difficult to ignore each other.

I don't know how long we stood there, not saying anything, exchanging covert glances, and pretending to look for something in our bags or a boat on the horizon.

Suddenly seeing the funny side of the situation, I went over to him and said with a broad smile, in the best English I could muster:

"As if the fire wasn't bad enough, we had to fall into the clutches of those vultures!"

At this he seemed inordinately pleased, and approached with open arms.

"So you're from abroad too!" he cried, as if the fact that we were both foreigners made us compatriots.

His English was less rudimentary than mine, but as soon as I told him where I was from he courteously switched to Italian, or what he thought was Italian, for to my ears it was incomprehensible. After I'd asked him three times to repeat the same sentence, he said it in Latin. That was a relief to both of us.

I soon found out quite a lot about him. He was a Bavarian, five years my senior, and since he was nineteen had lived in various foreign cities: Saragossa, Moscow for three years, Constantinople, Gothenburg, Paris, Amsterdam for three and a half years, then London for the last nine months.

"My house burned down yesterday and I lost everything," he said. "All I have left is in this bag."

He'd spoken lightly, as if rather amused, and I wondered at the time whether he wasn't more affected by the disaster than he was prepared to admit. But from speaking to him at length later, I'm sure he was acting quite naturally. Unlike me, he's a real traveller. For him, anything that ties him to a place – walls, furniture, family – eventually becomes unbearable. Anything that makes him move on, even if it's bankruptcy, banishment, war or fire, is welcome.

This passion seized him when he was still a child, during the German wars. He described the atrocities that had been committed in them: whole congregations slaughtered in the churches, villages decimated by famine, entire villages set alight then rased to the ground. Not to mention the hangings, the burnings at the stake, the beheadings.

His father was a printer in Ratisbon. The bishop had commissioned him to print a missal containing a diatribe against Luther, and both his press and his house had been burned down. The family emerged unscathed, but the father was an obstinate man and decided to rebuild house and workshop alike, exactly as they had been before and on the same spot. This swallowed up all his remaining fortune. And as soon as the work was complete, both buildings were burned down again. This time the printer's wife and an infant daughter died in the flames. The son, my new companion, vowed then that he'd never build a house of his own, or encumber himself with a family, or become attached to any piece of land.

He said he was called Georg Caminarius; I don't know his real name. He seems to have unlimited money at his disposal, but is neither prodigal nor parsimonious with it. He was always reticent with me about his income, and despite all my professional skill at sniffing out where money

343

comes from I was never able to make out whether his derives from a legacy, an annuity, or some lucrative business. If it's the latter it can't be very respectable: we had endless conversations during the next few days and he didn't mention it once.

But first I must get back to the account of my flight. After waiting for more than an hour, during which we waved our arms in vain at various passing boats, one did come alongside at last. There were only two men on board, and they said they would take us anywhere we liked so long as it wasn't Holland, and we paid generously.

Georg said we'd like to go to Dover, and they suggested taking us even further – to Calais. They asked four guineas for the trip, two guineas each. In normal times this would have been exorbitant, but seeing what we'd just had to pay for a journey twenty times shorter, we saw no reason to haggle.

The crossing was completed without incident. We stopped twice to take on food and water before emerging from the Thames estuary and heading for the French coast, which we reached on Friday, 17 September. A swarm of urchins descended on us at Calais. They were surprised and contemptuous when they found we had no baggage for them to carry. In the harbour and in the streets, dozens of people came up and asked us if it was true that London had been burned down. They seemed astonished at the news, but not heartbroken.

It was in Calais, the same evening, that, looking for my journal to write down some notes, I found that it was gone.

Had I dropped it as I made my way across London? Or had someone stolen it while I was on the boat? The deck was crowded, and the sailors were dishonest rascals.

Unless I'd left it in my room at the ale-house, or up in the attic. But I seemed to remember putting it away before I went to fetch *The Hundredth Name*. And I still have that in my possession.

Should I be glad that it's my worthless musings that have disappeared, rather than the book that made me travel round the world?

I expect so. I expect so.

Anyhow, I'm relieved not to have lost the florins I was given in Lisbon for Gregorio, and to have been able to give them back to him instead of increasing my debt to him.

There! My pen has got back into its old habits, and is stoutly beginning to keep a travel journal just as if I'd never lost my three previous notebooks, and London hadn't burned down, and the fateful year wasn't advancing inexorably towards its fulfilment.

What else can I do? My pen wields me as much as I wield it. I have to follow its path just as it follows mine.

But how late it is! I've been writing like someone eating after a fast. It's time I left the table.

24 October

It's Sunday, and this morning I went to church at Santa Croce with Gregorio and his family as if I were the son-in-law he'd like me to be. On the way there he took my arm and told me yet again that if I were to settle in Genoa I'd become the founder of a new dynasty of Embriaci that would put the fame of the Spinolas, the Malaspinas and the Fieschi in the shade. I don't despise Gregorio's generous dream, but I can't find it in my heart to share it.

Brother Egidio, my host's cousin, was present at mass. I had lunch with him in April, and gave him letters for my family. I haven't had any replies yet, but it takes three or four months for a letter to get to Gibelet, and the same for an answer to get back.

On the other hand, he told me that only yesterday he'd had some recent news by post from Constantinople which was very surprising and which he'd like to tell me about. Gregorio immediately invited him to come and bless our "humble meal", which he did willingly and with an excellent appetite.

He had the letter on him. It tells of things that happened six weeks ago, and I'm still not sure I believe what it says. It was written by a friend of his, a monk belonging to the same order, who is on a mission to Constantinople. According to the letter, the authorities there heard from a rabbi in Poland that Sabbataï was preparing to foment a revolt, so he'd been taken to the Sultan's palace in Adrianople and told that if he didn't perform a miracle immediately, he'd be tortured and beheaded – unless he repudiated the faith of his fathers and embraced that of the Turks. The miracle Sabbataï was asked to perform – Brother Egidio read me several passages from the letter – consisted of standing naked and acting as a target for the best archers in the Sultan's bodyguard. If he emerged unscathed it would prove that he really was an emissary from God. Sabbataï asked for time to think it over, which was refused. Then he said he'd been considering adopting the faith of Mahomet for some time, and there could be no more suitable place for his conversion than the presence of the Sultan. No sooner had he said this than he had to remove his Jewish skullcap and a servant bound his head in a white turban. His Jewish name was changed to Mehemet Effendi, and he was given the title of "capidji bachi otourak" – which means "honorary guardian of the Sultan's gates" – with the corresponding emoluments.

But according to Brother Egidio, and Gregorio agreed, Sabbataï's apostasy was only apparent – "like that of the Jews in Spain, who are Christians on Sunday and Jews in secret on Saturday". I still doubt whether the story is true. But if it is, and if it happened during the fire of London, how can it not be yet another disturbing sign?

Until other rumours arise and either remove my doubts or confirm them, I'd better go on with the account of my journey, lest new events make me forget the old.

Georg and I stayed only two days and three nights in our hotel in Calais, but that was enough to do us a lot of good. We had separate beds in a large room overlooking the promenade and with a splendid view of the sea. The mornings were windy, with a fine, persistent, driving rain. But the afternoons were fine, and we could see the townspeople strolling about enjoying the sunshine, in families or groups of friends. Georg and I joined them, after buying clean clothes and new shoes at inordinate prices from a cheat near the harbour. I call him a cheat because he sells shoes, though he's not a shoemaker, and clothes, though he's not a tailor, and I have no doubt that he gets his wares from porters and sailors who steal them from travellers, spiriting away one trunk and pretending to mislay another. It sometimes happens that travellers find themselves buying back their own clothes. One day I was told about a Neapolitan who found himself in this situation and demanded his things back: the receivers cut his throat to prevent him going to the police. But that wasn't in Calais. And after all, and in spite of the price we'd had to pay, we were glad to find some decent clothes so quickly.

As we walked along the promenade, talking of this and that, Georg called my attention to how the women about us tripped along holding the men's arms, laughing with them and sometimes resting their heads on their shoulders. And how men and women alike would kiss one another on the cheek when they met – once, twice, three or four times running, sometimes almost on the mouth. This didn't shock me, but it did strike me as odd. You'd never see men and women talking to each other so freely, or cuddling and kissing like that, in Smyrna or Constantinople, in London or Genoa. And my companion said he'd never seen anything like it in all his travels, from Spain to Holland, or from his native Bavaria to Poland and Muscovy. He didn't disapprove of it either, but he couldn't stop looking at it in astonishment.

At dawn on Monday, the 20th of September, we took our places on the public coach from Calais to Paris. We'd probably have done better to hire a coach and coachman of our own, as Georg wanted to do. It would have cost much more, but we could have driven faster, stopped at better inns, kept more convenient hours, and enjoyed some civilised conversation whenever we felt like it. As it was, we were treated grudgingly, fed on

347

left-overs – except at Amiens – made to sleep two in a damp and grimy bed, and woken up before daybreak. And there were four long days of it, being jolted up and down in something more like an ox-cart than a coach.

It had two banquettes facing one another, each of which would have seated two people comfortably but was forced to accommodate three. If one passenger happened to be rather stout, you were all crammed together like sardines for the whole journey. There were five of us: two were reasonably comfortable, but the other three could scarcely breathe, especially as only one of us was slender and the others were bursting with health. I myself have always been hale and hearty, and Bess's buttered beer had made me put on a few pounds. Georg is even more solid, though his height makes it less obvious.

As for the two travelling companions who joined us last, not only were they fat, but they had other weighty defects. They were priests, and they argued loudly with each other all the time. If one was silent it was only because the other had started up again. Their gabble filled the coach and seemed to use up all the air, so that Georg and I, who usually enjoyed chatting, did no more than exchange irritated glances and the occasional feeble whisper. The worst of it was that not content with deafening us with their opinions, the two men of God kept taking us to witness, not actually to ask us for our point of view but as if taking for granted it was the same as theirs and didn't need to be expressed.

That's the only way some people know how to talk. I've often met them, in my shop and elsewhere: they jabber at you at great length, inviting you to agree with them, and if you make some subtle reservation they assume it only backs them up, and carry on even more volubly. To make them register a contrary opinion you have to be quite curt, or even downright disagreeable.

The favourite subject of our two holy men was the Huguenots. At first I couldn't understand why they were arguing so heatedly, because they were agreeing with one another. Their theme was that the supporters of the Reformation had no place in the kingdom of

France, and should be driven out so that the country could once more enjoy peace and the favours of Heaven. They were treated too kindly, they said, and France would live to regret it. They rejoiced in France's misfortunes, and before long the King would realise they were traitors. The tone was unvaryingly threatening. Luther, Calvin, Coligny and Zwingli were compared to various kinds of noxious animals – snakes, scorpions and vermin – that ought to be crushed. Every time one priest expressed an opinion, the other agreed and went one further.

It was Georg who explained it all to me. During one of our silent exchanges he signed to me discreetly to look at our fifth companion. This unfortunate was gasping for breath; his gaunt cheeks were flushed, his brow gleamed with sweat, his knees were clenched together and he never raised his eyes from the ground. He was one of the "race" the priests were anathematising.

What saddened and disappointed me was that my Bavarian friend smiled from time to time at the cruel sarcasms raining down on the unfortunate Huguenot. We had an argument about it that first night.

"Nothing," said Georg, "will ever make me stand up for the people who burned my home down twice and caused my mother's death."

"But he had nothing to do with it!" I cried. "Look at him – he's never hurt a fly!"

"Probably not, and so I wouldn't do *him* any harm. But I wouldn't defend him, either! And don't talk to me about religious freedom – I've lived in England long enough to know that I, a 'Papist' as they call it, am not allowed any freedom or shown any respect for my religion. Every time I've been insulted, I've had to force myself to smile and go on as if nothing had happened, like a coward. And you, while you were there, didn't you always feel like hiding the fact that you were a 'Papist'? Didn't anyone ever insult your religion in your presence?"

He was right. And he swore he believed in freedom of worship even more than I did. But he said that in his view freedom must be reciprocal

– as if it were in the order of things for tolerance to be met with tolerance and persecution with persecution.

The persecution continued during the second day of the journey. And the two priests even managed to make me take part in it – in spite of myself! – when one of them asked me point-blank if I didn't think our coach was meant to hold four travellers, not six. I could only agree, glad the discussion was turning to something other than the quarrel between the Papists and the Huguenots. But the priest who'd spoken to me, encouraged by my answer, went on to elaborate on the fact that we'd be much more comfortable if there were four of us instead of five.

"Some people are not needed in this country," he said, "though they don't seem to realise it."

He pretended to hesitate, then went on, grinning:

"I said in this country, God forgive me, but I meant in this coach. I hope I haven't offended my neighbour."

On the third day the coachman stopped at a small town called Breteuil, and when he came and opened the door, the Huguenot stood up and made his excuses.

"What!" said the priests. "You're not leaving us already? Aren't you going on to Paris?"

"Unfortunately not," muttered their victim, leaving the coach without looking at any of us.

He stopped for a moment to collect his baggage from the back of the coach, then called to the coachman that he could go now. It was already dusk, and the driver whipped up the horses so as to reach Beauvais before dark.

If I go into all this apparently irrelevant detail, it's because I must relate the epilogue to this painful journey. When we got to Beauvais, a great shout went up. Our two priests had just discovered that the baggage, which all belonged to them, had fallen off the coach along the road. The rope securing it had given way, and in the clatter of hooves and harness no one had noticed when it fell off. The priests wrung their hands and tried to get the coachman to go back and look for their things, but he wouldn't hear of it.

On the fourth day, the coach was peaceful at last. The two talkers had no more to say against the Huguenot, though for the first time they had some reason. They didn't even try to accuse him of anything, probably so as not to have to admit that the heretic had had the last word. They spent the day with their breviaries in their hands, muttering prayers. Isn't that what they ought to have been doing all along?

25 October

I promised myself I'd write about my visit to Paris today, and then go on to my journey through Lyons, Avignon and Nice. Then on to Genoa, and how I found myself a guest in Mangiavacca's house again, though we hadn't parted very good friends. But something has happened that preoccupies me, and I don't know if I still have the patience to go back over the past.

For the moment, anyway, I shall stop writing about even the recent past, and concentrate on a journey still to come.

I've met Domenico again. He came to see his partner, and as Gregorio was out, it was I who sat with him. We started by going over shared memories – in particular, the January night when, trembling with cold and fear in the sack I'd been shut up in, I was hoisted aboard Domenico's ship, on which I was brought to Genoa.

Genoa. After the humiliation in Chios and instead of the death I expected, Genoa. And after the fire of London, Genoa. It's here I'm reborn every time, as in that game they play in Florence where the losers have to go back to the beginning.

As I was talking to Domenico, I had the feeling that this smuggler captain had a great admiration for me, though I don't think I deserve it. The reason is that I risked my life for the love of a woman, whereas he and his men, though they trifle with death on every voyage, do so only for gain.

He asked me whether I had any news of my beloved, if she was still a prisoner, and if I still hoped to get her back again. I swore to him that I thought of her day and night wherever I was, in Genoa, London or Paris, or at sea, and that I'd never give up trying to get her out of the clutches of her persecutor.

"How do you hope to do it?"

I answered without thinking.

"One day I'll set out with you, you'll drop me exactly where you picked me up before, and I'll manage somehow to get to speak to her."

"I sail three days from now. If you're still of the same mind, you're welcome to come with me, and I'll do all I can to help you."

As I started stammering my thanks, he did his best to play down his generosity.

"Oh well, if the Turks ever decide to get hold of me, I'll be impaled one day anyhow, because of all the mastic I've filched from them illegally in the last twenty years. It won't get me either a pardon or a worse punishment, whether I help you or not. They can't impale me twice."

I was carried away by so much courage and magnanimity. I got up, shook him warmly by the hand, and embraced him like a brother.

We were still hugging one another when Gregorio came in.

"Well, Domenico," he said, "are you coming or going?"

"It's a reunion!" replied the Calabrian.

They started talking business – florins, bales, cargoes, ships, storms, ports of call. I was so absorbed in my own thoughts that I no longer heard them.

26 October

Today I got drunker than I've ever been before, and all because Gregorio had just received six casks of *vernaccia* from his steward, produced in his own vineyards at Cinqueterre. He wanted to taste the wine straight away, and I was the only drinking companion handy.

When we were both very tipsy, Master Mangiavacca extracted a promise from me. He framed its terms, but I agreed to it with my hand on the Gospels. I undertake to go to Chios with Domenico. If I can't manage to get Marta away from her husband I give up trying to get her back. I then go back to Gibelet to sort out my affairs – to settle what needs to be settled, sell what needs to be sold, and hand my business over to my sister's children. Then, in the spring, I come back to live in Genoa, to marry Giacominetta in great style in Santa Croce, and work with Gregorio, who'll now really be my father-in-law.

So my future seems settled, for the coming months and for the rest of my life. But in addition to my name and that of Gregorio at the bottom of it, the agreement needs the signature of God!

27 October

Gregorio candidly admits that he got me drunk to make me promise; that makes him laugh. What's more, he managed to make me confirm my undertaking when I woke up and was sober.

Sober, but still very confused in my mind and queasy in my stomach.

What a stupid way to behave when I'm due to leave tomorrow!

How can I go aboard like this, as good as sea-sick already? I can hardly stand even on dry land!

Perhaps Gregorio was really trying to stop me going. With him, nothing would surprise me. But he won't get away with it. I shall go. And I shall see Marta again. And get to know my child.

I admit I love Genoa. But I can love it just as well from across the sea, as I've always done, and my ancestors before me.

At sea, Sunday, 31 October 1666

A strong north-east wind blew us off course to Sardinia; we'd been making for Calabria. As this ship, so the ship of my life.

When we berthed, the hull crashed into the quay and we feared the worst. But some divers went down to investigate, lit by the slanting morning sun, and when they surfaced again they told us the *Charybdis* was unscathed. So we're setting off again.

At sea, 9 November

The sea is rough all the time, and I'm constantly ill. Many old sailors are suffering just as much as I am, if that's any consolation.

Every evening, between bouts of sickness, I pray that Nature may be kinder to us, and now Domenico tells me he prays for the opposite. His prayers are clearly heard more sympathetically than mine. And now that he's explained his reasons I'll probably follow his example.

"So long as the sea is rough," he says, "we're safe. Even if the coastguards saw us, they wouldn't risk trying to come after us. That's why I prefer to go to sea in winter. Then I have only one enemy, the sea – and that's not the one I fear the most. Even if it decided to take my life, that wouldn't be such a misfortune – it would save me from being impaled, which is what I'm in for if I'm ever arrested. But death at sea is just a human fate, like death in battle. Whereas impalement makes a man curse the woman who gave him birth."

This speech so reconciled me with the swell that I went and leaned on the rail, letting the spray blow in my face and enjoying the taste of salt on my tongue. It's the taste of life, of the beer in London's taverns, and of women's lips.

I breathe deeply, and am steady on my legs.

At sea, 17 November

Several times in recent days I've opened this journal only to shut it again. Partly because I've been suffering from dizziness since I left Genoa, and that saps my energy, and partly because my mind is restless and I can't concentrate.

I've tried to open *The Hundredth Name*, too, thinking it mightn't rebuff me this time, and then I'd be able to make some headway. But every time my eyes went dark straight away, and I've shut it up again, vowing that I shan't try to read it at all unless it opens for me of its own accord!

Since then I've spent my time walking on deck and talking to Domenico and his men, who tell me about their favourite narrow squeaks and teach me, as if I were a lad, about masts and yards and rigging.

I take all my meals with them, laugh at their jokes even if I only half understand them, and when they drink I pretend to drink too. But I only pretend – ever since Gregorio got me drunk on his casks of wine I feel very fragile, and so close to actual nausea I'm sure one sip would tip the balance.

What's more, that *vernaccia* was pure ambrosia, whereas the wine we get on the ship is a kind of syrupy vinegar diluted with sea-water.

At sea, 27 November

We're approaching the coast of Chios like a hunter stalking his prey. The sails are furled, the mast has been lowered quietly, and the sailors keep their voices lower than usual, as if they could be heard from the island.

Unfortunately it's a fine day. A leaden sun hangs in the sky over Asia Minor, and the wind has dropped. Only a trace of cold air from last night reminds us that it will soon be winter. Domenico has decided not to move till tonight.

He has told me how he means to proceed. Two men, Yannis and Demetrios, will row to the island under cover of darkness: they're both Greek, but from Sicily. When they get to the village of Katarraktis, they'll contact their local supplier, who'll have the goods ready for them. If all goes according to plan – with the mastic ready and packed up, the customs men "persuaded" to turn a blind eye – and no traps are suspected, the two scouts will send Domenico a signal: a white cloth spread out on a patch of high ground at noon. Then the ship will get ready to come in close, but only after dark and only briefly. The cargo will be loaded and paid for, and the *Charybdis* will be off before first light. If by some mischance the white cloth didn't appear, the ship would stay where it was, waiting for the Greeks to return. If they weren't in sight by first light, the rest of the crew would sail without them, praying for their lost souls. That's the usual arrangement.

But this time it's to be modified because of me. Domenico's plan is –

No, I mustn't talk about it, I mustn't even think of it until my hopes are fulfilled, and fulfilled without harm to my friends. Until then, I'll just cross my fingers and spit in the sea, like Domenico. And muttering, like him, "By my ancestors!"

28 November

I can't remember any other Sunday when I've prayed so fervently.

Yannis and Demetrios's boat was launched during the night, and all the crew watched it until it vanished into the dark. We could still hear the slap of the oars, and Domenico was worried because everything was so quiet.

A bit later in the night, when I was already in bed, there were dozens of flashes of lightning in succession. They seemed to be coming from the north – and from a long way away, because we didn't hear the sound of the thunder.

Everyone on board has spent all day waiting. In the morning, waiting to spot the white cloth. Since then, waiting for dark so that we can draw in to the coast.

I share in everyone else's suspense, and I also have tensions of my own. My mind is full of them all the time, but I daren't write anything about them.

I do hope that . . .

29 November

Last night our boat anchored for a while in an inlet near the village of Katarraktis. Domenico has told me it's exactly the same spot as the one where, nearly ten months ago, he took delivery of the sack I was tied up in. Then I could hear all kinds of noises around me but couldn't see anything. Last night I could make out shapes coming and going, bustling about and waving their arms, both on the boat and on the beach. And all the sounds that had been unintelligible to me in January – now I could recognise them. The casting of the gangway; the mastic being set down,

357

checked, loaded; the supplier – a man named Salih, a Turk or perhaps a renegade Greek – coming on board for a drink and to be paid. Perhaps at this point I ought to repeat that Chios is almost the only place in the world that produces mastic, but the authorities make the peasants hand all of it over to them for the Sultan's harems. The state fixes the price to suit itself, and pays when it feels like it. Sometimes the peasants have to wait several years to get what they're owed: which forces them into debt in the interval. Domenico buys their mastic from them at twice, three times or even five times the official price, and hands over the full amount on delivery. According to him, he contributes much more than the Ottoman government to the island's prosperity!

Need I add that for the authorities this devil of a Calabrian is an enemy, to be captured and hanged or impaled? While for the peasants on the island, and everyone else who profits from this trade, Domenico is a godsend, manna from heaven. On nights like last night, they wait for him more eagerly than for Christmas. But they're frightened, too, for if the smuggler or his suppliers were intercepted the entire harvest would be lost and whole families reduced to want.

The whole operation didn't last more that two or three hours at most. And when I saw Salih embrace Domenico and, with the aid of a helping hand, totter down the gangway, I thought we were about to set sail, and couldn't help asking one of the sailors if this was so. He answered laconically that Demetrios wasn't back yet and we would wait for him.

Before long I saw a lamp on the beach and three men approaching in single file. The first was Demetrios. The second was carrying the light, so I could see his face fairly clearly; but I didn't know him. The third was Marta's husband.

Domenico had told me to stay out of sight and not show any sign of my presence until he called me by name. He'd stationed me behind a partition, where I could hear every word of their conversation, which was conducted in a mixture of Italian and Greek.

I should say, by way of introduction to what follows, that it was obvious from the outset that Sayyaf knew perfectly well who Domenico was. And he addressed him with respect if not fear. As a village priest might address a visiting bishop. I suppose that's rather an irreligious comparison. I only meant that there's just as clear a sense of hierarchy in the underworld as in the most venerable institutions. When a village brigand meets the boldest smuggler in the Mediterranean, he takes care not to behave disrespectfully. And the other takes care not to treat him as an equal.

The tone was set straight away, when Marta's husband, after waiting in vain for his host to tell him why he'd been summoned, finally said himself, in what sounded to me a hesitant voice:

"Your man Demetrios told me you had a cargo of cloth, coffee and pepper that you were ready to sell cheap . . ."

Silence from Domenico. A sigh. Then, as one tosses a damaged coin to a beggar:

"If he said so it must be true!"

The conversation collapsed again. Sayyaf was obliged to bend down and pick it up.

"Demetrios said I could pay a third today and the rest at Easter."

Domenico, after a pause:

"If he said so it must be true!"

The other, eagerly: "He mentioned ten bags of coffee and two kegs of pepper. I'll take the lot. But I need to see the cloth before I decide about that."

Domenico: "It's too dark. You can see everything tomorrow in the daylight!"

The other: "I can't come back tomorrow. And even for you, it would be dangerous to wait."

Domenico: "Who said anything about waiting or coming back? Come out to sea with us, and in the morning you can check everything. Feel it, count it, taste it."

I could hear the quiver of fear in Sayyaf's voice all the better because I couldn't see him.

"I didn't ask to check the goods. I trust you. I just wanted to look at the cloth to see how much I could sell. But it doesn't matter. I don't want to hold you up. You must be in a hurry to get away from the coast."

Domenico: "We're away from the coast already."

Sayyaf: "And how will you unload the merchandise?"

Domenico: "Better ask yourself how we're going to be able to unload you!"

"How?"

"I wonder!"

"I could come back in a small boat."

"I'm not so sure."

"Do you mean to keep me here against my will?"

"Oh no! No question of that. But nor is there any question of your taking one of my boats against *my* will. You must ask if I'll kindly lend you one."

"Will you lend me one of your boats?"

"I'll have to think it over."

I then heard the sound of a brief altercation. I guessed that Sayyaf and his henchman had tried to run away, but the sailors surrounding them soon overpowered them.

I almost felt sorry for Marta's husband. But not for long.

"Why did you send for me? What do you want of me?" he said, with a last vestige of courage.

Domenico didn't answer.

"I'm your guest. You asked me on to your boat, and now you try to take me prisoner. Shame on you!"

Some imprecations in Arabic followed. The Calabrian still said nothing. Then, slowly, he started to speak.

"We haven't done anything wrong. We haven't done anything more than an angler does. He casts his hook, and when he hauls in a fish he has to decide whether to keep it or throw it back in the sea. We cast our hook, and the fat fish bit."

"And I'm the fat fish?"

"You're the fat fish. I don't know yet if I'll keep you on the boat or throw you back in the sea. I'll let you choose. Which would you prefer?"

Sayyaf said nothing. Presented with such alternatives, what could he say? The sailors standing round were laughing, but Domenico made them stop.

"I'm waiting for an answer! Do I keep you here or throw you in the sea?"

"On the boat," grumbled the other.

It sounded like resignation, capitulation, and Domenico recognised it as such.

"Good, now we can talk properly. I recently met a Genoese who told me an odd story about you. Apparently you're holding a woman prisoner in your house, and you beat her and ill-treat her child."

"Embriaco! That liar! That scorpion! He's already been to my house with a Turkish officer, and they saw that I wasn't ill-treating her. Anyhow, she's my wife, and what happens under my roof is my business!"

It was at this point that Domenico called me.

"Signor Baldassare!"

I emerged from my hiding-place, and saw that Sayyaf and his henchman were sitting on the ground, leaning against some ropes. They weren't tied up, but a dozen or so sailors stood around ready to knock them down if they tried to get up. Marta's husband shot me a look that seemed to hold more menace than contrition.

"Marta's my cousin, and when I saw her at the beginning of the year she told me she was pregnant. If she and her child are well, no one will hurt you."

"She's not your cousin, and she *is* well."

"And her child?"

"What child? We've never had any children! Are you sure it's my wife you're talking about?"

"He's lying," I said.

I intended to go on, but a kind of dizzy spell made me have to lean against the nearest wall. So it was Domenico who continued.

"How can we tell you weren't lying?"

Sayyaf turned to his companion, who confirmed what he'd said.

"If you have told the truth, both of you," said the Calabrian, "you'll be at home tomorrow and I shan't bother you again. But we must be sure. So here's what I suggest. What's your name, you?"

"Stavro!" said the henchman, looking in my direction. I recognised him now. I'd only caught a glimpse of him before, when I went to Marta's husband's house with the janissaries. He was the man Sayyaf signed to to go and fetch his wife, while I was shouting and bawling. I meant to behave differently now.

"Listen to me, Stavro," said Domenico, suddenly less disagreeable. "I want you to go and fetch Signor Baldassare's cousin. As soon as she's confirmed what her husband says, they can both go. As for you yourself, if you do as I tell you you needn't even come back on board – just bring her back to the beach tomorrow evening and we'll come and fetch her in a boat. You can just go home, and you'll have nothing to fear. But if by any mischance the devil should put it into your head to deceive me, just remember that there are 600 families on this island who live on what I pay them. And that the highest authorities are beholden to me too. So if you talk too much, or if you disappear without bringing the woman back to us, I shall pass the word and you'll be made to pay for your treachery. And the blows will come from where you least expect them."

"I won't deceive you!"

As they launched the boat again, with Stavro in it and three sailors to escort him to the shore, I asked Domenico if he really thought the fellow would do what he'd been asked. He seemed quite confident.

"If he just disappeared without more ado, there's nothing I could do. But I think I've put the fear of God into him. And what I've asked him to do won't cost him anything. So he may very well do as he's told. We'll soon see!"

*   *   *

362

We're out at sea again, and nothing seems to be stirring on the island. Yet somewhere behind one of those white walls, in the shade of one or other of those tall trees, Marta is getting ready to come to the beach. Has she been told I'm here? Or why she's being sent for? She's dressing, making up her face, perhaps even putting a few things in her bag. Is she anxious, frightened, or full of hope? Is she thinking of her husband at this moment, or of me? And her child – is it with her? Did she lose it? Has it been taken away from her? At last I shall know. I shall be able to bandage her wounds. I shall be able to make amends.

Night's starting to fall, and I go on writing without a light. The boat is moving cautiously towards the island, though it's still some way off. Domenico has stationed a sailor called Ramadane, from Alexandria, at the top of the mast. He has the keenest eyes of all the crew, and it's his job to watch the beach and signal anything suspicious. It's because of me that everyone has to take excessive risks, but none of them shows any resentment. I haven't caught a single look of reproach or sigh of irritation. How on earth can I ever repay them?

We're getting nearer the coast, but the lights on the island still seem as faint as the furthest stars in the sky. Of course, we can't light any candles or lamps on board ship. I can hardly see the paper I'm writing on, but I go on all the same. But tonight writing doesn't give me as much pleasure as usual. On other days I write to record events, or to explain myself, or to clear my mind in the same way as one clears one's throat, or so as not to forget, or even just because I promised myself I would. But tonight I cling to the pages as if to a buoy. I haven't anything to tell them, but I need them near me.

My pen holds my hand. What does it matter if I dip it just in the black of the night?

Off Katarraktis, 30 November 1666

I didn't think our reunion would be like this.

I, eyes screwed up, on the boat; she, the dim glow of a lantern at midnight, on a beach.

When the lantern started moving from right to left to right like the pendulum of a clock, Domenico ordered three men to launch the dinghy. They were to use no lights and be very careful, scanning the coast to make sure there were no traps or ambushes.

The sea was rough and noisy, but not raging. The wind was from the north, and already typical of December.

On my cold lips, salt and prayers.

Marta.

How near she was, and yet how far still. The dinghy took a lifetime to reach the beach, and then stayed there for another lifetime. What were they doing? What could they be talking about? It's not difficult to take a person on board and then come back again! Why didn't I go with them? No, Domenico wouldn't have let me. And he'd have been right. I haven't got the practical experience that his men possess, nor their equanimity.

Then the dinghy did come back towards us. The lantern could be seen on board.

"God! I said no lights!" Domenico muttered.

As if they'd heard, they put out the flame. Domenico heaved a loud sigh and patted me on the arm. "By my ancestors!" Then he ordered his men to get ready to head out to sea as soon as we'd picked up the dinghy and its occupants.

Marta was hauled on board in a highly unceremonious manner – with the aid of a rope to which a plank was attached for her to stand on. When she'd been hoisted up far enough, I helped her step over the rail. She'd given me her hand as if to a stranger, but as soon as she was safely on

TEMPTATION IN GENOA

deck she began to look round, and although it was dark I could tell she was looking for me. I said one word. Her name. And she took my hand again, clasping it quite differently now. She'd obviously known I was there, though I'm still not sure whether it was her husband's henchman who told her or the sailors who picked her up from the beach. I'll find out when I have a chance to speak to her. No, no point – we'll have so many other things to talk about.

I'd imagined that when we were reunited I'd take her in my arms and hold her tight for a long, long time. But with all those bold mariners round us, and her husband still on board, waiting to be tried by our court of pirates, it would have been in bad taste to seem too intimate or eager. So the surreptitious pressure of her hand on mine, in the dark, was the only evidence of our closeness.

Then she felt unwell, so I told her to cool her face by holding it in the spray. But she began to shiver, and the sailors said she ought to stretch out on a mattress in the hold, under some warm blankets.

Domenico would have liked to summon her straight away, to find out what had become of the child she'd been carrying, to pronounce judgement and then sail back to his home port.

But she looked ready to give up the ghost, so he resigned himself to letting her rest till the morning.

As soon as she was lying down, she fell asleep – so fast I thought she'd fainted. I shook her a bit to make her open her eyes and say something. Then I felt ashamed of myself and came away.

I spent last night propped on some bags of mastic, trying without much success to get to sleep. I may have managed to drop off for a few minutes just before dawn.

During this seemingly endless night, while I was neither fully awake nor fully asleep, I was assailed by the most horrible thoughts. They terrify me so much I hardly dare write them down. But they arose out of my greatest joy.

I found myself wondering what I ought to do to Sayyaf if I found out he'd done Marta, let alone the child she'd been carrying, any harm.

Could I just let him escape unpunished? Shouldn't I make him pay for his crime?

Anyhow, I thought, even if Marta's husband had had nothing to do with the child's death, how could I go off and live with her in Gibelet, leaving Sayyaf behind to keep mulling over his revenge and return one day to haunt us?

Could I sleep easy in my bed knowing he was still alive?

Could I sleep easy in my bed if I –

Should I kill him?

I, kill?

I, Baldassare, kill? Kill a man, whoever he is?

And to start with, how does one set about it?

Me, creep up to someone with a knife in my hand and stab him through the heart? Or wait till he's asleep for fear he might look at me? No! God, no!

What about paying someone else to . . .

What am I thinking? What am I writing? Lord, let this cup pass from me!

It seems to me I shall never sleep again, either tonight or any of the nights that remain to me!

Sunday, 5 December 1666

I shan't re-read the last few pages – I might be tempted to tear them up. I wrote them, but I'm not proud of them. I'm not proud of having contemplated sullying my hands and my soul. And I'm not proud of having decided against it, either.

While Marta was still asleep, and to assuage my impatience, I wrote down the thoughts that visited me before dawn on Tuesday. Then, for the next five days, I wrote nothing. I even considered, once again, abandoning my journal. Yet here I am again, pen in hand, perhaps because of the rash promise I made myself at the start of my journey.

I've had three attacks of mental disarray, one after the other, in the last week. The first came when Marta and I were reunited. The next, in the confusion that followed. And after that, the fury, the spiritual storm that's raging in me now, shaking and battering me as if I were on deck in a gale with nothing to cling on to, lifting me up every so often, only to throw me down harder.

Neither Domenico nor Marta can help me now. Nor anyone else, present or absent; nor any memory. Everything that comes into my mind adds to my confusion. And so does everything around me, everything I can see and everything I can manage to remember. And of course this year itself, this accursed year. Only four weeks of it are left, but those four weeks seem simply insurmountable – an ocean without sun or moon or stars, just wave after wave after wave as far as the horizon.

No, I'm still in no fit state to write.

10 December

Our boat has left Chios behind, and my mind too is beginning to distance itself from all that happened to me there. It will take more time yet for the wound to heal, but after ten days I can at last think of something else sometimes. Perhaps I ought to try to go on with my journal . . .

Up till now I haven't been able to give a proper account of what happened. But it's time I did so, even if, when I come to the most painful moments, I have to confine myself to words devoid of feeling – "he said", "he asked", "she said", "seeing that", "it was agreed".

When Marta came on board the *Charybdis*, Domenico would have liked to send for her during the night and find out what had become of the child she'd been carrying, deliver his verdict, and set out straight away back to Italy. But as she could scarcely stand, he resigned himself, as I've already said, to letting her sleep for a while. Everyone on the boat had a few hours' rest, apart from the look-outs – in case some Ottoman ship should decide to intercept us. But the sea was so rough that night we must have been the only vessel there.

In the morning we met again in the captain's quarters. Demetrios and Yannis were there too, making five of us in all. Domenico solemnly asked Marta if she preferred to be questioned in her husband's presence or without him. I translated the question for her, into the Arabic that's spoken in Gibelet, and she said at once, almost imploringly:

"Without him!"

Her expression, and the way she wrung her hands, made it unnecessary for me to translate her answer.

So Domenico went on:

"Signor Baldassare has told us you were pregnant when you came to Chios last January. But your husband maintains you've never had a child."

Marta looked stricken. She turned to me for a moment, then hid her face in her hands and began to sob. I took a step towards her, but Domenico – taking his role as judge seriously – signed to me to stay where I was. He also signed to the others not to say or do anything; just to wait. When he thought he'd given the witness enough time to collect herself, he said:

"Go on."

I translated, adding:

"Speak. There's nothing to be afraid of. No one's going to hurt you."

But my words, instead of reassuring her, seemed to upset her even more. Her sobs grew louder. Domenico told me not to add anything to what he asked me to translate. I promised I wouldn't.

A few seconds went by. Marta's sobbing died down, and Domenico, with a tinge of impatience, repeated his question. Then Marta looked up and said:

"I've never had a child!"

"What do you mean?"

I'd cried it out aloud. Domenico called me to order. I apologised again, then translated just what Marta had said.

Then she said, in a steady voice:

"There never was a child. I never was pregnant."

"But you told me you were!"

"Yes, because I thought I was. But I was mistaken."

I looked at her for a long, long time, but couldn't once catch her eye. I wanted to see something that resembled the truth in her look; at least to understand whether she'd lied to me all along; if she'd lied to me only about the child, to make me take her back as fast as possible to her scoundrel of a husband; or if she was lying to me now. She only raised her eyes two or three times, furtively, probably to see if I was still looking at her, and if I believed her.

Then Domenico asked her, in a fatherly manner:

"Tell us, Marta – do you want to go ashore, back to your husband, or to come with us?"

I translated it as "come back with me". But she answered clearly, pointing, that she wanted to go back to Katarraktis.

With the man she hates? I didn't understand. Then suddenly it struck me.

"Wait, Domenico," I said. "I think I understand what's going on. Her son must be on the island, and she's afraid something would happen to him if she said anything against her husband. Tell her that if that's what she's afraid of, we'll make her husband send for the child, just as we made him send for her. Only *she* will go for the child, and we'll hold on to her husband until she comes back. Then he won't be able to do anything to her!"

"Calm down!" said the Calabrian. "I think all that may just be make-believe. But if you have the slightest doubt, I want you to say to her what you've just said to me. And you can promise her, in my name, that no harm will come either to her or to her son."

I then launched into a long tirade, at once passionate, desperate and imploring, begging Marta to tell me the truth. She listened with her eyes downcast. When I'd finished, she looked at Domenico and said:

"There never was a child. I never was pregnant. I can't have children."

She'd spoken in Arabic. She repeated what she'd said in faulty Greek, turning to Demetrios. Domenico glanced at him inquiringly.

The sailor, who so far had remained silent, looked embarrassed. His eyes turned first to me, then to Marta, then to me again, and finally to his captain.

"When I went to their house," he said, "I didn't get the impression there was a child around."

"It was the middle of the night – he'd have been asleep!"

"I banged at the door and woke everyone up. There was a great commotion, but I didn't hear a baby crying."

I tried to speak, but Domenico stopped me.

"That'll do! In my opinion the woman's telling the truth! We must let her and her husband go."

"Not yet! Wait!"

"No, Baldassare, I won't wait. The matter's settled. We're leaving. We've already made ourselves late to please you, and I hope one day you'll remember to thank all the men who risked great danger for your sake!"

These words hurt me more than Domenico could have imagined. I had been a hero to him, and now he saw me as a jilted lover, whining and making things up. In a few hours, a few minutes or a few words even, the noble and honourable Signor Baldassare had become a nuisance, a troublesome passenger barely tolerated, whom you could tell to be quiet.

If I went to weep in a corner away from everybody, it was as much because of that as because of Marta. She left as soon as the questioning was over. I suppose Domenico apologised to her husband, and I think he offered them the dinghy to take them back to the shore. I didn't want to be present at the farewells.

*　　*　　*

My wound has closed a little by now, though it's still very painful. I still don't understand Marta's behaviour. I ask myself questions so strange I don't like to write them down. I still need to think . . .

11 December

What if everyone lied to me?

What if this whole expedition was a trick, a deception, designed only to make me give Marta up?

Perhaps this idea is just a delusion arising out of humiliation, loneliness, and several sleepless nights. But it could be the truth.

Gregorio, wanting to make me give Marta up once and for all, could have told Domenico to take me with him and do whatever was necessary to make me never want to see her again.

Didn't someone tell me one day in Smyrna that Sayyaf was mixed up in smuggling – smuggling mastic? So it's likely that Domenico knew him, though he pretended he was seeing him for the first time. That may have been why they made me stay behind a partition. So that I couldn't see their nods and winks, and unmask their conspiracy!

And probably Marta knew Demetrios and Yannis too; she'd have seen them before, in her husband's house. So she'd have felt obliged to say what she did.

But when we were alone together in the hold, when she was lying down, why didn't she take the opportunity to speak to me in secret?

I must be deluding myself! Why should all those people have been merely acting a part? Just to deceive me and make me give up that woman? Hadn't they anything better to do with their lives than risk being hanged or impaled in order to dabble in my amorous intrigues?

My reason is as out of joint as my poor father's shoulder was once. It needs a good shock to re-set it.

13 December

For twelve days I wandered about on the boat as if I were invisible: everyone had orders to avoid me. If a sailor threw me a word from time to time, it was half-heartedly, and after making sure no one else was looking. I took my meals alone and surreptitiously, as if I had the plague.

But today people started talking to me again. Domenico came up to me and threw his arms round me as if he was just welcoming me on board. That was the signal for all the rest to mix with me again.

I could have sulked, refused the offered hand, let the braggart blood of the Embriaci speak. But no. The truth is, I'm relieved to be back in favour. I found it hard to bear, being an outcast.

I'm not one of those people who revel in adversity.

I like to be liked. Loved.

14 December

According to Domenico, I should thank the Almighty for arranging things His way rather than mine. These words, from a smuggler turned spiritual adviser, have made me think. Weigh things up, make comparisons. And in the end I don't think he's altogether wrong.

"Suppose she'd said what you hoped she'd say. That her husband ill-treated her, that she'd lost her child because of him, and she'd like to leave him. In that case I imagine you'd have kept her and taken her back to your own country."

"Of course!"

"What about the husband?"

"To hell with him!"

"Yes, but would you have let him go home, so that one day he might come and knock at your door and ask for his wife back? And what would you have told her family? That he was dead?"

"Do you think I never thought of all that?"

"Oh no, I'm sure you did. But I'd like you to tell me how you proposed to solve those problems."

We were both silent for a while.

"I don't want to torture you, Baldassare. I'm your friend, and I've done for you what your own father wouldn't have done. So I'm going to say to you what you yourself don't like to say to me. You should have killed that swine of a husband. No, don't make a face and look shocked – I know you thought of it, and so did I. Because if the woman had decided to leave him, neither you nor I would have wanted him to remain alive to come back and haunt us. I'd always have been thinking, every time I went to Chios, that there was someone there waiting to be revenged on me. And you too would have preferred to know he was dead."

"Probably!"

"But could you have killed him?"

"I thought of it," I admitted, but didn't go any further.

"Thinking of it isn't enough. Wishing for it still less. Wishing someone else was dead – that's something that can happen every day. A servant who steals, a difficult customer, a troublesome neighbour, even your own father. But in this case, wishing wouldn't have been enough. Would you have been capable of, say, picking up a knife and going up to your rival and sticking it in his heart? Or binding him hand and foot and throwing him overboard? You *thought* of it, and I *thought* of it for you. I wondered what would be the ideal solution for you. And I found it. Killing him, throwing him overboard wouldn't have been enough. You didn't only need to know he was dead; you also needed your neighbours to see he was dead. We'd have had to head in the direction of Gibelet, taking him with us, still alive. When we were a few cables' lengths from the nearby coast, we'd have tied his feet together, thrown him overboard, towed him along for an hour, say, then hauled him up again, drowned. Then we'd have untied his feet and laid him on a stretcher, and you and the woman

373

would have put on long faces and let my men take you and the corpse ashore. You'd have told everyone he'd fallen overboard and drowned that day; and I'd have confirmed it. Then you'd have buried him, and a year later you'd have married his widow.

"That's how *I* would have managed it. I've already killed dozens of men, and none of them has come back to haunt me in my dreams. But you – tell me, could you have done it?"

I admitted that I'd certainly have thanked God if our expedition had ended in the way he'd just imagined. But that I couldn't have committed a crime like that myself.

"Then be glad she didn't say what you hoped she'd say!"

15 December

I keep thinking about what Domenico said. If he'd been me, I've no doubt he'd have acted exactly as he described. But I'm a born merchant, and I have the soul of a merchant, not of a pirate or a warrior. Nor that of a brigand, either – perhaps that's why Marta chose the other instead of me. He, like Domenico, wouldn't have hesitated to kill to get what he wanted. Neither of them has any scruples about it. But would either of them ever have gone out of their way for the love of a woman?

I haven't forgotten yet. I don't know if I ever shall. Yes, one day I shall, and her betrayal will help.

Even so, I can't help still having a doubt. Did she really betray me, or did she say what she did to save her child?

There I go, talking about the child again, though everyone tells me it doesn't exist and never did.

But what if they're all lying to me? She to protect her child, and the others to . . . But no, that's enough! I must stop deluding myself. Even if I'll never know the whole truth, I must turn my back on my past and look ahead. Ahead.

Anyhow, this year is nearly over.

17 December

I looked at the sky last night, and it seems to me that there really are fewer and fewer stars. They're going out one after the other, while on earth the cities burn.

The world began in paradise, and is going to end in hell.

Why did I come into it so late?

19 December

We've just passed through the Straits of Messina, avoiding the whirlpool they call Charybdis. Domenico named his boat after it to try to ward off its dangers, but still he takes care never to go near it.

Now we're going to sail up the coast of Italy to Genoa. The Calabrian promises me a new life awaits me there. But what's the point in my starting a new life if the world is about to end?

I always thought I'd spend the last days of the "Year of the Beast" in Gibelet, so that all my people would be huddled together in the same house, comforted by familiar voices, if what must happen did happen. I was so sure I'd go back there, I hardly ever mentioned it – I just wondered about the dates and the routes. Should I go straight there in April, instead of following *The Hundredth Name* to London? Should I go through Chios or Smyrna on the way back? Even Gregorio, when he made me promise to go back to Genoa, realised I couldn't do so until I'd settled my affairs in Gibelet.

Yet here I am on the way to Genoa. I'll be there for Christmas, and that's where I'll be when the year 1666 comes to an end.

20 December

The truth is I've been hiding the truth from myself all the time, even in this journal, which ought to have been my confessor.

The truth is, I knew that once I was in Genoa again I'd never go back to Gibelet. I murmured it to myself sometimes, without ever daring to write it down, as if such a monstrous thought could never be put on paper. For my beloved sister is in Gibelet, and my business, as well as my parents' grave, and the house where I was born, and my grandfather's father before me. But I'm as much of a stranger there as a Jew. While Genoa, where I'd never lived before, has recognised me, embraced me, taken me to its bosom like the Prodigal Son. I walk head held high along its narrow streets, say my Italian name aloud, smile at the women and am not afraid of the janissaries. One of the Embriaci's ancestors may have been accused of drinking too much, but they have a tower named after them too. Every family ought to have a tower named after them somewhere.

This morning I wrote what I thought I ought to write. I could just as easily have written the opposite.

I boast about being at home in Genoa and only in Genoa, when in fact I'll always, till the end of my days, be Gregorio's guest here, and in his debt. I'm going to leave my own roof to live under his, abandon my own business to work for him.

Shall I be able to take pride in living like that? Depending on him and his generosity, when I think of him as I do? His enthusiasm irritates me, his devotion makes me laugh, and I've already had to make my escape because I'd had enough of his nudges and winks and of his wife's face.

I'm going to be given his daughter's hand as if it were homage from a vassal, a kind of *droit du seigneur*, because I bear the name of the Embriaci and he bears only his own. He'll have worked all his life just for me: built up his business, built his ships, accumulated his wealth and founded his family just for my benefit. He'll have planted, watered, pruned, tended the tree, and I'll just have come along and picked the fruit. And I have the audacity to take pride in my name and strut around Genoa, after abandoning what I built up myself and what my ancestors built up for me!

I shall end this year in Genoa, but if there are any other years to come, I don't know yet where I'll spend them.

22 December 1666

We sheltered from the swell in an almost deserted inlet north of Naples, on the alert for wreckers.

It seems some people aboard saw a big fire on the coast, on the outskirts of Naples. But I was in bed and didn't see anything.

I'm suffering from sea-sickness again. And a general unease at the approaching end of the year.

In ten days' time the world will either be definitely over the worst, or have sunk beyond recall.

23 December 1666

Neither Marta nor Giacominetta – when I woke up this morning I was thinking of Bess and her red hair, how she smells of violets and beer, how she looks at you like a mother who can't do enough for you. I don't miss London, but I can't think without sadness of its terrible fate. And though I hated its streets and its crowds, I made a tribe of strange friends there, all revolving around Bess.

What has become of them? What has become of their dilapidated ale-house with its wooden stairs and its attics? What has become of the Tower of London and St Paul's Cathedral? And all those bookshops and their heaps of books? Ashes, dust and ashes. Like the faithful journal I used to keep every day. Like all the other books except Mazandarani's. His book spreads desolation all around, but always emerges unscathed itself. Wherever it's been, there have been nothing but fires and shipwrecks. A fire in Constantinople, a fire in London, and Marmontel shipwrecked. And this ship now, which looks as if it might capsize at any moment.

Woe to whoever approaches the hidden name: his eyes are always dimmed or dazzled – never lit. Now, when I pray, I feel like saying:

"Lord, never be too far away from me! But don't be too close to me either!

"Let me admire the stars on the hem of Thy robe! But do not show me Thy face!

"Let me hear the rippling of Thy rivers, the sound of Thy wind blowing through the trees, and the laughter of Thy children! But Lord, Lord! let me not hear Thy voice!"

24 December 1666

Domenico promised we'd be in Genoa for Christmas. But we won't. If the sea were calm we might get there tomorrow evening. But the *libeccio* that's blowing from the south-west is getting stronger, and we'll have to take shelter on the coast again.

Libeccio . . . I'd forgotten the word. I used to hear it often in my childhood, when my father and grandfather would talk of it with a mixture of nostalgia and fear. They always contrasted it with the *scirocco*, and said, if I remember rightly, that Genoa has provided itself with defences against one but not against the other. They blamed the present ruling families, who spend fortunes on palaces for themselves but are like misers when it comes to providing for the common good.

Domenico told me that, until twenty years ago, ships wouldn't spend the winter in Genoa because the *libeccio* caused such terrible havoc there. Every year between twenty and forty boats – once, more than a hundred of all shapes and sizes – would be sunk. November and December were the worst months. But more recently a new jetty has been built, sheltering the harbour from the west.

"*We* shan't have anything to fear there – the dock's as smooth as a lake now. But we've got to get there first! My ancestors!"

25 December 1666

This morning we tried to get out to the open sea, then we had to fall back on the coast again. The *libeccio* was blowing harder and harder, and Domenico knew he wouldn't get far. But he wanted us to be be able to shelter in the cove behind the Portovenere peninsula, towards Lerici.

I'm tired of being at sea and ill all the time. I'd have been glad to travel the rest of the way to Genoa by road; it's only a day's journey overland from here. But after all the captain and his crew have done for me, I'd be ashamed to abandon them like that. It's only right that I should share their fate as they shared mine. Even if I have to heave my heart up.

26 December

Domenico said to a grumpy old sailor who told him off for breaking his promise, "Better be late in Genoa than early in hell!"

We all laughed except the old boy. I expect he's too close to his own end to see the funny side.

Monday, 27 December 1666

Genoa at last!

Gregorio was waiting for me in the harbour. He'd posted a man near the lighthouse, to let him know as soon as our boat hove in sight.

Seeing him waving excitedly in the distance, I remembered my first arrival in the city of my ancestors, nine months ago. I was on the same boat, coming from the same island, commanded by the same captain. But it was spring then, and the port was full of ships being loaded and unloaded, customs men, travellers, clerks and ordinary onlookers. Today, there was only us. No other boat was arriving or departing; no one was there to say hail or farewell to a traveller; there were no idle bystanders. No one. Not even Melchione Baldi: I looked for him in vain. Nothing but empty boats at their moorings, and quays that were practically empty too.

In this wilderness of stone and water, swept by a cold wind, one man stood ruddy and smiling, generous but intransigent. Master Mangiavacca, come to take delivery of 800 litres of mastic and a prodigal son-in-law.

I still make fun of him, but I've given up trying to resist him. And I bless rather than curse him.

Giacominetta blushed when she saw me enter the house with her father. She'd obviously been told already that I was coming back to Genoa, that I was asking for her hand, and that my request would be granted. As for my future mother-in-law, she was unwell because of the cold, and, I was informed, has had to keep to her bed for the last couple of days. I suppose it might be true.

*   *   *

There are three things I dislike about Giacominetta: her first name, her mother, and the fact that in some ways she's rather like Elvira, my first wife and the sorrow of my life.

But Gregorio's poor daughter can't be held responsible for any of these defects.

28 December

My host came to see me in my room very early this morning. He's never done that before. He said he'd rather no one else knew of our conversation; but it seems to me that what he really wanted was to make a solemn occasion of it.

He'd come for me to pay my verbal debt to him; he'll never ask me to repay the money I owe him. I expected it, of course, but perhaps not so soon. Nor in quite this manner.

"We've made promises to each other," he began.

"I haven't forgotten," I said.

"Nor have I. But I don't want you to feel bound – out of obligation to me, or even out of friendship – to do something you don't want to do. For that reason, I free you from your oath until the end of today. I've told them in the kitchens that you're tired after your journey and will stay in your room until the evening. Your meals and anything else you need will be brought up to you. Take a day off for rest and meditation. When I come back, you'll give me your answer, and whatever it is I'll accept it!"

He wiped away a tear, and left without waiting for me to reply.

As soon as he'd shut the door behind him, I sat down at my table to write these lines, in the hope that it would help me to think.

To think! How presumptuous! When you're thrown into the water, you flounder, you swim, you float, or you sink. You don't think.

*   *   *

Near to me on the table is *The Hundredth Name.* Should I regard it as a privilege to have it in my possession as the fateful year is ending? Are these really the world's last few days? The final three or four days before the Last Judgement? Is the universe going to burst into flame and then go out? Will the walls of this house crumple up like a sheet of paper in the hand of a giant? Will the ground on which Genoa stands suddenly open up under our feet, amid shouts and screams, as in some vast ultimate earthquake? And when the moment comes, shall I be able to pick up the book, open it at the right page, and suddenly see before me in shining letters the supreme name that I've never before been able to read?

To tell the truth, I'm not sure of anything. I imagine all these things and dread some of them, but don't believe in any. I've spent a whole year running after a book I no longer want. I've dreamed of a woman who has preferred a brigand to me. I've filled hundreds of pages and there's nothing left of them. And yet I'm not unhappy. I'm in Genoa, in the warm, I'm wanted, and perhaps even loved a little. I look at the world and at my own life as if I were a stranger. I wish for nothing, except perhaps that time would stop on the 28th of December 1666.

I waited for Gregorio, but it was his daughter who came just now. The door opened and Giacominetta came in, bringing me a tray of coffee and sweetmeats. She obviously meant to use it as an excuse for us to talk to one another. Not, this time, about garden trees or the names of plants and flowers. But about what's in store for us. Because she's impatient—and how can I blame her? My own questions about our future marriage take up a quarter of my thoughts. She's only just fourteen, and her questions about the matter must occupy absolutely all her time! But I pretended not to notice.

   "Tell me, Giacominetta, did you know your father and I have talked a lot about you and your future?"

She blushed and said nothing, though she didn't pretend to be surprised.

"We've mentioned betrothal and marriage."

She was still silent.

"Did you know I'd been married before, and am a widower?"

She didn't know. And yet I'd told her father.

"I was nineteen. My family arranged for me to marry the daughter of a merchant living in Cyprus."

"What was her name?"

"Elvira."

"What did she die of?"

"Sorrow. She'd wanted to marry a young man she knew, a Greek; she didn't really want to have anything to do with me. But they didn't tell me. If I'd known, I might have refused to go through with it. But she was young, and I was young, and we did as our fathers told us. But she could never be happy, and she didn't make me happy either. I'm telling you all this because I don't want the same thing to happen with us. I want you to tell me what you want. I don't want you to be forced to do anything you don't want to do. You need only tell me, and I'll pretend the difficulty's on my side."

Giacominetta blushed again, turned her face away, and said:

"If you and I get married, I won't be unhappy."

Then she ran out of the room. The door had been wide open all the time.

In the afternoon, while I am still waiting for Gregorio to come back for my answer, I look out of the window and see his daughter walking in the garden. She goes up to the statue of Bacchus that I gave to Gregorio, and leans against the shoulders of the recumbent god.

When her father comes back I shall ask him for her hand as I promised. If the world lasts out until my wedding day, I can only be glad. And if it doesn't, if it dies, and Genoa dies, and we all die, I'll have paid my debt, and I'll be easier in my mind as I go, and so will Gregorio.

But I don't want the world to end. And I don't really think it's going to. Did I ever? Perhaps. I can't remember . . .

29 December

While I was away, the letter I was expecting, the one from Pleasance, arrived in Genoa. It's dated Sunday, 12 September, but Gregorio didn't receive it until last week, and didn't give it to me until this morning. He claimed he'd forgotten about it. I don't believe him. I know perfectly well why he didn't give it to me before. He wanted to be sure no news from Gibelet would hold up my decision. But he was being too careful: there's nothing in the letter that could affect my relationship with his daughter or with him. But how was he to know?

My sister says both her sons came home safe and sound. But she has no news of Hatem, and his family is very worried. "I try to reassure them, but I don't really know what to say," she writes. She begs me to let her know if I have any news.

I reproach myself for not asking Marta about it when I saw her. I meant to, but I was so shaken by the way things turned out I didn't think of it. I regret it now, but what good does that do me? And what good does it do poor Hatem?

I'm particularly affected by this piece of news because I didn't expect it. I didn't have much confidence in my nephews. One was motivated by his desires and the other by his crazy ideas, and they both struck me as weak and vulnerable. I had been afraid they might refuse to go back to Gibelet, or get lost on the way. But I was used to emerging unscathed from difficult situations with the aid of my clerk, and I'd hoped he'd manage to get to Smyrna to take charge of Habib and Boumeh before they left.

My sister also tells me that a parcel arrived from Constantinople, delivered by a pilgrim on his way to the Holy Land. It contains the things I had to leave behind at Barinelli's. Pleasance mentions some of them, but she doesn't say anything about my first notebook. Perhaps they didn't find it. But it may be that my sister didn't mention it because she doesn't know how important it is to me.

She doesn't say anything about Marta either. It's true that in my letter to Pleasance I merely said she'd joined us for part of the journey. I expect her sons have put her in the picture about our idyll, but she chose to say nothing about it. That doesn't surprise me.

30 December

I went to thank Brother Egidio for bringing Pleasance's letter. He spoke as if it were understood that I was going to marry Giacominetta, praising her piety and that of her mother and sisters. When it came to Gregorio, he lauded only his good-nature and generosity. I didn't argue. The die is cast, the Rubicon crossed, and there's no point now in fussing about the details. I didn't really choose to get mixed up in all this, but does one ever really have any choice? It's better to go along with the ways of Providence than spend your whole life consumed with regret and resentment. Surrendering to fate is nothing to be ashamed of; it was an unequal contest, so honour is satisfied. In any case, you always lose the last battle.

In the course of our conversation, which lasted for over two hours, Brother Egidio told me that, according to travellers recently arrived from London, the fire was eventually put out. It's said to have destroyed most of the city, but not many people were killed.

"If He had wished it, the Almighty could have wiped out that country of infidels. But he just gave them a warning, so that they might renounce their errors and return to the merciful fold of Mother Church."

In Brother Egidio's opinion, it was the secret devotion of King Charles and Queen Catherine that persuaded the Lord to be lenient this time. But one day the perfidy of the English themselves will exhaust God's infinite patience.

A crowd of different thoughts crossed my mind as he spoke. While I was hiding up in the roof of the ale-house, it was rumoured that it was because of the King that God had punished London – because of his secret devotion to the "Antichrist" in Rome, and because of his marital infidelities.

Was God too hard on the English? Or not hard enough?

We ascribe to Him such sentiments as vexation, anger, impatience and satisfaction, but what do we know of His real feelings?

If I were He and presided over the whole universe for ever and ever, master of today and tomorrow, master of birth, life and death, I don't think I'd ever feel either impatient or satisfied. What is impatience to Him who disposes of eternity? What is satisfaction to Him who possesses everything?

I can't imagine Him being angry or outraged or shocked, or vowing to punish those who turn away from the Pope or stray from the marriage bed.

If I were God, I'd have saved London for Bess's sake. After seeing her rush about and worry and risk her life to save a Genoese, a passing stranger, I'd have stroked her tousled red hair with a little breeze, sponged the sweat from her face, removed the debris that barred her way, scattered the raging mob, and put out the flames encircling her house. I'd have let her go up to her room and lie down, and fall asleep with an untroubled brow.

And is it possible that I, Baldassare, miserable sinner that I am, could be kinder than He? That my merchant's heart could be more generous than His, and more inclined to mercy?

*　　*　　*

When I look over what I've just written, carried away by my pen, I can't help feeling rather scared. But I shouldn't be. A God who deserves my prostrating myself before Him can't be petty or easily offended. He must be above all that, He must be greater. He *is* greater, as the Muslims say.

So, whether tomorrow is the last day before the end of the world, or just the last day of the present year, I mean to stick to my Embriaco uppishness and not take anything back.

31 December 1666

This morning, all over the world, lots of people must be thinking today will be the last day of the last year.

But here in the streets of Genoa, I haven't noticed any trepidation, or any special religious fervour.

But Genoa has never prayed for anything but its own prosperity and the safe return of its ships, and never had more religion than is reasonable. God bless it!

Gregorio had decided to give a party this afternoon to thank Heaven for restoring his wife to health. She got up yesterday, and really does seem to be well again. But I have a feeling my host is already celebrating something else. A sort of disguised betrothal. Disguised like the writing in this journal.

Dame Orietina may be quite well again, but whenever she sees me she seems to get a pain in her face.

I still don't know if she looks at me like that because she doesn't want me as a son-in-law, or because she thinks I ought to have solicited her daughter's hand humbly, instead of just accepting it with my nose in the air as something due to the name I bear.

*   *   *

Gregorio had engaged a viol player and singer from Cremona to entertain the guests at the party. He played the most delightful tunes by various composers, including, if my memory serves, Monteverdi, Luigi Rossi, Jacopo Peri, and someone called Mazzochi or Marazzoli, whose nephew is supposed to have married one of Gregorio's nieces.

I didn't want to spoil my host's pleasure by telling him that the music, even the gayest pieces, made me feel sad. That was because the only other time I'd heard anyone playing the viol was soon after my first marriage, when my family and I went to Cyprus to visit Elvira's parents. I was already very unhappy, and listening to music that was at all affecting only made me feel worse.

But today, when the man from Cremona began to play and the large room was filled with his music, I immediately found myself drifting into a gentle daydream where there was no room for Elvira or Orietina. The only women I thought of were those I've loved, those who held me in their arms when I was a child – my mother, and the black-robed women in Gibelet – and those I have held in my arms as a man.

Among the latter, none arouses such tenderness in me as Bess. Of course, I do think of Marta a little, but now she causes me as much sadness as Elvira – the wound is taking a long time to heal. Whereas my brief and surreptitious stay in Bess's garden will always remain a foretaste of paradise for me.

How glad I am that London wasn't destroyed!

For me, happiness will alway have the taste of spiced beer and the smell of violets – and even the creak of the wooden stairs that led to my kingdom up at the top of the ale-house.

Is it right that I should be thinking of Bess like this in the house of my future father-in-law, who is also my benefactor? But dreams have nothing to do with houses or proprieties, promises or gratitude.

Later in the evening, when the man from Cremona, who had had supper with us, had just left with his viol, there was an unexpected storm.

It couldn't have been far off midnight. Lightning, long rumblings, gusting rain – and all the time the sky, though cloudy, looked calm. Then came the sound of a thunderbolt, with a deafening crack like a splitting boulder. Gregorio's youngest daughter, who was drowsing in his arms, woke up and started to cry. Her father comforted her, saying lightning always seems much nearer than it is, and that this bolt must have struck up near the Castello, or in the docks.

But he'd scarcely finished reassuring the child when there was another thunderbolt, this time even nearer. Now the crash was simultaneous with the lightning, and several of us cried out.

Before we'd got over our fright, a strange thing happened. We'd been sitting round the hearth, and suddenly, for no apparent reason, a tongue of flame shot out of the fireplace and started advancing across the floor. We were all sat silent, trembling, terrified, and Orietina, who was sitting close to me but up till then hadn't looked at or spoken to me, suddenly clutched my arm so tightly that I could feel her nails sinking in.

In a whisper so loud that everyone could hear it, she hissed:

"It's the Day of Judgement! They weren't lying to me! It's the Day of Judgement! May the Lord have pity on us!"

Then she fell on her knees and took a rosary out of her pocket, signing to us to do the same. Her three daughters and the maids who were there started muttering prayers. As for me, I couldn't take my eyes off the tongue of flame, which by now having reached a sheepskin that happened to be lying there, took hold and set it alight. I was shaking in every limb, I admit, and in the confusion of the moment it struck me that I ought to rush up and get *The Hundredth Name* from my room.

In a few strides I was on the stairs, but then I heard Gregorio shouting:

"Baldassare, where are you going? Come and help me!"

He'd stood up, grabbed a large jug of water, and started to pour its contents over the burning sheepskin. The fire died down a bit, but didn't quite go out, so he began to stamp on it, leaping about in a sort

389

of dance that in other circumstances would have made us all laugh till we cried.

I ran back and joined in, and we both went on jumping on the tongue of flame every time it revived, as if we were trying to crush a column of scorpions.

Meanwhile some of the others got over their terror, and first a young maidservant, then the gardener, then Giacominetta ran and fetched various receptacles filled with water, which they proceeded to pour over anything that was still burning or glowing or smoking.

The upheaval lasted only a few minutes, but it was around midnight, so it seems to me the "Year of the Beast" must have ended with that farce.

Soon Dame Orietina, now the only one left kneeling, rose to her feet and declared it was time we all went to bed.

As I went up, I collected a candlestick which I put down on the table in my room so that I could write the above lines.

Superstition dies hard. I shall stay up until the sun rises, to write down the new date.

It's now the 1st of January of the year one thousand six hundred and sixty-seven.

The so-called "Year of the Beast" has ended, yet the sun is rising over my own city of Genoa, which gave me birth a thousand years ago, then forty years ago, and now again today.

Ever since dawn I have been overflowing with happiness. I feel like looking at the sun and talking to it like Francis of Assisi. We ought to rejoice every time it begins to give us light again, but now men are ashamed to talk to it.

So, neither it nor the other heavenly bodies have gone out. I couldn't see them last night because the sky was cloudy. Tomorrow, or the next night, I shall be able to see them, and I shan't need to count them. They are there, the heavens haven't been extinguished, the cities haven't been destroyed – Genoa, London, Moscow and Naples are all still there. We still have to go on living on earth day after day, with all our mortal woes. With plague and fever, with war and shipwreck, with our loves and our wounds. No divine cataclysm, no august flood will come to drown our fears and treacheries.

It may be that Heaven only reflects our own promises. Nothing either better or worse. It may be that Heaven lives only in terms of our own promises.

The Hundredth Name lies there beside me, and still it sometimes troubles me. I wanted it, I found it, I got it back again, but though I opened it it has remained closed to me. Perhaps I wasn't really worthy of it. Perhaps I was too afraid of finding out what it conceals. But maybe it hadn't anything to hide.

I shan't open it again. Tomorrow I shall leave it discreetly on a shelf in some bookshop, so that one day, years hence, other hands may take it up and other eyes look avidly into it, eyes which may by then be able to read it.

In pursuit of this book I have crossed the world over land and sea, but if I were to sum up my peregrinations as the year 1666 is left behind, I'd say I've only gone a roundabout way from Gibelet to Genoa.

It's midday by the bells of the nearby church, and I shall now put down my pen for the last time, shut my notebook, put my writing things away, and open myself and the window wide to the sunshine and sounds of Genoa.